Also by Isabelle Ronin

Chasing Red
Always Red

Spitfire IN LOVE

ISABELLE RONIN

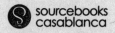

sourcebooks
casablanca

Published by Sourcebooks Casablanca, an imprint of Sourcebooks
P.O. Box 4410, Naperville, Illinois 60567-4410
(630) 961-3900
sourcebooks.com

The author is represented by Wattpad.

Printed and bound in the United States of America.
OPM 10 9 8 7 6 5 4 3 2 1

To Adam, my love

Chapter 1

Kara

I WAS ABOUT TO MAKE A HUGE MISTAKE.

This wouldn't be the first time it happened, nor would it be the last. I knew all the reasons why I shouldn't—the painful consequences were so familiar to me. But that didn't stop me.

I closed my eyes, silently counted to three, and took a long, deep breath.

Then I took a giant bite of the cheesiest veggie lasagna they served once a week in the campus cafeteria.

"Ungghh…" I sighed lustily, savoring the creamy, salty, addicting flavor of cheese in my mouth. The softness of the noodles. It was my reward for being such a good citizen this week, and I deserved—

"Why are you doing this to yourself?"

My eyes snapped open. My best friend Tala, all four feet eleven inches of her, stood in front of me with a look of disappointment but no surprise on her pretty face. She placed her books on the table, dumped her bag on the floor, pulled out a chair, and sat.

I shot her a mischievous grin and took another bite.

"You're lactose intolerant," she pointed out uselessly, watching me chew in ecstasy.

I licked the warm cheese on my lips, took another bite, and moaned. "I had a crappy morning at work today. I owe myself this cheesy perfection."

"I know you're happy now," she continued. She opened her bag and fished out a pink square Tupperware with pictures of cute cats all over it. The scent of spices filled the air as she opened her lunch box. "But remember what happened in Professor Balajadia's seminar last time?"

I made a face. "I took the pills."

She shook her head, pulled out a folded paper towel from her bag, and unwrapped it. It was her spoon and fork. Even though she had immigrated to Canada ten years ago, she'd grown up in the Philippines, where they usually use both utensils. "You know they don't work on you."

I glared at her. "You're ruining my moment here. And aren't you going to microwave that?" I pointed at her lunch with my fork. It was rice and adobo today.

She gave me an embarrassed look. "And get sued? No thanks."

I rolled my eyes. To show how much I loved her, I hit pause on my romantic date with the lasagna and grabbed her lunch box, heading straight to the microwave. Bonus: there were only three people in line.

Tala's mom always prepared lunches for her, and it was usually rice and meat. When heated up in the microwave, the smell was so pungent it filled the room. The first time she used the microwave in the campus cafeteria, people complained about the smell of her food clinging to their clothes, so she never did it again.

Well, this *was* the cafeteria. Where else would she

heat up her food? Under the sun? People would just have to deal.

I met Tala our freshman year in college. We were in the same accounting class. One of the girls in the class said something nasty about Tala being overweight, and I reacted accordingly. Two years later, we're still friends, so the friendship must be real. She's one of the best people on planet Earth.

When it was my turn, I put her food in the microwave for two minutes. Thirty seconds later, the overpowering smell of spices and meat filled the air. I could hear grumbles from people behind me, and I glared at them defiantly, daring them to say something.

When they didn't, I turned around and stared at the microwave's timer screen. When it hit two seconds, I jerked it open like my life depended on it. I hated the beep it made when it hit zero.

Why couldn't they make it a single beep? Or a nice catchy song?

I hit Clear to reset the timer, pulled down my sleeves to cover my hands so the Tupperware wouldn't burn my skin, and went back to my table.

"It's not your Gaspard Ulliel," I teased. She was obsessed with him. "But enjoy." I shoveled another sinful bite of lasagna into my mouth.

She giggled. "It's all right. You're forgiven. You know that cute archi student I told you about? We had a moment in the library this morning. He *looked* at me," she gushed. "I think he can have my babies."

"Oh really?" I raised a brow. "Like the nursing student you want to marry in Vegas? You cheater."

She laughed and flicked a piece of rice at me.

The cafeteria was filling up quickly now. People eyed our table, gauging how long we'd be staying to eat our food, so they could take over our spot. I made eye contact with one of them and flashed a sympathetic smile that said, *I feel you*.

"Don't you think, with the ungodly tuition we pay, they could afford to build us a skyscraper for a cafeteria? Dusted in gold," I said, sneering at the wobbly table and orange plastic chairs.

"Seriously. Don't forget the sexy servers." She ate a spoonful of her food. She used to offer to share her food with me, until I told her I didn't eat meat. "Anyway, how do you like being back in college?"

"It's good," I answered, scraping the last bite of cheesy goodness from the plate and sucking the fork clean.

Money was and continued to be a problem in our household, so I had taken a little over a year off from college to help my dad with expenses. It didn't help that I had a deep and lasting love affair with clothes and makeup, but I knew my priorities.

I had been working two part-time jobs and one full-time: I worked full-time at a personal care home, and on weekdays, when my schedule allowed, I worked part-time as a clerk at our auto repair garage, where my dad and younger brother worked. On weekends, I worked as a cashier at a coffee shop. When I went back to school, I had to quit the full-time job.

"It's a little bit of an adjustment," I added truthfully, debating whether I should lick my plate clean. "But I'll get used to it. I'm taking one of the advanced elective classes they're offering for second- and third-year students."

The semester had just started, and I already felt like

I had so much catching up to do. I didn't mind college, but it wasn't exactly my favorite. Some people knew from the start what they wanted in life. I'd say to them, *Congratulations! I don't like you.*

I had *no* idea what I wanted to do with my life…yet. So just like any practical college student who couldn't decide what they wanted, I majored in business. Hopefully, I'd have a lot of options when I graduated.

"That's great, that's great," Tala said, chewing on her lip.

I watched her for a few seconds. I knew what was coming.

Tala was a self-proclaimed psychic. I didn't believe in that sort of thing, but I also didn't *not* believe it. What I believed was that I was not a very patient human being, so I asked, "What is it?"

She put her spoon and fork down. *Huh. Must be serious.* "Have you…met anyone new today?"

"Like someone not stupid?" Screw it. I licked my plate. "Nope."

"Kar!" she admonished, but she was smiling.

Satisfied, I wiped my mouth with a napkin as gracefully as possible, leaned back in my chair, and patted my food baby. "Am I going to win the lottery?" I asked dryly.

"Hmm," she said absently.

Whether or not I believed in her psychic abilities, I couldn't resist the possibility of something exciting. So far, my life had been as exciting as a rock on a deserted island.

I'd never even had a boyfriend. I was a lifetime member of the Single Since Birth Club. Yay.

"He'll find you," Tala said after a moment.

"You're being creepy right now. Who will find me?"

She had a faraway look in her eyes, like she was watching a movie in her head. "You'll find him. Or he'll find you. I'm not sure."

"The guy I owe money to?" I was being flippant, but the hairs on my neck stood up…and inside my chest, my traitorous heart skipped a beat.

"You'll see" was all she said before she gathered her things and left for her next class.

I couldn't really put stock in what she said. Sometimes she'd predict things correctly, and other times she was dead wrong. It was the same thing as asking a random person on the street if it was going to rain next week or not. Their guess was as good as mine.

Deciding to forget what she said, I quickly wiped our table before snatching my backpack to leave. Sure enough, two girls quickly snagged our seats. I gave them a thumbs-up.

I had another hour or so to spare before my next class started, so I decided to head over to my department's lounge area to pass the time.

The hallways had lockers on one side and floor-to-ceiling glass windows on the other, flooding the interior with rich sunlight. Students sat on the floor or stood, leaning against their red lockers, chatting with each other. I'd once heard from a transfer student that they didn't have lockers in college in their country. In Esther Falls College in Manitoba, Canada, we had lockers. I counted myself very lucky.

I stopped in my tracks when I remembered that I needed an ID card to get into my department's lounge. I pulled my backpack in front of me, rummaging for my ID card when I was suddenly compelled, for some reason I couldn't identify, to look up at that precise moment—and saw him.

His face belonged to a dark archangel, and his hair was as dark as Lucifer's soul. It curled below his jaw, flirting with the collar of his shirt.

My brain stopped working. All I could think was *Are they shooting a movie on campus? Who is he?*

He continued walking, unaware of everything—that or he didn't really care. His stride was confident, as if he owned the damned place. Broad shoulders, long legs.

Everything on him was black: black shirt, black jeans, black combat boots, black backpack. So much so that when I looked up in his eyes, the impact was like a punch to the stomach.

His eyes were piercing blue.

It was only a moment—a very brief moment—when our eyes met.

But I knew.

The lasagna wasn't the biggest mistake of my life.

He was.

Chapter 2

Cameron

"Shit."

I stood in the street in front of my house and looked up at the bright morning sky. Closing my eyes as the heat of the sun pounded against my lids, I tried to find my calm. Counted to five.

One. Two. Three—

Didn't work. I lowered my head and took a deep breath before I opened my eyes.

There was a deep gouge on the fender of my motorcycle.

Curling my hand into a fist, I bit my knuckle.

A quick inspection found more scratches all over the side fairing and the engine cover was completely busted. *Hit-and-run*, I thought, grinding my teeth. Someone had crashed into my bike, and whoever hit it took the time to put it upright before fleeing the scene.

Thank you very much, motherfucker.

I crouched in front of it, stroking the once-smooth surface, now all banged up—the metal felt ridged and sharp under my fingertips. I'd had this ride for so long it felt like a piece of me.

Someone was going to pay.

I stood up slowly. When my phone rang, I didn't even look to see who it was and grabbed it like a lifeline.

"Yeah?"

"Hey, Cam."

It was Caleb.

I probably should have said something nicer, but all I could grit out was another sharp "Yeah."

I tamped down the anger and tried to concentrate on what he was saying.

"You know, it completely slipped my mind," he began. He sounded like he just woke up. "It's not Saturday today, is it?"

I kept rubbing the scratches, hoping they'd disappear. "You're such a genius."

"I hear that all the time." He paused. "Give me a ride to school?"

"You dying?"

"Don't think so."

I blew out a breath when I spotted a rip on the leather seat. "Then no. I'm not giving you a ride."

"My bike's at the shop."

Where mine was going to be very soon.

He cleared his throat. "And I left my car at the club last night. Took a cab this morning."

He sounded guilty. That meant he had slept at some girl's house again, took a cab to get back to his place, and hadn't bothered picking up his car.

"Actually, I changed my mind," he drawled. "I *am* dying and—"

Whatever he was saying was drowned out by a series of horn honks blaring behind me. I turned around just in time to see a beat-up Honda Civic speeding toward me like a bat out of hell.

It happened so fast. I yelled, jumping back to avoid getting clipped, and bumped into my bike in the process. I could only watch in horror as my motorcycle fell over with a loud crash.

There was a sound of metal bouncing against pavement. I looked to my right. It was my side mirror.

My mouth opened in shock, but nothing came out.

I stood dumbly and watched as the Civic came to a full stop, brakes screeching like a banshee, two houses down, across from my place. It idled for a few seconds before it reversed like a jet to the house across the street from mine.

I could feel my body bracing for a fight, my anger so close I could taste the bitterness of it.

What came out of it was a tall, willowy brunette ready for war. She wore some sort of uniform—a green dress shirt and slacks, her long honey-brown hair down her back—and she marched to the front door like she was going to give someone a come-to-Jesus talk.

She rang the doorbell incessantly, and when that wasn't answered after ten seconds, she started banging on the door with her fists.

Spitfire was the first word that came to mind. *What a spitfire.*

I had been living in my place for a couple of years now, but I kept to myself and especially stayed away from my neighbors. I'd only ruin their lives if I let them too close. It was easier this way.

I had no idea who lived there, but this girl clearly was going to eat that poor person for breakfast.

The door finally opened to reveal a frail old man with a cane. He looked like he'd be toppled over by a gust of wind. He wore a checkered shirt with suspenders and boxers, like he had forgotten to put on his pants before answering the door. Not surprising, since it was way too early in the morning.

What in the hell could her business be with the poor old-timer?

I could tell she wasn't expecting him to open the door. She stepped back, hesitant. I couldn't hear their words, but she seemed to be apologizing. When she finished, the old man pointed at the house next door.

She must have gotten the wrong house.

I couldn't help but laugh.

Looking contrite, she walked away with her head bowed low. When she raised it, the look in her eyes had transformed from penitent to billowing fire. *Interesting.*

She was tall and gangly, no curves on her body. From what I could tell, her features were relatively plain: small, straight nose, pale-pink lips. Her hair was something else altogether. It was thick and shiny, and in the sunlight, my eyes snagged on shades of honey gold mixed with the brown.

She wasn't my type. Of that I was sure. So why was I so completely, unquestionably fascinated with her?

She clenched her fists as though she itched to punch someone. Her walk was purposeful, deliberately intimidating to whichever unlucky bastard caught her anger as she headed to the house next door.

She might not have been a striking beauty, but it was hard to tell from my distance. All I knew was that she commanded my attention like no one had before.

I couldn't help the smile that split my lips. I wanted to see this.

Her gaze briefly met mine, and I swear to God my whole body jolted. I knew that I would always remember this moment. Her presence was too powerful to forget. My whole body froze, scared that if I moved, I'd realize this was all an illusion.

Before she could hit the doorbell, a Camaro parked in the street in front of the neighbor's driveway. I heard a car door open and slam closed, but I couldn't be bothered to look. I couldn't seem to remove my eyes from the spitfire. She froze, then turned with painful slowness toward that someone I still had yet to look at.

Her mouth moved, upper lip curling into a sneer. She shouted something unintelligible, and I wanted to see more, hear more. My mind was unconsciously moving my body toward her. I've never been in a trance before, but I thought this was what it must feel like.

I didn't have to move far because she started to walk down the driveway toward her new target, still shouting, hands flailing with temper.

Did I really think she was plain? I thought, staring at her unabashedly.

She was magnificent. Strong. Powerful.

Her eyes were glowing like fiery embers, beaming deathly daggers.

"You fucking piranha," she snarled.

I glanced quickly away from her to see who she was chewing into pieces, and I stopped cold when I realized who—or *what*—it was. It was a monster. The guy was as wide as a house, neck as big and thick as her torso. Tall and hairy as Chewbacca.

What the hell is she doing? Does she have a death wish?

I was going to come and help her out, wondering how in the blue hell I was going to fight this mother-fucker. He was heavy so he'd be slow, and I could use his weight against him. I'd probably lose a couple of my teeth and get my nose broken by the end of the day.

She drilled a finger into his chest, shouting in his face. "Remember the guy you harassed earlier, the one who came here to collect your car repair bill? That's my brother, you fuckwad dingle dick!"

She didn't look like she needed my help. The guy stepped back and raised his hands in defense. He looked like he was willing to take her crap to get a chance to check her out.

I gritted my teeth. Should I interrupt? She didn't look like she was in danger. I leaned against a parked car on the street across from them, alert and watching. It would only take me about five seconds to jump in the middle of them if needed.

"Listen here, sweet tits, your brother owes *me* money. You're not getting a dime out of me!"

She narrowed her eyes at him, as if she'd like to squish him like an insect. "Listen carefully, potato face, because I'm not repeating myself. What's between you and my brother has nothing to do with what you owe our business establishment. You're gonna have to pucker up and spring me some money right now or else you won't like the consequences."

He sneered, puffing up his chest. "Do you really think a little twig like you can scare me?"

I felt my body go on full alert. I pushed away from the

car, ready to attack him if he made a wrong move. That
movement caused him to finally notice me. I placed my
hands in my pockets, staring at him. He looked away.

"Oh, probably not," she shot back. "But the cops
will." She shook her phone right in his face. "Does your
brain have the capacity to recognize this as a phone?
Why, let me tell you what I'm going to do with this
shiny phone. I'm going to call the cops right now and
tell them how your vehicle was delivered to you in good
working order and you refused to pay. How's that sound
to you, Mr. Dingle Dick?"

Mr. Dingle Dick didn't like that one bit. He turned
an ugly shade of red and his left eye began to twitch.
He opened his mouth, stopped, and threw another
glance at me.

"You get off my property right now," he growled at
her. "You're trespassing."

He turned around and lumbered back to his house,
slamming the front door closed.

I straightened, expecting her to turn around and
finally acknowledge my presence. But she just stood
there, hands balled into fists. I could feel her anger and
frustration.

I was going to say something, but she spun on her
heel and hurried to her vehicle. I jumped behind the car
behind me just in case she had any ideas.

Tires squealing, her car jumped the curb, crushing
the two lawn gnomes that were happily sitting on the
corner of his front yard. There was a loud popping noise
over her screeching tires as she ground the gears back
into first.

I watched as the broken head of one of the porcelain

figures bounced across the street and rolled to a stop by my feet.

I looked up, eyes fixated on the little Honda as it zipped down the street and turned the corner until it disappeared out of my sight.

Wow. Just…wow.

I had to see her again.

But first, I had something to take care of. I pressed the doorbell and waited on Dingle Dick's porch. His face was confrontational as he opened the door but cleared when he spotted me.

He must have been expecting her. I suppressed my smile.

"Hey," he said, blocking the doorway from me.

I didn't blame him. People were usually wary of me. My best friend, Caleb, said it was my size. I towered over almost everybody. I was lean, and working in construction, with all that heavy lifting, had filled me out. He also said, "Sometimes, when you turn all quiet and dark, you get this look that freaks people out. You look at them as if you're assessing them and you can see right through them. You're not afraid and that makes you unpredictable. It's really cool. Like Batman, bro."

The truth was I knew how cruel and ugly people could be behind the masks they show the world. I also knew how to be like them when needed. And I despised it. Maybe that was why I was so drawn to her. She didn't hide anything. She was so…real.

"You're the guy who lives across the street, right? The one with the cool-ass bike."

"Yeah."

He scratched his head. "Look, man, I don't want no trouble."

I nodded, trying to appear friendly. "I figured. See my bike out there?" I pointed with my thumb over my shoulder.

He shifted. His eyes bugged out as he spotted my bike. "Son of a bitch. What happened?"

I gave him the saddest look I could muster. "*She* happened."

His jaw fell open. "You mean *she* did that?"

I looked at him solemnly. Not agreeing, not denying. Well, technically she did. "I may have forgotten to pay my bill."

He sighed, scratched his beard. "It was just a hundred and thirty bucks, man."

I shrugged. *What a piece of shit.* "Mine was only fifty."

"Well, shit." I could see the wheels in his head turning. "I really don't want no trouble. My old lady will be back tomorrow."

"I heard this other guy owed her money and she phoned his work, his parents, his grandparents, his girlfriend, his neighbors a few times a day. She stalked him everywhere he went until he cracked and paid."

He looked horrified. "Well, shit." He hung his head. "I guess I better pay that bill."

My mind was so busy thinking about her that it wasn't until I was on my way to the gym when I realized I had no idea where she worked. I could ask Dingle Dick, but then I'd blow my cover and he might not pay her at all.

Son of a bitch. How the hell was I going to find her?

My phone vibrated as I was storing my things in the gym locker. It was my dad. Automatically, as if my brain was conditioned by it, my body braced for a fight. Resentment whirled in my chest. What the hell did he want now? I ignored it, slamming the locker door closed. I don't know how long I stood there, brooding, getting sucked back to that hateful place, before I shook my head to clear it. I headed to the pool.

It was still early in the morning, so I had the pool to myself. Just the way I liked it—alone.

I raised my arms and did a good, long stretch before I dove in the water. As soon as the water surrounded me, muting the sound of everything, I started to relax.

I cut through the water, and an image of her flitted in my head. I smiled.

Her eyes had that upward tilt at the corners. I felt sudden regret that I hadn't been close enough to see the color of them. They could've been green or brown, I couldn't be sure.

And her legs. Jesus. That girl had long, long legs. I wondered what they'd look like in a skirt. Or tight jeans.

She was fearless and reckless, confronting a man four times her size. I pushed off the pool wall, did another lap, laughed as I remembered her driving over those garden gnomes, and choked on pool water.

When I got my breath back, I continued my lap.

Was it really a surprise that I was drawn to her? Most of the people in my life bottled everything up until their resentments and disappointments started to spill over, poisoning everything around them. And I knew a part of me turned out to be exactly like that. And I despised it.

And myself.

I reached the wall, pushed off, and did another lap. And another. And another.

———————————————

After a quick shower, I quickly pulled on my black shirt and pants, hiked up my boots. Swinging my backpack over one shoulder, I grabbed my phone and headed out to the gym parking lot.

"Hey, cutie," I heard a girl holler behind me. I kept walking.

"Damn," I muttered under my breath as a quick Google search of car repair shops in the city of Esther Falls produced more than a hundred. How was I supposed to find her?

I filtered my search to just the businesses around my area and narrowed it down considerably. Thinned it out some more by searching "family owned." I figured since she personally came to collect the bill from Dingle Dick, her family probably owned the business. Maybe, maybe not.

Was I really going to search every damn shop to find her? What the hell was I doing?

I needed to get my bike fixed anyway, so it was killing two birds with one stone. I was being practical. No BFD.

The thought of my broken bike was starting to piss me off. I still had yet to call insurance, but that would make it too real and I wasn't ready to deal. I needed to find out who did it. There would be hell to pay, I thought as I hopped in my company truck and drove to campus.

The temperature had dropped a little, so I cracked the

window open to let the cool breeze inside. I turned the radio on and cranked up the volume.

I wondered what it would be like to have her in the truck with me. I had a picture of her standing up through the sunroof. The grin on my face felt stupid, but I really didn't care.

I parked my truck, considered staying in it for a few minutes until lunch break was over. I didn't like crowds and avoided them like the plague, but I was feeling thirsty after my workout and needed to hydrate.

I took the stairs two at a time, then turned the corner toward the cafeteria to get a drink. When I spotted the crowd in the hallway, I slowed down and didn't bother hiding my annoyance. I'd rather have been somewhere else.

I dug in my backpack for my earphones and, when that took too long to find, gave up and kept walking. I wondered if Caleb was on campus now. I might not have given him a ride to school, but that guy could easily get any one of his girls to pick him up. He was usually in the hallway with the team or in one of the lounge areas with girls.

I scanned the hallway, looking for him. And froze. It was *her*—spitfire! I was about to do a double take when I felt someone pull my pants down from behind me. I caught the top of my pants just in time and whirled around.

"You fucking asshole," I barked, watching as Caleb dissolved in laughter.

I punched him on the arm and turned back around. But she was gone.

I swear I saw her.

"Cheapo," Caleb said. "Thanks for not picking me up. Appreciate it, bro."

Was that really her, or was my mind playing tricks on me? Man, did I have it bad. I blew out a breath, shaking my head at the ridiculousness of it all.

"Who're you looking for?" Caleb asked. He placed his hands in his pockets, leaning against the locker as he tilted his head and studied me. He usually did that when he was trying to figure out something.

I shrugged.

"Hmm. That's an eight," he said appreciatively as a blond passed by and smiled at him. Caleb had a thing for blonds.

We usually did this to pass the time, but I wasn't in the mood for it today. Not when *she* was still in my head.

What the hell was happening to me?

"Need some Gatorade. Be right—" I paused when my phone rang. It was my dad. Again. I let out a long breath.

Caleb gave me a knowing look. "Which one of them this time?"

He knew that only my parents could put me in this mood. "My dad," I said grimly, staring at my phone.

"You going to answer it?"

I balled my hand into a fist and bit my knuckle. *Fuck it.*

"Yeah," I answered.

There was a pause before my dad spoke. "You might want to answer your phone more politely than that, lest people think your mother didn't raise you properly."

There was disappointment in his voice. As usual.

"She didn't," I said.

He scoffed. "How's your friend Rick doing these

days?" His tone was condescending. "Is he still begging people for money?"

We both knew he was trying to get a rise out of me. He knew how badly it affected me when he talked about Rick that way. Rick had been there for me when everyone had left.

"Nothing to say?"

I gritted my teeth and said as calmly as I could, "Why don't you tell me why you called?" *So we can both move on with our lives. You've never been in mine, anyway.*

"Just checking up on you, seeing how you're doing with your studies."

"I have no time for this."

He chuckled but not with humor. It was patronizing. A parent talking to an errant child. He'd never shown me anything other than contempt. There were moments I thought I felt his concern, but they were brief and left me confused. I remember one day he took me for a short flight in his plane, though I barely recall what he was like as a person. What made that day unforgettable was when we got home. My mother, Raven, was furious. I could only watch helplessly as she hit my dad with her fists and scratched at him with her fingernails. She hated anyone who took me away from her. My dad rarely attempted to reach out to me after that. On the rare occasion when he did, Raven would pick a fight with him and he'd end up leaving for weeks at a time. He became a stranger to me, a man who owned the house I lived in. The more emotional Raven became, the colder my father became toward me. Maybe it was to punish my mother. Maybe he just despised me. I had long stopped wondering about it. I had long stopped caring.

"Your mother's back. She called me. I need you to see her and calm her down, so she can stop harassing me. Be a good son, won't you?"

"Why?" I could hear the bitterness in my voice. "You've never been a father to me. Why don't you do one thing, just one thing, and get her off *my* back?"

I hung up, closed my eyes, and pressed my fingers to them. I hated showing any emotion to my dad.

The last time I saw Raven was a year ago, and it didn't go well. There were only two things Raven loved in this world: money and herself. She despised Esther Falls and preferred big cities like Toronto, but when she got bored, Raven always went back to her favorite hobby: torturing my dad. And me. My dad didn't want to deal with her and would always pass her off to me.

I could feel my mind shutting down, feel the anger taking over me. I needed to walk it off, do something before I exploded.

"Hey, Cameron."

A flirty voice. I opened my eyes and found Lydia standing in front of me.

"You free tonight, Cam?" she asked, batting her lashes at me suggestively. "My parents won't be home and—"

I reached for her wrist. "I'm free now," I answered. "Let's go."

Chapter 3

Kara

MEETING HIM WAS A MISTAKE.

A beautiful mistake.

The sharp curve of his jaw.

His neck.

The shape of *his mouth*.

His mouth.

The long lines of his arms.

His mouth.

He had lion eyes, heavy-lidded and piercing—the kind that could make your knees weak if he glanced at you even for just one second. Or slash your heart and make it bleed if he dismissed you.

I thought those sharp blue eyes were uncaring, somehow detached from everything around him. But they looked sad somehow.

And that sadness made me want to look longer, made my greedy heart *want.*

I want to know why he's sad.

I want him to want to tell me.

I want to be beautiful enough to be with him.

And *that* last part woke me up from my daydreaming,

like scalding water splashed on my hand. I saw his friend sneak up from behind him and pull his pants down.

As soon as he turned away from me, I flipped my hoodie up, face burning, and ran the opposite direction.

What the hell? *Beautiful enough to be with him?*

I'd be damned if I let the same insecurities I had when I was a kid plague me again. Beautiful faces don't affect me anymore. Well…to be honest, maybe a little. But it had been a long time since a gorgeous face had triggered me to wish I were someone else.

Getting physically and mentally bullied for my looks, my height, the fact that my family was very poor, and my mother running off with another man had made me feel insecure. It made me wish to be someone else, made me believe that if I were beautiful, maybe the world would be easier on me.

I knew better now. It made me wary of everyone, made me learn how to fight, made me defensive and combative.

So what was it about him?

I decided I didn't like him.

In fact, I hoped I'd never see him again. I had no business thinking about a boy who wouldn't pay attention to me anyway and that *I* normally wouldn't pay attention to.

I was sure I wasn't even a blip on his radar.

The girls in the hallway gave me a wide berth, throwing a nervous glance my way before turning the corner.

I rolled my eyes. I was having a moment here.

There must have been something in that lasagna. Or, if I was being honest with myself, the disappointing inability of my body to process dairy.

The instant I thought of it, my stomach began to cramp.

Oh shit.

Something was trying to bubble out of me.

And from the unearthly sounds my stomach was making, I knew I was going to *suffer*.

I knew it. I *fucking* knew it. And in my head, I knew I deserved it for being a greedy pig.

The line to the washroom was past the door. It was five minutes before classes started, and everyone wanted to do their business last minute.

Assholes. Everyone was an asshole. I would lock all the bathroom doors five minutes before the end of the world, so no one could use them. Later, I'd laugh at the ridiculousness of that. But it wasn't later yet, and I was dead serious about it.

There was no other choice. I had to go to the third-floor bathroom. Correction, the third-floor *fuck* bathroom.

Students nicknamed it that because it was where couples go to…well, fuck. You had to climb three flights of stairs to get there and walk a whole floor, since it was located at the end of the corridor. No one in their right mind who needed to take a piss would take a long hike to get to that toilet.

No one but me.

"Oh *fuck*."

A cramp so sharp I felt it in my soul. I grabbed the railing on the stairs, breathing heavily as I rested my clammy forehead on my arms.

You can make it. Steel, baby. You are made of steel.

I pushed away from the railing, tightened my butt

muscles, and ran. I could hear my heavy footsteps echoing, felt the cold sweat trickling down my face.

I was wheezing by the time I reached the washroom door, losing my balance and almost sliding to the floor with my rush to get my butt to the toilet. I slammed open the first stall I could reach, fumbled the lock home, and let go.

Have you ever had to go so bad that you brace your arms against the stall walls, close your eyes tightly, and hold on for dear life as you moan like a pig and *pushhh* with all of your might…but only air comes out?

Yes, it was *that* kind.

I was in the middle of doing this when I heard the bathroom door open and then moaning and the rustling of clothes. It sounded like someone was going to get down and dirty, *literally*, on the bathroom floor.

"You feel so good, Cam," I heard a sultry feminine voice purr.

Prrrrrrrrrrrtttttttttt!

That was me passing gas. Blowing wind. Farting. Like a choo-choo train on Christmas.

Silence.

I heard more rustling, like they were putting their clothes back on, and then the door opening and closing.

Thank fuck they left.

I finished my business quickly, sprayed some perfume in the bathroom so the next poor soul wouldn't have to deal with my stink. I washed my hands in the sink thoroughly, reapplied my lipstick, opened the door into the hallway, and froze in my tracks.

There he was with his piercing blue eyes and Lucifer black hair.

He was leaning against the wall across the bathroom, hot as hell and twice as dangerous. His arms were crossed in front of him, a lollipop in his mouth.

His eyes widened when he saw me. We just stood there for what seemed like forever, staring at each other.

Then…he grinned.

Chapter 4

Kara

MY MIND TURNED BLANK. COMPLETELY, BLESSEDLY BLANK.

It was like trying to watch a movie online and suddenly the screen turns into fuzzy images and text appears: *Your brain is buffering 7%...*

He was watching me with that beautiful crooked smile. As if he had all the time in the world, he shifted his shoulders lazily and pulled out the red lollipop from his mouth.

It was one of those flat, round lollipops they sold in the cafeteria, and I was surprised he liked them.

Deep, deep blue eyes focused on my face. I heard myself swallow.

Leisurely he opened his mouth and gently placed the lollipop there again, but instead of sucking on it, he trapped it between his teeth.

And bit.

Crunch.

There go my ovaries.

I saw that his tongue was stained red from the candy.

Soon, I thought, I was going to run out of saliva to swallow.

He finished the candy, flicking the stick in the trash

can. I thought that his focus on me couldn't get any more intense.

I was wrong. A wicked glint flickered in his eyes.

Uh-oh.

His first words to me were "Your wind was so strong it blew me away."

I choked on air.

There was a cry like that of a trapped animal burning in the back of my throat. I was never the type of person to be rendered speechless. I always had something to say, but at that very moment, I wanted the sky to open wide and beam me to space.

His lips twitched. "You owe me one, Spitfire."

Spitfire? I should say something. I knew there was a comeback floating somewhere in my brain, but where the hell was it?

Buffering 7.001%...

"What's your name?" he asked, still watching me, still so *focused* on my face.

I gulped. I tried to speak. Nothing.

Now his eyes were laughing, those big, deep blue eyes crinkling at the corners. And then he looked down as if he couldn't contain his amusement, brought his fist to his beautiful mouth, and... Was he biting his knuckle?

Oh Jesus. Why is that so sexy?

His eyes flicked up to mine.

I think I peed a little.

"Cat got your tongue?" he asked teasingly.

Now if it were a different person who asked that or maybe if I just had my wits about me, I would have annihilated them and chopped them up for dinner.

But I did not. My batteries died, and I needed to recharge.

"Tell me."

He seemed like a person who didn't say please, and if he did, he would have been quite uncomfortable, but somehow I heard it in his voice.

Tell me your name. Please.

"K-Kara," I stammered. My voice sounded weak. "Kara," I repeated, strongly this time.

A pitiful attempt at getting back control.

My eyes felt wide open. Had I blinked yet?

I tried, but my lids wouldn't cooperate. They just took him in, filing everything like a screenshot in my head.

The way his black hair glinted almost blue in the sunlight filtering in through the window behind him.

The way he tipped his head, with the black-blue strands silkily sliding to touch the side of his face and cover part of his eyes.

The way he was leaning against the wall…with just the right amount of recklessness.

He was tall. God, he was tall. Lean but muscular. Like a swimmer. His shoulders were wide, tapering down to a slim waist.

"And your number?" he asked.

This time, there was no *please* in his tone. It was as bold as brass. All confidence.

I told him.

His smile was wicked as he entered it into his phone. He looked like a little boy who had gotten away with something.

What was I doing? This wasn't me. Someone had possessed my body. I had *never* given my number to a guy like this, but something about him compelled me to do it.

He'd sucked away all my powers from me. I had to get away. But my legs wouldn't move. Traitors!

He pushed away from the wall, straightening. For a moment, I felt panic climb up my chest. Not because I was afraid of him. I was afraid of what I was going to do.

He started to walk closer, closer. But he wasn't looking at me anymore, and I wondered if it was just a test. A game.

He kept walking, staring straight ahead. There was a small smile playing on his lips as he walked by me, inches away from where I was standing. My eyes closed involuntarily.

And then…I felt a light touch on the back of my hand. Featherlight, as if a butterfly's wings were hovering near my skin.

My eyes opened. Holding my breath, I looked down. It was like watching something happen in slow motion. We stood side by side, facing different directions. Slowly, gently, the tip of his finger stroked mine, tracing the outline of it.

I felt his head lean down a little toward me, felt his body heat, smelled his masculine scent. Something that reminded me of the sea: deep, blue, and sensual.

And then he was gone.

Chapter 5

Kara

As soon as I got home from campus, I took off my shoes and made a beeline for the bathroom. But this time, it wasn't to take a dump.

I sat in the empty bathtub, still fully clothed, chin on my knees, hands on my neck. I stared at the yellowed spots I couldn't get rid of no matter how hard I scrubbed the surface of the tub and let my mind wander.

It was quiet except for the *drip, drip, drip* from the faucet. And if I really listened to it, I could hear the creepy grandmother clock in the living room ticking heavily. It needed to be adjusted again or, in my opinion, thrown out, but my dad loved to hoard junk—*useful junk*, according to him—so it stayed.

I should have asked my dad to fix these things, but I tried to make it as easy on him as I could because I knew how exhausted he was every day. In the back of my mind, I was thinking that if only my childhood friend Damon were here, the dripping and the heavy ticking would have been taken care of already. He was a pretty good handyman, among other things.

But he wasn't here. His last text said he was

somewhere in British Columbia. Doing only God knows what.

My eyes hesitantly traveled up from my feet to the other end of the tub, where I had placed my cell phone. It mocked me with its dark screen. I narrowed my eyes at it, like it was my archenemy.

I should turn it off.

Why didn't I?

Was I actually waiting for him to call?

And oh God. He smelled my butt burp. My *loud* butt burp.

I slapped my face with my hands, covering most of my mouth, and screamed. Torture. This felt like torture. And to think that I was fantasizing about him just a few minutes before he saw me in the hallway outside of the bathroom…or *heard* me inside the bathroom…

Shit.

Why would he ask for my name? And my number? He couldn't possibly be interested in me…*right?*

But the bigger question was why the hell did *I* give him both?

I thought of the way he'd asked for my name. Like a whisper. Like a secret he wanted to know. His voice held just a little hint of desperation.

Tell me.

Tell me your name. Please.

How could I have refused *that*?

I snapped my eyes shut. Why? Why did he want to know?

He had sounded so cocky by the time he'd asked for my number, so confident, so *in charge*. And why the hell not? He probably thought, *This girl is easy.*

Easy! Me? Easy? Ha! The thought made me itchy.
I wanted to punch and kick something…preferably his
gorgeous face.

Cam.

That was his name. I heard her say it.

And there was my answer.

I could have refused *that* because he was making
out—scratch that—giving the dirty salami to his girlfriend in the fuck bathroom just a few minutes before
he'd asked for my number.

So he thought he could cheat behind his girlfriend's
back with me, did he?

I gritted my teeth. That made me angry. Cheaters were
on my blacklist. My mother was one after all. She ran
away with a vacuum salesman, leaving my dad to raise
two kids by himself. Good riddance, if you asked me.

I glanced at my socks and noticed my big toe poking
through a small hole. These were my favorite cat socks.
One more thing to add to his growing list of offenses.

I was feeling anger, and that was fine, but there was
something else too.

Disappointment.

I leaned back, glaring up at the ceiling. A lot of idiots
cheated on their partners. It wasn't a surprise. So why
was I disappointed that someone I had no idea even
existed until today was a cheater?

Why?

I had never seen or heard of him before. Granted, it
was a huge college, but someone as attractive as he is
was bound to be one of the hot topics on campus. Also,
I had taken more than a year off. Of course I wouldn't
be updated. Maybe he was a transfer student. Or a

freshman. I shook my head at the absurdity of that. He wasn't freshman material. He was *huge*. And tall.

I was taller than most people I know, but he was taller. That alone would've gotten my attention. It was like finding a beautiful pair of shoes in my size at the store. I was size eleven and stores almost never carried my size. So naturally I had to take a closer look. I had to check it out, touch it, try it on for size.

That was it! That was why I gave him my name and number. That was why I was disappointed. The shoes didn't fit. Total huge disappointment.

Satisfied with my conclusion, I grabbed my phone and got out of the tub, ready to put it all behind me.

An image of him standing beside me, his head leaning closer to mine, his skin touching mine appeared in my mind.

My heart started to beat faster at the thought. Now I was angry not only at him, but also at myself for still thinking about him. I shook my head, clearing my thoughts. I refused to think about him for one more second, and if he disturbed my peace again, I would release the kraken.

I dare him to call me!

My phone rang.

"Sumbitchmotherfuck!" I screamed.

I scrubbed my face, gripped my hair. Was it him calling?

I thought for a second of throwing my phone, but then it might break. I still had a few months on this plan, and I wasn't going to pay for repairs or a new phone.

He wasn't worth it.

Heart hammering in my chest, I closed my eyes so I

didn't have to see who was calling. I gripped it in my hand, letting it ring and vibrate for a second, savoring a kind of sick pleasure from my misery, taunting myself with the possibility that maybe it was him and maybe I would answer it.

And say what exactly?

Maybe I'd give him a piece of my mind, how about that?

Annoyed with myself, I opened my hand and let my phone slide to the sink before I stepped out of the bathroom and closed the door behind me. *This is all his fault. That lying, cheating baboon.*

The doorbell rang.

"For fuck's sake." I let out a loud breath and dragged my feet to the door. "Do I need to sell my soul to get some peace and serenity on this earth or what?"

I glanced at the clock. It was home time for my dad and brother.

If they forgot their keys again, I swear to God...

The permanent sour face of my uncle Andrew and the round, kind face of his wife, Charity, greeted me as I opened the door. The car shop was owned by Andrew and my dad, and the tiny two-bedroom house we lived in was behind it. Andrew loved to remind us how lucky we were that we didn't have to pay him half the rent, since he co-owned the house with my dad.

And since, in his mind, this was his property, he could come and go whenever he wanted. He had asked my dad if he could have a key to our house *in case of emergencies.* I told my dad he'd find me in Salome Avenue working with Faye, a family friend who was a sex worker during the weekends. My dad didn't give him a key.

Andrew settled his scrawny butt on one of the stylish chairs I had refurbished in our living room. His eyes were assessing as he scanned our house. Charity sat beside him.

I couldn't boast about the size, and I might not be the most organized or cleanest person on the planet, but I knew how to spice up the place. Most everything we had was secondhand—stuff I'd picked up from Value Village or the Salvation Army that I'd revamped or repainted, hand-me-downs from relatives and friends. Stuff my dad picked up everywhere. But I was meticulous in choosing what stayed and what didn't. Damon and my brother, Dylan, had to build a shed on the property for Dad to store all the junk he collected and thereby prevent me from murdering him.

"Why is it so hot in here?" Andrew complained. "It's not even that cold outside. Do you know how much heating cost nowadays? Living here for free doesn't mean you can waste, kid. Turn the heater off."

What did he think I was, a cold-blooded mammal? I narrowed my eyes at him. And leaned against the wall. Defiantly.

When he realized I wasn't going anywhere, he looked at me with a disapproving curl on his lip.

"Make us some coffee. A little hospitality won't kill you," he said.

He just said it was too hot in here.

I raised an eyebrow. "Well, I don't know. I'd have to boil water using the kettle and electricity costs money. Are you sure that's a good idea?"

Charity let out a snorting laugh, then coughed to cover it up. Andrew glared at her.

"Out of all my nieces and nephews, you're the only one who gives me a headache. Why are you always so disagreeable?"

He had said different variations of this to me while I was growing up. It stung back then, and it still stung now. I crossed my arms. "Am I? Maybe because you're not particularly my favorite person."

He didn't hold back, so why would I?

He sneered. "I heard you're back in college now," he said. "You should stop fooling around and just finish your studies. Look at my son, John. He's a successful pharmacist now. My daughters, Chloe and Judith, are both teachers. Your other cousins too—Cecille, Miriam, Naomi—they all graduated with degrees. What about you and Dylan? Your dad—"

I could tolerate *some* insults about me—I'd had so many thrown at me by nasty kids at school—but if he thought I'd let him get away with insulting my dad, he was very wrong. I was going to boot his bald ass out.

"Oh, but I'm very proud of my kids, Drew," my dad announced cheerily. He stood at the front door, wiping his shoes on the outdoor rug on the porch before entering. He was lanky like me, and his six foot two inches were very hard to ignore. He took off his gimme cap and shoes and put them in the storage closet by the door. "They haven't murdered anyone…yet." My dad winked at me. "How's it going, Charity?"

He trooped toward the kitchen sink to wash his hands of the grease that he could never get rid of entirely. For as long as I could remember, my dad's hands were always stained with it. He wiped his hands with the dish towel hanging on the fridge handle and put water in the kettle to boil.

"You should encourage your kids more, Mike, so they can have big dreams, unlike…"

Unlike you was what he wanted to say.

Son of a bitch. I opened my mouth to deliver a killing blow, but my dad popped a piece of bread in my mouth. He sat on one of the barstools under the kitchen island that served as our dining table.

"I only need them to be decent human beings." He smiled indulgently at Andrew. "Kara helps me with paperwork, and I'm training Dylan in the shop. They're both with me. Healthy, happy. All I need, Drew. All I need."

Andrew's children didn't ever visit him. They were too busy with their lives to bother with their parents.

Out of the corner of my eye, I saw Charity look at my dad with longing. I heard from my dad's sister that Charity liked my dad when they were younger, but my dad fell in love with my self-absorbed mother, who broke his heart and left him in the end.

Maybe that was why Andrew always looked down on my dad. He was still bitter. My dad, however, always respected him. When my grandparents' farm wasn't doing well, Andrew had sent money until they were back on their feet again. My dad always told me to have patience for my uncle because he owed a lot to him. I understood that. Why did he think I hadn't murdered Andrew yet?

But right now, I really needed to put some distance between me and my uncle. Besides, four people in the house felt a little claustrophobic to me, so it was either escape to my room—which would upset my dad because he'd think it was rude—or leave, which was the safest bet. I'd tell him I needed to go to the library and study like a responsible college student. But first, my phone.

I tuned them out and stopped at the closed bathroom door, listening. My heart started beating faster at the thought of my phone ringing, but there was no sound on the other side. Taking a deep breath, I opened the door.

Ten missed calls.

From Dylan.

What the hell did he do now?

I turned the faucet on—I was sure I would hear a heartfelt lecture about paying the water bill from Andrew when I came out—and stood in the tub so they wouldn't hear me. The walls in the house were paper thin.

"Kar? Why the hell weren't you answering your phone?"

I scratched the back of my neck. Itchy. Frustrated. "Just so you know, Sour Face is here."

"Ah. Glad I'm not there then."

"Where are you?"

"At a friend's house. Kar…I need your help."

Pause.

"Did you kill anyone?" I asked.

"No."

"Did you put someone in the hospital?"

"No."

"Are *you* in the hospital?"

"No. I told you, I'm at a friend's house."

"I don't have money, Dylan. I told you—"

"It's not that. I… You know this morning when I tried collecting that bill for the Camaro?"

"Well, you failed that one big time, and if I hadn't

had classes this afternoon, I would have nagged that hairy giganotosaurus a little more to pay his bill. And what's he saying, that you owed him money? What's between you and—"

"Kar, focus. Listen to me."

The urgency in his voice made me stop.

"Kar," he said quietly.

I waited.

"I…" His deep breath rattled in my ear. "I hit someone's motorcycle."

Chapter 6

Kara

"WAIT. BACK THE HELL UP." I SMASHED THE PHONE AGAINST my ear. "Did I hear you say you hit someone's motorcycle?"

There was a moment of silence on the other end of the line before I heard Dylan's quiet reply. "Yes."

I gripped the phone hard and swallowed the panic threatening to climb up my chest. "Which one were you driving?"

This time the moment of silence was longer.

"Bertha," he answered.

I snapped my eyes closed. Bertha was the ancient GMC truck rotting away in the garage's lot for years.

Dylan had a weakness for classic trucks. He had begged my dad to let him drive the one we had in the lot—so he could show off to his friends—but it needed a lot of work done to it before it was even safe to drive. Hell, it needed a blessing from Jesus to make it safe to drive.

And, more importantly, it wasn't insured.

I felt a headache trying to worm its way into the base of my neck. The idiot must have sneaked out with it.

"I'm going to kill you," I hissed.

My dad was tapped out for cash from buying new

equipment for the shop. Dylan was in high school, and Dad was still training him in the garage. I thought of the money I had worked so hard to save up sitting in my bank account.

All those times I had to wake up at four in the morning to do my shifts at the coffee shop. The backbreaking twelve-hour shifts at the personal care home and hospital. The odd jobs I had to take on the side, so I could add all that income to my savings.

It was supposed to pay for my tuition fee for next semester and buy off Andrew's shares from the shop.

Now a huge chunk of it was going to pay for my brother's stupidity.

I thought of the lecture my uncle pompously spouted at me every chance he got about me having a direction in life and finishing my studies. How could I when every time I took a step forward, something always slapped me in the face, reminding me it was all one big fat joke? Tears threatened to spill, but I held them off.

Steel, baby. I'm made of steel.

"Tell me what happened," I said. "If you lie to me, I'll cut off your dick, so help me God."

"Okay, okay." I could hear the whine in his voice, and the underlying fear in it.

Dylan was easily scared. Ever since we were kids, it was the trace of fear I heard in his voice, that same fear glittering in his eyes, that always, *always* got to me. And never failed to soften me up, raise my protective instincts.

It was one of my many weaknesses to want to protect him and bail him out of whatever trouble he was in or share that trouble with him.

Whenever Dylan had nightmares as a kid, he would always call out for me. When he got bullied by the kids at school, he'd come home crying to me. Of course, I'd beat them up for him—and usually dragged Damon to be my sidekick.

When my brother got teased at school for wearing the same clothes over and over again or for wearing the hand-me-downs of the brothers and cousins of his classmates that the ladies at church had donated to us, I'd persuaded my grandma to ask her dressmaker friend to teach me how to cut and sew, so that I could redesign the hand-me-downs. I wasn't going to win an award for best dressmaker of the year, and it didn't stop the teasing completely, but it lessened.

I raised Dylan as much as my dad did. I never had a mother, but I learned how to be one out of necessity.

"After I tried to collect the money from Big Tony—"

"That giganotosaurus said you owe him money," I said.

"It was a stupid bet. We were joking around. I had no idea he was serious about it."

The headache had spread to my temples. Dylan was naive, especially about his "friends." I tried to protect him, but I could only do so much. Maybe I was the root cause of it. I had sheltered him so much that he didn't know how to spot users and had no street smarts. "Tell me about the motorcycle."

"Big Tony threatened to beat me up if I didn't pay him," he said carefully.

I knew this already. It was why I drove to the customer's place to collect his bill this morning.

"I was freaking out when I reversed the truck from

his driveway. I didn't know I reversed that far and veered off. I never even saw the motorcycle. It was an accident," he whined.

"You idiot!" I pressed my finger to my eyes, sighed. Opening the medicine cabinet, I grabbed the bottle of aspirin, shook two into my mouth, and drank from the tap. "Did you damage it?"

"It was only a couple of scratches, I think…"

"You think? I need you to gather all your working brain cells right now—those that aren't infected by your stupidity."

"I was in a hurry! I didn't get the time to inspect it. I got out of the car and lifted it back up. Maybe I didn't damage it after all. I mean, it stood well enough. What do you think?"

"What do I think? You little shit. Dad told you not to drive Bertha!"

"I know. I'm sorry!" he wailed.

"You're a spoiled kid, is what you are. Don't you dare tell Dad about this. He's already got so much on his plate without you adding to it."

"What if someone saw me? My life is over. What if someone took a video on their phone and uploaded it online? What if I'm in the news tomorrow? Should I just come clean to the owner?"

"Calm your tits. Let me think." I placed my hand on my neck, mulling it over. "So you're saying there might be a chance you didn't damage it at all."

"I… Maybe."

I heard the hope in his voice. Maybe in mine too. Maybe he didn't damage it and he could get away with it. Maybe we were both just freaking out. If the owner saw him, he would have reported Dylan by now. The police would have been here by now.

"You think someone saw you?"

"I don't know, Kar..."

"Listen. I'm going to drive by that house. You better start praying on your knees right now that motorcycle isn't a wreck and is sitting in the driveway or I will sell your organs to pay for it."

He sighed. "Do you want me to come with you?"

"No. Besides, I'm going to stop by your friend's house and try to collect his bill. If he doesn't pay this time, I'm calling the cops."

"Aw, Kar. Don't be like that."

"Don't you 'Aw, Kar' me. You're lower than a worm right now."

"What if his motorcycle is not in the driveway? What if I damaged it? What if he has a camera on his front porch and recorded everything? He'd see my license plate. My face. My gawsh."

Judging from the tone of his voice, he'd be crying in a minute. I sighed. "What if you started sprouting wings out of your ass and flew to outer space? Man up." And because I knew he was seriously freaking out and could have a panic attack, I softened my voice. "Look, Dyl, I'll take care of it, and if there's more to it, I'll let you know. For now, I need you to come home and just... don't touch anything. You got that?"

"I got it. Thanks, Kar." His voice broke. "Thanks."

I hung up and placed my phone in my pocket.

I got this.

I grabbed my keys and left.

I parked my car three houses away from Mr. Motorcycle's place. Not too close, just in case someone in the neighborhood got suspicious. Not too far, just in case I needed to make a run for it.

The screen dashboard in my car indicated 7:00 p.m. It was dark. The streetlights were on, good folks tucked away in their lit-up houses, probably having a homecooked dinner or relaxing in their overpriced, comfortable beds.

Which I should be doing. Instead, I was here on a mission to save my brother's ass.

I grabbed my thick hair—it was too long, and I needed to give it a trim—twisted and squished it under a cap. *Should've brought my shades to be more incognito*, I thought as I slid out of my car. Mr. Motorcycle's house wasn't that far from ours; someone might recognize me.

I shivered. Must be the cool night air, I decided as I zipped my oversized jacket closed. It was absolutely not because I was nervous. Or excited. Nope. Normal people stalk all the time. It was a legit pastime.

I always do it on social media.

Correction. Not stalk. *Research.* I was here to do research. I was just going to look around, see if the motorcycle was in the driveway. Maybe it wasn't as bad as Dylan suspected.

What if the owner came back while I was sneaking around? I stopped in my tracks. Maybe I should bring the flyers from church I had in the car. If Mr. Motorcycle caught me around his house, I could simply hand him a flyer and say I was distributing it around the neighborhood. Genius.

Giving out flyers at seven-shit-o'-clock at night is genius? Really.

I shushed the bitchy voice in my head and spun around to return to my car to fetch the flyers.

Mr. Motorcycle's house looked like a modern bachelor pad. Tall privacy-glass windows, sharp angles, lots of concrete. It seemed like a spare house for a drug lord's youngest son. Not too big, but luxurious and expensive.

If my hunch was right, Dylan was going to be in an enormous pit of trouble. And it wouldn't be just him in that pit. It'd be him, me, and my dad.

There was a long, wide driveway that led to the garage. On the driveway was a muscle truck, but no sign of a motorcycle. Why was his truck on the driveway and not in the garage?

Maybe there was more than one person living in the house. That would make it a little more complicated, but nothing my investigative skills couldn't handle.

A six-foot-high fence extended from the side of the windowless garage with a door I assumed led to the backyard. There were no lights in the house except for the soft glow of the porch light. No one was home.

I imagined an evil grin on my face, rubbing my hands in glee at this golden opportunity. I cracked my knuckles. *My body is ready.*

Maybe I should whistle casually.

Overkill much?

Swallowing the nervousness down, I walked closer. There were no trees or bushes I could jump in to hide. My eyes scanned for any cameras attached to the exterior of his house. In the darkness, it was hard to see every nook and cranny, but I was 97.9% sure there weren't any.

My heart beat madly as I studied the fence. I looked behind me to check if I was still alone. Everything was spookily quiet except for my loud breathing and the occasional scratching sound my shoes made against the concrete as I stopped in front of the fence.

I laid my palm carefully on the door, pushed gently. It was locked. Damn it. It was too high to see over, and there were no gaps between the wood posts to peek through.

There should have been something in the front yard I could use to step on, so I could see what was behind the fence, but he didn't care to have anything on his lawn but grass. My eyes shot to Big Tony's house. He still owed us money, and he was next on my list. I marched quickly to his front yard, unapologetically grabbed a fake wood stump made of plastic surrounded by funny-looking gnomes, and returned to Mr. Motorcycle's fence.

There, I thought, dusting my hands off after positioning the stump. I stepped on it, looking down to make sure it didn't wobble. When I looked up, my jaw dropped.

La-dee-freaking-da. A huge pool sat empty in the backyard—probably didn't bother filling it because it was too cold to swim outdoors now—but the blue lights on its walls were on and some fancy lampposts scattered in the garden, casting an eerie glow around the yard. Mature trees, beautiful stonework. I loved good landscaping, and this was first-class.

I almost forgot my mission. The motorcycle. Peace of mind was imperative, and I just had to make sure this wasn't going to bite us in the ass later. Still, there was no sign of the motorcycle. I could very well be honest about it and knock on his door and confess everything, but what if this guy proved to be a psycho? I didn't want to risk it.

Should I climb the fence and see if he had another door behind the garage? Maybe it was open, and I could sneak inside quickly. But…what if he had a dog?

Focus. If there were a dog, it would be barking by now.

Gathering my powers, I laid my hands flat on top of the fence. I was going to lift myself up, hook one leg on top, when I heard a noise behind me. Every hair on my body rose.

Holy shit, I'm going to prison tonight.

"Who are you?" A very deep, very male, very *cold* voice said behind me.

Everything inside me froze.

Run!

But my limbs were frozen. Legs weak, I let gravity take over and lower me to the ground, tripping when my foot missed the stump. I squealed, grabbing the fence to maintain my balance. All the jostling loosened my hat, spilling my hair down my back.

I heard a sharp intake of breath behind me.

Silence.

"Who are you?" he repeated. There was still suspicion in his tone, but this time, there was also…curiosity. And that curiosity killed the cat.

Slowly, painfully, I turned around. And I realized…I was the cat.

I knew he could see me. Where I had been grateful for the porch light earlier, now I hated it. It illuminated my face in all its glory for him.

He, however, was surrounded in darkness. I couldn't see his face, but I could make out his shape. He was tall, his shoulders wide and muscular.

There was something awfully familiar in the way he

leaned against the truck. As if I had met him before. His posture told me he was unbothered, like he had made himself comfortable watching a show. Suddenly, I had the urgent need for him to reveal his face in the light. At the same time, I dreaded it.

Do I know him?

He straightened and stepped forward. I backed away until I bumped against the fence behind me. I was gripped by the moment. I wanted to look away, but I was transfixed.

"What are you doing here?" he asked. This time, his voice was like velvet. Teasing.

An uneasy feeling took over me. I'd heard his voice before.

"Tell me," he said.

Tell me.

Why was that so familiar?

And then…he stepped into the light.

All the blood drained from my face. A horrified, strangled noise came out of my throat.

Not him! You gotta be shitting me.

Someone told me I wasn't supposed to get punished for my sins until I die. I'm not dead yet! Then why, oh why?

His smile was infuriatingly cocky. His eyes locked onto mine as he kept coming toward me.

"Stay where you are!" I yelled.

He didn't even pause. Not one bit. Instead, the smile on his beautiful mouth widened, showing his white teeth.

"Stop!" I warned again.

He did. But I had a feeling he didn't stop on my account. Inches from me. The smile on his face disappeared.

A lock of his coal-black hair fell silkily on the side of his face. My eyes followed its movement until it settled on his cheek. I couldn't help as my gaze traveled from his cheek to his mouth, and I just…stared.

In the dark, under the soft glow of the porch light, his face was sinfully beautiful.

And then that smile appeared again. It was a *knowing* smile. An unapologetic, cocky smile.

My eyes shot up to his.

Boom.

I felt it. I *felt* it.

"I didn't expect to see you so soon," he whispered in the same seductive voice. "Miss me already?"

I heard his words, but the signal connecting my ears to my brain was on airplane mode. My eyes and nose, on the other hand, had full bars of signal. LTE.

He must have been out for a run before he caught me trying to climb his fence. He was wearing sweatpants and a T-shirt, despite the cold, that molded to the contours of his body wonderfully. Mouthwateringly.

He smelled of male sweat and soap. An intoxicating combination.

He reached out, gently pushing my hair over my shoulder, but not before the tip of his finger grazed the sensitive skin on my neck.

I shivered. I felt a shock travel from where he touched me reverberate *everywhere* in my body.

And why are my lips tingling?

"Cold?" he asked.

I shook my head vehemently, and that same lock of hair slid over my shoulder again.

"Kara."

It was almost…erotic. The way he said my name. The way his mouth formed the syllables.

"It suits you," he murmured, twirling the ends of my hair around his finger. "I forgot to tell you mine."

I already know it. Cam.

"Cameron," he said when I didn't answer.

Cameron.

My mouth seemed to be under construction again.

This was like our first meeting. This had never happened with anyone else. What was it about him?

It was the beautiful masculine face, I admitted grudgingly. *There!* I admitted it. I was attracted to the face and that was totally fine. I wasn't going to do anything about it. It didn't mean I liked *him*. It didn't mean anything at all except that I was a healthy human being with an eye for beauty.

In defense, I put on my poker face. An emotionless face. If I couldn't speak, fine, but he was not getting any reaction from me.

As if he heard my thoughts, a playful glint appeared in his eyes, and he asked, "How's your stomach?"

It felt like a splash of cold water. I had this sudden urge to cover my face, run, or disperse my molecules into thin air. I glared at him instead.

Who the hell does he think he is to remind me of that mortifying experience?

I'm going to take you down! I vowed angrily, but then he said, "I know why you're here."

That stopped me cold. *Shit.* I had forgotten why I was here.

"I saw what happened this morning," he continued.

No!

I closed my eyes in defeat. Most people wouldn't have kept pressing, but he was persistent.

He must have seen everything. Somehow, this guy saw Dylan.

As soon as I got home, I was going to fry my little shit of a brother in a tub of boiling canola oil. But right now, I had more pressing matters on my hands.

Daydreaming is over, sister!

I had no right to be taking out my anger on him—*he* should be the one angry, *he* was the victim after all, but I couldn't help it. The thought of dealing with the consequences of my brother's actions again and the helplessness and panic gripping my throat drove me over the edge. I opened my eyes and flattened my palms on his chest to push him away. He didn't even budge.

"Move!" I said in the sternest voice I could muster. My voice sounded rusty. Maybe that was why he looked amused—and, okay, sexy as hell—as if he was enjoying the show.

How could he not be angry about his motorcycle right now? Or the fact that he caught me about to sneak inside his yard?

Is there something wrong with his brain?

"I said move."

He moved closer.

I inhaled sharply. He was so close. He sucked on his bottom lip, trapping it between his teeth.

What is it like to kiss him?

As soon as the thought crossed my mind, I killed it mercilessly. Squished the thought like a bug.

No way I was going to kiss this guy! Not his type. Not ever.

What was he doing to me? I was just angry a moment ago, and now I was thinking of kissing him. His proximity was driving me insane, and I wanted to step away, but if I did, that would mean he won. "Get your face away from my sight right now or I'll—"

"Stare at it some more?" he provided. "I think we both established how much you like my face."

Unbelievable!

"We didn't establish shit," I snorted. "But you know what? I do like it."

His eyes glittered with satisfaction.

His smile looked smug until I said, "I'd like to smash it against a rocky surface."

He lost the smile. And since I counted that as a win, I figured it was okay to step away, which I did.

As soon as my nose was far enough not to smell his scent, my brain cells started activating again. "Look, I'm here to negotiate with you," I said.

He looked at me but didn't say anything. And I realized as long as I was gazing at his vivid blue eyes or his sexy mouth, I couldn't think straight, so I looked at his chest. But that was distracting too, so I looked down at his pants. But the—

"Negotiate what?"

I jumped at his voice. Blushing, I looked at his ear— what peeked through his hair anyway. "You know," I croaked. I cleared my throat. "About your motorcycle."

When he didn't reply, I looked up. The playful glint in his eyes was gone and had turned into danger.

I swallowed.

I raised my hands in surrender, backing away from him. Away from his murderous glare. But he kept walking toward me, stalking me, looking like a pissed off archangel.

"Why don't you start from the beginning?" he whispered. His voice was as soft as a feather, as sharp as a knife.

"B-beginning?" I parroted stupidly. I looked past him, gauging how fast I could get away and to my car.

"Don't even try it," he warned.

Nothing pisses me off more than someone telling me I can't do something. We looked at each other for a heartbeat. Waiting. Waiting. And then I sprang for the car.

His hand shot out, gripping my arm. His hold didn't hurt at all, but it was firm. The look he shot me told me this wasn't going to be as easy as I'd hoped it would be.

"You're unbelievable," he said.

I sighed in defeat. "I won't try to escape again, so can you let me go?"

I relaxed my arm and his grip loosened. I shook him off. He let go, but his stance clearly stated that he was just going to catch me again if I tried to run.

I raked my hands in my hair, gathering my thoughts before I spoke again.

"I'm sorry," I said quietly. Sincerely. Because the truth was he was the one wronged. He hadn't asked for any of this, and even though I wasn't exactly Miss Do-It-Right, I'd *try* to do my best to make up for it.

"I'm really sorry," I repeated. "My brother didn't mean to hit your motorcycle this morning."

He closed his eyes, looking like he was praying for patience. I could see the muscle in his jaw ticking. "Your. Brother. Hit. My. Motorcycle."

"Well, yeah. You saw what happened this morning,

right? That was my brother." I waited a beat. When he didn't reply, I continued. "I have a deal for you. A deal only an idiot can refuse. Want to hear it?"

He opened his eyes. He was mad. He didn't speak, just narrowed his eyes at me.

"Do you have security cameras here?" I prodded. "Did you call your insurance yet?"

Again, he didn't answer.

"Listen. I'm taking responsibility. I'll pay for your repairs. In fact, we'll do them."

He crossed his arms. I really should shut up, but his silence only made me want to confess my sins more.

"We own an auto repair shop. I hope you haven't phoned your insurance yet, but if you have, you can probably phone them and cancel the claim. Tell them you settled. If you report it, my brother's insurance will demand his firstborn child in payment."

We looked at each other. I watched as the anger in his eyes faded eventually. I could tell he was thinking.

"What's in it for me?"

I had wanted him to respond, but now that he had, I realized I preferred his nonverbal cues. He looked like a cunning fox.

"What do you mean? We're doing your repairs for free. You won't have to pay your deductible."

Now he looked bored. "The deductible's not a problem."

I bet. "Well…we'll add in an extra service."

He grinned.

I would have smacked his face, but I was trying to get him to show me some mercy, not execute me. It had nothing to do with the way my heart skipped a beat at the sight of that grin. Or what I thought he was thinking by *extra service*. Nothing at all.

Also, it had nothing to do with the way he looked at me. No one had looked at me like that before.

Like he wanted me.

You're fucking crazy. He has a girlfriend. He's a cheater!

I rolled my eyes at the voice in my head.

Yeah, duh. I know. It's not a sin to find something beautiful. Even flies like poop. Nothing's going to happen here. Not ever, so zip it!

"We'll throw in some add-ons," I continued. "If you like. Some accessories. At a reasonable price. Or we can give you free basic maintenance checks for three months. Pick one."

Suddenly, I wanted to get away from him. Fast. I pulled out my wallet from my jacket pocket, fished out our business card, and shoved it and the flyers in his hand.

"Here. All our information is there. Come tomorrow morning. I usually open the shop, so I'll be there." I was rambling. "And you...you have my number."

I flushed at the reminder of how he got it. I started walking down his driveway back to my car. "Which I totally didn't want to give to you, for your information!" I called out to him. "You caught me in a...private moment and I was totally vulnerable. If you have any objections, tell me now or else I'll take this as a yes." I got in my car, started it, reversed. I looked over and saw him still standing there with a mysterious smile.

My heart was knocking so hard in my chest it started to hurt. When I stepped on the gas, I let myself breathe.

"Good job, good job. You did a great job," I muttered to myself. "He totally agreed."

I glanced at my rearview mirror. And found him standing in the same spot, watching my car, before I turned the corner and he disappeared from my sight.

Chapter 7

Cameron

"Don't think the shop's open yet," Caleb said, slamming the tailgate closed after we'd muscled my motorcycle out from the bed of his truck to the ground.

I shrugged.

"You sure about this?" he asked dubiously, surveying the surroundings. He knew how scrupulous I was when it came to my motorcycle.

"Yeah," I answered, turning around to look at the area with him.

The shop was an old, gray, rectangular box built in the middle of a dirt lot. There was a big sign on the roof with the words *HAWTHORNE AUTO REPAIR SHOP*, with their phone number in smaller block font on the lower right. The paint on the *W* was peeling. The roof still held but looked ready to be replaced.

Cars were parked neatly in two rows on the front left side of the building, and on the right side was a dirt road leading to the back of the lot.

"All right then. Let's go get me some coffee," he announced.

"Get a job so you can afford it."

"You could've driven the company truck, but I have

a heart of gold and still drove you here, didn't I? So pay up, cheapo."

"I bought last time. It's your turn, asshole."

"No, it's not, dumbass."

"Sure it is," I said easily.

"Basketball practice on Monday. Loser buys."

"You got it."

His phone chirped.

"It's Rick," he said after reading the text message.

"Better get your ass to the site, then. I'll get a cab as soon as I'm done here and meet you there."

He leaned against the side of the truck, tucked his phone in his jacket pocket, crossed his arms, and yawned.

"Rick's used to me being late," he said. "But, man, the guy's a tyrant. Remind me again why we haven't quit."

Because he saved both our lives, I thought. I knew Caleb was thinking the same thing.

The night I flew to Esther Falls City in Manitoba, the night when my dad picked me up from the airport, was the same night I met Rick for the first time.

I'd lived there before, until I was eight years old, and then my parents divorced and Raven had moved us to Toronto. Then one day, she sent me to Esther Falls for good. I hated it. I found out later that the court gave my dad full custody of me. He didn't want me, but it was a way to hurt her. Even when I lived in his house, I rarely saw him. We never spent time together.

I was the new kid in town. A teenager who hated everything and everyone. An angry kid looking for trouble wherever he could find it. And when I didn't find it, I created it.

Instead of having dinner with my dad, I escaped into

town and looked for trouble. Trouble came in the form of a newly constructed building. It was ten stories high and so pristine that the windows gleamed.

I broke in and found it empty. Some of the walls still needed paint. I found unopened cans of paint, brushes, and tools. I opened the cans, abandoned the brushes, and threw the liquid on walls and ceilings instead. I picked up tools and used them to break thousands of dollars' worth of windows and doors.

That was when Rick found me. He was the contractor, and he came to check the building that night. He was so angry I thought he was going to kill me. But I was confident that I could beat him up if he tried to hurt me.

I ran away, but he caught me easily, shocking me with his strength. He told me I could pay for the damages by working for him for free. I told him to fuck off. He said he'd call the police on me if I didn't. The next day was the first day I started working for Rick.

I didn't know what compelled him not to report me to the police. Didn't know what made him take me under his wing, train and teach me the ins and outs of the business. But he changed my life.

When he thought I was ready, he introduced me to one of his big-shot clients who bought a cabin and wanted it renovated. That became my first freelance gig and earned me a big, fat check. Word spread around, and I got so many projects that I had to quit school for three years and keep working, building my rep. Now I had more than enough saved up to choose which projects I wanted to work on or if I wanted to take a break from my own projects—like I was doing now—and help out Rick now and then. As much as he wanted me to be on my own, I knew he missed me and it made him happy when I worked with him.

I'd paid for those damages with my labor a long time ago, and now he was the one paying me. I'd have worked for him for free if he'd let me.

Caleb and I first met at one of Rick's reno projects. We were troubled teens, angry at the world and blaming ourselves and everyone else around us for the mess that was our lives. We were uncontrollable, didn't give a damn about anything, and on our way to throwing our future to whatever trouble we could find.

I was already doing demos for Rick for a couple of months before Caleb started. The crew knew to stay away from me. I didn't want to talk to anyone, didn't give a rat's ass about eating lunch with them or going for drinks after work. I wanted to be alone and destroy as much as I could. I hated everything.

Especially myself.

And then Caleb Lockhart showed up. His brother, Ben, was friends with Rick and had asked him a favor to let Caleb work doing demolitions. I heard Ben quit a semester into college to focus on his troubled brother. Just for that, he had my respect.

The Lockhart brothers were what the crew called "pretty boys." They came from a wealthy family and clearly didn't need the work. They had a gleam of sophistication even when they were covered in dirt and doing grunt work, and both seemed to enjoy it.

After Caleb started working for Rick, my peace and quiet went out the window. *Alone* seemed to be a foreign concept to Caleb.

He annoyed the hell out of me, picked on me until I

gave him what he wanted. What he wanted was someone he could fight with and who could fight back and
didn't hold back. He found it in me.

It didn't take much to rile me back then, and we beat
each other up almost every time we saw each other.

Eventually, Rick sat us down, and we figured it would
be less painful and would save us money on medical
bills if we focused our anger on demolitions instead.
And then one day, we became friends.

It happened in the middle of summer when we were
doing a demo for a twenty-story apartment building. It
was scorching hot, the air heavy with humidity. It was
the kind of day where breathing alone made me sweat.
The windows were open, but there was no wind coming
in. I glugged water like a camel and seemed to sweat it
out instantly.

I was irritable, hungry, and desperately needed a
shower, but I kept pounding the brick fireplace with the
sledgehammer. I found satisfaction in destroying it.

"Hey, asshole."

I turned around. It was Caleb and he had two monster
sandwiches in his hands. He placed one on top of my
backpack.

"Want a sandwich? Made two. You can have this
one. My dog didn't want it."

I ignored him and went back to work. A couple
of hours later, the foreman called for a lunch break. I
kicked the sandwich to the ground before grabbing my
backpack and walking toward the elevators.

"Hey!"

It was Caleb again. I kept going.

"Does your mama know you're an asshole?"

I stopped in my tracks. This mouthpiece just wouldn't shut up. I was about to turn around and read him his last rites when I felt something hit the side of my face.

I smelled mustard, ketchup, and the mouthwatering aroma of burger meat. I grabbed the tomato on my cheek, popped it into my mouth. Chewed. Swallowed.

My anger faded.

We looked at each other, assessing, watching.

"Got another one?" I asked after a moment.

Surprise flickered in his eyes.

Then he grinned. "Yeah. I got two more, but you're paying for drinks."

I studied his face and determined I didn't detect any deceit. I thought about it for a beat. "Deal."

From then on, Caleb Lockhart has been my friend.

Rick gave us both the chance to purge our anger by giving us sledgehammers to break walls, destroy fireplaces, rip Sheetrock. Eventually, we were promoted to framing, replacing shingles on roofs, painting, and everything else in Rick's business.

I had taken to it naturally. At first, I went because I wanted to focus on something other than my miserable life, but eventually I came to look forward to doing renos after school. It was something I was really good at and I found joy in it. It gave me a sense of purpose. It made me…less miserable and not focus so much on my problems. To forget about that day I regretted the most, that day I desperately wished I could go back to and change.

"I'm going to ask you again. You sure about this?" Caleb indicated the building behind me.

"Yeah, I'm sure. Go ahead to the site. I'll come over soon as I'm done here."

He yawned again. I yawned. "Get your ass out of here, man. You're making me sleepy," I grumbled.

"Need that first." He nodded at my beanie. "Cold as hell for a demo today."

I thought about it.

"You owe me for this morning," he pointed out.

That sounded reasonable. He hated waking up early, and he had to be at the site before nine today, so he'd had to wake up even earlier to drop me and my motorcycle off at the shop.

"You're right," I acknowledged and threw my beanie at him. "Don't sleep with it under your pillow tonight."

He caught it easily, put it on, and shot me a grin. "Hey, how'd you know?" He gave a dainty wave of his fingers before sliding into his truck.

He slid his window down. "Cam," he called out.

"Yeah?"

"Want a sandwich?"

I heard him laughing as he drove away.

Chapter 8

Cameron

As soon as Caleb left, I turned to study the auto repair shop again.

It looked old but clean and decent enough. Appearances could be deceiving though, so I didn't get my hopes up.

I gave my motorcycle a regretful we'll-survive-this-buddy pat on the side.

Suddenly, the shadiness of it all hit me like a freight train. I had no idea who this woman was, what she was capable of. She asked me to come to her shop early in the morning, when no one would be there...

I looked around again. The structure reminded me of the abandoned places where serial killers take their victims to torture them.

Damn Caleb, making me watch all those scary movies. Now I had them in my head.

Why are you here?

Even as I asked myself this, I was already looking for a place to park and hide my motorcycle safely.

Hey, it's your funeral.

There were at least ten cars parked out front. They were either already repaired and waiting to be picked up or still due for repair. That meant they had customers.

Unless those were the cars of their *victims*.

On the right side of the building where the dirt road was, someone had parked a big tandem truck to block the way just enough so a vehicle couldn't pass through.

What were they hiding out there?

More dead bodies, possibly.

But as I reached the dirt road, I saw that there was still a good amount of land behind the shop. Thirty feet away from the shop was a tiny, yellow barn house with pale-blue trim. A toolshed stood beside it. They were in considerably better shape than the shop and made a pretty picture among the pine and poplar trees scattered around the edges of the property.

Was that where she lived?

I scanned the place, looking for her, but there wasn't a soul around. A quick glance on my phone told me it was 8:15 and that I was stupid for being early—too early. Before the shop even opened.

Why are you here?

I sandwiched my motorcycle between the building and the tandem truck, making it hard for anyone to spot it. It looked like it would be safe there. I walked to the edge of the building, then I looked up.

And my heart staggered at the sight of her.

She was coming out of the yellow house and seemed to be having trouble closing the door. She opened it again with a swift kick of her foot, then pulled it closed with considerable muscle and force.

She looked like she'd just gotten out of bed, put on her necessary outerwear, and marched out of the house.

She was still in her pajamas, boots the color of Pepto-Bismol, and a black parka with a hoodie that drowned her body.

She was sniffing from the cold, pushing up the huge eyeglasses that she hadn't been wearing last night. Her thick hair was a nest on top of her head, with pieces of it escaping.

She looked grumpy.

Why are you here?

Wasn't it obvious?

I was here because of her.

Something was not right with me.

I needed coffee. Coffee would zap me back to reality.

I watched as she headed to the back of the shop, where there must be another entrance. I wasn't in her line of sight, although if she looked slightly to her left, she would see me. But her steps were purposeful, her gaze straight.

She was like this yesterday too. Yesterday. It didn't feel like we just met yesterday. It felt like I'd been thinking about her for a long, long time.

It was clear to me that she had a one-track mind. She was like a missile. Once she locked on her target, that was all she could concentrate on.

Yesterday morning, when she was marching to Dingle Dick's house, she passed in front of me as if I didn't exist. And last night, while I was out for a run, trying not to think about her, debating whether to call her or not, she appeared in my driveway. She was sneaking around like a thief and didn't even notice that I was behind her, watching her.

I had thought it was a tall, lanky guy in a large,

shapeless hoodie trying to do a B and E. I would have attacked. And then her hair had spilled out from her hat.

And somehow, I knew it was her.

I thought she'd vandalized Dingle Dick's house, maybe got spotted and was looking for someplace to hide and picked my house.

I didn't expect the words that had tumbled from her mouth after that.

And now I was at her shop, watching her again.

She tried to open the back door of the shop with her key, but it looked like it wouldn't turn. Must have frozen overnight. She muttered under her breath. Instead of walking to the side of the building where I was standing, she circled around the opposite side. I walked back to the front of the building.

Success, I thought as I watched her twist the key and unlock the front door. At least this door didn't give her grief. She raised her head slightly, and our eyes connected.

She froze, eyes wide in shock, before she pulled out her key—or tried to. It was stuck.

I watched her struggle, almost in a panic trying to yank the key out. When she did, she grabbed the door like a lifeline and disappeared inside. The decisive snap of the dead bolt was loud. I laughed quietly.

Man, she was a riot. She saw me and definitely locked me out.

I walked to the front door, leaned against the wall. Tapped my knuckles on the door.

Nothing. I waited.

Was she pretending she hadn't seen me?

It took a couple of minutes before I heard the lock open. The door opened a crack.

Hazel. Her eyes were hazel. More green, like crisp grass in the morning, than brown.

Those eyes glared at me, razor-sharp blades ready to make me bleed. We stood there for a beat.

My gaze slowly shifted down.

She had a beauty mark on the upper side of her lip. So faint you could barely see it unless you knew where to look.

I wanted to do more than look.

Her hands flew to cover her mouth.

"Back off!"

Or I thought that was what she said. Her hands had muffled the sound.

"Morning," I said. I propped my arm on the doorjamb, gave her a smile. A friendly, nonthreatening, I'm-as-safe-as-they-come smile. It usually worked. This time, it didn't.

She glowered at me. She had zipped her parka closed, hoodie in place to cover her messy hair.

"Do you know how to read?" she demanded, still covering her mouth with her hand.

I pushed the door open and walked inside the warmth. She stepped back.

"I'm getting tutored every Wednesday," I answered, closing the door and facing her. "Right now, I'm having trouble reading"—the door was fogged up with condensation; I wrote on it with my finger—"this. Can you read that for me?" I asked.

I spelled *HIT-AND-RUN*.

She pursed her lips, rubbed away what I wrote with her fist, and jotted *9 AM*.

"Can you read this? You're early. The card I gave

you yesterday clearly stated the shop's not open till nine on Saturdays."

I could have waited at a coffee shop, walked around the block, but I didn't because…

I wanted to see you.

"Where's your motorcycle?"

I shrugged. Her jaw hung open.

"You…you didn't bring it?" She backed away a few feet. "I mean, did you change your mind about bringing it here?"

"What made you think I'd made up my mind?"

"Last night! You agreed—"

"Did I?"

She sputtered. I wanted to smile but figured that wasn't a smart thing to do, so I sucked my bottom lip into my mouth.

"Listen," she started. "I don't know what else you want, but I'm giving you a deal here. A really good deal. And if you need me to repeat it again until your brain can absorb it, I will."

"Why are you covering your mouth?"

"I forgot to brush my teeth!" she yelled. "Okay? You happy now?"

She looked like she was going to stomp her foot. "I can't talk to you like this. I need my powers. I'm going home to brush my teeth. Stay here. Don't steal anything. I'll be back in five minutes."

She locked the front door and proceeded to the back of the shop. There was an impression of clean floors, tools, a couple of cars suspended from the ceiling, the smell of motor oil, solvent—good, strong smells of a hardworking garage.

"I like your hair," I said as I followed her outside. And meant it.

She threw me a withering look. "Don't make fun of it. It's my antenna for my brain. Keeps me reasonable, you know? That's why I haven't murdered you yet. Get it? Why are you following me?"

She sure talked a lot, but I really liked the sound of her voice. "Need coffee."

She laughed.

It was so unexpected I stumbled. I wished she'd do it again.

"Don't we all?" There was sympathy in her voice. "Go back to the shop and I'll bring you some."

She stopped at the door of her house, pulled out her key.

"Kara," I said softly.

She froze. Slowly turned around to face me, her hand still on the doorknob. Maybe that made her feel safe. Having an anchor.

There was something between us. I knew she felt it.

"Invite me inside," I said.

I saw her throat working.

"You do this to me a lot." Her voice was raspy.

"Do what?"

"Nothing. I'm not going to be alone in my house with you. Do you normally sneak behind your girlfriend's back to go to another girl's house?"

"I don't have a girlfriend."

"Liar."

"Not this time."

She looked at me for a moment, her eyes direct and searching. She must have liked what she saw because, without a word, she went inside and left the door open for me.

I took my time. By the time I came inside, I saw her closing a door to what I assumed was the bathroom.

I saw her parka on the couch, where she'd carelessly thrown it, and her shoes by the door, so I removed mine before going in and took a seat on the sofa. There was a pink note posted on the wall that said *SHOES OFF!* And another one by the light switch that said *LIGHTS OFF BEFORE YOU LEAVE! CHECK STOVE!* I figured her mom probably posted them there. It was obvious by the knickknacks around the house that she didn't live alone, but where was her family?

The tiny house looked bigger on the inside. It was one of the older houses in the neighborhood and it was clear they'd renovated it at one point in time. Broke down the walls, so it was open concept now, added windows to let in more light. I had renovated houses like these with Rick before. It gave me a warm, good feeling to be in her home.

Fifteen minutes had passed when she came out of the bathroom. She stood outside the door. Her hair was up in a neat ponytail now. She had put gloss on her lips and did something subtle with her eyes that made them look bigger. She had changed into tight jeans and a sweater the color of sunshine.

My hands itched to touch. Her skin, her hair, her lips.

"How do you take your coffee?" she asked stiffly.

"Black."

"I ran out of the good stuff. I only have instant."

"That's fine."

She walked to the kitchen and put on the kettle to

boil. I got up from the couch, followed her there. There was another pink note. This one said *NO SPOON IN MICROWAVE!* I chuckled.

"What's so funny?" she asked, pouring hot water in a cup.

I gestured toward the note.

"I'm the only female in this house, surrounded by men who can't function by themselves. I have to put reminders on everything or else they forget."

I wondered where her mom was but didn't comment.

She cleared her throat. "Answer this for me. Who was that girl in the…" She blushed. "In the bathroom with you?"

So, back to that. I looked down, so she wouldn't see my smile. When I looked up, she was placing the mug of coffee on the counter beside me, then moved as far away from me as the tiny kitchen allowed.

"I never had a girlfriend before."

"You want me to believe that?"

"I think you already do. I wouldn't be in your house if you didn't, would I?"

Her eyes sparkled, and a hint of a smile flirted on her lips. She was enjoying this.

"You've never gone out with any girl for more than a couple of weeks?"

"If I did, it never meant anything."

"What was the longest time you dated a girl?"

This time, I let her see my smile. "Why do you want to know?"

"Just…an experiment. You're an experiment," she stammered.

"An experiment?"

Slowly, I stepped toward her. Her eyes were wide, watching my every move. The pulse on her neck was pounding.

"You want me to be your experiment?"

She swallowed.

"What do you have in mind for me?" I whispered.

I placed my hand on the soft skin of her neck, gently stroked the side of it with my thumb. "I might say yes if you tell me."

She closed her eyes, her muscles relaxing and her body swaying softly toward me. I wrapped an arm around her waist to support her.

"How about I make you a deal?" I continued. She smelled of peaches. Ripe, sweet peaches. "You said your brother doesn't have insurance. See, you shouldn't have told me that. Now I've got an ace."

Her eyes flew open. She slammed her hands on my chest and pushed me away.

"Get off me!"

I stepped back. "You're too honest for your own good."

She scoffed. "Oh, believe me when I say that I'm not!"

"Maybe," I allowed. "But in my book, you are."

"What do you want?" she spat it out. Her stance was confrontational, her voice dripped with venom.

If she thought that would turn me away, she was mistaken. I wanted more of it.

I leaned against the counter, reached for the cup of coffee she'd made for me. "If I go to my insurance, my bike will be fixed."

"But you're going to have to cough up your deductible—"

"I can pay for my deductible easily. And I can take it to the mechanic who's been servicing my motorcycle for years. Why should I go to a shop that I have no idea if they'll do a good job or not?"

If looks could kill, I'd be decapitated by now.

"Have you heard of subrogation? My insurance will go after your brother. It's also a hit-and-run. The police will be *very* interested."

I gave her a moment to absorb that. Then I said, "So now that we know where we both stand, let's make a deal."

I took a sip and very nearly choked. It was too strong. When I saw her face, I knew she'd deliberately made it undrinkable.

This girl would cut me off at the knees without batting an eye. Why did that excite me?

Damn. I'm in trouble.

"First, tell me why you're doing this for your brother."

She crossed her arms in front of her. "I don't need to tell you dick."

My mouth twitched. "Tell me why the hell he isn't owning up and paying for his mistake."

"You're not going after him for this. If you do, I'll castrate you."

"You like making threats, don't you?"

"I like putting them in action too. Try me and you'll find out."

"Oh, I think I want to. I'm looking forward to it." To prove it, I took another sip of her coffee without breaking eye contact with her. "Tell me where he is."

"I won't let you—"

"I'm not going to hurt him. Don't you think he owes me an apology? Or do you think that's too much to ask?"

She opened her mouth, closed it. Sighed. "No," she said, capitulating. "It's not too much to ask. He went fishing with my dad."

"So…" I looked at her lips. Her bottom lip was fuller than the top. I moved my gaze up and met hers. "You're alone with me."

She narrowed her eyes. "Yeah. And no one would know who murdered you when I hide your body in the shed."

I paused and threw my head back laughing.

"I like you," I said.

"Listen, I don't go out with guys. Ever."

I paused. There was something about her expression that told me she wasn't feeling as firm on this as she sounded. "Girls?"

"No."

"Never had a boyfriend?"

"Never met anyone who measured up."

"To what?"

"My standards."

"Tell me what they are."

"You're playing with me."

"Am I?"

She let out a huff and walked to the living room. "Let's talk about this deal so you can leave. I have a very busy day."

"Sure." I poured the coffee in the sink and rinsed the cup before following her to the living room. I sprawled on the couch. She leaned against the wall opposite me, eyeing me warily.

"That's my dad's bed. Feel free to soil it or anything."

The house looked like it had two bedrooms and

a bathroom. The two rooms must be for her and her brother.

"I like sleeping on the couch too," I said. I stopped for a moment. I hadn't meant to tell her that.

She gave me a bored look. "What's the deal?"

I looked her directly in the eye. "Give me a ride."

She blinked slowly. "Come again?"

"Until my motorcycle is finished to my satisfaction, you're going to drive me where I need to be. Not your brother. Not your best friend. You."

"Have you lost your mind? What, do you think I have all the time in the world?"

"Since I saw you trying to break into my house last night, I'm going to have to say yes."

"You have a mint truck in your driveway! That's yours, isn't it?"

"That's not mine."

It was the company truck assigned to me, which would make what I said technically a lie, but I couldn't let her know that or she would never agree.

"You can get a rental!"

"Are you paying for it?"

"This is blackmail."

"You make it so easy. Rule number one: don't expose your weakness to the enemy."

"Are you my enemy?"

"Wanna find out?" I stood up, walked toward her.

She stood her ground. Unflinchingly.

"If I do this, you'll let my shop fix your motorcycle? You won't file a claim with your insurance?"

"Yeah."

I want to know what your lips taste like.

"No accessories," she added.

What they feel like.

"And no maintenance," she finished.

She'd drive me to bankruptcy if she could. And laugh while she was at it. She could shut me down and kick me out if she really didn't want the deal, but some part of her was thriving on the tension between us. I could feel it in the way her body turned toward me, the way her eyes flashed with excitement, and the hint of a smile on her lips she tried to hide.

"The deal includes maintenance." Before she could open her mouth to protest, I added, "But you can get out of it. Easily."

"Why don't you tell me how, oh wise one?"

I rubbed the stubble on my jaw. It was getting itchy. Time for a shave. I headed to the front door and put on my shoes. I opened the door, then tossed her my keys.

"I'll let you know."

Chapter 9

Kara

THE MOST IMPORTANT THING IN LIFE IS THAT YOU HAVE YOUR health. Because once that was gone, nothing else would be the same. Food wouldn't taste as good. And that would be really bad. Really, really bad. Because food is important. And health is important. As important as food. It's the most important thing in life. Food.

So why the hell was I melting on the floor, feeling like he just took everything important with him when he went out that door?

All my food was still in the fridge.

Nothing was out of place.

But nothing felt the same.

He was like a black hole. His presence had sucked out all the energy, all the light in the room, so that when he left, the room felt too bright.

Too empty.

I wanted to lock myself in the bathroom. I wanted to *think*. Stress out and freak out about what had just happened. Replay everything in my mind, obsess about every detail, every word he'd said, every look he gave me...

Every response I could have said *better*.

It felt like I just signed a contract with the devil.

I could always say no. I had a choice. I hadn't signed anything. I hadn't even agreed to anything.

Who am I kidding?

We both knew that I would. And that was what galled me. He *knew* that I wouldn't say no. He had cornered me. Herded me like he was a damn border collie and I was a sheep.

Even though he was being logical like a damn lawyer, pointing out the facts and consequences of Dylan's actions, every word out of his mouth felt like a threat. And it pissed me right the hell off.

What was disturbing was that I had no idea what his intention was. Why was he doing all this? Was he bored and thought it would be fun to play with me? Or did he just really want payback for his damaged motorcycle? But why did he want *me* to drive him and not Dylan?

What if I said no deal? Would he actually make good on his threat and file the claim?

Yes, I realized, gripping his key in my hand. Yes, he would.

He looked like someone who would go to great lengths to get what he wanted.

So what if he was get-naked-for-me-baby kind of gorgeous? *So what?*

He was clever and calculating. Manipulative and threatening. You never knew where he was leading you until he was good and ready to reveal it to you. Although, if I were being honest with myself, I would admit that he was… exciting. Different from anyone I have ever met before.

His sheer size was threat enough. Combined with his electric-blue eyes and sharp tongue, he was lethal.

But I could handle him.

If he was dangerous—and he was—I was danger.

The sound of feet stomping at the front door woke me up from my mental torture. My head jerked up.

"You!" I pointed to Dylan. "We need to talk."

Saturdays at the garage were busy. There were already five cars lined up outside the door by the time Dylan and I headed to the shop.

I'd usually have already set up the coffee maker and bought donuts from across the street for our weekend customers, but thanks to a fuckboy showing up too early and scaring the living daylights out of me, I hadn't had time to do anything.

Hours later, I still hadn't caught up, but at least I had managed to get the coffee going.

"Here you go," I told a customer, handing her a set of keys and the receipt for an oil change. "Have a great day, Mrs. Chung."

"Oh, I would have brought my car in on Tuesday, so your dad could take a look at it. I do think Mike's the best mechanic in the city," she said conversationally, folding her receipt. She opened her purse and stashed it there. "The brakes were making weird noises while I was picking up my grandkids, and I was scared something would go wrong with the car. So I went to another garage. The one outside the city, near that soil company. It's close to where my grandkids live."

Mrs. Chung had been our loyal customer for years. Her white puff of hair reminded me of cotton candy. She always smelled like cigarettes and the mint candy she chewed on. She pulled out one and offered it to me.

"Thanks, Mrs. Chung."

"They're really good. I just don't like it when they crack my dentures."

I smiled at her while I unwrapped the candy, popped it in my mouth.

A picture of Cameron biting that red lollipop invaded my mind. The candy made a cracking sound as I bit on it hard, imagining it was his hand.

"Oh dear, be careful. Might crack your teeth. You don't want dentures, you don't."

"Might take a while before I need them, Mrs. Chung. Maybe by then, they'll have invented uncrackable ones that can bite through metal."

"Technology, eh. Gotta love it." She nodded. "I'd have preferred to bring my car here," she continued. She wasn't done with the topic. Mrs. Chung sure loved to chat. I smiled at her. "Your dad doesn't come up with ten other things to repair just to make a quick buck. He's honest, Mike is. Good-looking too." She winked at me. "But they have that shuttle service over there. Makes it convenient for me because I had my hair appointment that morning. They picked me up too when my car was ready."

"That's great, Mrs. Chung."

"I do miss those times when you had that shuttle service."

I didn't bother sighing. In an effort to increase sales during the weekdays, we had offered the shuttle service twice a week for a while before we kiboshed it.

It increased the number of our weekday customers, but work orders were barely finished on time. Dylan and Ekon, both our maintenance mechanics, had to postpone their work to drive customers around. We simply didn't have the manpower or a budget to hire a driver. Unless I cloned myself or suddenly shit a million bucks, it was a no-go.

"Say hi to your dad for me, won't you? Where is he?"

"He went to Lockport this morning to pick up car parts for a friend."

"Did he go fishing too?"

My dad and Dylan had left at three this morning, so they'd have time to go fishing before picking up the car parts. Dylan told me Dad had to stay there for a few hours to help his friend cut a giant tree on his property that was damaging his house.

"You bet your sexy tush he did."

She giggled. "Tell him to give me a ring if he has fish to spare. They don't sell them that fresh at the store anymore." She tucked her purse in her armpit. "I'll see you on my next oil change, dear. Bye now."

I went back to my desk and was just about to sit down when another customer came in. I sighed and put on my sweet-girl smile. "Hi there. Here to pick up your car?"

When she left, I glanced at the clock. It had been a long, tiring day, and it was almost time for my shift at the coffee shop. I gulped my coffee and started closing.

I grabbed my phone, debating whether I should look at it or not.

Had the son of Satan texted yet?

It drove me apeshit wondering, waiting.

"Hey, Kara Koala." My dad propped his elbow on the counter.

"Hey, Dad. I didn't know you were back already.

You just missed Mrs. Chung. She said give her a call if you got extra fish."

"Sure thing."

I tapped my cheek. "Got something there."

He grabbed the rag from his back pocket—the one with more grease on it—and wiped his cheek. It only added more.

I let out a sigh, reached for the baby wipes I kept in my desk drawer.

"Left cheek, boyfriend," I said.

He rubbed his eyes and leaned on the counter, turning his cheek to me.

I wiped it off.

"Am I handsome yet?" He looked tired. Really tired and—

"Heartbreakingly handsome. How's the tree?"

"Stronger than me. You still going to Tala's tonight?"

"Uh-huh." My dad usually lingered when he was chewing over something on his mind he wanted to discuss with me. "What's up?"

He took his time. He went to the water cooler and grabbed a cone paper cup. "Getting colder now. It'll be winter soon."

"Dad, spit it out."

He just gave me a smile, his eyes patient. And worried. "It's one of our busiest seasons. People wanting to get their vehicles ready for winter."

"I'm sure they all don't want to ride their dog sleds to work."

"Smartass." He winked at me and took a sip of his drink. "Want some?"

I shook my head. He finished his water and pitched

the cup into the wastebasket before he walked back to the counter.

"Your uncle thinks we need to let go of Ekon."

"What? Why? We need Ekon!" My words came out in a rush, angry and hot. "A lot of our customers come for oil change, brake checks, inspection. Dyl and Ekon are our only maintenance guys. And you and Vlad do the heavy work orders. What's going to happen if we get bombarded with customers wanting an oil change? Turn them away?"

"I already—"

I was so furious and frustrated I made a fist and slammed it on the counter.

"Just because Andrew comes here twice a week to help, he thinks he can fire people who are more useful and hardworking than he could ever be?"

Andrew's face was very clear in my head, and so was my fist as it connected with it.

"He doesn't even stay a full day, Dad. He leaves whenever he pleases. Always complaining about his bunions. Charity said he doesn't even have them! He thinks he can act like King Kong, king of the jungle, *oh-em-gee*, raise your hands up in the air! King of the jungle!" I snorted derisively. "More like *joke* of the jungle."

My dad snorted out a laugh at that. But I wasn't done. I was so fired up.

"Dylan won't be able to do all of it if you let Ekon go, and you or Vlad are going to have to help him. You know both of you are more than busy enough. I'm going to have to give that guy an epiphany and talk to him. He's dumb as a doorknob, Dad."

His dumbness was oozing out of every orifice, and I

was going to plug every one of them so that he wouldn't be able to infect us.

"Don't worry, Kar," my dad said placidly. "I already told him I don't agree with him. I just wanted to tell you, so you know what's happening if he brings it up."

"Ekon has been working for us for years." I heard the whine in my voice now. "He's going to school. He needs this job."

"I know, sweetheart. He's not going anywhere."

I let out a sigh. I could always count on my dad.

He had built a good reputation in the community, both in business and socially. Business was good, but we were only breaking even.

Since the shop was owned by my dad and Andrew, the profits were split fifty-fifty. But instead of putting the profits back into the business, like my dad did, Andrew insisted on keeping his share.

A huge chunk of the savings in my bank account was to buy the leech out, and that money I refused to touch until it was ready. I wouldn't even use it to pay for my tuition. It was going to buy Andrew's share of the shop. He'd already told me his price.

"Sorry, Dad. Rant over. I don't like your brother." I took out my parka from the closet, shrugged it on, and grabbed my purse. "Time for my shift at the coffee shop. I'll see you tomorrow morning."

"Are you sleeping over at Tala's?"

"No, but I'll come in late. Don't wait up for me."

"I always wait up for you."

The couch in our living room was my dad's bed. There were only two bedrooms in our tiny house, and he refused to sleep in the same room with Dylan. My brother snored like a freight train.

"Don't forget to turn off the TV. Don't you dare wash the dishes. It's Dylan's turn. Flo is coming by to pick up the couch I refurbished. She owes me two fifty for that. Make sure you count, Dad. I've been working on that for two months during my spare time."

"I'll write it on my body so I don't forget. Anything else, ma'am? I think I still have room on my back to write on."

I laughed. "Don't forget to call Mrs. Chung."

"Will do. Have fun tonight. Love you, sweetheart."

"Love you, Dad."

T: Wanna Netflix and chill?

I laughed as I read Tala's text.

K: As long as you keep your hands to yourself, we won't have a problem.

T: Why? You do know I only want you for your body, right?

K: Yeah, but you never pay tho. This shit's not for free yo.

K: P.S. I'm a block away. Get the milkshakes ready!

T: You're such a gold digger. See you soon xoxo

I tucked my phone in my parka, pushed the door open, and stepped out of the coffee shop.

I'd just finished my four-hour shift and was seriously

thinking of walking to her house instead of driving there to save gas money.

It was three blocks away.

I disliked any form of exercise that didn't involve earning money by the hour.

Well, there were always exceptions.

Although I wished I could get paid for breathing.

Wouldn't that make things easier?

I needed to double *super* save now—more than ever before—just in case my blackmailer proved to be a diva and asked me to drive him all the way to Timbuk-fucking-tu.

It was necessary to talk to him about his terms— and *mine*—and get all of it in writing. You can't fully trust people nowadays. Especially someone as slick as he was.

I gripped my phone in my pocket.

There had been no text, no call—nothing, nada, zilch—from him.

I'd been looking at my phone on and off at work to the point of getting the stink eye from my manager, Ramandeep. Couldn't blame her, really.

It was driving me batshit crazy.

When did he want me to pick him up? How often? Where?

I'll let you know.

What did he mean by that? Did he already have something in mind, or was his computer brain still processing it?

For him, it was all about who had the upper hand. *I* would show him who had the upper hand. But first, I had to make him think I was following the rules.

Thinking about him made me hungry for food. And when I was hungry, I was grumpy.

Vlad said it would only take two weeks—three tops—for the parts to arrive and be installed before his motorcycle would be done. Then I'd be free.

Can't wait! It was my mission in life now.

I turned the corner, spotting Tala's house. It was an architectural beauty of stone and wood, with two tall pillars on the front porch.

It would've been better if it wasn't painted the color of fresh salmon, and it could definitely go without the puke-green trim.

It needed flowers, I thought, pressing the doorbell. Colorful, fat blooms on the porch, a couple of rocking chairs, traditional lanterns in bronze on each side of the door, repaint it a gorgeous shade of white and soft gray for the trim, and *voilà*! Instant curb appeal.

"Kara, honey, come in." Mrs. Bautista swiveled her wheelchair back as I stepped inside.

"These are for you, Mrs. B." I handed her a box of her favorite donuts from the coffee shop, noting the dark circles under her eyes. Her black hair was pulled in a tight bun, accentuating the sharp angles of her thin face. Her clothes hung loosely on her body. "How are you feeling today?"

"My arm's bothering me a little bit, but nothing I haven't dealt with before." She waved her hand in dismissal. "Tala's in the kitchen."

"Over here, pimp!" Tala called out.

"Tala didn't give you a massage today, did she?" I asked Mrs. B. "That lazy ass. Let's give you one in a few. Get the blood flowing a bit, huh?"

She looked haggard today. She patted my hand and smiled. "You spoil me every time you come here."

My mother had left me, but a few women had taken her place.

Mrs. B was one of them.

"I do this for a living," I said, referring to one of my many jobs.

I had just quit my full-time position at the nursing home because it conflicted with my class schedule, but I told my manager that I'd like to be kept on as part-time. I also picked up shifts at a hospital if they phoned, which wasn't often. Full-time positions were limited, so it wasn't unusual for a healthcare worker to work in more than one institution.

"I got mad skills. Mad massaging skills."

I pushed Mrs. B's wheelchair to the kitchen, appreciating the delicious scent of Filipino food. Tala was at the stove, transferring food from a pot to a big bowl.

"Ma made pancit."

Due to an accident, Mrs. B had lost both her legs. She had full range of motion in her arms, but her left one bothered her quite a bit.

"Sit down, Kara. Tal, give her a plate."

"I won't say no. I'm starving."

"I made a vegetarian version just for you. Tal, pack some food for her dad and brother before she leaves."

"Why don't we just give her the fridge?" Tala asked.

"Your pantry too." I gestured my fork at Tala before taking a huge bite. Damn, this was good noodles.

"Want some rice with that?"

I looked at her plate, which was a mountain of noodles on top of rice.

I shook my head. "Man, aren't you tired of rice? Even squirrels eat other shit"—I glanced at Mrs. B—"stuff, I meant stuff, Mrs. B—aside from acorns."

"Girl, don't you be throwing shade at my rice. I'd rather die than not eat rice. See, I know you're half Asian—Filipino and Chinese, right? But the problem is that your Asian soul never settled in your corporeal form. You're a fake Asian. Whatever. If you don't grasp my love affair with rice, you're a hopeless Asian."

"That's because I'm part Spanish, Italian, French, and German too. I'm a mongrel. A mix. A kaleidoscope of everything unicorn-y."

"Guess what? I wish I'm a magical unicorn with wings. That way I could flap away from your bullshit."

"You love my bullshit. That's the truth."

"Let me tell you the truth. I can eat meat the size of my finger, but my serving of rice has to be the size of my head."

"That's why she can't lose weight," her mom said. "She keeps on eating rice. I told her just one cup every meal. Then eat one cup a day as soon as she gets used to it, but she wouldn't listen. Talk to your friend, Kara."

"Mrs. B," I said in a strict voice. I looked at her directly, then I pointed at my ass. "Do you know how hard I wish I got her curves? Look at these babies." I shook my tits. "Look at hers. I wouldn't change a thing about her body."

"You look like a model, Kara."

"Why, thank you, Mrs. B. I do love how clothes look on me. That's why I have a love affair with them. Naked is a different story."

Tala laughed and started cleaning up.

"Don't clean up while Kara is still eating. You know what they say when you clean up while a single woman is eating."

"What do they say, Mrs. B?"

She knocked on wood. "You won't be able to marry."

If the image of my gorgeous-as-sin blackmailer's face came to mind at the word *marry*, I told myself it didn't mean anything. "Good! I'm finished anyway." I got up and brought my plate to the sink. "I'd just be a butterfly, hopping from one flower to the next."

"Until someone catches you and breaks off your wings," Tala interjected.

"Whoa, whoa. Such bitterness. What's wrong with you?" I wanted to talk to her about Cameron, but it could wait until we were alone.

Tala didn't talk until we were in her room, after I'd helped Mrs. B use the commode, settled her on the bed, gave her a bed bath and a massage, and turned on the TV so she could watch her Filipino soaps. She was settled in for the night.

I could do this in my sleep. When I was working at the nursing home, I had to get eight patients washed and ready before breakfast. In other nursing homes I worked at or the hospital, it was more. And night shifts could easily triple that number.

But today had been a long day, and I was starting to feel it.

"Thanks for coming today. Her worker called in sick. She didn't want a different one to come in."

"Anytime. She looks exhausted."

"She's almost always depressed. She wants to go home."

Home meant the Philippines.

"So why don't you take her on a vacation? On Christmas break. You'd get two weeks."

"No, Kar," she said in a grave voice. "She wants to go home. Permanently."

My heart fell to my stomach. "What?"

"Maybe it's the depression that's talking. I don't know."

"If she goes, you go too, right?"

"Let's not talk about it. There's no point in stressing over it right now."

"No, let's talk about it now."

"No. Let's really not. But…" She sighed. "I don't know how to make her happy anymore. I'm doing everything she wants. I'm taking business, just like she wants. She can't wait until I graduate, so I can take over our stores in the Philippines. But…"

"It's not what you want."

She looked at me helplessly. "That's the thing, Kar. I've been following my mom's plan for so long, I don't even know what I want anymore."

She plopped on her bed and turned on the TV. She shook her head at me, a sign that she really didn't want to talk about it, and patted the space beside her. I sighed and lay down beside her. I wanted to talk to her about my blackmailer, but the timing was off. She had so much on her plate that I didn't want to burden her more with my problems. We watched one of her shows for a while before I said goodbye.

It was still early when I got home, still preoccupied with my conversation with Tala. Ever since Mrs. B's mother passed away a year ago, Mrs. B's health had declined. If she wanted to move, it wouldn't be a problem for them financially. Tal's family was loaded.

What I couldn't get out of my mind was the helpless anguish in Tala's eyes.

The back porch light turned on as I looked for my house keys in my purse. Tired to the bone, I prepared myself to have a hard time opening the door, but it opened easily. Dad must have repaired it already.

The house was ancient, and the wooden door became swollen from moisture. Dad had to trim it. It should've been replaced, but doors were pretty expensive.

I heard the sounds of the TV before I pushed it open.

"Hey, Kara Koala, you're early. How was your girl night?" His smile turned into a frown when he saw me. "What's wrong?"

I stored my boots in the closet, dumped my keys in the bowl on the console table, hung my purse on the hook, and walked to the kitchen to get something to drink. The light from the fridge made a yellow slash on the floor.

"I think Tal's mom wants to go back to the Philippines for good."

He sat up from the couch and muted the TV. "Hmm."

My dad knew me enough not to say anything. To give me time to formulate my thoughts. The more people demanded what I was thinking or feeling, the more closed off I got.

I took my time, storing the Tupperware filled with pancit that Tala gave me in the fridge, boiling water, cutting up lemon wedges to make honey lemon tea for me and my dad.

I handed him the cup and sat beside him. We watched TV for a while. I was lost in my thoughts, and I didn't realize there was no sound from the TV until I heard my dad sipping his tea.

"Dad?"

"Hmm?"

"You never asked me to be anything," I said quietly, staring intently at my cup. "You never told me what you want me to become."

He took another sip. Sighed deeply. "That's because you already are what I want you to be."

I felt the threat of tears.

"You know what your favorite sentence was when you were a kid?"

I sniffed. "Gimme food?"

He chuckled. "You eat like me, but we never gain weight, do we? I got supreme genes, I tell you."

I nodded. "That you have, Mr. Hawthorne. That you have."

The light from the TV was playing on my dad's features when I looked up at him.

"Your favorite sentence was *I can do it*." He laughed as if remembering a funny memory.

"I don't know if you remember, but you were five years old, and you were watching me wash the dishes. All of a sudden you tugged at my shirt and said, 'Dad, I wanna do it.' I remember how big the plate looked in your hands and I thought you were going to drop it. I tried to take it from you, but you got mad and said—"

"No, I can do it."

He smiled warmly, nodded. "Same thing when you were tying your shoes, picking out your outfit. You wanted to do it all by yourself. Those moments made me realize how strong and independent you are. It's very hard for a parent to step back, watch his kid struggle. But I'd learned that protecting you too much wasn't doing you any good."

He looked down for a moment. "One day," he continued, "I'll be gone, and I want you to be strong when that time comes. Before that happens, you have to learn how to handle pain. When you're sick, when you're sad, when people hurt you. If it hurts you, it hurts me more. How can it not? You're my life."

"Dad." I sniffled. I couldn't bear the thought of him gone.

"When your ma left, I was terrified. How the hell was I going to do this alone? I know I'm not perfect. And I'm lacking so many things. But then I look at you. And I know I did something good on this earth. And that's all I need. That's all I need, my baby girl."

I stayed with my dad for another half hour after that, trying not to cry, sipping on my honey lemon tea, watching TV. When I collapsed in bed, my body was exhausted, but my mind was buzzing with everything that had happened that day.

Everyone was trying to control someone's life in some way. It didn't matter whether they had good intentions or bad.

Andrew, the joke of the jungle, trying to suck the life out of everything as usual.

Mrs. B's depressive state and her need to control Tala's life.

Tala's helplessness and anguish. She might move away soon. She was going to leave me. I tried not to think about that.

And last but certainly not least, my blackmailer, the right-hand man of Satan. Leaving me little choice but to be his chauffeur ninja. Be at his beck and call. Like a circus monkey.

I'm a strong woman who takes control of her life. I can't control what others do around me, but I can control my reaction.

And my reaction is to go to my blackmailer's house right now and demand what the hell he wants. The terms and conditions. Make a contract. Take back control.

I sprang up in bed. Cracked my knuckles. Stretched my neck.

I'm ready.

Chapter 10

Cameron

"THANKS, MAN."

I hopped out of Caleb's truck, slamming the door closed. He gave me a salute before driving away.

It was dark by the time we'd finished at the site. The guys who did overtime with us were going out for beer, and Caleb with them, but I wasn't in the mood to socialize.

I'd told Caleb I'd take a cab, but he wouldn't hear it. It was easier to agree than argue with the guy.

I walked up my driveway, thinking I'd give up a limb for a shower right now. Ice-cold beer too. I just preferred drinking it after the hot shower. And having no one flapping their lips at me, especially when I was this exhausted from a reno.

The porch light flashed as I walked closer to the front door, then I stopped.

I smiled as I spotted something in front of the fence. It was a fake wood stump. The one she'd used last night to boost herself up and climb the fence.

I walked to it, my muscles screaming at me to take that hot shower as I crouched down to pick it up.

Where the hell did she get it from? Did she bring it with her?

I chuckled as I pictured her carting this thing from her car. She was resourceful if anything. I tossed it to the other side of my fence.

I was keeping it.

Why was she trying to climb over my fence anyway? I wondered as I opened my front door. I took off my boots, so I wouldn't get dried mud on the floor, stored them in the mudroom. I'd clean them tomorrow.

I doubted she was trying to steal from me. I stripped off my dirty clothes, threw them in the washer, pressed the right settings. Then I hopped in the shower and programmed the right temperature and pressure.

Closing my eyes, I groaned in relief as the hot water cascaded down my body, washing away the dirt and muck.

I'd ask her why she was trying to get in my house next time I saw her. Which would definitely be on Monday. There was a whole day of not seeing her tomorrow.

I could have called her to pick me up tonight, but I was too filthy after working at the site. I wanted to look good when I saw her.

I reached for a towel, dried off, then tied it around my waist. The thought of shaving flitted in my mind for a second, but I dismissed it as I padded to the kitchen. Too tired, too exhausted for anything other than a beer and the couch. Maybe order some pizza, watch TV then crash.

I frowned as I opened the fridge, scowling at the crap inside it. Caleb and Levi, one of the few guys on the team I actually liked and who stuck to Caleb like glue, always brought snacks over and stored them in there. I reached for a beer.

Now why did I feel disappointed at the thought of not seeing her for one day?

It had only been yesterday that I'd met her.

I dismissed that thought too, popping open the can of beer as I strode to the living room.

Ah. That's what I'm talking about, I thought as I took my first sip.

The aches and pains from working manual labor were welcome to me. They were a distraction from my dark thoughts.

I was exhausted, but that was what I wanted. Needed, even. I had a lot of energy and putting that to use made me feel good. Useful. I should look into taking another project again. I could live very comfortably for a few years off what I had in my bank account. I didn't need much, but that money wasn't just for my living expenses. It was a ransom for myself. Pretty soon, Raven would show up, and the only way I could get her out of my life was either relocate again where she couldn't find me or stay where I was and give her money. She was rich, having inherited her parents' wealth when they passed away, but Raven was obsessed with money.

I would give anything to make her stay away. She always brought trouble with her demands and needs and manipulation. She also reminded me too much of my childhood, of my guilt. And I didn't want to go back to that dark place.

Kara. I had no business mixing her life with mine, but I was…drawn to her. I should leave her alone. Soon, but not yet. Not yet.

I sank into the couch, moaning in relief as I finally let my body relax. I lifted the beer to my mouth, eager to down it, when the doorbell rang.

What the hell?

I leaned my head against the couch, sighing at the irritating interruption. Pressing my fingers to my eyes, I willed it to go away.

Who could it be?

It was late. Unless it was Caleb returning to insist that I go with him to wherever the hell he and the guys were going this time.

Pissed, I slammed my beer on the table, tightened the towel around my waist, and pulled open the door.

She was standing there. Mad as hell.

Well, well.

I smiled. "I was just thinking about you," I drawled.

The fire in her eyes faded, glazing with desire as they slowly traveled from my face, lingered on my shoulders and stomach, froze on my towel for a beat, then snapped back to my eyes.

She bit her lip.

I grinned. "Had your fill yet?" I asked.

She blinked at me slowly, her eyes still glassy. I don't think she heard me.

She was still wearing the same clothes from this morning—pants and the sweater the color of sunshine. Her face had been scrubbed of makeup.

I could look at her all night.

"Would you," I said, staring at her mouth for as long as I liked before looking back up at her eyes, "like to come inside?"

She opened her mouth, but nothing came out. Enjoying the moment, I leaned against the doorjamb.

"Kar, he's asking you a question!"

Surprised, my eyes shifted to look behind her.

"Hey there! I'm Dylan." He waved, smiling widely as if he'd been my long-lost best friend. "Her brother."

The smile on my face disappeared. So this was the asshole who hit my motorcycle and fucked off. I pushed away from the doorjamb and fixed my gaze on him.

The memories of yesterday morning when I found my damaged motorcycle came crashing back. The scratches, the cracks, the *pain* of seeing something you'd been taking care of so painstakingly disregarded so blatantly by someone who didn't even have the guts to own up to the crime.

The lack of remorse on his face—as if he were entitled to everything—warranted a good punch in the mug. Maybe I'd knock out a few of his teeth. That would be punishment enough.

And then I looked at her. And held off.

It would scare her off if she saw how angry I was. I needed a moment to cool off. "Gimme a minute, will you?" I gritted out.

I clenched my jaw, turned my back on them, but left the door open. Frustrated, I rubbed my hands over my face as I walked to my bedroom.

"Hey! I'm talking to you. Where the hell do you think you're going?"

I heard her voice catching up to me. I slammed my bedroom door closed and dropped my towel.

She barged in.

"Holy fuck!" she screamed.

Shit.

I expected her to avert her eyes, like a normal person would do, but she was still staring.

I reached for the towel for cover just as she slapped

her hands to her face, spinning around so fast she almost lost her balance.

She'd sure had an eyeful.

I let out a frustrated sigh, hiked up my pants, zipped them closed. Staring at her back, I pulled a shirt out of my closet, put that on.

"I need to talk to your brother," I said between clenched teeth. "Alone."

Pissed, I walked past her. All I'd wanted was some damn peace and quiet tonight.

"No, you're not."

"Oh, yes, I am."

"Not alone, you're not."

I stopped abruptly. She almost crashed into me, but her hands flattened on my back before her body did.

I turned around, looked at her quietly, waiting for her to calm down. Her face was red, her eyes glittered—from anger or embarrassment, I wasn't sure. Maybe both.

"You don't see anything wrong with this scenario?" I asked.

She placed her hands on her waist. "The only thing that's wrong here is you trying to bully my brother. I'm not letting you or anyone do that to him again. You hear me?"

My anger was fading. Why did she look so cute when she was telling me what to do?

But when she defended the people she cared about and put herself before them to take the blows, she was irresistible.

I softened. "You're aware," I started, wanting to erase the dark circles under her eyes, "that you're only making it worse for him, right?"

She blinked.

"You should let him fight his own battles," I continued. "You're doing more harm than good. You're enabling him."

She looked stricken.

I waited.

She wet her lips. "All right," she said, defeated. "Did you talk to my dad or something?"

"What?"

"Just be careful. He had…issues when he was a kid. Don't be too rough, all right?"

She looked as exhausted as I felt. I wanted to pull her on the bed and lie down with her. Just to sleep, I realized. Just so she could rest.

That was something new. I'd never brought a girl to bed just to sleep before.

I wanted to take care of her.

I scowled. Where the hell did that come from?

"Did you hear what I said?" she demanded.

"What?"

"Never mind. Where should I stay?"

"Kitchen. Off the living room, to your left."

"Fine."

She marched past me. I followed her to the living room.

"Kar! Where are you going?" Dylan asked.

"I'm going over there." She pointed to the den, walking briskly in the wrong direction for the kitchen, where I told her to wait. "And you're staying over there."

"But…"

His words cut off as I stood in front of him. He was young, probably in high school. But old enough to have a sense of responsibility. And she wanted me to put on the kid gloves just because he had issues?

How many times had he used that one to skid over his own responsibilities and pass them on to her? No matter how strong and aggressive she was, she had a soft heart for people she cared about. I bet she felt guilty for the past, and he knew how to wield that against her. It was a kind of power he had over her.

I knew because I was, in some way, like him when I was a kid. I attacked and swung with my fists. He, on the other hand, used them to cover up blows thrown his way and huddled in the corner like a scared mouse.

Different issues, different ways of dealing with our problems, but the core was the same.

Selfish. Needy. Entitled. Like I was. Even now I knew there was still a lot of those things left in me.

"I'm Dylan. Hi."

I just looked at him, saying nothing.

He didn't look like his sister. His hair was blond, his face round and had the chubby look of a well-fed pet.

"Right. I said that before. We're fixing your motor-cycle, so we're cool, right? We'll make it better than it was before. You're going to love it!"

No apology whatsoever. No remorse on his face. In fact, he looked like *I* should be thanking him.

I still had that selfish, angry kid inside me trying to take over, but I was stronger than he was now. But sometimes, I let him take the reins.

"Listen here, you little shit."

He recoiled from me.

"You're the one who hit my motorcycle, then fucked right off." I watched him swallow and back up a step. "Aren't you?"

"B-but we're going to fix it, and it's going to be better

than it was before. I'm a good mechanic, and Vlad is the best on motorcycles. He'll be working on yours. You'll be happy that this happened. You'll see!"

"Happy?" My jaw ticked.

One clean punch right in his pug face. That was all I needed. Just one. Lucky for him, he was her brother. She would probably murder me if I harmed a hair on his head.

"My sister said your name is Cameron. I've heard about you. I mean I've seen you play. You're savage on the basketball court. I mean, *wow*. You're a monster. Maybe we can play sometime after your bike's fixed. I can even fix your other cars for you. Or your friends'. I have a weakness for classic trucks. Just let me know. You want my number? I can—"

He must have seen my thoughts on my face because he stopped talking and started backing away from me.

"Listen, man, I didn't mean to hit your bike. I was trying to run away from Big Tony. The guy's massive. Bigger than you are. And I mean you're already huge, you know? Just look at those guns. But Big Tony, I don't have a chance of survival with him."

"And you think you have one with me?"

"I mean you're friends with my sister, right? Aren't friends supposed to take care of each other? We're practically family, right?"

Was he being sarcastic? Or was he really this gullible?

"You see, I had this bet with Big Tony, but I thought we were joking around, you know? Turns out, he was serious. So he didn't pay his car bill when I came to collect yesterday morning. But my dad said he paid by phone that afternoon, so we're all square, you know?"

He moved his shoulders. He was just getting warmed up.

"Anyway, he chased me out, would've probably beaten me up when I insisted on him paying. But I got away, you know? It was just that…I panicked, man. Panic mode activated. I backed away and hit your bike, but I wasn't sure if it was damaged or anything because I put it right back up and it stood pretty good, man."

I clenched my teeth. The reminder of what he did to my motorcycle and his nonstop yapping grated in my ears like nails scraping on a chalkboard.

"So I told Kar, and she said she was going to see if your bike was really damaged, because I didn't even hit it that hard, man. She said she made a deal with you and that—"

"Quiet."

He shut his trap.

"It's bad enough that you hit my motorcycle. You didn't even have the decency to own up to it. And you don't even feel any remorse. But dragging your sister to clean up your own mess?" I curled my lip in distaste.

He pulled the collar of his shirt down. "S-she doesn't always do that for me—" He stopped, looking at me cautiously. "Yes," he said almost inaudibly. "Yes, she does."

"You drag her down quite a bit, don't you?"

He shook his head in denial. "It's just a motorcycle!"

Just a motorcycle? Easy for him to say when it wasn't his property that was trashed. It wasn't *just* a motorcycle to me. It had sentimental value.

The fact that he was playing it lightly, and the lack of accountability, as if damaging my motorcycle were as insignificant as spilling a drink, pissed me off as much as that he'd done a number on it.

"You think because you had it rough when you were a kid you get a pass for fucking up someone else's life? You think you're the only one?"

I couldn't count how many times I had to defend myself as a kid. Every day, I let anger take the driver's side because it was easier. The world would see how miserable I was and maybe, just maybe, give me a break.

But it didn't work that way, did it?

The world never let up. You just learned how to fight back.

If she loved this kid, and I knew she did, she'd have to toughen him up.

"I just…I know I'm no good," he started, his voice thick.

I paused. Suddenly, he looked very young, just a kid trying to fit in and figure out the world—a vicious world that could crush him.

A picture of a boy in dirty clothes and vulnerable face flashed in my mind. Fire. Screams. A boy frozen in fear. My head started to pound.

I can't get involved again. I tried to help someone before and… I'll just destroy this kid's life. Like I did before.

I was about to tell him to go home when he continued.

"It's hard when I can't even invite my friends over because our house is so small. I can't even ask a girl out because I'm a loser," he said. "I love working at the garage, but it seems there's no point to it. My dad works like a horse and we're barely paying the bills because of my uncle. We don't really have a choice, you know? So my dad's always broke and my sister's working herself to the bone trying to support us…and I'm…I'm just a loser."

I closed my eyes and lowered my head. The helplessness in his eyes spoke to me. *Bothered* me.

I made a fist and bit my knuckle, hoping for some inspiration. "Look, man. You did a wrong thing but you're not a loser."

Rick should be here, talking to him. Not me. I had my own issues. What the hell do I tell him when I didn't even have my own crap together? And what if I just made it worse? Like I always did.

"Thanks. It would be nice…" he said hesitantly. "To have you as a friend."

I let out a sigh. Damn kid was going to make me cry.

I frowned, trying to remember what Rick said or did to calm me down back then. Nothing came to mind but the feeling of someone who finally cared.

"I've been in your shoes before. You have to try. Just…try. Because from where I'm standing, you're not even doing that. Damn it, where the hell is my beer?"

I grabbed my beer from the table and finished it off. When I saw Dylan still looking at me, I decided I needed another one. I went to the kitchen and opened the fridge. I popped open a beer and glugged. I could feel his presence behind me, waiting.

"Want a beer?" I asked.

This time, his face broke into a smile. "I wish," he answered. "I'm not eighteen yet."

Well, damn. I opened the fridge again, looked through the debris.

"Ah." I grabbed an item, pierced it with a straw, and handed it to him. "Juice box?"

This was probably Levi's.

"Nah, man. Give me a pop or something. I'm not a kid."

"What's wrong with a juice box?" I took a sip.

"I like pop."

"Yeah, but pop doesn't give you these." I lifted my shirt and showed him my six-pack.

He broke into laughter. "Ooooh!" The pure happiness on his face was innocent. "Yeah," he said. "I like a juice box. What flavor is it?"

"I don't know, man. It's got vitamin C. Just take it."

He sipped and was quiet for a few moments. I considered it a miracle.

"I'm sorry about your motorcycle."

I nodded to him in acknowledgment.

"We're cool, right?"

I thought about it. I was still pissed, but going after him felt cruel. Like kicking a puppy. Besides, I liked his sister. A whole damn lot.

"Yeah," I answered, walking back to the living room. "We're cool."

"Can I hang out with you?"

I was saved from answering when we heard heavy footsteps coming.

"Hey!" She was frowning as she stepped in the living room. "Are you guys done? Is that beer? You gave him beer?"

She glared at the beer I was holding.

"Calm down, Kar." He waved his hand. "It's not beer."

"What is it?"

She squinted as he shook it in front of her. "Just a juice box."

"I have to talk to your sister," I told him, but I was looking at her. "Alone."

"Kar?" There was worry in his voice.

She narrowed her eyes at me. Distrustful.

I gave her a small smile, challenging her.

You can't handle being alone with me, can you?

Her smile was sharp.

Oh, yes, I can. I can crush you if I want to.

"Go ahead. I'll see you at home."

"I'll wait for you outside."

"It's going to take a while. Go home, Dylan."

"You sure?"

She nodded, shooed him away.

I looked at Dylan. "I got her. I'll take her home."

He must have seen something in my face that reassured him. He patted his sister's shoulder, told her he'd see her at home, and left.

Then the door closed.

And I was alone with her.

At last.

Chapter 11

Kara

CAMERON'S BLUE EYES WERE EVEN DEEPER, SOMEHOW more intense, in the muted glow of the light. They were patient as he followed Dylan to the front door—no, not patient. They were waiting. Anticipating what was to come.

I heard my brother's footsteps and Cameron's, then the click of the lock.

The echo it made in the room was as loud and heavy with meaning as a declaration of war.

Then those eyes, with those deep-blue irises, shifted to mine.

Conquer me, they challenged, *before I conquer you.*

It was bait.

And I wanted to bite.

I curled my hands into fists and instinctively stepped back, stopping when the back of my knees hit the couch.

The effect he had on me was undeniable, and I didn't care for it. I didn't like the way I felt defenseless around him, how he could strip away my reasoning just by looking at me.

As if he heard my thoughts, his lips, slowly and deliberately, formed into a smile.

I got you, his smile said, *exactly where I want you.*

Strength and controlled power showed in every movement of his body as I watched him cross the room toward me. His body was big and sleek, like a stealthy cat roaming the jungle, patient and hungry.

My eyes took in the long lines of his arms, the ripple of muscles, the veins that stood out like cords, his thick wrist. Every part disciplined, tight, and masculine.

He stopped in front of me.

"Kara." He whispered my name. His voice was deep and rich, and my name sounded and *felt* so carnal coming from his lips. "Tell me why you're here."

I tried to answer. God knows I tried, but my body wouldn't cooperate. It felt so easy, so sinful, like a soft, silky feather stroking my skin, to give in. Let someone else take control for once. No, not just someone. It had to be him. I closed my eyes in defense. I was losing, and surprisingly, I didn't seem to mind. Was this what it felt like to want? To need?

The air was thick with tension, and I felt it shift before his fingers stroked the inside of my wrist. Once, twice. Then it was gone.

My lips opened a fraction, letting out a sharp breath. An expulsion, a way my body dealt with the surging desire in the aftermath of his touch.

Or maybe, maybe, it was a silent demand for more.

"Open your eyes," he said softly.

I kept them closed.

"Kara." His voice was soft as velvet, coaxing. "Look at me."

But what would happen if I did?

This was something I'd never felt or experienced

before. I'd never been this close to anyone nor had I wanted to be.

I was teetering between two worlds—the one where I would stay the same if I stepped away from him now, and the other one where the world I knew would end and change to something unfamiliar.

Which one would I choose?

I always put others before me. Responsibilities, commitments, family. When was the last time I did something just for the hell of it?

I opened my eyes. And stared right into the blue of his.

He was ruthlessly beautiful. The straight, dark brows, the deep-set eyes, the long, straight nose, the full lips. And all that beauty framed by soft, black hair.

I had thought he looked like a dark archangel when I first laid eyes on him. I still did.

He was as deep and dark as a cave, and I was standing right at his entrance. Should I go in or leave?

I made up my mind.

His lips parted in surprise as my finger slowly traced his collarbone, marveling at the warmth of his skin, at the smoothness of it. I thought I'd be satisfied just by feeling it, but I wanted to do more.

His muscles tensed as I moved my fingers to the long line of his neck, rubbing the stubble on his jaw, tickling myself.

I smiled but didn't say anything. I usually had a lot to say, but I wasn't myself right now. I was different when I was with him. I felt more beautiful, more aware of myself as a woman.

The pulse at the base of his throat jumped as I focused

on his lips and continued my exploration there. They were full, pink, with a prominent Cupid's bow.

Suddenly, he opened his mouth and caught my finger between his lips, between his teeth, then with his tongue. And sucked.

I gasped, my eyes snapping to his as I snatched my finger away, feeling like my whole body was on fire.

There was so much emotion raging inside me. My skin prickled. I felt hot, itchy, needy. I wanted…more. Just *more*.

"You're driving me fucking crazy," he whispered. His voice was husky, more than a hint of frustration in it.

Where every move before had been disciplined, he now radiated restless energy. It felt like having a big, edgy cat in a small cage.

His eyes grew heavy, hungry. "I'm waiting for you to run away," he said quietly.

When I didn't reply, his arms fell dejectedly to his sides.

"I don't want you to."

I bit my lip at his confession. He made me feel wanted. That I shouldn't deny myself what I wanted. Even just for this moment.

The way he looked at me felt like heat gliding across my skin. Hot, palpable, alluring.

He looked so good, so unapologetically *male*.

"Kara."

I looked up at him. He held his hand out to me, palm up.

"Come here," he said huskily.

As if in a trance, I placed my hand in his. His hand was wide, with long, tapered fingers, and rough, with calluses and scrapes. A working man's hand. A capable, strong, gorgeous man.

My eyes shifted to his. There was a delicious hot curl in my stomach at the approval and hunger I saw in his eyes.

He kissed my palm and placed it on his chest. His hands banded on my hips, his fingers pressing intimately, possessively, as he sprawled on the couch, pulling me to him and settling me on his lap.

I gasped as our bodies made contact, as I straddled him. He was wide, and *God*, so big that my legs stretched to accommodate him.

Up close, he was even more beautiful. Almost unreal. His features were perfect, his skin creamy and smooth.

His hands slipped under my sweater, fingers stroking the skin on my lower back. I shivered at the delicious rough texture of them.

When his lips touched my ear, I jumped. He let out a deep, low laugh.

Butterflies whirled in my stomach at the sound. Even his laugh was sexy.

"Can't stop thinking about you," he murmured.

He dragged his lips from my ear to my jaw, inhaling long and deep. My hands gripped his arms, waiting, wanting him to keep going, wanting to feel what was going to happen next.

His hands left my back, gliding up my arms, gently securing both sides of my neck. His thumbs stroked the hollow of my throat. My head fell back as I savored his touch. Back and forth and back and forth on my pulse that had gone mad.

He leaned forward until his lips were almost touching the side of my mouth. Almost.

"Kara," he whispered. "Won't you kiss me?"

I hissed out a breath.

I thought he would just take, remove the decision from me and just take, but he waited until I was ready. Until I made up my mind.

I felt his body poised for my rejection or my surrender. But there was no question in my mind.

I closed my eyes and took his bottom lip between mine. I heard him growl, as if he'd been starved and I'd just served him what he'd been craving.

Then he took over.

His tongue traced the seam of my lips, seeking entrance to my mouth. I opened up to him and he slid inside, shocking me with the arousal that bloomed inside me.

He tasted like orange and mint with a hint of the beer he had been drinking earlier.

One of his hands moved to the back of my head, securing me in place, as his mouth slanted against mine, wanting more, *demanding* more.

He moaned, deepening the kiss. And I was lost.

I pressed my hands on his back, pulling him closer, rubbing my body against his.

He was hard everywhere, his muscles rippling and tensing as I placed my hands under his shirt, glided up his chest. His skin was burning hot.

His hands settled on my heels, sliding up to my calves, swirling at the back of my knees, up my legs, then cupping my ass.

Then his hips surged up. *Oh God.*

His hands reached for the zipper on my pants. My eyes flew open.

"Stop."

I pushed against him, but it was like pushing a car, he was so big and heavy. But he stopped, his hands falling to his sides.

I untangled myself, standing up and away from him, breathing hard.

His mouth was wet, rosy, his eyes smoky with desire. "Kara."

"No," I said.

His hands shook as he raked his fingers in his hair. "I won't do anything you don't want me to."

He reached out, his hand closing on my wrist.

"Don't go," he pleaded.

I shook my head, pulled away, but he was ten times stronger than I was. There was no way I would be able to escape him.

"Let. Me. Go."

He looked at me for a moment. There was a vulnerability in his eyes I hadn't seen before. It nearly undid me.

And then he opened his hand and let me go.

I ran to the door, feeling claustrophobic. I needed space, time to think.

I held the doorknob in my hand, twisted.

"Kara."

I turned my head, looked at him one last time, and left.

Chapter 12

Kara

YOU HAVE FAILED THE QUEEN MOTHER SHIP.

Blood pounded in my head as I raced out his door, down his driveway, almost tripping in my haste. I kept running until my couch potato lungs gave out on me.

My legs went weak and I had to stop. I crouched on the sidewalk, burrowing my head in my knees, trying to catch my breath.

What the hell was that?

My lips *throbbed.* Sore, but a delicious kind of sore. Like I'd been doing something bad, and it was a secret because it felt too damn good to share.

I could still feel the imprint of his lips on mine, still taste him on my tongue, still hear the sounds he made.

The sexy moans and growls he made at the back of his throat.

I made a tight squealing sound that sounded like a hyena giving birth.

God!

That's right. Only God can help you now. You have failed the fort! I repeat: you have failed the fort! Retreat!

I have failed nothing! I just kissed him…

That's right! You gave your first kiss away just like that? And note, it wasn't just a kiss. There was dry humping involved. Girl, you wild thing, you!

Shut up!

After protecting the castle for twenty-one years, you're going to lower the drawbridge to a guy you just met yesterday? What's wrong with you?

I wasn't going to sleep with him. I just…I just wanted to feel…wanted. For once.

That's not the whole truth.

Yes, it is.

There have been a couple of guys before who liked you, but you never paid them any attention. Granted, one didn't shower, and the other one hardly blinked. And neither of them was as hot as Cameron, but who is? Still. There's another reason. What is it?

There's no other reason.

You like him.

I slammed my hands against my ears, trying to shake off the voice in my head.

You like *him. There's never been anyone who challenged you like Cameron has. He's not intimidated at all. No matter what you dish out at him.*

I just met the guy yesterday!

It's going to be midnight soon, so two full days now, FYI. But you're deflecting. Why you deflecting, sister? That's not what I asked.

Leave it alone.

You eavesdropped on their conversation when they were in the living room.

I didn't hear all of it! Only toward the end because I was actually really trying to give them privacy but…

You sly grandma, you! But what you heard, you liked. You heard him going easy on Dylan when other guys would just dismiss or laugh at him. Or worse, bully him. He was kind to him. And that, my friend, was your downfall. Cameron's kindness was your downfall, wasn't it? And when they came back from the kitchen, you saw how Dylan looked at Cameron.

Dylan already adores him.

Don't be falling for him now! With all your talk of standards, where are they now, huh? You gave in so easily. I'm so disappointed.

I'm going to bash your head in two seconds if you don't shut the hell up.

He didn't even want foreplay. He wanted the pearl in the shell right away. The caramel in the middle. The egg yolk.

You're just like any other girl to him. He was horny, and you just happened to be there. You were supposed to talk to him about your contract, not suck his face.

You probably didn't even kiss that good. He dominated that kiss in epic proportions.

"Enough!" I yelled into the night, ignoring the uneasy flutter I felt in my belly. "He's an experiment. That's all he is to me. He'll be gone after his motorcycle is fixed."

He'll stay because you're amusing, but once he gets bored, he'll be gone. Just like your mother. Just like everyone.

I rose, dusted off my hands, and shivered. I hadn't grabbed my jacket when I'd left my house earlier because I was so pumped. I hadn't noticed the cold either when I left *his* house. But now I did.

I crossed my arms and rubbed them for warmth. Then

screamed and jumped in fright when I felt something land on my shoulders.

I spun around, moved into a karate position, got ready to run—and choked on air when I saw that it was *him*.

He picked up the leather jacket that fell on the ground when I spun around, shook it, and offered it to me. His face, too beautiful even in the dark, was set in severe lines. His eyes, when they looked at me, were indifferent now.

Why did my stomach drop suddenly?

It wasn't the reaction I'd expected to see on him after…what happened in his living room. But then again, he didn't get what he wanted from me, did he?

So why was he here, holding out a jacket for me?

It was all so confusing. And frustrating.

Was there a training center I could enroll myself in to get an education in this?

He was looking at me, but I couldn't figure out what he was thinking. His shields were up. The shields that kept people out. I sensed them around him before, but I'd never gotten the full effect of them until now.

It made me…sad.

"You're freezing," he said. No hint of the warmth in his voice that had been there before. "Why don't you wear this?"

But the way he said it wasn't a request. It was an *order*. The arrogance in his tone was enough to cause my temper to flicker.

"You're not the boss of me."

I sounded like a sulky five-year-old, but I couldn't have cared less.

He looked at me for a moment before he said, "I told your brother I'd take you home."

I closed my mouth. His words, delivered so matter-of-factly, sounded sweet to me. Sounded so kind and thoughtful.

The guy was a walking contradiction. How the hell was I supposed to figure all this out?

Be strong, girl. Don't give in. Don't give in. Really, don't.

My house was a twenty-minute walk from his house. I turned away from him and started walking home. He needed to stay far, far away from me right now.

He was confusing me, and I needed to be on my A game, especially now. This close to the fruition of my plans, there was no room for interruptions. If I wanted to buy another life for my family, at least give them a comfortable life free from my uncle's greedy claws, there was no room for weakness. My eyes should always be on the prize.

Fantasies were all I could afford right now. And how pitiful was that?

My steps faltered when I felt something warm settle on my shoulders. Something that smelled like leather and man.

"Don't," he warned when I started to remove his jacket from my shoulders. "I'll just put it on you again."

"That's really not the way you should talk to me if you want me to do something." I shrugged off his jacket and threw it at him. I don't know why I was suddenly angry. But I was. My skin felt flushed, my breathing sped up, and I wanted to hit something.

"You can keep your jacket right where the sun don't

shine, babe, and you can go back to where you came from. I've been walking home my whole life without you," I said, and my voice failed me when it broke.

That weakness in my voice, that chink in my armor that he heard made me angrier.

"I'm not going to start needing you to find my way back home anytime soon. Because you know what? I can take care of myself and mine just fine. I've been doing it since I was a kid, and I don't need you or anyone else to tell me what the hell to do!"

It was unfair to take it out on him. I knew that, just as I knew I was going to beat myself up for it later. But he represented something I couldn't even let myself want.

He was a great fantasy, one that was being dangled in front of my nose. Life was cruel. Because I was realistic enough to understand that was all he could ever be. He wasn't meant for someone like me.

He'd be gone soon, and it would be like we'd never met. And the sorry thing was, I'd be left with all the memories.

People always left me memories. As if I were a box where they could just dump whatever crap they no longer wanted.

Just memories. Always memories.

What the hell could I do with those? They wouldn't put food on the table or pay the electricity or the number of bills piling up in the mailbox.

And if I wanted to forget and get lost in the kisses of a man who was gorgeous as sin and for once be a memory to him, then by God, I had every right to!

Feeling the threat of tears, I threw up my hands in frustration and started marching home. I could feel him following me.

What did he want? Wasn't freaking out on him enough to turn him away? What was wrong with this guy?

I walked faster, hoping he'd just leave, but it had been a very long day and I was starting to feel it.

The wind whistled loud and mean in the streets, blowing cold and strong. I sucked in my breath, trying to keep my hands to my sides so he wouldn't know I was freezing my ass off.

I heard him sigh loudly behind me before he started walking faster, until he was walking right in front of me.

Did this guy have a death wish?

The wind blew again, but this time the force of it didn't blast my face and body. Instead, his body took it.

He walked ahead of me because he wanted to block the wind from hitting me.

Something warm was forming in my chest.

It was just a reaction to his kindness. That was all. Nothing more.

I watched his broad shoulders move as he walked, the fascinating muscle play on the back of his shirt, the dark, curly hair that flirted with his collar.

He had the leather jacket folded and hanging over his left shoulder.

He never said anything, never even turned around to look at me. I kept waiting for him to say something, grow impatient, or say *Fuck this shit, I'm out*. But he never did.

We walked together like that until we reached the entrance to my family's shop.

The quiet between us was palpable, and it wasn't comfortable. He stopped walking and stood beside the tandem truck that blocked the dirt road leading to my house.

I could feel his massive body tense as I walked past him, could feel his eyes tracking me as I crossed toward my house. But like him, I kept walking and didn't look back.

The porch light came on as I stopped at my front door. The wind howled, and I wanted to look back so badly to see if he was still there.

Forget about him. Eyes on the prize, girl.

I grabbed the keys under the flowerpot, pushed the key in the lock, and opened the front door. I stepped inside, closing it quietly behind me so I wouldn't wake up my dad.

The house was asleep. The only sound I heard was my dad's soft snoring and the white noise the electric fan made.

I should go to bed, call it a day, but I leaned my forehead on the door instead. Something was screaming at me to do something. I wasn't sure what.

Damn it.

I took a deep breath and opened the door. He was almost at the entrance of the shop. He must have heard me because he stopped, and slowly, he turned around. Looked at me for a moment.

I couldn't see his eyes because of the distance, but I knew they weren't indifferent anymore. I wished I could see his eyes. I wished I knew what he was thinking, what he was feeling. I wished this day had never happened.

And I wished he would never forget.

Because as much as I wanted to, I knew I wouldn't.

Before I could decide what to do, he turned his back to me and walked away.

Chapter 13

Kara

THE NEXT DAY, I FELT LIKE I HAD A HANGOVER.

The birds outside my bedroom window were competing for which of them could destroy their voice box first and, unsurprisingly, couldn't give a rat's ass if they woke me up from a dream I could barely remember now.

I was contemplating throwing a pillow outside to shut them up and go back to sleep, but the knock on my door squashed that plan.

"Kar?" It was Dylan. "Dad said it's time for church. You're not up yet, so I'm going to use the bathroom first, okay?"

I heard the words, but they didn't register in my brain. Everyone in my household knew my brain was in sleep mode until I had my coffee.

I got up, groaning at the slight dizziness I felt. What the hell? I hadn't even drunk alcohol last night, but I had a slight headache and my tongue felt furry and gross.

Eyes closed, I grabbed my bath towel and walked to the door, squeaking when I stepped on an empty can of beer. *Oh, will you look at that.* I guess I drank last night after all.

Funny how some things you just choose to forget, I thought as I made my way to the kitchen and poured myself a cup of coffee. Like last night. I almost didn't remember what had happened last night.

Almost.

At the first sip, I felt like I was out of solitary. At half a cup, I had shed my jail clothes. At a full cup, I was out of prison. Perfect. Brain activated. I poured another cup.

"Good morning, sweetheart."

I had just noticed my dad at the stove, cooking something that smelled like eggs. He and Dylan had taken over cooking duties in the kitchen since I tend to burn everything.

"Morning, Dad. I'm going to shower."

"Dylan beat you to the bathroom."

"Nooo." I sighed.

It was going to be a steamy, wet bathroom. Dylan didn't seem to get that he was supposed to shower in the confines of the tub with the shower curtain closed and not on the floor of the bathroom.

"Want toast or cereal?" he asked as he turned around.

He wore the apron I'd bought for him for Christmas. It had a picture of a naked bodybuilder's physique with a glittering Christmas ball covering the dingdong.

We paused, looked at each other for a beat, and started laughing.

"You look so cute," I chuckled. I sat on the island, sipped more coffee. "Can I have cereal, please?"

"I didn't hear you come in last night," he said as he shook cornflakes into a bowl, poured almond milk, and placed it in front of me.

I ate a spoonful before responding. "I got home late. You were asleep."

"What were you up to?"

I took another bite, chewed slowly. "I had to talk to a…friend," I said carefully.

"Tala?"

"Nope."

"You mean you have friends other than Tala?" He chuckled teasingly.

I rolled my eyes at him and turned back to my cereal. I knew he was looking at me, waiting for me to elaborate. But I couldn't. Not yet. Maybe not ever.

"Tell me when you're ready, Kara Koala."

I nodded, finished my breakfast as he turned to the dishes.

I have other friends, I thought as I stepped into the shower. But I was the type of person who chose the people I spent time with very, very carefully. Because once I let them in, I got attached quickly.

I had a strong preference for deep, long-lasting relationships. Relationships that meant more than *let's hang out*. I only had so much time in a day, and I was very careful where I invested it. Once I committed to a relationship, I made sure to carve out time to nurture it. And so, I only had very few people in my life.

That was one of the many reasons why I couldn't let *him* in my life, I decided as I reached for my towel, dried off, and moisturized. I walked to my bedroom, reached for the hair dryer. He was going to be out of my life as soon as his motorcycle was done. So I really should stop thinking about him.

Can't stop thinking about you…

He'd said that to me last night. Did he mean it?

My face was flushed, I realized as I looked in the mirror, getting ready to put on my makeup.

Did he actually like me? Or was he the type of guy to blurt out anything to get laid?

I felt that familiar uneasy flutter in my belly at the thought. He didn't seem to be the type, but…how would I know what was real and what wasn't?

I *just* met him.

Didn't stop you from kissing him though, did it?

No, I admitted, it didn't. I touched my bottom lip, rubbing it. The memory of his tongue tasting my lips was so strong I felt it.

Suddenly, my knees felt weak and I had to sit down on the floor.

So that's what a french kiss feels like.

I'd always wondered about it, imagined it, dreamt about kissing the boy that I would fall in love with someday. But nothing had prepared me for the real thing.

He was pure sex.

At first, I had been nervous. I could hear my heart pounding in my ears. I was as surprised as he was when I made the first move to touch him. But the way he'd looked at me, the way his sharp blue eyes *watched* me… He was irresistible. He made me feel craved.

As if he *hungered* for me.

There was no hesitation in him—just pure confidence. He knew what he wanted, knew how to get it, knew he'd show it to me. And he had.

The way his lips had eagerly taken from me, the way his tongue had played inside my mouth, the way his fingers had stroked and squeezed. The way he'd *moaned*.

He'd *enjoyed* it. Or at least he'd looked like he had.

So I didn't feel sorry or embarrassed for what I'd done because he made me feel his presence, that he was *there* with me. He made me feel like I was the only girl in the world. The urge to touch him had been unstoppable. I couldn't have stopped myself even if I'd wanted to.

Until he tried to unzip your pants, that is.

Was that all he wanted from me?

What else could he possibly want from you?

I was scared he wanted something more from me, and I was scared that he didn't.

Something was stopping me from thinking there was more than that. My heart couldn't afford to think there was more than that.

Impossible.

Because…what came next after that? I'd have to give up something. There was always something valuable taken away in exchange.

And I wasn't ready to change my life. I wasn't ready to give up anything.

And I was scared that this man would make me want to.

A heaviness was forming in my chest. It wasn't disappointment, I realized. It was…sadness. And resignation.

I usually enjoy and pay more attention during Sunday mass, but trying to get enough sleep, especially this week, was about as easy as finding Nemo.

Not that I was complaining. I had set out down this road by my own choice, and even though my mind and body were screaming at me to slow down, it would be a sin for me to stop now. I was so close to saving enough money to buy off my uncle's share of the shop.

By the time the first reading was over, I was falling asleep on my feet. Dylan was beside me, and he would elbow my side or pull the hairs on my arm to wake me up, but nothing worked. The hymns they were singing felt like lullabies to my sleep-deprived body.

"Kar!"

I jolted and slapped Dylan's cheek for waking me up. By the time I realized where I was, I noticed people were moving. Was mass over?

Dylan drilled his finger into my forehead. "It's time for communion, dummy," he whispered, trying to suppress his laugh.

My dad was sitting in front of us and, like a normal dad trying to keep his little kids from misbehaving, glared at us to be quiet. I winked at him and he sighed.

My dad was a devout Catholic. Rain or shine, he took us to church every Sunday. When we were little kids who had too much energy, we'd run around the church like little shits. Until my dad learned to bribe us with McDonald's if we behaved.

People from the front pews were lining up in the middle and sides of the church to receive the *hostia*. I figured I had another thirty seconds to close my eyes before it was our turn. But just as I was closing my eyes, I froze.

There was a tall guy sitting four pews to my left in front of us. His hair was black and curly, his shoulders wide, and his back looked very, very familiar.

Suddenly, I was on full alert, my heart beating like a drum in my chest. It was his pew's turn to line up for communion. My eyes focused on him like a laser, but when he turned, I realized he wasn't who I thought he was.

The guy caught me looking at him, and he looked back at me curiously. I looked away, breathing a sigh of relief. I wasn't sure if I could deal with my black-mailer's potent magnetism today.

"Let's go, Kar. I have a lot of sins to atone for," Dylan muttered under his breath.

We made our way to the line and the choir started singing "Hosea," my favorite church song, when my phone started vibrating.

My heart skipped a beat. Was it him? I wondered if God would forgive me if I quickly checked my phone.

What am I doing? What's happening to me?

It felt like there was no hour that I didn't think of him. That needed to stop—stat. I grabbed my phone, gave it to Dylan, and told him to turn it off.

"You have one missed call."

"Just turn it the hell off."

He looked at me curiously but didn't comment. *At least it woke me up*, I thought as Dylan, my dad, and I made our way to the exit when mass ended. My dad was stopped by a few people, inviting him for birth-days, asking him advice about their cars. Dylan and I hung back, waiting for him to finish. I knew I should've brought my own car, but my shift at the coffee shop didn't start until after lunch today.

"Kara!"

"Tita Didi, how are you?"

Everyone called her Tita Didi at church. An active volunteer, she mainly organized events and was a loyal customer to our shop.

"I'm good! Oh, your makeup is so pretty. You have to meet my nephew. He's *pogi* and single too. He's an engineer. Good, right? I'll set up a date between you two. You want?"

She also loved setting me up on blind dates with her nephews or cousins or coworkers. She thought being single was a disease and her mission in life was to cure the world of it. I was fond of her though.

"No, Tita. I'm still trying to get over my dead boyfriend, remember?" I deadpanned.

I'm lying in church. God would understand. Right?

She was always after me on this boyfriend crap, so I had to come up with creative ways to discourage her.

"I'm good, really. I have to go to work. See you next week!" I waved and hightailed my ass out of there. I'd wait in the car for my dad and Dylan.

In the afternoon it rained a little as I drove to the coffee shop. *Free car wash*, I thought. It wasn't until I was on my break when I checked my phone again. It was my supervisor at the nursing home. Shit. I phoned her back right away and was happy when she told me the shift was still available.

It was a four-hour constant care. The patient needed one-on-one care because she was confused and at risk for falling, but my supervisor reassured me that she was an easy patient.

Some voice inside me told me I should just go home, but I felt bad turning down an easy shift.

A female's intuition was really powerful, and I should've listened to it.

My constant-care patient ended up being very restless. And because I had overdosed on coffee all week to keep myself up, my brain and body were starting to shut down. I was changing my patient's diaper when she started feeling very agitated. She was trying to stop me from closing the diaper around her hips. I should've seen the signs, really.

"It's the last one, Mrs. Gonzalez. I promise."

And because I was distracted, I didn't see the fist coming at my face until it was too late.

After my supervisor asked me to write a report and suggested I go to the emergency room so they could check my bruise, I gathered my things and drove home on autopilot.

I could feel hot tears trying to worm their way out, but I held them off. Tears were useless to me. But I knew my emotions were brewing very close to the surface. I knew I was close to the breaking point. I wasn't sure how long I could keep doing this. I didn't even know what was holding me together anymore.

"Steel, baby. You are made of steel."

But it didn't feel like that when, physically and emotionally spent, I crawled into bed and fell asleep.

I woke up in the middle of the night hungry as hell. I felt for my phone and looked at the time. When I saw a text message from an unknown number, my heart skipped a beat.

Sitting up, I typed in my passcode. My lips parted, and a quick, soft breath came out as I read the message.

8 a.m. tomorrow. My place.

Chapter 14

Kara

THE SKY WAS AS BLEAK AND DARK AS MY DAY PROMISED TO be. I shouldn't even be able to function right now—exhausted as I felt—but my body was keyed up for some reason.

I slid into my car with sluggish movements, flicked back my hood that was wet with rain. There had been a deluge late last night, and the forecast today stated that it was going to rain all day. Perfect day for a murder, wouldn't you say?

The rain would erase most of the evidence.

I threw my backpack on the passenger seat, yawned, and fitted my coffee cup in the holder. The mud on my boots stained the plastic mat on the floor of my car. It looked like smeared shit.

The dials on my ancient stereo system were worn, the color faded. There was a coffee stain on the passenger seat the size of Texas, and the smell inside my car didn't scream *Yo, I clean this once a week*. It smelled more like *Yo, I clean this once a month...or year. Maybe.*

I should've taken Ekon's offer to detail my car the other day. I turned on the ignition and the windshield wiper blades, blasted the heat, and leaned back against the seat.

He was going to be here in a few minutes. Inside my car. With me.

Shit.

That was the reason why my body was on edge.

My heart was doing somersaults inside my rib cage, and I sucked in deep breaths to calm it.

"It's fine, it's fine. If he doesn't like it, he can kiss my fine flat ass."

That he squeezed the other night.

Screw you, voice in my head. Screw you.

Anything pertaining to what happened *that night* was taboo.

I shook off my thoughts, nudged the rearview mirror, yawned again, checked my makeup. I had done a great job hiding the bruise under my eye. I couldn't tell it was there. The huge, chic glasses covering half of my face also helped.

"Your eyebrows are on fleek." I winked at myself, fixed the rearview mirror back into its place. "You're gorgeous. You're perfect. You're all set. Let's do this."

7:48 a.m.

It was a five-minute drive to his place. Why did I leave early?

Could it be that you're excited?

"Of course not." I rolled my eyes. "*Puh*-lease. Be serious."

I just didn't want to be late. I wanted to show him I was a pro at adulting and serious about fulfilling my part of the deal.

The heat often emphasized smells, made them

stronger, I thought as I eased my foot on the gas pedal. Maybe a couple sprays of perfume would make the car smell better.

Eyes on the road, I zipped open my bag using my right hand, felt around inside for my perfume, and spritzed a couple times. Five seconds later, I was hacking my lungs out.

"Holy smokes, what the fuck?"

I cranked open my window—it wasn't automatic— and gulped cool, fresh air. Eyes still on the road, I quickly reached over to open the passenger window, heard the sharp zap of the seat belt as it locked in and snapped me back, nearly choking me.

Pissed, I pulled over to the side of the street, slammed my brakes, unbuckled my seat belt, and, finally, thank God, opened the two windows.

The source of the terrible smell was lying happily on the mat on the passenger's side.

It was the same boxy shape as my perfume—except it wasn't my perfume. It was Dylan's cologne.

What the hell was it doing in my backpack?

I blew out a defeated breath, leaned my forehead against the steering wheel.

8:03 a.m.

I was late.

He was waiting outside for me.

Under the portico where he was shielded from the rain, he leaned against the wall, wide shoulders, long legs crossed at the ankles, hands in pockets. He looked dark and broody and so brutally beautiful.

He was wearing black sweatpants and a thick, dark-blue sweater with the sleeves pulled up just under his elbows so that the thick, corded muscles of his forearms were visible. He had a backpack slung carelessly over his shoulder.

The wind rose and blew his loose, dark curls, covering his eyes. I couldn't see the blue of them, but his head came up, a proud lion sensing prey, as I rolled my car in his driveway.

My hands curled tightly around the steering wheel. I could feel the pulse in my neck beating wildly. Slowly and surely, his eyes found me in the rain.

I shivered.

But it was only because the windows were both open and the cold wind had soaked into my bones.

He didn't take his eyes off me as he walked to my car. Confident, long strides that ate up the ground in a matter of seconds.

I faced forward, refusing to turn my head so I could watch him. My heart jerked as the passenger side door creaked open. He reached in, grabbed my backpack, and gently threw it along with his into the back seat.

Butterflies danced in my belly as he slid his big body inside my small car. I jumped a little when he slammed the door closed.

Then we were locked in together. And the air around me changed.

In my peripheral, I saw him crank his window closed, then push the seat way back to accommodate his long legs. I heard his soft groan as the seat jolted to a stop and his body rocked slightly, then settled back.

His broad shoulder nearly touched mine. I would have moved a little to my left if I could, but I was paralyzed.

God, he was just so *big*. It was impossible to ignore his presence or even pretend to.

I gripped the steering wheel harder as I felt his eyes watching me.

"Can I?" he asked quietly. Whispered it.

I didn't even know what he was asking, but I nodded. I gasped as he carefully reached over, grazing my arm as he reeled my window closed.

"You're shivering," he said, a hint of frustration in his voice as he turned the heater on full blast.

He grasped the back of his sweater, pulled it off. The black shirt he had on shifted up, showing the hard muscles on his stomach.

"Here," he said, offering his sweater to me.

I closed my eyes when, without warning, he placed the sweater on my head, pulled it down.

I blinked, strands of hair falling on my face, my glasses fogging up. His mouth twitched into a hesitant smile.

I saw his throat working. In a husky voice, he asked, "Can I touch you?"

There was that same need I'd heard from him the other night. But there was no regret, no hesitation in him letting me know his intentions. He wanted me to know exactly what he wanted.

He wanted me.

No apologies.

I nodded.

He brushed my hair to the side—fingers stroking, sliding softly—and tucked it behind my ear. I trembled as my skin absorbed the warmth from the pads of his fingers.

"Right arm." His voice was rough.

I pushed my right arm into the sleeve.

Normally, I would protest at being taken care of like this, but with him, in this moment, I craved the intimacy.

"Left."

His sweater drowned me. It was three times my size, at least. It was warm, and it smelled...blue. Blue. I couldn't help associating the color to his scent—it was fresh, sweet, cool ocean air. I wanted to pack his fragrance and eat it like candy if I could. I wanted to savor it bit by bit. It was perfect.

"Are you warming up?" he murmured.

"Yes."

We stared at each other for a moment, the air thick with tension. His gaze was intense on my face, watching my every reaction.

Then he moved back.

"If you're trying to get out of this deal by freezing me to death"—he whispered the words, but the challenge, I realized, was there—"you're going to have to come up with something more creative. This"—he swept a hand at the window—"is child's play. You're only going to get yourself sick."

What?

"You're not getting out of this deal," he continued. His jaw was hard, his eyes glittering with a dare.

I was so shocked by the words coming out of his mouth that mine hung open. He thought I deliberately made it cold inside the car to get out of the deal.

"Unless your word means nothing to you," he finished.

He meant my principles.

Where did this guy come from? How was it so easy for him to unearth the perfect words to get the perfect response he wanted from me? To find my weakness, to *use* it without shame, to goad me, to get what he wanted…

And why was I playing in his web? I had to find *his* weakness and use that against him to level the field. Or turn the tables on him.

I'll find his weakness. If it's the last thing I do.

My nostrils flared. "Listen up, *buddy*—"

"You called me *babe* the other night," he interrupted.

"—if you think… What?"

"I said you called me—"

"Shh. Shh. Shh."

"—babe the other night."

My face felt hot.

Just as I was finding my footing, he pulled the rug out from under me again. He'd opened the box filled with our dark secrets from that night. We weren't supposed to talk about it until X amount of days had passed or some bullshit rule someone had made up that I was totally willing to follow if it would save me from this.

Too late.

I was engaging with a player who broke every rule in the game.

"I called you *babe* that night as an *insult*."

His thumb grazed the corner of his mouth, going back and forth, back and forth, as if he was contemplating something.

"Tell me," he started. A small smile appeared on his lips. And still, he kept rubbing. "Did you kiss me that night as an insult too?"

Oh, he did *not* just go there.

If I were a volcano, my lava would have been all over him by now.

"Because," he continued, looking at me like he wanted to eat me in one big bite, "I want more."

Oh, no, no, no. He's not doing this to me again.

I blinked rapidly, shaking my head. Resetting it.

Focus. Call upon your inner Jedi. She's in there somewhere.

"Is that why you reached for my zipper the first chance you got?" I shot back. "I mean, that was my first kiss!"

His eyes widened in surprise.

Aha! Finally!

But at what cost to me? I didn't mean to blurt that out. I had just handed him another golden weapon he could use against me.

"I'm not sorry about that night, Spitfire," he said.

Spitfire. That nickname he'd given me the first time we met. It felt…funny, like a tickle in my belly, hearing him say it again.

My arms started to hurt. I realized I was still gripping the steering wheel. I let my arms fall to my sides and slumped back against the seat.

"But I *am* sorry for…going too fast." He looked down, hiding his face from me. "I'm not used to taking it slow." When he turned his gaze on me, the full power of his eyes penetrated my shield. "Next time, babe, we do what you want, when you want it," he said with a huskiness in his tone that made me shiver. It felt like a promise.

Holy smokes. My face felt hot again, and it was dangerously and quickly spreading throughout my body. I wanted to bite my lip, but I was afraid he would be able to tell that I was…turned on.

No! I was *not* turned on.

I leaned away as far as I could, closed my eyes, and took a deep breath.

His scent had taken over every bit of air space in this car. It was drowning me. I opened the window a crack. Better.

"We have"—I cleared my throat—"to discuss this deal. I'm not going to be at your beck and call just because you need a ride. I have a lot of responsibilities."

"Give me your class schedule."

"You're not getting my class schedule. What are you, my keeper?"

"If you want."

"I *don't* want," I said. "I'll give you the times I'm available, and you can call me if you need a ride then."

"No. That's cheating."

He was so disagreeable. So damned argumentative. It frustrated me because it was so damn…interesting. And exciting.

"How is that cheating?"

"You could only give me the times you *want* to be available, not when you actually are."

"What the—"

"Why don't I give you my schedule too? Although I should warn you that it's all over the place."

Suddenly, he moved closer. His face inches from mine as he asked in a soft, seductive voice, "Kara?"

Air. I needed air.

"Hmm?"

"What time is your class?"

"Eleven."

"I woke you up too early," he said softly.

"I-I was going to study and do homework anyway."

His hand reached out to touch my cheek. I wanted to lean closer, rub my face against his wide palm like a cat. Instead, I leaned away, gathered all my battery charge so I could find the strength not to succumb to him.

"This isn't happening again," I said. "That night—it was a mistake. A mistake I don't intend to repeat." Suddenly, my body felt heavy, and I slumped against my seat. Was exhaustion catching up to me?

He was silent for a moment. Then, "I'm driving," he said coldly. "Get out of the car."

"You're not driving."

"Yes, I am."

"This isn't even your car!"

"It is until you finish my motorcycle."

How did the conversation suddenly come to this point? We were just...

He slid out of the car and pulled open my door.

"You can barely keep your eyes open. I'm not letting you drive like this."

He was right. I was very tired; I could hardly lift my head. I felt like the cheese in my whiz was gone, the fizz in my pop evaporated. I was too exhausted to argue with him.

The car was warming up considerably, and I thanked God that I could barely detect Dylan's toxic cologne. I yawned, covering my mouth with my hand.

I only had three hours of sleep last night and just a little more than that every night this past week. Trying to fulfill both my work and school duties was taking its toll. And it was so easy to just give up trying to control everything for a while. Just for a little while.

Instead of getting out of the car, I crawled to the passenger side as slow as a turtle, taking my sweet time. I heard him sigh, then suddenly, he was on the other side of my car, closing the passenger door.

How the hell did he get there so fast?

"Did you teleport?" I asked him sleepily when he settled in the driver's seat.

"What?"

"Nothin'."

"Seat belt," he said.

I was going to put it on, but now that he said it, I didn't want to.

"Kara," he growled.

I turned away from him, lowering the seat so I was lying at a comfortable angle. I was so exhausted I couldn't keep my eyes open anymore, let alone argue with him. Maybe I could relax for a bit while he drove us to school. It was so warm in here. His sweater smelled so good, felt so comfortable. If I had my own place, I'd want this scent to cover every surface of it. I let out a contented sigh, closed my eyes, and fell asleep.

Chapter 15

Cameron

THERE WAS A MAZE IN MY CHILDHOOD THAT I WOULD NEVER forget. It had been a refuge for me when I was a kid, trying to escape from everyone's expectations. Trying to just *be*.

It had been a safe haven until that vicious night when life sharpened its claws and made me bleed. Before everything fell apart because of one mistake.

It had been a welcome surprise when I found the maze. Raven and I had just moved to a new neighborhood—for the sixth time that year. I was eight years old, but Raven had made me pack our bags so many times that every place and every face started to look the same.

It only got worse when my father divorced her and remarried. Before, her attention had been divided between me and my father; now, it was concentrated solely on me. It was toxic.

If the kid inside me yearned for an adult to lean on, or for a friend, it was easily squashed by the reality that was my mother. Raven's demands and emotional instability stopped me from reaching out to anyone.

People stopped mattering to me—just as I stopped mattering to them. It was easier to stop caring.

But at night, when I was alone in a huge house, with my mother out partying or doing whatever the hell she pleased, and when the confines of that house started to represent what was lacking in my life that an eight-year-old boy couldn't fathom, the maze had been my sanctuary.

She'd lock me in the house, but a kid could escape if he had half a brain and enough guts.

Funny how I despised the nights I was locked up. Funny how miserable I thought they were when the worst was still yet to come—the night that shattered everything.

But I'd locked away those memories. Locked them tight.

It didn't take long to find the maze. The kids in my class often talked about a haunted mansion on my street. They said it was cursed, that whoever entered it would be cursed as well, so there weren't a lot of people in town who had the balls to venture inside.

The mansion stood on twenty acres of land. It was owned by a writer who never left her house. Rumor had it that it took a year before they found her dead body in the mansion and that she still haunted it up to this day—especially the intricate maze she had built for her lover behind it.

It was a siren's call to an angry, lonely boy, but I wasn't afraid of a stupid ghost or a stupider curse. I wasn't afraid of anything.

Armed with a flashlight and nothing else, I broke into the mansion. A flimsy board served as the front door, as if it didn't need protection from anything. As if it were daring anyone to smash the board and go inside. All the windows were boarded up with drywall now covered in graffiti.

I only made it to the foyer that first night before my imagination got the best out of me and I ran back to my house, trying my best not to piss my pants.

The dark, cold, and damp room freaked me out; it felt like an evil clown was hiding in there, waiting for me.

It took me a whole week before I tried again. I had cut classes and sneaked out of school, so I'd have the light of the day to guide me.

I climbed the long winding staircase that was covered with unidentified debris, stopped when I reached the landing. There were impressive floor-to-ceiling windows that dominated the wall. I walked toward them, wiped away the thick dust on the glass at eye level, and gawked at what I saw behind the mansion.

The maze spread out before me. The magnificent green of it, the fascinating twists and turns. I was mesmerized. My immediate fascination with the maze overpowered any lingering fear I may have had for the house and I ran straight to it.

The maze was massive. Tightly packed bushes and trees as high as a house served as walls—some of them dead and brown, some green. A few of the partitions were made of steel and wood, buried in vines so thick and fat I could barely see what was behind them.

But if I kept looking, and I did, I saw what hid behind them were secret passages and doors.

And those secrets hid more mystery. Winding in sharp turns and curves and bends and dead ends that I could easily get lost in and leave me confused. Every time I thought I had it figured out, it would change its pattern.

I could have easily gone up to the roof and uncovered

its secrets, but that felt like cheating. Besides, where was the challenge in that?

Kara reminded me of that maze.

I stared at her back, watching the rise and fall of her shoulders as she slept restlessly. Even in sleep, her mind hadn't fully relaxed.

There was something inside me that yearned to comfort her. I wanted to gather her in my arms and tell her everything was going to be okay, that I'd take care of her troubles if she'd let me.

I nearly laughed at the ridiculousness of my thoughts. I couldn't take care of anyone. And she'd laugh in my face if I told her that anyway.

It was the confined space, I thought as I turned to face the windshield, watched the rain slide lazily down the glass, listened to the drumming sound it made on the roof. I was alone in a car with the most alluring girl I had ever met. A girl I hadn't stopped thinking about since I met her. A girl who was fighting the strong pull between us. All these things lulled my brain into dreaming up foolish thoughts.

It didn't make sense that, of all the girls I'd been with, she was the one I'd want. She'd bite my head off if she had the chance. She never listened, was stubborn as a bull, and always disagreed with me. Except when we were kissing. That was a different story.

She turned onto her other side, facing me now, whimpering in her sleep. Her long hair slid down to cover half of her face. I held my breath, hoping she wouldn't wake up.

She looked so soft, harmless, like a pretty kitten, but that would be a dangerous assumption to make. She was as safe as a ticking time bomb.

So why couldn't I stop thinking about her?

I released my breath when her breathing steadied again. My hands itched to touch her, to skim my finger over her skin and tuck that lock of hair behind her ear, so I could see her face.

I couldn't get her face out of my mind. Her hair. Her eyes. Her lips.

Her body.

Her fire.

I should be happy that she thought of me as an experiment. But goddamn that had pissed me the hell off when I'd heard her say that on Saturday night.

I'd decided I was going to forget about her the next day, but when I was at the site doing a reno, she was all I could think about.

I had a scratch on my back to prove it. I was distracted and didn't see the sharp edge protruding from the wall. It ripped my shirt off.

The color of the bricks reminded me of her hair. Dark brown and gold. But then I realized it was the wrong shade. The color of her hair was richer and deeper.

Even the fucking lettuce I slapped on my burger reminded me of the flecks in her hazel eyes.

It was annoying the hell out of me. She was like an itch on my back I couldn't reach.

I shifted in my seat when I saw her lips part. She was snoring lightly, and I couldn't for the life of me figure out why I found that so damn adorable.

Had she changed her mind about our deal? I had a feeling she'd bow out because of what happened on my couch two nights ago.

Especially when she came to pick me up with her

windows down, freezing her ass off, and the hint of an unidentifiable stench in her car. It smelled like some poison they sprayed to kill cockroaches.

She was unpredictable. Every time I thought I had her figured out, she changed the pattern on me.

I wanted more. I wanted to know her, memorize every piece of her.

Just like I wanted to taste every part of her.

Maybe once I had my fill, this constant wanting would stop.

Her lips closed, then parted slightly.

Then she opened her eyes.

And I was lost.

I realized a few things all at once. The maze in my childhood both scared and excited me. I was always afraid that I would never find my way out the deeper I explored it, but somehow, it showed me clues, kept its doors open for me to come and go as I pleased.

I always found my way out.

Kara was like that maze. The only difference between them was that I might not make it out this time.

And maybe, I thought as I stared in her eyes, I wouldn't want to.

Chapter 16

Kara

IT FELT LIKE MY SOUL WAS DETACHED FROM MY BODY THE moment I woke up. I blinked and tried to focus, but my brain wouldn't engage. It kept on chanting *coffee, coffee, coffee.*

Someone beautiful was staring at me. He looked awfully familiar, like I should care about him somehow, but like everything else, he felt unreal.

I sat up—slumped, really—and realized I was in my car, parked in someone's driveway. I stared at the windshield and watched as rivulets of rain ran down it.

There was something wet on the side of my mouth. Drool, probably. I should wipe it, but it seemed like a lot of work. Besides, my arms felt heavy.

I heard a deep chuckle coming from somewhere in the car. I moved my head to search for it, and my eyes landed on the mug of coffee in the cup holder. Some sort of yearning sound came out of my throat, and I grabbed it possessively, glugging it down like medicine. It was cold, but it was this-shit's-gonna-make-me-human-again cold.

A few minutes of this and my senses were starting to come back. Suddenly, I became conscious of everything around me. The toasty warmth of the car, the soothing pitter-patter of the rain, the scent of it—something unpleasant mixed with fresh, cool blue that my nose wanted to inhale. But most of all, I was painfully aware of a compelling presence beside me. My heart skipped a beat.

"Better?" A deep, masculine voice. A hint of amusement.

I jumped.

Cameron.

When did he become *Cameron* to me and not *my blackmailer* or *the spawn of Satan*? Must have been some really magical coffee I just drank.

"I can make you a fresh cup." I glued my eyes to the windshield, refusing to look at him, but in my peripheral, I saw him gesture to his house. "But you'd have to come inside."

Something told me that wasn't a good idea. He sounded like a dark sorcerer who came to offer me the best deal of my life...in exchange for my body.

Okay, soul.

"Want to?" he asked softly.

I must not look at him. I must not.

"No thanks," I croaked, feeling warm. "Listen," I started, cranking the window open just a little to cool me down. We needed to discuss important things, and right now was the perfect time. *The time!* "Holy shit. What time is it?"

I couldn't help it. My head whipped in his direction. He moved his head slightly, toward the clock on the dash.

His hair, as black as crow's wings, was rumpled boyishly as if he'd been sleeping. His clear blue eyes were gleaming with amusement. And the way he sat in the seat… Well, he *took over* the space.

"It's 10:15," he provided. "You've been sleeping for two hours."

"I thought you had classes in the morning!"

"I did."

"Why didn't you wake me up?"

"It looked like you needed some sleep."

"But you…skipped classes?"

He shrugged. "I'd rather stay here with you."

I didn't know what to say to that. I didn't even know how to feel about that. It seemed…sweet.

He's not really sweet. Remember what he wants from you. Don't get taken in now. You know what happened in that movie because of a pretty face.

"Right. I haven't forgotten why I'm here," I said, putting my seat belt on. "I'm supposed to drive you. I don't want you to come back later and say I didn't hold up my end of the bargain."

When I looked at him again, the warmth in his eyes was gone. "Is it just me, or are you like this with everyone?"

Was he upset? "What do you mean?"

"What does it take for you to accept kindness? Or do you just really not trust me?" His voice had turned cold. "Is that it?"

Kindness? Had it been kindness he was bestowing upon me all this time? I must have missed the damn memo.

"Well, you didn't really do anything to earn it, did you?"

Suddenly, he moved away as far as he could from me in the confined space of the car, and it dawned on me how close we were leaning toward each other. In defense, I mirrored his actions and crossed my arms in front of me.

"Seat belt," he growled.

I already have it on, Mr. Grouch. "You should be in the CIA. Your observational skills are so on point."

I looked outside my window, watching the rain. It was only drizzling now, but the dreary sky promised more of it.

"You were already late this morning," he said. "Is that what you meant by holding up your end?"

His temper was nasty, but so was mine. I faced him.

"Why don't you kiss my fine, grade-A ass? You're not worth an explanation. Start the damn car and let's go."

"Know what?" he said, his voice had turned low. Dangerous. "Why don't you drive?"

"Why don't I?" I shot back.

Kindness? This is why I don't accept your kindness, you stupid, muscular, pig-headed baboon.

His black temper pushed him out of the car, and he slammed the door closed. And while he walked around the front to the passenger side, I locked the door.

In a frenzy of movements, I unbuckled my seat belt, leaped to the driver's seat. Adjusted it so my legs reached the pedals, put the gear in reverse. I waited until he was about to reach for the door. Then I stepped on the gas and reversed.

Just a couple of feet away. Just enough to send him a message that he couldn't intimidate me. I would match his temper with mine.

His glower could have burned villages. I gave him a smile.

The rain was slowly soaking his black hair. It curled under his sharp jaw, over his forehead, and dripped rain on his face.

We stared at each other for a few seconds—two fighters unwilling to budge. I could feel my skin prickle with electricity at his challenging stare, at the silent invitation in it.

And then he shook his head. He looked down and bit his knuckles, his shoulders shaking. Was he laughing at me?

Talk about hot and cold.

I blew out a breath. He swaggered the few feet to my car and opened the door. I heard the thump of metal as the lock prevented him from opening it. He rapped his knuckles on the window, leaned down so his face was visible to me.

He was smiling.

"The accessories I want cost a couple grand," he said through the crack in the window I hadn't closed.

Goddamn it. I threw him the nastiest glare I could manage and unlocked the door. He got in, a smug look on his irritatingly handsome face.

I gritted my teeth, contemplating the cost of paying his insurance company instead, the premiums in Dylan's insurance, the negatives in his credit. Besides, how bad would it be if Dylan spent some time in jail? He could use the time to reflect.

The spawn of Satan closed the window. As if he owned the car, he lowered the back of the seat—lower than I had it before—and relaxed back into it. He closed his eyes.

"Like I said the other night," he said lazily, "you drive me fucking crazy."

He didn't sound too bothered by it.

"I don't want to drive you anything," I said. The last thing I wanted to remember was that night. "Just to your destination, thank you very fucking much."

His lips twitched. Cool as a cucumber.

The one thing that pissed me off more when I was already pissed off was when the person I was supposed to be pissed off with wasn't as pissed off as me.

"You can take a picture of me if you like," he said easily, opening his eyes and catching me looking at him. "Or you can drive me to my destination."

"I'll drive you to your *final* destination, all right."

He replied by closing his eyes and laughing softly.

I gritted my teeth and stepped on the gas.

I was painfully aware of him sleeping lightly beside me. He crossed his arms across his chest. Probably protecting his stone-cold heart from the ancient, cursed dagger that I wanted to bury in there.

But I couldn't resist glancing at him. He was like a black panther in the jungle. Too beautiful to ignore. Sleek and dangerous. Even when he looked relaxed, there was an edge to him that kept my gaze coming back.

I released a sigh of relief when I saw the campus sign.

"I'm parking on the street," I said. "I can't afford to pay the campus parking."

He shifted his wide frame, adjusting his seat so he could sit up straight. The top of his head grazed the roof of the car.

"I got it," he said. "Just drive us to school."

"What do you mean, you got it? You're paying for parking?"

He shrugged.

"Do you know how much parking is on this campus?" I asked. It cost a fortune.

"I don't want to walk a couple of blocks just to go to school," he drawled.

I threw him a quick glance from top to bottom. If he was this lazy, where did he get all those muscles from? They must be silicone. That was why they felt big and hard. They didn't...feel like silicone though. They felt real and warm and *good*. I kinda wanted to feel them again...

No you don't!

"Really," I croaked, erasing the memories that started to bombard my mind.

I found it hard to believe that walking a couple of blocks would bother an athletic guy. What I knew for sure was that he always had an ulterior motive. What was it this time? What would it cost me? He had another reason he was hiding.

"I'll pay for gas too."

Now that was really shady... I stopped at a red light and threw him a suspicious look. "And you're doing all this because you don't want to walk a couple of blocks?"

He shifted in his seat, his body turning toward me. My eyes were suddenly drawn to his lips. His lips...

"What do you think?" he purred.

My face felt hot. I could feel his gaze roaming over every part of my body. Was he checking me out like I was checking him out earlier? Why did it always turn sexual around him? Some guys just seemed lame and gross when they tried, but with him...it felt as if I was playing with a pro. And the worst of it was, it bothered me...in a good way.

"I think you have a sinister plan for me again. And I want to know what it is."

He didn't respond.

"Well?" I prodded.

"A student was robbed at knifepoint last week in one of these streets," he said quietly.

My heart did a slip and slide.

"I just want you to be safe when I'm not there to protect you."

Slip and slide. Slip and slide.

I didn't know how to process this side of him or this side of me that was feeling all these emotions for the first time. I put my signal on, preparing to turn left at another traffic light, onto a campus street. It looked deserted, light fog and rain covering the grounds.

"Fine," I said. It seemed fair to give him my schedule, something to give him in return for what he'd…offered. I gave him the schedule I'd memorized. "Weekends are tricky. I work at the coffee shop from one to five in the afternoon, but I'm always on call for night shifts at the nursing home or hospital. Weekdays too, but they don't call all the time."

I threw him a look when he didn't say anything. I sighed. "Look, I can still drive you. If I can't, Dylan will."

"The deal was that you'll be giving me the ride. Not your brother."

Before I could say anything, he added, "My schedule's more flexible. I'll work around yours. If I need a ride, I'll borrow your car to get around and I'll come pick you up from work."

I shifted in my seat. That seemed too…personal.

"How much do you get paid?" he asked, straight as

you please. I didn't think we were close enough for him to ask me that question.

I glared at him. "Why do you want to know?"

"I don't think you're getting paid that much at the coffee shop. Are you?"

"At least I work. Do you?"

"I'm only a part-time student, but I need you to pick me up and drop me off at work."

I snorted out a laugh. "You work?"

"I freelance. Flipping houses," he said. "When I don't have a project, I work for a friend."

That put me in my place. "Oh." Hence the god body and the hard hands.

I glanced at him quickly when he wasn't looking. He owned a business? Looks could be deceiving, I thought. He looked like someone who bossed around people to wash his underwear.

I pulled into a spot in the campus parking lot. I put the gear in Park and turned off the ignition.

"You should take care of yourself," he said softly. "You're working yourself sick. You don't even have a day off."

"I don't need you to—"

"Just an observation. Your eyes were really tired this morning." I held my breath as he leaned close to me. I could see worlds in his eyes. Hundreds of galaxies in different shades of blue.

"You're beautiful," he whispered. "Spitfire."

My lips parted, and my body involuntarily drew closer to him.

"I'm going to kiss you now," he whispered.

And then he did. I closed my eyes, my breath

hitching as his lips touched mine. It was only a meeting of lips, barely. So soft, so swift it was over even before I could blink.

"I'll see you later," he murmured, brushing my bottom lip with his thumb. "Kara."

_____

My heart was still beating a crazy rhythm by the time I reached my lecture hall. I chose a seat in the back, sitting behind a tall guy so I could hide. Just in case I needed to take a quick nap. Although at the rate my heart was skipping, I'd be awake till Christmas.

He was a master manipulator of my senses, I realized as I caught myself touching my bottom lip. Trying to re-create the way he'd brushed his thumb over it. Trying to remember the feeling of his kiss a few minutes ago in my car. The kiss that wasn't really a kiss.

It was so different from...our first one. But no less powerful. Not at all.

I looked around the hall, checking if someone had read my thoughts or could read my face. Most of the students were listening to the professor standing on the podium, his hands animated as he explained something to the class.

"What does it take for you to accept kindness? Or do you just really not trust me?"

Maybe he was right. I was too harsh on him. I shouldn't have responded that way. There was something about him that activated my defensive mode.

Maybe because I knew he could take it. He wouldn't be put off by it. Or was I trying to put him off with it? Testing to see how long he could go until he gave up and left?

Because the truth was I liked him.

I *liked* him.

And I didn't want to.

But that was my problem, I realized as the professor dismissed the class. Rejecting someone who was trying to be kind to me, as he'd put it, was vicious. And my dad didn't raise me to be like that.

Although the guy didn't make it easy when he started bossing me around. *I* was used to bossing people around, not the other way around. I guessed we were similar in that regard, so it was only natural we'd butt heads. But, I thought as I let out a sigh of resignation, I knew that I'd stepped out of line.

Contrite, I fished my phone from my pocket. I bit my lip as I scrolled to his name in my inbox, read his only text from last night.

8 am tomorrow. My place.

A man of few words. What should I text him to let him know I wanted a truce? *Did* I want one?

A few of the classes in the lecture halls had ended. Students filled the corridor, some heading to their next class in another building, others hanging out to chat and blocking the way. Since I didn't want to squish between them, I leaned against the wall and started typing him a message.

Want some food?

Erase.

Need a ride after class?

Erase.

Are you over your period cramps?

Erase. He might think I was looking for another fight with that one.

This was hard. All the tips and tricks I'd read about men in magazines flew out the window when I was faced with an actual one. I needed to brush up on the subject again.

Frustrated, I combed my fingers through my hair and looked up. The hallway was now empty, as if the fire alarm had rung and everyone had escaped except for a few rebels who believed it was only a drill.

My eyes scanned the space.

And froze.

There he was, sitting on a bench outside the lecture hall in the corner. He sat like a maverick. Sprawled, really. He leaned back lazily, long legs spread, muscular arms propped on the back of the bench.

The rain had stopped, and the sun had finally come out of hiding. Its light pierced through the skylight, kissing his hair and turning the color to blue black.

This was where I'd first seen him.

I saw two guys walk up to him. A short, muscular guy with spikes in his blond hair and the gorgeous Caleb Lockhart. Popular basketball player slash Lothario who was rumored to have boned every gorgeous blond on campus.

They were joking around, hitting him on the arm. His mouth moved a little, a hint of a smile, but he remained the way he was. A little aloof, as if he was selfish with his personal space, and a lot sexy.

"Hi, Cam!"

A beautiful redhead as short as my thumb sashayed in front of him. She bent down, her torpedo cleavage in his face, and wrapped her arms around his neck. Kissed him straight smack on the lips.

And then his eyes lifted and met mine.

Motherfucker.

Cameron

"Saint Laurent!"

I almost missed the ball when it zoomed in front of me. I grabbed it before it hit my face, spun around, and took my shot.

"Stop daydreaming, asshole!" Caleb called out, laughing. I gave him the finger in the spirit of friendship.

Another hour went by, and another, and my lungs and legs were screaming for me to take a break, but I kept going. I loved the burn, the distraction from my dark thoughts. And darker mood.

It made me stop focusing on the missed call I'd gotten just as I'd pushed away the redhead. I was going to go after Kara, but that missed call had stopped everything in my world for a moment. It was from the person I was hoping wouldn't contact me for a while. Or forever. But that was asking too much.

Coach blew the whistle, ending practice. I lifted my shirt to rub the sweat off my face. I was out of breath, bending as I propped my hands on my legs to slow down my breathing.

"You got good game, son!" Levi slapped my back as he headed to the showers.

I took off my shirt, slung it over my shoulder.

"Cam!"

I caught the bottle of water Caleb threw at me. He motioned for me to go ahead without him. He was talking to a couple of girls on the sideline. It looked like he was going to be a while.

I twisted the cap, glugged water, and just for the hell of it, poured some on my head to cool off.

"Hey, Cam."

I turned. It was the redhead. I was an asshole for not even remembering her name. What was it again? Lisa? Maria?

"It's Siobhan."

"Hey."

She flicked her hair over her shoulder. "Do you want to hang out in my dorm tonight?"

"Listen," I said, raking my fingers in my hair. The water dripped on my shoulders and back. I just wanted a damn shower. "That night was fun, but that's all it was. I thought you weren't looking for anything else."

Her lip curled into a sneer. "I'm not. Bye, then. Asshole." She gave me the finger and walked away.

Before I could respond, I felt a kick in my ass and turned.

"Hey, hey!" Justin sniggered. "You're hoarding all the girls! Ya gotta leave some for me, dickhead."

I narrowed my eyes, feeling the heat shoot through my veins.

"Do that again. I fucking dare you."

He looked shocked, then raised his hands, palms up. "Someone's got her panties in a twist."

I curled my hands into fists, got in his face. "Say that again?"

Justin backed off, looking behind him for help. "I was kidding! Dude, chill."

"Cam." It was Caleb. "Cool off."

I looked down, flexed my fists. What the hell was wrong with me?

The guys were looking at me like I'd sprung a leak in my brain. They weren't used to seeing my temper. I was usually coolheaded around them, usually shrugged off their ribbing.

But those days had been free of *her*, Raven. I headed to the shower, turned on the cold water. Even after not seeing her for years, she still had the power to tie my guts into a knot just by a single missed call. What could she want now?

I had changed my number a few times, but she always found a way to get it. My father probably gave it to her just to get her off his back.

"Hey, bro." Justin tossed me a towel just as I wrapped one around my waist. "Didn't know you didn't like your ass kicked. Sorry. About earlier, I mean." His voice still held resentment from what happened, but I didn't blame him.

"Yeah. Me too," I said and let it go. I walked to my locker, using the towel he gave me to rub my hair. A sign of peace.

I felt exhausted but not better. I already knew what was coming in the next few days. Dread was already pooling in the pit of my stomach.

"Need a ride?" Caleb asked as I pulled on my pants.

"Nah, I'm good. Thanks."

The light from my phone sucked the breath out of me, but I saw the screen before I could dismiss it.

Spitfire: I'm in the gym, sicko.

The knots in my stomach started to loosen. As soon as I saw her text, my shoulders released a tightness I hadn't even been aware I was holding.

"Hot date?" Caleb asked. He saw me smiling.

"Yeah," I replied. "Really hot."

And when I saw her waiting on the bleachers, I grinned.

"Hungry?" I called out to her.

"No." She jumped off the bleachers as soon as she saw me, throwing her backpack over her shoulder. "I want to drop your ass home, so I can do the hundred errands I need to do."

I wondered if she was even aware that she was still wearing my sweater. She'd folded up the arms a few times, but it still reached her wrists. It gave me a warm feeling in my stomach seeing her in my clothes.

She wasn't wearing her glasses anymore, but she had her hair up in a ponytail again. It swung back and forth as she walked ahead of me. Damn, how cute was that?

I wanted to hold her hair in my fist, feel the softness of it in my fingers. Did it smell like peaches too?

"It's late," I said, walking beside her, matching her steps. "What do you need to do?"

"I need to find the cure for cancer."

"What about bullheadedness?"

"That's next."

My mouth twitched. She always had a comeback for everything. I wanted to come up with something stupid to pester her with just to hear what she was going to say.

"Hold up," I said when she kept walking toward the exit. "I need a drink."

I went to the vending machine. It was two dollars and fifty cents for a bottle. Just as I was inserting the last dollar, I curled it in my palm, and hid it in my pocket.

"Got a dollar?"

She huffed out an impatient breath. "Why didn't you just text me that you wanted a drink? I could've saved myself a dollar. Here." She threw it at me.

I caught it easily. She didn't look impressed.

"Don't choke on it," she added. She looked like she wanted me to do the opposite. She was in a bad mood, her movements punchy. I popped open the lid, heard the fizz, and took a sip. "You can bring me a drink next time."

"Says who?"

I opened the door leading to the parking lot, let her pass first. "Well, start bringing a dollar or two for me every time you pick me up then."

She shot me a glare that could boil water before opening the car door with her key. It wasn't automatic. Once she was inside, she had to reach over and unlock the passenger side.

She looked really pissed. I reached for the dollar in my pocket and rolled it around my fingers before I slid into the passenger seat.

"Kara."

She didn't respond but placed her key in the ignition.

"Wait," I said, reaching for her hand. It was cold. I wanted to warm it up between my hands, but I knew she wouldn't let me. Slowly and gently, I unfurled her fingers one by one, savoring the feel of her skin, wanting to linger, wanting to caress, but I stopped myself.

Her eyes were wide as they searched my face and dropped when I placed the dollar on her palm.

"I was just kidding," I murmured.

Her gaze lifted to mine. And I knew she felt it too.

God, I wanted to kiss her.

The noise from a group of students exiting the building broke the moment. She moved away and drew a deep breath.

"Don't talk to me," she said and turned the radio on high before starting the car and zipping out of the parking lot.

I just smiled. Fine by me. It was enough to be around her.

Her car looked cleaner and smelled fresher too. Hopefully got her useless brother to detail it for her this afternoon maybe. The seats were still a little damp, but I didn't mind. I could sit on a rock for all I cared if she was beside me.

I cranked the window open a little, letting the wind swirl in the car. Watching it tease her ponytail. What would she do if I pulled it, releasing her hair so it could flow down her back and shoulders?

She'd probably open my door and push me out.

She threw me a worried look when I chuckled.

I watched her hands for a moment. She had long fingers and nails painted hot pink. I wondered if she'd painted her toes the same color.

Her hands were capable on the wheel. She drove a little over the speed limit. With her music way up high. She was singing under her breath, and I wished I could hear her.

But right now was enough for me. More than enough.

The drive felt too quick as she parked at the edge of my driveway.

"Sayonara," she said. "Off you go. Back to the pits of hell."

I turned the radio down.

"You want to come in?"

"You want to live?"

I looked at her, daring her to come inside.

"Tell me why you're in a bad mood, Kara."

Her fingers tapped on the wheel impatiently. "Every time I'm around the spawn of Satan, I'm in a bad mood."

"It's not because you saw a girl kiss me earlier, is it?"

She sputtered. The play of emotions on her face was a joy to watch. "Pardon the hell out of me but I think it's time for your drugs, boyo. The voices in your head are getting out of control again."

"I didn't kiss her back."

She narrowed her eyes. Hazel fire.

Spitfire.

"I don't even remember her name."

"And what does that say about you?" she asked.

"That I'm an asshole."

"That's right. Shoo. Go away now." She waved her hand.

"I've never claimed otherwise, but"—I leaned close, and when she leaned away, I leaned closer, until our faces were inches apart—"you make me want to be something else."

Her eyes turned glassy, and I could hear her trying not to breathe.

"You sure you don't want to come in?" I whispered. "Re-create your *first* kiss?"

She turned red. Fucking adorable. She recovered quickly, snorting derisively. "You call that a kiss?"

Now I smiled. She was challenging me.

"Why don't you let me show you?"

"Get off me, creep."

"I haven't touched you. Yet," I pointed out. "And you weren't saying that last time when you were on top of me." I knew I was being a dick, but she was too adorable not to tease.

I waited for her cutting remark, but she didn't say anything. I could feel the sharp edges of her temper whirling around her in waves, but she just bristled in her seat, glaring at me. I almost laughed out loud when I slid out of her car.

"See you tomorrow," I said easily, almost smugly. "Same time."

As soon as I closed the door, she reversed her car a few feet away. I paused, watched her curiously. What was she up to?

We stared at each other for five seconds. Then she pointed two fingers in a V toward her eyes before pointing them back at me, the universal sign for *I'm watching you.*

It was too late before I realized.

Her tires spun, roared, and accelerated, splashing a giant puddle I hadn't noticed. Dirty, muddy rainwater from last night's downpour sprayed all over me. I could feel the grittiness of it dripping down my face and my neck.

I wiped my face and mouth with the back of my hand. Then I cursed her. I saw her give me the finger as she drove away.

And then I laughed.

Missing her already.

Man, oh man. I was in big trouble.

Chapter 17

Cameron

I WOKE UP HUNGRY.

But that was nothing unusual. I always woke up with my body craving food.

I groaned as I sat up on the couch where I slept. Leaning forward, I propped my elbows on my knees and rubbed my face with my hands.

The sun wasn't up yet. Working for Rick since high school had programmed my brain to wake up the same time every day. I didn't even set up the alarm anymore.

I got up, folded my blanket, and tried to reach the itch on my back, but it was too far away.

"Shit."

Normally I'd do my workouts first—it was easier to lift weights when my stomach was empty—but sometimes I gave in to more basic urges.

I turned on the lights, staggered my way into the kitchen still sleepy, still trying to reach that itch with my fingers. Then my stomach growled.

I opened the fridge, grabbed one of the boxed takeout meals I must have had this week—hopefully. Sniffed it. Smelled okay.

Pulling open a drawer, I reached for a fork, used that

to scratch the itch—damn, that felt good. Wolfed down the food.

When that didn't satisfy me, I got a bowl and poured cereal and milk and ate that too. Still hungry. Grabbed a couple of bananas. Crunched on an apple. I made a mental note to buy some peaches at the store.

Is she still sleeping?

She was probably still asleep, I thought as I took a leak, then turned on the shower, closing my eyes as the warm water washed away the rest of the sleep from my body.

And once she woke up, I imagined her going straight for her cup of coffee, bumping into walls on the way to the kitchen.

Hair in disarray. Clothes rumpled. Skin warm. Lips soft. What did she wear to bed? Did she wear anything at all?

I got out of the shower, reached for the towel, and wrapped it around my waist. Brushed my teeth, reached for the razor to shave. I wondered what she'd feel like, smell like in the morning.

She'd be unaware of her surroundings, and I could wake her up with a kiss on her neck, nuzzling her sensitive skin there. It would be warm, and her scent would be concentrated there. My hands would travel down—

"Shit."

I winced as my hand slipped and I nicked myself with the blade.

Even thinking about her was ruining me, I thought as I washed the cut with freezing water. I grabbed tissues, put pressure on it.

I couldn't help but laugh when I remembered the events from last night. Her temper. That puddle. She was…larger than life. Bigger than the world I chose to live in, it seemed.

I put on jeans, then headed to the kitchen to grab a cup of coffee. I looked out my window, standing at the sink, sipping coffee as I watched the sun rise. Smiled as I remembered the sewage coffee she'd served me in her home.

What a spitfire, I thought as I stepped in to my office.

It was easier to conceal my real self from people. There was a darkness lurking inside me. It was there, burrowed close to the surface, waiting. I could feel it even now.

I knew most people couldn't handle or accept the real me. But with her…a little bit of the real came out. She demanded it, and it seemed I was helpless not to give in.

It alarmed me a little. I wasn't used to it. I wasn't sure if I liked it or not, but I must have because I wanted her to…stay. For a little while longer at least.

Never wanted a woman to stay before. The thought disturbed me. I dismissed it, tucked it away for now.

I sat at my desk, opened my laptop. Checked my business email, replied to the urgent ones. I hadn't seriously decided about expanding my business, although I toyed with the idea now and then. With a lot of help from Rick, I had built my connections and clients and fattened my bank account over the years of working for and with him. I quit college for three years to work on big projects that earned me a huge bank account. I only came back to study because of Rick. He wanted me to get a degree. I didn't mind, but I would do it on my own time.

My company was a one-man operation, but it suited me just fine. I could pick up or drop projects whenever

I wanted. I hired people to work for me for one project or two when needed, and after that was done, we both moved on. I answered to no one, was shackled to no one once a house was done. It was what I wanted.

Leaning back against my chair, I glanced at the clock. It was early, but I knew Rick was already awake. I grabbed my phone and called him.

"Mornin', kiddo," he greeted. "You working for me today?"

"No, sir."

"Got a flip you're doing?"

"Not yet." I had one on the line though. It'd bring me a couple hundred thousand potential profit with all the upgrades I was planning, but it was a big job, and it would take up a lot of my time. "Thinking about it."

"I got one for ya if you want. Not even on the market yet. I'll get Deb to send you the details."

"Sounds good. Speaking of Deb. She going on maternity leave soon?"

"Yeah, why? You helpin' her deliver the baby?" he chuckled. I could hear him moving around. He was probably at a site already.

"I heard she broke Logan's fingers when she had their daughter. Think I'm keeping mine intact for now."

He laughed heartily. A hacking one. He had a raspy voice from years of smoking. Started smoking cigarettes at nine years old out of boredom, he'd said.

He grew up in a trailer park, in a town where there was nothing to do. So he'd smoked a lot, but never did drugs. He watched his brothers waste their life in prison because of drugs. Eventually he left his hometown and made something of himself by working in construction in the city, then eventually for this man who saw potential in him and taught him everything he knew about building houses.

Rick got his certificates and licenses and owned his company now. Just like everyone in the business, he experienced a rough patch when the market crashed and lost a bunch of properties. He had to ask everyone he knew for loans to keep his business afloat, but eventually, he'd bounced back. He was one of the very successful contractors in Manitoba now.

I owed this man a lot. I guess he saw himself in me. He took me under his wing, treated me like his son and student. He was one of the very few important people in my life. I would give up my limbs for him if he asked.

"Women are strong, powerful creatures," he said. I could hear him scratching his beard. He and I usually forgot to shave when we were busy with a project. "What is it, Son? Spit it out."

He knew me well. "Got a favor to ask you."

"All right."

All right. He'd said it simply, without a thought. He'd been my father when mine couldn't be bothered with me.

"I know someone who might be able to take over Deb's job. I can vouch for her." I cleared my throat. "You'd need her twice a week and weekends at the office, right?"

He didn't say anything for a moment and then, "Sure, makes my job easier if I don't need to interview a bunch. A girl, huh? Yours?"

"Ah." *I think...I'd like her to be.* "A friend."

He chuckled. "Let's grab a beer sometime this week. Come by the house, kiddo."

"Will do."

"You doing good with your studies?"

"It's only a couple of classes, but yes, sir. I am."

"Good. I'm heading up north to check on that project I told you about. See you when I get back, Son."

After I hung up, I sent a text to someone and got the ball rolling. Half an hour before eight, my phone chirped a text.

> **Spitfire**: Hey, bigfoot, how did you like your swim last night?

I chuckled and read on.

> **Spitfire**: Can't pick you up this morning. Sorry. I worked the night shift and my replacement at work just called in sick. I'm pulling a double. Will drive you home tomorrow night after your basketball practice.

I sat up when I saw three dots on my screen. She was typing another message. I waited. Waited. But it disappeared without a new message from her.

How bad did she need the money? Did she really have to work this obsessively? She worked the night shift, so that meant she'd go to school without any sleep. How did she do it?

I leaned back in my chair, grabbed a lollipop from my stash. I unwrapped it, placed it in my mouth. Then I started thinking.

I only had one class in the morning, and when it was over, I had no reason to stick around campus. I hopped into my truck and was about to pull away when my phone rang.

"Yeah?" I mumbled.

"Seven days."

"Fuck off, Lockhart."

He must have been watching scary movies again.

"Need you to do me a favor," he said.

"I don't do favors."

"I'll drop you off at your girl's shop again if you need."

"Deal."

"Whipped," he chuckled. "Did you know Jack had an accident?"

Jack was our painter. He was fifty-five, looked like a mad bulldog, and barked at everyone who talked to him, but he was excellent at his work. I liked him.

"Broke his hip," Caleb continued. "Rick asked if I could visit him today. He has no family."

"Why can't you do it?"

"I have this charity ball thing I need to attend with my mom. Can't bail."

I scratched the scruff on my cheek. "Do I have to do it?" I asked.

"Yep."

I sighed. "All right."

"Make sure you bring him something."

"Like what?"

"Oh, I don't know. Last time I talked to him he said he was looking for a girlfriend."

Only Caleb could get Jack to tell him that.

"I don't know what to bring the guy. You know I don't do this kind of thing."

"That's why I want you to do it. Jesus. Bring the man a fruit basket. Bring him beer. Maybe a TV."

"You want me to bring him a TV?"

"Why would you bring him a TV? They have one at the hospital."

I blew out a breath. "You just told me to bring him one."

"Son, sometimes I worry about you. I worry about you a lot."

"I'll get him a TV then," I said, just for the hell of it.

He snickered. "Don't forget the remote."

I bought Jack a fruit basket at one of the kiosks at the hospital. He looked grumpier than usual and said he didn't much care for visitors. He told me to leave as soon as I got there. Except for a cast on his arm, he looked healthy. I stayed for ten minutes and left, but before I did, he told me to hand him an apple. That was his way of saying thanks. I gave him a salute and walked out of his room.

The ward was a long hallway, with rooms on both sides facing each other. A couple pieces of bulky equipment, some chairs, patients and staff walking in the hall. It was too bright and smelled of antiseptic. I couldn't wait to leave.

"His name is Cameron."

I stopped. Someone had just said my name in a very familiar voice.

"Oh, so that's his name," another female voice said.

"That's his alias. His real name is Spawn of Satan and I *don't* like him."

I felt the smile spread across my face. That was definitely *her* voice. What were the chances? I headed toward the voices.

"Oh, well now. It sounds like he's just pulling your pigtails because the boy likes you."

"Amanda, you're supposed to be on my side."

"Well, why else would the boy want to be around you?"

I liked Amanda. She was a smart woman.

I leaned against the wall beside the door so they wouldn't see me and carefully peered inside the room.

Kara was wearing deep blue scrubs and white sneakers, her hair flowing down her back, just the way I liked it. She looked very pretty in her uniform—and made me imagine all sorts of things.

"He kissed another girl! You really think I…"

"Can I help you?"

I turned my gaze from Kara and saw a woman in scrubs looking at me expectantly.

"I'm good," I answered. "Just visiting."

I thought she'd leave but then she asked, "Which patient?"

"Jack. Room 204."

Her name tag said her name was Sue, Nursing Assistant. I wished she'd leave.

"204. Mr. White," she said in a flirty tone. "Charming." When I didn't reply, she asked, "Did you have a good visit?"

I nodded at her and she seemed to get the idea I wasn't interested in a conversation. She wished me a good day and strolled into the room where Kara was just as Amanda walked out.

Wait. Is Sue going to tell Kara I was hiding here?

How the hell would she know?

"Kara," I heard Sue say. "The charge nurse wants

us to move the equipment in room 201 to free up some space."

"What? The equipment in there is heavy. Did she say why and where?"

"She's expecting supplies to come in five minutes and we don't have enough space in the supply room," Sue answered. "You don't need to move them to another room. Just push everything to the back."

"*I* need to move them?"

"It's time for my break. You good?"

There was a pause. "If you're asking if I'm good if I break my back, Sue, then no. I'm not good. It's a two-person job and you know it."

"I'm not postponing my break to move that stupid equipment. I've worked enough today."

"You sure did work enough today," Kara said with sarcasm. "Are you tired from hiding in the bathroom when you hear the patients' call bell?"

I heard a *hmph*, then Sue exited the room. Her eyes widened in embarrassment when she saw me.

"Good job," I said.

She turned red and walked away in a hurry.

"You gotta be shitting me," Kara exclaimed, her eyes wide with accusation and incredulity as she gawked at me. "Why are you here? Omigod are you stalking me? Is this what's happening now?"

I could see why she would think that.

I held my hands up. "No. I was visiting Jack, room 204."

She had a pen tucked behind her ear and her glasses on. The ones with the big round frames. Cute.

"Liar! This is my place of work and—"

"Still here?"

We both turned at the voice. It was Jack. He was in a wheelchair and a nurse was pushing his chair toward the elevator.

"Go home, Cam," Jack said before disappearing inside the elevator.

When they were gone, I turned to Kara expectantly, but she was already walking away. I chuckled and followed her.

"Aren't you going to say sorry?" I asked.

Her sneakers made a squeaking noise on the floor. One of them was untied.

"You're the one who invaded my territory, genius."

"I'm not leaving until you do."

She glared at me over her shoulder. "Well, the hospital is open twenty-four hours."

She stopped in front of a closed door and let out a long, deep sigh before pushing it open.

Son of a bitch.

This must be the equipment room. There were various machines that looked too heavy to move, a recliner that could sit a buffalo, wheelchairs, a bed. Where exactly would she move all of it? My eyes scanned the back of the room. That was full of crap too. She'd have to organize that part of the room first before she could move anything.

She was right. This was a two-person job.

I glanced at her and felt a squeeze in my chest. She leaned against the wall, her shoulders drooping, her face looking exhausted.

Without a word, I pushed my sleeves to my elbows and started arranging the equipment at the back.

"Don't," she said. Her voice was small, tired. "You're not even supposed to be here. I'll get in trouble if anyone sees you."

"They won't."

And even if they did, I'd file a damn complaint against them for making her work by herself—especially that woman who was supposed to help her.

"Sometimes," she started, "I just want to disappear. Do you ever feel like that?"

Yes.

We worked silently for a while. I told her to sit down and let me do the work, but she wouldn't listen. All I could do was grab the heavier stuff from her.

"*Street Fighter* or *Mortal Kombat*?" she asked. She was so random with her questions. I really liked it.

"*Street Fighter*, hands down."

She nodded. "Good choice. Superman or Batman?"

"Batman."

"Everyone likes Batman," she pouted.

"That's because he's real. He's just a man, but he can do all these cool things without supernatural power. He gives hope to mortals that we could be amazing like him. Batman is the shit. Batman is cool."

"You do know one finger flick from Superman and Batman is down for the count, right?"

"Not when—"

"Shh! Enough. Next question: Spider-Man or Venom?"

"Please." I shot her an *are you kidding* look. "Venom."

"Really." She made a humming sound. "It makes sense you'd choose Venom."

I suppressed my smile. She was trying to figure me out with her random questions. Like she wanted to know more about me. "Venom is a very misunderstood character. Sure, he's portrayed as a villain, but you have to remember Venom hates bad guys too. He just has a very…different way of expressing himself compared to Spider-Man. Sometimes it's hard to see the truth when you only use your eyes."

There was a clanging noise behind me. A pile of metal basins had fallen on the floor, and she was already picking them up.

"Sit down, Kara."

But she wouldn't listen.

"Stop," I said. I grabbed a wheelchair. She had folded them neatly behind the bed, so I opened one and gently pushed her to sit down. When she opened her mouth to protest, I added, "Please."

She stayed. I wished I could take her home. I bent on one knee and knelt in front of her.

"Cameron, what are you…"

I tied her shoelaces carefully.

"Do you see my truth?"

"And what is that?" she asked in a small, vulnerable voice.

"Will you stick around a little bit?" I asked. "I think I…I want to show it to you."

I froze. She had placed her hand on my hair, her fingers playing with the strands. I closed my eyes for a moment, savoring her touch. Then I looked up.

"Thank you," she said softly.

I held my breath as her finger traced the bridge of my nose, sliding down to my lips.

"Kara, can you help me with Mrs. Gonzales? She's—oh. Sorry. Am I interrupting?"

Like guilty children, we both jumped away from each other. It was Amanda. She had a happy smile on her face. I assumed she was Kara's friend and wouldn't tell anyone about me.

"No," Kara answered, rising from her chair. "I'll be right there."

Amanda winked at me and left.

"I'll finish the rest," Kara said. "You can leave now."

There was no way I'd let her. I'd finish everything before she could come back.

Before she stepped out of the room, she looked back. "Thank you."

She looked tired and a little sad. I wanted to make her smile.

"Shirt and pants," I said, pointing at mine. She had splashed me with that muddy water last night. "You still owe me."

She cracked a smile. Mission accomplished.

Chapter 18

Cameron

THE NEXT DAY WAS BETTER. SHE WORE HER HAIR IN A HIGH ponytail.

I leaned against the locker, watching her walk out of the lecture hall. Classes had just ended. Students spilled out from classrooms, crowding the halls. She stopped where she was, braced her side against the wall as she waited for the coast to clear.

She looked tired but so damn cute in her blue knit sweater—the one that looked like a dress sack and ended just above her knees. She had on those dark leggings that girls wear all the time and boots. Her usual backpack was on her shoulder and her usual water bottle in her hand.

She ignored everyone around her.

It seemed like she was in her own world, waiting for everyone to get the hell out of her way so she could move on.

My eyes shifted to a guy standing a few feet from her. He looked interested as he eyeballed her up and down. He walked closer, trying to get her attention. But she didn't even look at him, didn't even know he was alive, didn't care that he was trying to breathe in the air she exhaled.

She shifted, ready to move. The guy deliberately blocked her way but made it look like an accident. He stood in front of her, smiling.

She moved to the left; he moved to her left. She moved to the right; he moved to her right.

My jaw ticked.

When I noticed she was looking at him with dead eyes, I nearly laughed. She stopped, waited for him to move, but he wouldn't.

He looked at her as if he was undressing her, looking down his nose at her. Son of a bitch.

I was just about to walk up to them when I heard her say, "Is it filled with air?" Her voice sounded sweet.

My eyes narrowed, watching her with rapt attention. She only sounded sweet when she was going to deliver a blow.

The guy, clueless, took it as an invitation. He smiled at her and stepped closer. "What's filled with air?" he asked.

"Your brain. I don't want to look at you all day. Can you move?"

The guy glared at her but backed off.

Coward.

That's right. Move aside, I thought, watching the guy slink off. *You're not the one for her.*

"And you are?" I heard Levi say. I scowled at him, found him flirting with a girl. For a moment, I'd thought the question was for me.

And you are…the one for her?

Am I?

I watched her fill her water bottle from the fountain. She'd bulldozed a guy who wouldn't stand up to her.

She could be blatantly rude, and her jagged edges could cut like a chainsaw to wood.

She wouldn't want a gentle or weak man who capitulated to her every whim. She'd get bored with him easily. She needed a guy who could match her temper, who could take her sharp jabs and see them for what they really were. They were her line of defense. Her thorns. Her walls.

I knew firsthand how high and thick those walls were. And I also knew that if I kept hacking at them, she'd put her defenses down and let me in. She'd already done it a few times. She'd put them back up quickly, but she'd let me take a peek.

She presented a tough exterior to the world. She had to, but I knew what she was hiding, what she was protecting so fiercely was her soft heart.

I saw her glance at the bench where I was sitting yesterday. She craned her neck to see inside the other lecture halls, almost hitting a trash can in front of her.

My smile felt huge on my face as I walked to her.

"Looking for me?" I asked.

"Oh shit."

She jumped, backing up a step, her hand flying to her chest. She looked guilty—like a little girl caught trying to sneak a little kitten into her room.

"Why would I look for you?" She sounded embarrassed. "I don't even know if your classes are in these lecture halls. I'm looking for my friend."

"Uh-huh." I couldn't wipe the smile off my face. "You're definitely looking for me."

She ignored me, walking faster. I followed her. My teammates were looking at us weirdly. They hadn't seen me show this much interest in a girl before.

"Where are you headed?" I asked.

"Why? You want me to drive you to your next class too?"

"Well, you didn't drive me yesterday. Or this morning."

She kept going, kept ignoring me.

"At least you're not talking about me today. Yet."

She glared at me over her shoulder, but her eyes were smiling. She kept walking.

At this rate, she'd disappear before I could get her attention.

I grabbed the hair tie holding her ponytail together, pulling it down her hair. She squeaked, spinning around to glower at me.

"What the hell is your problem? Do you know how long it took me to do this hair?" She looked red.

"I'm keeping this," I said, shaking the blue hair tie at her. "See you at the gym later."

I whistled, walked away. And laughed.

After practice, I showered quickly, got dressed, and didn't stay around to chat with the guys. I felt...excited. I hadn't felt this way in a while, and it felt damn good. It felt like how Christmas should feel.

I walked back to the gym and laughed softly when I saw her there.

She was sleeping.

Without a care. Like a little child who'd gotten tired and needed a nap, she'd stretched out on the lowest bleacher seat, arm covering her face, hair spilling around her like a halo. Her other arm hugged her backpack in front of her. Her water bottle was by her feet.

Carefully so as not to wake her, I sat on the bleacher seat above her. I'd watched her sleep before, but watching her now, it felt like the first time.

I only saw half of her face. A little bit of her small nose and her mouth. Her lips were pale, a little dry. And somehow, seeing that…I felt a pang in my chest.

She always had a water bottle with her, but I bet other than water, it was coffee she sipped most of the time. Always trying to stay awake to keep up with her responsibilities.

She was strong. There was no doubt about that, but even the strong needed rest.

I should've told her to go home and get some sleep, but if I didn't ask her to pick me up today, I bet she'd have picked up another shift.

I removed my jacket and draped it over her.

A lock of her hair touched the floorboard. I held it in my fingers, feeling the texture. It was soft, silky. The color reminded me of burnt caramel—gold and dark brown. I leaned down, close enough to smell it.

Peaches.

Thirty minutes passed, an hour. And then the janitor came in. That woke her up. She pulled her arm away from her face, and her hazel eyes found me.

She looked confused and so damn adorable I wanted to wrap her in my arms.

"It's time to go," I said, and remembering yesterday morning, how she needed coffee to wake up, I reached for her water bottle, opened it. I smelled coffee. "Here."

She sat up slowly and drank dutifully. Without a complaint this time. A few seconds later, the caffeine had hit her system. She looked exhausted but a little more awake.

"Ready?" I asked.

She nodded.

She walked mechanically, hugging her bag to her chest like a shield. Her hair hid her face from me.

The only time I'd walked with her without talking was that night when I'd first kissed her. And still, I had felt impatient energy coming off her in waves.

Tonight, that energy was not present. She felt subdued, as though she was hiding herself from the world.

"You can hold on to me," I whispered. "If you want."

She shook her head and kept walking. When at last we were seated in her car, she leaned her head against the headrest and just closed her eyes.

I sucked in a breath when I felt her rest her head on my arm.

"Five minutes," she said softly, her voice breaking. "Five goddamn minutes. Let me just…"

"You can take more than five minutes. You can take…" I stopped myself before I said anything stupid. "Take all the time you need, Kara. I got you."

"I'm so tired."

"I know, baby."

Her breathing was uneven, her chest rising and falling fast. I was expecting her to cry, but there were no tears.

We sat in the parking lot for a quarter of an hour. I didn't dare move, just in case she was asleep again. I didn't want to wake her up but realized she was awake and was just quiet.

"What's your last name?" she asked randomly.

I knew hers was Hawthorne.

"Saint Laurent," I answered.

"You're no saint though," she laughed softly, teasingly. It sounded so feminine that I wanted to kiss the tip of her nose.

"Sometimes I feel like one," I said.

I had a feeling she rolled her eyes at me. "Middle name?"

"Jeremiah."

"Jeremiah," she repeated. "That's one of the prophets in the Bible. He's an ass kicker."

She pulled away. I could still feel the imprint her body heat had made on my arm.

Her voice was soft, whispery. Like we were talking in candlelight.

"You look like a Jeremiah," she added. "Not Jerry though. Jeremiah."

My lips wanted to twitch. "What's yours?"

"Cammilla."

I said her name in my head a hundred times.

"Doesn't it sound like a stripper name? Don't obsess too much on it though."

This time, I smiled.

"We're still waiting for some of the parts on your motorcycle. Just letting you know, in case you're wondering."

I shrugged. As long as she had it, she was bound to me. It was more than fine if she kept it for a while.

It seemed she was getting nervous, filling up the silence with chatter. I wondered if she was thinking what I was thinking—about that moment she rested her head on my arm.

"Tell me what you like," I said.

She stilled at my question. I heard her breath hold for a moment, a split second before it released. I frowned.

"You have a way," she said.

"What way?"

"Like you're seducing me with your words."

My face relaxed into a lazy smile. "Am I?"

"See?" She blew out a breath. "Put a lid on it, all right? I got it."

I chuckled. "Tell me."

She looked up at the ceiling, then breathed deeply. She muttered something under her breath. I thought I heard *Lord have mercy*, but I wasn't sure.

"Hold on." She cranked her window open a little more. "Hmm, let me think," she started, chewing her lip. "Like, what I do for fun? I like decorating. And designing."

I was hoping she'd answer my other question—if I was succeeding in seducing her with my words. But I liked her answer too.

"Houses?"

She nodded. "I probably would have taken interior design if I had the money, but that's what the internet is for, right? I just watch videos about it and I learn a lot."

She preferred an eclectic style, I knew, remembering the time when I was in her house.

"What else?" I prodded.

"When I was a kid, I had this huge swing at our old house. Whenever I felt sad or angry or misunderstood, I'd just go there and swing the day away. If I had money to spare, maybe I'd buy some candy or a milkshake, and I wouldn't get hungry while I was there. I didn't have many friends so…" She jerked a shoulder. "I was too much for girls my age, I guess."

She placed her hand on the steering wheel, her thumb rubbing the groove on it. "Dylan sometimes came with me, but mostly he stayed in the tree house. He and my dad built it and I decorated it. I think that's where I started to love decorating."

She pulled her seat back, tucking her long legs under her and leaning against the door so she was facing me. I liked that. I liked that a lot.

"I like fireworks too. When we were kids, Dad used to take me and Dylan to the Forks in Winnipeg. We'd drink milkshakes and eat spaghetti and feed the ducks in the river."

The smile on her lips looked tender. Her childhood memories were happy ones. I wished I could tell her the same.

"Dylan wanted to ride the boat, but Dad didn't have money. I don't remember us having enough money ever." She frowned. "I used to ask my dad every year to buy me new shoes for the new school year. I was a kid and didn't know better, until I heard Andrew giving my dad shit about paying off his debts or something like that. I thought at the time, because I was so young, that I didn't understand what they were talking about, but I realized I did. Because I never asked my dad to buy me anything after that."

"Tell me more."

"Hmm. I like makeup. I feel pretty with makeup."

"You look pretty without it too."

She snorted, not taking compliments from me. I wondered if she knew I meant every word.

"What about you?" she asked. "What do you like?"

"I like *you*."

She blushed, then said, "Do you sleep around a lot?"

I paused. "Do you really want to know?"

She looked at me directly. "I guess I know."

I was surprised how much that hurt coming from her.

"It didn't mean anything to me," I said. "And I feel like shit talking about it to you."

"Why?" she asked.

"Because it's…you."

And since I had a feeling she'd ask me more about myself, questions I wasn't ready to answer, I asked, "Why do you have a bruise on your face?"

I tried to soften my voice, hiding the anger I was feeling. It wasn't the same anger I felt when I was a child. Back then, I was angry for and at myself—for being mistreated, the unfairness of the world, for being weak and not growing fast enough, so I could run away from everyone. The anger I felt now was for…her. Anger so hot and sharp I wanted to destroy something out of helpless wrath because I couldn't protect someone special to me.

Was that what she was to me? Special?

I'd seen her bruise earlier when she got up from the bleachers. I knew she was confrontational. Had she been in an argument and someone had hit her?

She sniffed. "I thought I hid it pretty well with makeup."

"You did," I answered calmly. "But I think you wiped it off when you were sleeping."

"A patient got confused and hit me." She was whispering, and so was I.

"Does that happen a lot?"

"I've heard stories from coworkers, but it was my first time."

She exhaled softly, her hand on her lap curling. I wanted to hold it. No, I wanted to do more than hold her hand.

Slowly, I turned toward her. It was getting dark now. The lampposts in the parking lot were on, and only a couple of cars were scattered in the huge parking lot.

The car felt like our own little world.

Her eyes looked vulnerable. I held her face with both my hands, my thumb stroking her lip. I wanted to kiss it, taste it, but I leaned closer and kissed her bruise instead. I felt her body soften and lean into me.

I want to take care of you.

There was a hunger I felt for her inside me. It was always there, so strong I'd never felt it with anyone else before. But it felt like I was taking advantage of her vulnerability if I kissed her now.

"I'll drive," I said. Damn, my voice sounded rough. I'd drive her to her place, park her car, and walk home.

"No. I got it." She pulled away from me and ran a hand on her hair. "I just needed a moment. Thanks," she said softly. "Cameron."

That was the first time she said my name. It sounded... good coming from her lips.

Would it be all right to reach for her hand right now? I'd never wanted to hold anyone's hand before. I wondered how her hands would look in mine. They looked dainty. Mine would swallow hers whole.

"I got you a drink," she said.

What did it mean, I thought, when my heart jumped

in my chest at what she said? When warmth was sneaking in like a thief?

"I got it because I didn't want to give you a dollar," she added.

"Where is it?"

"At home." She laughed. "Just kidding. In my bag."

She grabbed her bag, unzipped it, and reached inside. There was something so soft and sweet about her when she was like this. I must've stared at her longer than what was normal because she nudged me with a can. It was ginger ale.

I cleared my throat. "Thanks."

"You're welcome," she said, starting the car. "Thanks for helping me yesterday too."

She threw me a smile—a genuine one. I thought there was affection in the way she looked at me. Maybe it was my imagination. Maybe, but I was keeping it.

She didn't turn the radio on this time. She'd opened her window a little wider, letting the wind inside the car. I noticed she liked doing that while she drove.

We were quiet, but it was comfortable. It surprised me. I'd never had a comfortable moment with a girl before. Not like this. There was usually an expectation to be met—between the sheets. I never wanted anything else after that.

I could see how empty, how shallow all of it was when I was sitting beside her. I raked my hands in my hair, feeling uneasy. When she threw me another look, another smile, every thought in my head quieted down.

And…I relaxed.

She slowed down when she reached my street. When she laughed softly, I turned to look at her. I'd been trying not to look at her all throughout the drive—just in case it freaked her out. We'd reached some sort of truce tonight, and I didn't want to ruin it.

"What's funny?" I asked.

"You're right. I owe you a shirt and pants. You made me very mad at—"

The rest of her words didn't register when I saw the black Ferrari as we pulled up to my driveway.

All the blood drained from my face. My hands felt cold, clammy.

"What's wrong?" she asked.

"Nothing." My hands turned into fists to prevent them from shaking. "Go. I don't need you anymore."

She laughed.

There was a big ball of dread in the pit of my stomach.

"Stop joking around. Don't worry. We'll go shopping and I'll get you a shirt and—"

"Leave," I whispered.

She looked at me, confused, then her eyes turned to the car in my driveway, then back at me again.

It took everything I had to lift myself out of that car. She opened her mouth to say something, but I cut her off.

"Leave!" I said it more forcefully. "I'm done with you."

I slammed the door closed and walked up my driveway.

My heart was beating like a drum in my chest. She hadn't moved. I heard the car running and felt her eyes throwing daggers at my back. And then I heard her tires squeal and the car zooming away.

I turned, watching her car disappear. I knew it would

end, knew it would come to this. I just didn't expect it would be this early. I thought we'd had time. I was wrong.

I clenched my fists, trying to tamp down my anger, and faced my house. I closed my eyes as I held the doorknob, took a deep breath, and opened it.

"Hello, Cameron."

Time to confront reality.

Chapter 19

Cameron

"Hello, Cameron."

Love, guilt, and hatred rolled into one big ball that lodged in the pit of my stomach at the sight of my mother.

Raven lounged on the couch, comfortable in her own skin. She had always been that way, as though she owned everything she set her eyes on. That, or she knew she could buy anything and own it.

Everyone had a price, she'd said, and if there wasn't one, she'd find out what was important to them and use it to get what she wanted.

People say I look like her—same black hair, nose, mouth—except for the color of our eyes. Hers were dark. When I was kid, I watched this movie about a shark that enjoyed killing people. Its eyes were black and soulless. It wasn't until later when I realized the shark's eyes reminded me of Raven's. Sometimes, she'd have that dead look in them; sometimes, there was a gleam of danger when she was thrilled about something, as though she had scented blood and craved the kill. It never failed to disturb me.

"How did you get in?" I asked.

She crossed her legs and leaned forward, tucking

her hand under her chin. Her nails were long and painted a dark color. "You still don't lock the basement window," she answered with a knowing smile. "I know you so well."

I clenched my jaw.

She rose and walked toward me, her high heels clicking on the hardwood floor. The light caught the gleam of her diamond earrings. She loved to be draped in expensive jewelry and silk.

"Didn't you miss me?" she asked.

I shrugged her off when she tried to hug me.

"Come on now, sweetheart. I missed you terribly."

"What are you doing here?"

"I came to see you, silly. Can't I just say hi to my baby?" She placed her hand on her chest, her expression hurt. It was all an act. There were very few things that could hurt Raven, but I knew what they were. "You give such a warm reception, Cam."

I hadn't seen her in a year. She'd come and go as she pleased. As long as she knew where I was, she stayed relatively sane. There was one time when I ran away, and no one knew where I was. My dad had told me she'd gone ballistic. She and I had made a deal that if she stayed out of my life, I wouldn't disappear again. No matter how selfish she was, I knew she loved me in her own way. But she was toxic.

"Now that you've seen me, you can go," I said.

"All I want is for us to be best friends. Why are you so angry at me all the time?"

"Pick one. Or do you want me to find my long list?"

She gave a dramatic sigh. "You know you're going to miss me one day when I'm dead and they bury my fabulous corpse in the ground. Just make sure they don't touch my rings, won't you?"

I looked at her for a moment. When I couldn't hold it any longer, I snickered. Sometimes she could be funny.

"I heard that." Her face lit up. "I can still make you laugh. Now am I allowed to have a drink?"

The faster I gave her what she wanted, the faster she'd be gone. She followed me to the kitchen.

"Give me a glass of champagne. I have something to celebrate."

"Sorry, I'm fresh out." She lived an extravagant lifestyle and she never understood why I didn't. I opened a can of beer, and because it was her, I poured it into a glass and placed it on the counter in front of her. "What did you do this time?"

She reached for the glass. "Oh, honey, you don't want to know."

"It's not money you're after."

"Oh, God no. I have so much money I'm sick of it."

"What then?"

"Oh, you know how it is. Men in high positions are so demanding. They beg and I'm there." She looked young for her age. She was tall, beautiful, and smart. Growing up, I knew men fell at her feet. It was a thorn in her side that my dad wasn't one of them.

"And here I am, dancing like a puppet for them," she continued. "Yachts, jewelry, and men. Oh, my life is tiring. I'm so bored."

"You're still playing with people's lives. When are you ever going to change, Raven?"

"I told you to call me Mom."

Never. "I might if you ever acted like one."

The air around me changed.

The shark was back. This was the real her.

She strolled over to the sink and poured the beer down the drain. Then she placed the empty glass on the edge of the counter, so close that it could fall and break into pieces with the tiniest tap.

"I noticed you have a new friend. Who is she?" She raised an eyebrow. "Should I be interested?"

If there was one thing I wanted to protect and hide from her, it was Kara. Raven was smart and cunning. She'd know it right away if I acted suspicious.

"Do whatever you want. I don't care."

Now she smiled. "One of your playthings?" She clucked her tongue. "They can't stay away, and they can't catch you. Those poor little girls. You know what they want, don't you, Cameron? Don't forget what I taught you. You don't need them."

She clinked a fingernail against the glass and it teetered dangerously.

"You remember what happened to that poor boy, don't you?" she asked. "That poor foster child in that godforsaken town. Do you think anyone would understand what you did to your only childhood friend? Don't get close to anyone. Remember, it's just you and me against the world."

"Get the fuck out," I said quietly.

She grinned. "I'll be back." She crossed to me and gave me a kiss on the cheek. "See you soon, my love."

Chapter 20

Kara

I SHUT MY BRAIN OFF AS I DROVE HOME.

Because if I didn't, I would drive back to his place, and my anger would make Voldemort's wrath seem like a Sunday ride in the park.

There was a heaviness in my chest that had me breathing fast.

Was that his girlfriend's car in his driveway?

No, no. Don't think.

How could he?

My hands shook on the wheel. The tips of my fingers tingled as though all the blood in my body had concentrated there.

Stop thinking. You're almost home.

I had no idea how I got home. As soon as I stepped inside, I took off my shoes, kicked them aside. I didn't bother putting my things away and just dumped them by the door. My keys made a clanging sound as I tossed them on the console table.

I registered the noise from the TV and something sharp and sweet hit my nostrils as I headed to the bathroom. I needed to cool down.

"Hey, Kara Koala," my dad greeted cheerily.

He and Dylan were sitting at the kitchen island, eating dinner.

"Kar!" Dylan chirped. "My friend got you an interview for a job! It's really good pay and—"

"Code Red," I said.

Code Red meant that they should know better than to talk to me. I realized my jaw hurt. I'd been gritting my teeth all the way home.

The moment I locked the bathroom door behind me, I turned on the shower, hopped in the tub fully clothed. Three minutes later, I let my legs fold under me, pulling them close to my body.

I shut my eyes, letting the anger roll through me now, in the privacy of the bathroom, with the cold shower pounding on my heated skin.

It was his girlfriend, wasn't it? The owner of the black Ferrari.

Why else would he look furious, almost desperate, to get me the hell out of there? As if he didn't want whoever was there to see me.

As if I was some dirty little secret he wanted to hide.

My heart hurt.

Leave! He'd said it so quietly at first, then with more force as if he couldn't stand being around me anymore. *I'm done with you.*

His cold and impersonal tone was as shocking as a slap in the face. I curled my hands into fists, wishing I could punch something. His nose preferably, just to see him bleed.

The way he was making me bleed now.

I was a game.

That was all I was to him, wasn't I?

Was this his revenge because of what I did last night when I splashed the puddle on him with my car? Or maybe it was because of the whole motorcycle incident. Maybe he was really that furious about it.

But was he really that small and heartless to make me believe that he was genuinely interested in me when all this time he was just stringing me along?

He was good. Fuck, he was good. Oscar-fucking-worthy good.

Because…I was starting to believe him. I thought he was different. I had thrown him almost every rude behavior in my book to push him away, but he just kept coming back. And I thought…I thought…

Tears threatened to flow, but I held them off.

I had mistaken his tenacity for sincerity.

He'd told me he liked me. Twice. I remembered each moment.

The first one was when he showed up in my shop and followed me inside my home. *I like you*, he'd said with that dangerous, amused smile. Those lying lips.

I didn't believe him then, thinking he probably said that to all the girls he wanted to bone. I should've kept on not believing him.

But then tonight happened. And he'd melted my resolve.

I hadn't had a proper night's sleep in weeks.

I was so exhausted and feeling so vulnerable and alone. And when he and I walked from the gym to my car and I saw the time, I realized what he'd done for me.

I had fallen asleep while waiting for him in the gym. And he had waited for me.

He must have been tired and hungry after practice, but he didn't wake me up or complain.

And it struck a chord inside me. I felt like he *cared*.

And so I opened up to him.

I like you, he'd said again. And I believed him.

I felt that he was serious. That somehow, I was more than a little special to him. I thought I felt his sincerity. But I realized now that I just *wanted* to believe it.

A huge part of it was my fault. And that made me angrier more than anything else.

Because I should have known better.

I fell for his act. I was weak, and I prided myself on being strong. It was a blow. If I wasn't strong, then what was I?

I'd fallen for his act just because he was kind and sweet to me a handful of times. Was I that desperate for his attention? But why?

There had been other guys out there I could've made a fool of myself with, but I hadn't. So…why him?

I was embarrassed and pathetic. But he was worse.

Because he was cruel.

Maybe his goal was to get me in the sack, and now that he realized I wouldn't give it up, he'd decided to humiliate me or get back at me in a different way—to make me like him and then throw me away. He'd succeeded. And now he didn't want anything to do with me.

Maybe there was no girlfriend. Maybe that was his Ferrari in the driveway. And he really just wanted me to leave because he'd gotten what he wanted.

Maybe he'd made a bet with other guys. Or girls. It wasn't the first time it happened to me. My own girl "friends" had made bets with other guys off me before.

Mean ones. Nasty, vindictive ones. *Get Kara—the poorest, plainest-looking, tallest girl in the class—to go out with you, sleep with her, and post it on social media.* That hadn't quite worked out the way they'd wanted it. I'd escaped before any physical damage was done to me. Emotional scars were different though.

Did he make a bet with his fellow basketball players? With the whole team?

Why did I want to cry?

Worse things have happened to me and I didn't cry then. I sure as fuck wouldn't cry now.

I knew there was a possibility I was blowing this out of proportion, and my history was clouding my judgment.

I turned the shower off and lifted myself out of the tub. My wet clothes dripped all over the floor. I looked up to the ceiling, prayed for patience. A wet floor was a pet peeve. Just one more thing to add to his list.

I took my clothes off and wrung them dry. Using the washing machine would be costly. I had to wash these by hand now or else they'd smell tomorrow. I was adding that to his list too.

And when I searched for a towel and remembered I didn't get my things before I jumped in the shower, the anger came back. It always did.

I shouted for Dylan to get me a towel. I wrapped myself in it and ran to my room.

His sweater was on my bed.

And I just saw red.

I slammed open my dresser, put on panties, shirt, and jeans.

Girl, what about a bra?

Fuck the bra. I didn't need it anyway.

My hair was still wet, but I didn't care. I marched past my dad and Dylan in the living room, put on my parka, grabbed my keys, and leaped in my car.

I was ready for war.

―――――――――――――――

It started to rain again just as I got into my car. Little pellets of hate from the night sky that my windshield wipers couldn't completely clear away. Just like the hot anger I felt for him. Except that mine was building into a storm.

I felt hot, burning. I cranked the window open a little, letting the night air cool me down. The lights from the oncoming traffic blinded me as I put my signal on, turned right onto his street. I was hoping the drive to his house would calm me a little bit. Not a chance.

My body was poised for a fight. The adrenaline rush and the anger made me blind to everything but confronting him. My breathing quickened as I spotted his house, as I pulled up to his driveway. The Ferrari was gone.

I sat there for a moment, trying to convince myself to let it go. He wasn't worth it. Forget about him and move on. He certainly didn't care about me.

I gripped the steering wheel, focusing on the feel of it in my hands. The squeaking sound of the wiper blades as they slid back and forth on the windshield every few seconds. The sound of the rain as it hit the roof of my car. Focusing on anything other than all the things I wanted to hurl at his face to hurt him as much as he had hurt me.

Leave! I'm done with you. His voice was strong and clear in my head.

I gave myself another minute to calm down. Inhale, fucking exhale. Inhale, fucking exhale.

Fuck it.

I slid out of my car and slammed the door closed. The bright beams of my headlights illuminated the door of his garage.

My hands curled into fists as I marched to his front door. The porch light came on as I rang the doorbell once. Twice. Ten times. And when it didn't open fast enough, I started banging on it with my fists.

Open up, asshole.

And then he did.

He filled up the doorway. He stood there, looking tall and mercilessly beautiful. I was tall, but he was taller. He had to lower his head to look at me this closely.

His eyes, deeply blue in the daylight, had gone dark and cold. He reminded me of a silent lion before it attacked. It felt like I was looking at a different person.

I wanted to tear right into him.

I'm done with you. His voice kept banging in my head.

"You fucking asshole," I said. My voice had gone quiet and thick. "How could you?"

I waited for him to say something. Anything. His lack of response cut me more than his words could.

"Aren't you going to say anything to me?"

Nothing. The man who said he liked me was gone. His mouth looked hard. His masculine face had no softness or compunction over what happened just a couple of hours ago.

Filled with hate, I drilled a finger into his chest. "How dare you! What right do you have to play with my feelings? Or anyone's? Do you think it's okay to make me like you and when you get bored you can just throw me away? Fuck you!"

And still there was no emotion on his face. It made me angrier, spurred me on.

"You think you're someone special?" I snarled. "You're not. You're not the first asshole who tried to pull this crap on this girl. There's one of you on every fucking corner of every fucking street. Did you make a bet with your teammates to get me to like you? Have fun with the fucking virgin, get you some dough while you're at it. How much was it, huh? Was it enough to pay for my gas money?"

Something flickered in his eyes, but he hid it so quickly I wasn't sure if it really happened.

"Was that your girlfriend coming to visit you? She caught you, didn't she? You motherfucker. You deserve to be alone." I raised my chin, daring him to respond. "You deserve to be with girls like you who don't give two shits about you. I don't give a fuck about your bike, I don't give a fuck about your shit, and I don't give a fuck about you."

I spun around, dismissing him. I took a step, two, and then stopped. I clenched my hands into fists. I wanted to punch him, make him feel something. Get a damned response out of him. I turned to face him again.

He hadn't moved. His face was the same impenetrable wall that screamed at me how much he didn't care.

"You're just like everybody else," I said softly.

With finality.

If he had something to say, I didn't wait for it. I ran to my car.

My lungs felt full, my heart beating fast. I could feel

the blood pounding in my head. I closed my eyes and hung my head, trying to calm myself.

I said what I came here to say. That was all I wanted. Right?

So why did I feel…empty? Incomplete. Something was missing and unfulfilled.

After a few seconds, I looked up. He was gone.

My throat tightened. I felt my body tense as I stared at his closed door. I was waiting. Waiting.

For what?

Waiting for what?

And then his porch light flicked off.

I got my answer.

The anger I was nursing inside fell away. Just fell away. But what replaced it was worse.

Rejection.

It felt like a heavy cloak had wrapped around me and a weight had settled inside my chest.

"Fuck him," I whispered in the dark. "Fuck him."

I reversed out of the driveway quickly. I should get the hell out of here, but my hands were shaking. My car idled for a moment as I looked down, took a deep breath. Took another.

"Okay." I nodded. "Okay."

I hit the gas. And screamed.

"Oh shit!"

I slammed on my brakes hard, my car screeching to a halt. And there he was, standing in front of my car.

The light from the streetlamp lit his face. He looked big and solid, his shoulders wide, his legs long and thick. It had stopped raining, but it was cold outside, and I noticed he wasn't wearing a jacket.

"What the fuck?" I yelled.

I stared at him, he stared right back. The light revealed the change in his eyes. I couldn't see the blue of them from the distance, but I knew they weren't cold anymore. They were wild, intense, and filled with an emotion my heart refused to recognize.

For a moment, I thought about running him over. Oh, I was tempted to. It would teach him not to toy with anyone's feelings. Or let him know how much he had hurt me.

Then he pulled away, straightened. Slowly, carefully, he walked to my side of the car. There was a ringing in my ears as I watched him stop beside my window. He waited.

He could've opened the door. It was unlocked. But I knew that he knew he'd lost the privilege to do that now. He wasn't allowed anymore.

I looked at him accusingly as he leaned down to face me.

"Kara."

How unfair was it that his face could still get a response out of me after everything he'd done? Or maybe it was his deep, dark voice that sounded so remorseful. Or his searching, blue eyes. I could tell from them that he'd let his walls down, but not completely. The walls were still there, ready to come back up the moment he felt threatened.

"Let me talk to you," he implored.

Unbelievable!

"Please," he added. So softly, so sincerely it made my heart skip a beat.

There was an undeniable pain in his voice that tightened my throat.

When I met him, I knew he was the kind of person

who didn't say *please*. And I was right. What made him say it now?

I didn't trust him. My mind rejected anything to do with him. It was telling me to drive away, forget about him. Do the logical thing.

But my heart was screaming something else.

"I…" He lifted his hand as if he was going to offer it to me to hold, but it fell away instead. "You can drive away now, and I would understand. But…" I saw his throat working. His hand shook as he rubbed his mouth. "Please don't."

I looked at his eyes directly.

"You're an asshole," I said.

"I know."

"Why should I listen to you?"

"You shouldn't."

"All right. I'm fucking out."

"Kara."

I took a deep, shaky breath. I licked my lips. They felt dry.

"Open your window."

I cracked it open a little bit.

"A little more," he said. Was there a hint of a smile on his mouth?

How dare he smile right now?

"Will you come out of the car and talk to me?"

"That depends."

He waited.

Oh, I knew he could be infuriatingly patient. We were complete opposites. I didn't have any patience. But that wasn't what mattered now. Why should I give him a chance? Why should I listen to him now?

There was no explanation. My body was already doing it before I even made up my mind. He moved away as I pushed the door open and got out of the car. I stepped away from him. Far, far away from his reach.

"Talk," I said. As coldly as I could.

"Will you look at me?"

"No," I said, crossing my arms across my chest. "I will not look at you."

But he waited.

I blew out a loud breath and glared up at him. "What?"

"I'm sorry," he whispered. "I'm sorry, Kara."

My traitorous heart jumped in my chest. He was releasing the heaviness wrapped around it, melting it away. I fought it. Fought it hard.

"You think saying sorry is enough?"

He looked down for a moment, then lifted his eyes back up to mine. He looked like a man fighting with himself.

Since I'd met him, he'd always looked confident, sure of himself. But now as he stood in front of me, he looked uncertain for the first time.

He opened his mouth, about to say something, then closed it. He looked up at the sky, blew out a frustrated breath. Rubbed his hand over his face.

I wanted to tell him to spit it out, whatever the hell he wanted to say, but I was afraid he'd close up again if I did. I shouldn't be with this man. I shouldn't give him another chance, but the raw need I saw in his face—the need for me to stay and listen to him—was clear to me. And it struck something in my heart.

Your heart can't be trusted.

"I've never felt the way I feel about you with anyone before. And…" He raked his hands in his dark, silky hair. "And it's fucking killing me. I don't want to screw it up, but I ruin everything around me and I don't want... with you... I don't know where I'm going with this."

There were butterflies in my stomach. And they were fighting with each other.

"There are things that you don't know about me and that I can't tell you right now," he said. "That I need to protect you from."

"I can take care of myself."

"I know that. I know you can. But can you protect yourself from me?"

"What do you mean?"

"I don't want the things around me...around you. Everything always turns to shit around me." I saw his throat working.

What was he hiding from me? He was so closed off. So private. So careful of what he shared about himself. Everything around him was shrouded in mystery. I practically didn't know anything about him.

"There is no bet." His voice was hard, his eyes looked at me directly.

I looked at him, confused. It took me a few moments to catch up to what he was saying.

Oh. He was addressing what I'd said earlier when I was in the middle of my tirade.

"I would never do that to you."

I believed him. I was so screwed.

"I don't air my business to anyone. Not even my friends," he continued. "I told you before, and I'm telling you again: I don't have a girlfriend."

"Who was that, then? The one who owned the Ferrari?"

He loomed over me. I should've been intimidated by his sheer size alone, but oddly enough, I felt safe with him. I knew he wouldn't let anything happen to me. Physical harm, at least. And for now, he wanted my forgiveness. I knew my heart was safe with him. At least for now. But I also knew that could change. I wasn't naive anymore. Or I wanted to think I wasn't.

"No matter what, it's not somebody you have to worry about. I won't let anything hurt you," he said.

Was that what he was doing earlier when he told me to leave? Would the owner of that car really hurt me? Why?

I won't let anything hurt you, he'd said. But he already had. And I realized with shock that the only thing that could hurt me was him. My stomach flipped. Why would he have that power over me? Why had I handed it to him? In so short a time too.

"That's not good enough," I told him. "I need to know more."

"It's going to have to be good enough for now. All I know is that I don't want you mixed up with the bad things in my life. I can't let that happen. You are," he said, his voice deepening. He paused for a moment, his eyes searching mine. "You are important to me."

His words, spoken with certainty, were a balm to my heart. I had no clue what was going on with his life, but it seemed like he wasn't ready to tell me. *I can't tell you right now*, he'd said. So maybe someday he would.

Someday? Was I already thinking about us being together in the future? Shit, why?

"What now?" I asked.

He crossed his muscular arms over his chest. "I don't know." He sounded defensive.

"If you can't explain it right now, then just tell me something about you. I hardly know who you are."

He opened his mouth, about to say something, and stopped when he looked behind me in the distance. His eyes widened. I was going to turn around, see what he was looking at when he said, "You should stay away from me."

Frustrated, I glared at him.

"You shouldn't have come here tonight," he added.

"What?"

He was doing it again. He was pushing me away.

"Are you going to tell me to leave again?" I demanded.

He looked at me without saying anything. But it was clear in his eyes.

Yes. I'm telling you to leave again.

I thought that we'd progressed somehow after our conversation. Progressed in this...relationship, whatever the hell it was, but it was turning out that nothing changed.

"You're a piece of fucking work!" I yelled at him.

"Go home, Kara."

"You know what? I will!"

Because if I didn't, I had a feeling I'd punch him eventually. He was so stubborn. I slid in my car, realized that the engine was still running.

Damn it. My gas.

Adding that to his list. I'm making a fresh list.

I stepped on it. I could see him bathed in the light of my car's taillights. An angel pushed out from heaven, trying to find his way back. So lonely. Solitary. Refusing everyone's love. His eyes showed how needy he was, but that was where it ended. He wouldn't speak it.

I let out a sigh, stepped on my brakes.

I'm done. It's either now or never.

I reversed my car. I saw him startle, his eyes widening as he jumped back. Some memory in my brain told me that looked familiar, as if I'd seen him do that before.

I reversed too far before I hit the brakes, but I was in a hurry. I swung the car door open, jumped out of it, and walked to him. Faster, faster until I was running.

His eyes were on me. So focused on me. As if I were the only one who existed in his world.

I heard his sharp intake of breath as I wrapped my hands around the collar of his shirt, pulled him down to me. And I kissed him.

I kissed him because he was lonely, and I wanted to remove the sadness in his eyes.

I kissed him because I had to. I wanted to.

I kissed him because… Goddammit. *I'm falling in love with him.*

I didn't wait for his reaction. I jumped back in my car, stepped on the gas.

Damn, I thought. *I'm happy.*

———————————

There seemed to be a permanent smile on my face as I drove home, as I walked to where my dad was sitting on the couch, watching TV.

It was late, but I knew he was waiting for me. He was probably worried because I'd stomped out in anger earlier. He looked sleepy and tired, but I knew he wanted to talk to me and check if everything was okay. His eyes, the same color as mine, studied me as I sat beside him.

He muted the TV, just as he normally would when there was something we needed to talk about.

I was smiling like a loon. We looked at each other. Five seconds, ten, fifteen. And then he smiled too.

"All good?" he asked.

"All good, Dad."

He nodded. "Good. Your hair's wet."

"It's raining." I yawned.

"You should get something to eat. Want me to heat up some food for you?"

"I'm tired. Going to bed." I got up.

"Sometime, I'm going to sit you down and I'm going to have to CIA-interrogate you about what's going on."

I laughed nervously. "I know. I'll tell you. I promise, but not yet."

He nodded. "All right. Make sure you do. Love you, sweetheart."

The moment I closed my bedroom door behind me, I squeaked out a joyful "Eeeee!" and jumped in my bed.

I grabbed my pillow, hugging it tight in my arms. Was this how it felt to be in love?

As if nothing could go wrong, as if nothing could piss me off. Everything was just so damn *good*.

But wasn't this just too fast? Even though it felt like we'd known each other for a long time, the truth was it'd only been a few days. It couldn't be real yet, could it?

Was love at first sight real?

I thought back to the very first day I saw him outside the lecture hall when, somehow, I had known—no, I'd *felt* that he was going to be a part of my life.

I turned on my side, closed my eyes, hugged my pillow with both hands and feet. So, do we date now?

I bit my lip, so I couldn't squeal like a super-excited seal.

Cameron Jeremiah Saint Laurent.

Wow. How *hawt* was his name? Scorching.

I wanted to get to know him better. I wanted him to open up to me, without hesitation. I was going to peel him like a sexy banana, until I knew everything about him. It was just so weird feeling this way.

But if he wasn't ready, that was fine. I knew how hard it was to get him to talk about himself. I could be patient.

I knew though that he wanted to get to know me better. Like *his* version of *better*. That was fine. I guessed I wanted that too. But not right away. Maybe in a few years.

Making out was fine. Maybe even…second base?

He's a guy though. Guys nowadays aren't interested in a relationship without sex. Hello? What century are you living in?

I sat up quickly, my hair flipping against my face. I flicked it off.

Besides, you do remember that make-out sesh you had with him, right? He had no qualms letting you know what he wanted.

Well, I'd just have to have a talk with him. Communication is the key with these things. He knew I was a virgin. He knew where I stood when it comes to sex. If he didn't, I'd let him know.

I didn't play games when it came to relationships. If I did, I'd have gone out with a number of guys already. My dad had never even dated after my mom left him. I wouldn't make the same mistake he did. I'd seen how hurt he was after she left. I didn't want that for myself, and I didn't want my dad to watch me experience that. It would just be another heartbreak for him. I had been very careful.

I didn't date just for the moment. Or *just* to have fun. If I decided to be with a guy, it was because I was serious. I had forever in my mind.

What was the point in continuing to date him if I knew he wasn't going to be the one?

Maybe he was the one, maybe he wasn't. But I was going in with the knowledge—or hope—that maybe... maybe he was.

Take it slow for now. Get to know each other. Don't be rash and say he's the one. For goodness' sake, you just met the guy!

He's the one, though. I can feel it.

Maybe I was scared a little. Okay, a lot. But if I had a pyramid of emotions, feeling scared wouldn't be dominant. Happiness and excitement were.

I grabbed my phone, hoping I'd see a text from him. I felt a little disappointed when I didn't.

But that was fine. He wasn't the type to text. Should I text him though? Maybe he needed a prompt. I should start, and maybe he'd do the same.

I opened my inbox, laughing quietly when I saw his contact name.

SOS meant *Spawn of Satan*. I should change it.

I went to my contacts and changed it to *Cameron*. Then changed it to *Cameron Jeremiah*. Then changed it to *Saint Laurent*. Then changed it to *Bigfoot*. Then *My Crush*. In the end, I settled for *Cameron*. And typed a text message to him.

> See you tomorrow, Skyscraper. Same time. Good
>   night.

Damn, I forgot to add an emoji.

I sent a smiley emoji after that.

I hugged my phone to my chest, waiting for his reply until I fell asleep.

————————————————

The next day felt like a present. The day was a little brighter, happier. Well, it was raining a little bit, but what did it matter? I was going to see him soon. My heart was happy.

I didn't even need coffee.

All right, I did, but that was beside the point. I meant figuratively. After coffee, I hopped in the shower, did my morning routine. Put makeup on carefully. I was smiling all the while. *I should add a second coat of mascara*, I thought, since I wanted to wear my glasses today.

My hair was still damp. Just like last night when I kissed him in the rain.

Something squealed. And it came from my throat. Was that me?

That kiss was so romantic. I wanted another one.

It took a little while longer to pick out clothes. *Maybe I should wear a blue top,* I thought as I walked to my dresser. *Just because it reminds me of his eyes.*

"Ugh."

I looked down and saw that I'd stepped on my phone. I grabbed it right away, hoping it hadn't cracked. It hadn't.

Did he reply last night? I had fallen asleep and hadn't checked yet. I pushed the Home button.

I gasped. There was a message from him. I opened my inbox.

I held my breath as I opened the text.

Cameron: I don't need a ride.

Chapter 21

Kara

I BLINKED AT THE TEXT: I DON'T NEED A RIDE.

My heart fell into my stomach.

What the hell is happening?

He had sent it last night. Probably right after I fell asleep.

Did he mean he didn't need a ride *today*?

I shut the voice in my head up before I started jumping to conclusions and blowing this out of proportion like I had last night. I should just ask him what he meant.

Not that he'd give me any clear answers. His answers just raised more questions on top of questions.

I sat on my bed and read his text message over and over, waiting for another one from him. As if he'd just sent it and was about to send another one. I needed him to clarify. Was it his hobby to be as unclear as possible?

Of course, there wasn't another text coming. I typed furiously.

Kara: Okay. You need a ride tonight?

I stared at the screen, waiting. Willing him to reply. There was no sign that he'd read it. Nothing. I wasn't sure which one was worse: if he'd read my message and ignored it or if he hadn't read it yet.

There was a nagging and unsettling feeling in my chest that something was wrong. My intuition was telling me that there was more to his text. And the last time I ignored that intuition, I got socked in the face by a patient.

Still. Maybe my senses had dulled because I was seeing everything with my emotions. Could I still trust my intuition? How did I know it was my intuition and not just my feelings for him clouding my judgment?

I bit my lip, debating whether I should give him a call or not. I didn't want to annoy him by being a pest.

Whoa, whoa, *whoa-t?*

Why was I hesitating to call him? It was just a phone call. It's no big deal. It wasn't like I was in a game show where I could only phone a friend once. I could phone him as many times as I wanted. Not that I would. This woman had enough pride for that. Still, he made me feel so unsure. The prick. Or was that my own insecurities getting the better of me?

Get your head out of your ass, girl. Be in love if that's what you want, but don't lose your head. Be practical.

What the hell was happening to me? The heart eyes didn't fall off my face. I flicked them off.

I phoned him. I ignored my heart when it started to beat fast. But it went straight to voicemail.

A feeling of gloominess was starting to descend onto my head. I kept convincing myself that this didn't mean anything. Nothing had changed. I'd see him on campus later. He'd probably text me later to tell me to pick him up tonight after his practice.

Later that day, I found myself looking for him in the lecture hall. I saw his teammates, but I didn't see him anywhere. What if something had happened to him? Last night, he'd told me that there were things he wanted to protect me from.

Was it the mafia? Was he an undercover agent? An assassin? A superhero with a dark past? A fallen angel? Or maybe it was as simple as his own complicated issues?

What the hell?

Calm your tits, girl.

When I exited my last class, I walked to the water fountain even though I didn't need a refill. He probably had something planned with his team or an appointment. Or a million other things. He had a freelancing business he was running after all. He could be having a meeting with Iron Man and Captain America. Who the hell knows?

But the thing was...why didn't he answer my text or call me back? And why was I obsessing about this?

I was loitering, I realized, annoyed with myself. I had a mental picture of me looking like Humpty Dumpty in *Puss in Boots*, creeping in the background, shady as hell, spying on Puss.

Thirsty much?

But it wasn't even thirstiness that was propelling me to the campus gym to see if he was there. It was out of concern now.

The gym was empty.

Frustrated, itchy, I lingered there, debating with myself. A picture of him lying bleeding on the floor of his house pushed me to leave campus. And following my intuition, I drove to his place.

His place looked and already felt empty as I pulled into his driveway. Still, I got out of my car, walked to his front door, and pressed the bell.

I wanted to show him I could be mature, especially after last night, so I waited for another thirty seconds before pressing the doorbell again.

He's gone.

I worried my lower lip with my teeth. Sure, we talked last night. And he confessed some intense feelings he had for me. And I kissed him.

But there were no promises.

Calm the hell down. Holy crap, girl. You're not even a couple yet and one time he doesn't reply to your text and you're freaking out? If I were him, I'd hide from you too. Man, you're wacko.

Right, right. I was overreacting. He was just probably in the bathroom, pooping.

Suddenly, I felt a prickle at the back of my neck. I felt edgy, as if someone was watching me. I turned around.

And saw the black Ferrari parked two houses away.

It was idling. It was already dark outside. Coupled with the dark-tinted windows, I couldn't see who it was behind the wheel.

Watching me.

My body felt cold, numb, an instinctive response when there was danger in the vicinity. I felt…scared. And when I felt scared, I got angry. And when I got angry, I fought.

I forced myself to walk down the driveway, ready to confront whoever the hell was hiding behind that tinted windshield. And then the car moved. Slowly, quietly, as if it were telling me that it wasn't intimidated or worried about me approaching it.

It stopped for a second or two in front of me, as if sending me a message.

I've seen your face, and I know who you are now. Be very careful.

And then it accelerated. I watched as it disappeared around the corner.

The hair on my arms stood up. Who the hell was that?

I jumped as I heard a banging noise across the street, my heart in my throat. I let out a relieved breath when I saw Dingle Dick throw me a glare as he dumped his trash in the recycling.

Wrong bin, genius.

"Hey!" I called out, striding across to his driveway.

He eyed me suspiciously. He looked like a giant, grumpy cockroach.

"What's up, psycho?" He leered at me. "What are you doing at my neighbor's house?"

"You know him?"

"Of course I know him. Why? You here to suck his soul out? He said he already paid his bill. *I* already paid my bill, so stay off my property, will you?"

What bill?

"He said he paid his bill?"

"Well, yeah. That morning right after you left, he came here to tell me what you did to get your money back, so I better pay my bill if I don't want the same thing happening to me. Wack job," he muttered under his breath.

I wanted to kick his micro baby maker, but I needed

information from him. I tried a sweet smile. "How did he even know you owed me money?"

"He was right there behind you all the time. What's wrong with you?"

He was?

"What did he say exactly?" I asked.

"As if you don't know."

"I hit my head a lot when I was a kid, so you know, sometimes I have this tendency to forget. Why don't you remind me?"

He scoffed. "He said he knows this guy who owes you money and you phoned everyone in his life, even his dentist and the girl who does his pedicure."

I narrowed my eyes. "Is that right?"

"Don't act like you don't know. He came to warn me because he cares about me. He's a good neighbor. Not that you know anything about being one."

Idiot. He came to tell you because he was helping me. But that meant…he knew about me even before I met him that day. This was all so confusing.

He backed away a few steps. "Don't tell me you came here to harass me next. I already paid my bill." Then he eyed me up and down. And sneered. "You could use a little more here"—he cupped his chest—"but you're pretty when you got makeup on. Make sure you put it on every day, eh? Just a little advice from a friendly neighbor."

The pig. I wanted to dropkick him in the forehead, but I needed more information. I batted my lashes. "Thanks. I could sure use the advice."

He looked pleasantly surprised. "Yeah?"

"Sure. Listen, I was supposed to meet him"—I

pointed at Cameron's house—"at his house five minutes ago. He wanted my shop to fix his vehicle, but he's not answering the door. Have you seen him this morning?"

He scratched his head. "Yeah. Late last night, actually. He was throwing a big duffel bag into the back of his vehicle. Some tools. I asked him where he was going, but you know the guy. Tight-lipped son of a bitch. Didn't say nothing to me. Just drove off."

"Have you seen a black Ferrari in his driveway or just around the area?"

"No, can't say that I did. Hey, you busy tomorrow night or any night this week? Wanna…?" He lifted his eyebrows suggestively.

Now I sneered at him. "What exactly do you mean by that?"

"Oh, come on. You know. Booty call. What do you say?"

I wanted to puke at his face. "You have a wife, don't you?"

"Well, yeah, but she's pregnant and…" He trailed off. He probably saw the absolute disgust on my face. His brows knitted together. He looked like a mean rotten potato.

"You're not even that pretty," he spouted. "Are you telling me you have the right to be choosy? Seriously? You know," he continued, sounding irritated now, "those garden gnomes you drove over and destroyed? My mom left me those."

I curled my upper lip at him and started to walk back to my car. "I'd be more worried about that face your mama left you with!" I called out.

I slid into my car, reversed out of Cameron's

driveway, and left Dingle Dick watching me with his jaw on the ground.

——————————————

I drove home with dark thoughts about that black Ferrari. About where Cameron might have gone. About why he would leave just like that without saying anything. What about the deal he'd manipulated out of me? He had been so tenacious trying to get that deal, and suddenly he just disappeared? Either he had a house to flip, or he was running away.

Tools, Dingle Dick said. He was throwing a duffel bag and tools in his vehicle. *Vehicle?* What vehicle? Didn't he tell me he only had his motorcycle? If he had another vehicle, why did he want me to drive him around in the first place?

I checked my phone again when I got home and before I went to bed. Still no text from him.

Damn, chica. He might just be gone today. He has a life and a business, you know. Tomorrow he might be back or he might even text you tonight.

But he didn't.

Pride kept me going the whole week. He was gone. Just gone. He kept his phone off, so I couldn't even talk to him. I left him two voicemails. After that, I was done. I wasn't going to chase after him. The silent, arrogant prick.

It hurt as much as it confused me.

Where the hell is he? Is he okay?

Who's driving the black Ferrari?

Why did he leave? Is he coming back?

He should have been going to classes, at least. As far as I knew, the campus policy was that after three consecutive absences, the professor can boot the student out of the class. Assuming the professor even checked attendance. If Cameron had two classes and they were only once a week, that meant he could still be gone for another couple of weeks before he was forced to come back.

Assuming he hadn't quit college yet. What about his freelancing business? He flipped houses. He also said he worked for a friend when he didn't have a project. Why the hell hadn't I asked the name of it? He couldn't just leave his responsibilities, so he had to come back some time.

I drove by his house again last night. Scared that I'd see a for sale sign in his front yard. I was putting a stop to it tonight. It was getting ridiculous already. And I felt like a creepy stalker.

I had worked at a casino for a short time before, as housekeeping. I once saw a lady playing those slot machines. She kept on inserting coin after coin, her eyes glued to the screen, hoping she'd hit the jackpot. But she never did. Her winnings never came. I felt like that lady. Hoping I'd win eventually if I just inserted more coins, but what it was doing was actually making me broke and leaving me with an empty wallet. I could keep investing my emotions in him, but I was only getting a negative in return. If he was going to leave, then why did he have to confess all that to me that night? He could've just left it at that. It was crueler to say all those things to me, make me hope and wish for what could've been between us. I hadn't even known the guy that long. Why was I acting like I'd lost my husband of sixty fucking-till-death-do-us-part years?

This was the part I hated about myself. Once I let

people in, I got attached and it was hard for me to let them go. But I tried. I had a lot of practice letting go of people who had been a part of my life before.

It was a chilly Thursday, and I was at the campus cafeteria with Tala, staring at the food menu board on the wall when I realized I'd completely missed out on my veggie lasagna.

The cafeteria didn't have a fixed schedule for it, just as long as they served it once a week. So you had to check the menu every day.

And they had served it two days ago.

"Motherfucker! This is all his fault. I missed my veggie lasagna," I muttered under my breath.

The girl behind the glass food display case smiled sympathetically. I noted how beautiful she was with her dark cat eyes and dark hair up in that white chef hat and wearing the white apron the culinary arts students wore. I smiled back at her and moved on.

"My psychic powers tell me something is the matter with you." Tala frowned at me as I placed my tray on the table—I'd bought fries, a miserable half cucumber sandwich, and a cup of coffee—and took the seat across from her.

I shook my head and reached for my sandwich. It tasted exceptionally good today, but I couldn't fully appreciate it or anything else in the state I was in. I checked my phone and found a text from Dylan.

Dylan: Rmembr when I told U that one of my many friends got U an interview! It's really good money. Will tell more when I see you @ home if interested! I know U R!

He'd mentioned it before, but I hadn't been in the mood to listen to him then. Because it was Dylan, I was skeptical, but I sent him a quick reply just in case. I looked up and noticed Tala watching me with sad eyes.

"I feel like I'm not your best friend anymore," she said quietly.

"What?" Shocked that she'd say this, I gaped at her.

"I know how strong you are, Kar. But you never share."

I placed my sandwich back on the plate. "That's not fair, Tal. I do share things with you."

"Yeah, but it takes you forever to tell me what's bothering you, and even then, the crisis has already passed, and there's no way I could help you. You don't want *me* to help you. Why are we even friends when you can't lean on me?"

I let out an exhausted breath.

"I can see you're tired of this. *Nagbago ka na*," she said in Filipino, which if I remembered correctly meant that I've changed. "I have to go to class."

"Tala…"

But she was already striding out of the cafeteria.

Feeling helpless and frustrated, I massaged the back of my neck. It hurt that she'd think that way about me, but it hurt more that she felt sad and upset because of me.

Why did every unfortunate thing start happening at the same time? If it wasn't one thing, it was another. I couldn't let Tala feel like this all day. I had to clear things up with her. But when I sent her a text asking if we could have coffee after our last class in the afternoon, she didn't reply right away like she used to.

I headed to the lecture hall for my next class, feeling

like a sad and depressed zombie. Tala was right, and I hadn't even realized it.

Shit. It felt like my life was falling apart. And I wanted to blame him for all of it. I knew that couldn't be true. But I blamed him anyway.

The sound of male laughter caught my attention as I passed the lockers near the lecture hall. My heart skipped a beat as I scanned the tall, athletic bodies of the basketball team, hoping I'd see him. But just like last week, he wasn't there. My chest felt tight.

His friend, the campus Romeo, Caleb Lockhart, was there though. I marched up to him.

"Hey," I said. "Can I talk to you?"

All male eyes turned to me. Including Lockhart's. The gorgeous boy. Shiny, thick brown hair, green eyes. Tall, hot bod. Just standing there, I could tell he was charismatic.

But his face didn't make my heart race. His eyes didn't excite or challenge me. Not the way Cameron's face and eyes did.

"Sure," he said.

We moved away a little, but his teammates were watching us. He waved them away and told them to go ahead without him.

"Wow. Mind control?" I said, gesturing toward his team when they followed his orders like the Unsullied followed Daenerys.

"I can turn invisible too. It's just not working right now." He smiled.

Yes, he was definitely gorgeous. Charming smiles that could easily lure a girl's heart. But it didn't affect mine.

Mine was already given to someone who didn't want it.

"I see your cart, but where's your donkey?" I asked.

He blinked, confused. I wondered if he was wearing fake lashes. They were so long. "Donkey?"

"Yeah, you know. The one with the black, curly hair and as tall as a yeti and as muscular as a bull. The idiot one."

His eyes twinkled. "Cam?"

"Caleb! Break's over. Let's go!" one of his teammates called out as he passed by us.

Caleb waved him away.

"I just want to know…is he okay?" I asked.

His green eyes warmed. "He's okay. Don't worry, Kara."

I lifted my eyebrows. I was surprised he knew my name. Did Cameron tell him about me?

"He told me about you."

He did?

I gave him a smile. He was nice. "Thanks," I told him. "You're not so bad."

"You're not so bad either."

We both cared for the same person. That was enough for me to like him. I turned to leave.

"Kara!" he called out.

"Yeah?"

He angled his head, studying my face. After a moment, he asked, "Can I tell you something?"

"Go ahead."

"He gets into these moods now and then. He leaves town for a couple weeks or so to reset. This time, he asked our boss if he could be sent up north for a project. Don't worry, he'll be back."

"Hi, Cal!"

"Hey, B!"

I said goodbye as the petite blond possessively wrapped her arms around his waist and walked to my class.

Now that I knew he was okay and was not getting tortured or bleeding on his floor and was just in a *mood*, I felt stupid. And angry. What the hell was his problem? I was worried and obsessing over him for nothing. He couldn't even send me a courtesy text? I didn't even need him to tell me where he was. *Sayonara. It's been nice, but I don't want you to give me rides anymore* would've been enough instead of leaving me up in the air. I curled my hands into fists.

The professor was droning on and on about marketing when I felt my phone vibrate in my pocket. My breathing picked up. When I looked at the message, it was Tala.

T: How about dinner? At my place.
K: Sure. If you behave, you might just get lucky.
T: Put out or get out, girlfriend.

And that, I realized as I smiled like a loon, was all I needed from her to feel better.

———————————

"It's either *The Notebook* or anything Keanu Reeves. *John Wick*, maybe? Or how about *Despicable Me*? Hurry up! Pick one already," Tala said, comfortable in her unicorn pajamas.

I was wearing monkey pajamas, which reminded me of Bigfoot. I refused to let it ruin my mood. I'd get over him pretty soon. He was old news to me now.

We were lying on her bed, gorging on pizza we'd ordered and some healthy fruit smoothies she made. To "balance the pizza out," she'd said. I wanted a milkshake, but since I wanted to be a supportive, awesome best friend tonight, I let her have her way. I convinced her to switch to beers eventually, and I happily sucked on one, enjoying the lull it gave my body. I gave myself another couple of hours before I needed to bless their bathroom. Being lactose intolerant was a real struggle.

It was getting late, but we both had afternoon classes tomorrow, so we had agreed it was time for a girls' night. I just had to make sure I woke up early tomorrow to do an assignment and review for a quiz.

Mrs. B was sleeping over at her sister's place, which was unusual because she didn't like to leave her house. I asked Tala about it.

"I'm so glad she's spending more time with her siblings. Her mood's definitely improved. She doesn't nag me as much," she said, sounding happy. "Can we binge-watch *Game of Thrones*?"

Picking out a movie or show usually took us a half hour before we settled on one we both liked. I reached for another slice of pizza. I felt like a bloated whale, but I couldn't stop eating.

"You made me do a GOT marathon just a couple of weeks ago," I reminded her.

She rolled her eyes at me and started singing a Taylor Swift song, then she played it on her phone, hooking it up to her speakers. I jumped from her bed to the floor, started singing the song at the top of my lungs. Tala joined me. We butchered it, but I thought we made up for it by doing some cool-ass moves that got us breathing fast. The music changed, and we just kept at it.

"Tala and Kara here to break it down for ya, yo. Ya ready?" she laughed.

"OMG this is so damn cringey. I love it. I love you, girlfriend. Okay, but watch this, Tal. Guess what this epic move is!" I wheezed, swishing my hips left and right with my arms doing the helicopter.

"It's an octopus mating dance, baby. Make sure you do it when your crush walks by. Guess this one!"

We were laughing our asses off, and we were both happy and young, and we didn't care about responsibilities, and nothing could have pierced our bubble. And then she started laughing and yelping in pain as she fell on the floor and cradled her crotch.

"Cramp, cramp. I think I ripped something. My vagina. Shit. Shit. Hold on, I gotta lie down," she laughed-snorted-sobbed.

"Don't break the vag before you use it, baby," I said, laughing with her.

That brought on more giggles. When our laughter died down, we just stretched out spread-eagle on the floor together in comfortable, happy silence.

"I like someone," I blurted.

So much for old news, huh?

I sighed and turned my head so I could see her reaction. "I think it's more than like, actually."

She blinked slowly. "What? Like in love?"

I nodded slowly.

"First, does he know you exist?"

She asked it in a girlfriend way. The way where you just knew each other so well and there was nothing mean or petty, whatever question you threw at each other. It was all about honesty.

"I met a boy—no, a man." It seemed ridiculous to call Cameron a boy. "And we kissed. Twice. No, three times."

She sat up quickly, gawking at me. "Bitch, what? Tell me I was in a coma and that's why I never heard of this before. What's going on?"

"Calm your tits. I just met him."

She didn't say anything for a moment. I knew she was thinking about it. And then, "Was that why you started pulling away from me?" she asked quietly. "I knew something was up. You usually don't text or ask to hang out with me when you're going through something."

"Do I really do that?"

She nodded.

"I'm sorry, Tal."

"S'okay. I know you're super strong. And I know I'm...not as strong as you are. But I want you to know that you can still talk to me, and I'll try my best to listen and be there for you. Aw, Kar, what's wrong?"

I wasn't crying, but my throat felt tight. I sat up, rubbing my neck with my hands. "A week and four days. That's how long he's been gone."

"What? Girl, you scared him off already?"

I chucked a piece of mushroom at her as a self-deprecating laugh trickled out. "Maybe I did. I think I did, just as I do with everyone around me." The last part I said under my breath, not meaning to say it, but she heard.

"Aw, girl, that's not true." Now she looked mad. "You take care of the people you keep close to you. You make them smile and cheer them up just by being near you. It's your aura. It's so strong people can't help but want to be around you."

She shifted so she was facing me. "It's like everyone is worried about what other people say about them," she continued. "But not you. You just do you, because you know what's important. You say what you think or feel regardless of what other people will say, and you go for the things you want. Without apologies. Without giving a damn about other people's expectations...unlike me. And you know what? People feel that, and they're drawn to it because it's fearless. And it's so freaking cool. Do you want me to continue kissing your ass with the truth?"

She laughed when I threw myself at her and hugged her.

"Now talk to me and tell me everything."

And so I did. She was just quiet, listening without interruption. Her face showed her reactions though, and I laughed at some of them. Some parts I left out, needing to keep them to myself. I'd always been that way, even when I was a kid, leaving details out, not revealing enough, but I thought I had gotten better.

"So," she said after I finished. "Python?"

I shook my head.

"Oh." She frowned. "Garter snake?"

"Far from it."

"Wild boar? Starfish? Crocodile? Tell me! I'm running out of animals!"

I bit my lip.

"Tell me," she said breathily.

"Anaconda."

We both looked at each other for a moment, eyes

shining with suppressed laughter. And then we started giggling like little girls.

"Ayayay!" She wiped her eyes. "For real though?"

I nodded, a creepy smile on my face.

Her mouth formed into an O. "Whew!" She blew out a loud breath, fanning her face. "Did you touch it?" she asked in a whisper.

I burst out laughing. She was so cute. "No."

"And you guys didn't have sex, right? I mean you don't have to touch it to have sex." Her nose twitched. "I'm sure of it. I mean I'm in college and I'm still a virgin, but I'm pretty knowledgeable about these things. We've researched enough of it, you and I. So"—she took a breath—"you guys didn't…?"

I shook my head, feeling my face grow hot. "It's funny, you know, when we talk about sex and blowing a guy's brains out because, you know, we're so hot, but when faced with it in real life, it's…it's pretty scary."

"I wouldn't know. Tell me, tell me, tell me." She bounced. "Wait. You mean his massive penis scared you, right? That's what you mean?"

"No, Tal! You shithead." I barked out a short laugh. "Well…I guess, yeah. I mean, *come* on. No pun intended."

I waggled my brows and she laughed.

"But that's not what I'm trying to say. It's like…" I paused, gathering my thoughts. "Sharing your body with someone…it doesn't feel like it's just your body you're giving to him. It's your heart and mind and soul. Your vulnerabilities, your *trust*, the entirety of who you are—you're giving him all of that. You're entrusting all that to him and believing and hoping that he will cherish it and not use it to destroy you. And knowing that, once you have, you can never get back that part of you ever again. And it's terrifying."

"That was so deep. I love it. And yes, I know what you mean," she said. "Are you really falling for Mr. Complicated and Mysterious?"

I rose, grabbed another beer. My throat felt dry. I finished half the bottle, wiped my mouth on my sleeve, and said, "I think I don't want to be in love with him."

"But why?"

I glared at her. She was already on Team Cameron. I could see it in her eyes. "Maybe I was just caught up in the moment. The rain, his confession, the kiss, the man—it was perfect. Maybe I'm just infatuated."

"He scares you, doesn't he? Because he's already gotten under your skin and you can't get him out even if you wanted to. He's like a tick. The more you try to pull out those fuckers, the more they burrow."

I laughed without humor, drank more beer. "He wanted me to trust him, not ask him any questions and just trust him, then he left. Without a word. How the hell does that translate to *you are important to me*? I'm not asking him to spill his life story to me, although I want that, yes. But I just need him to…trust me too. It's a two-way street. He's asking me to trust him when he can't do the same thing for me."

I sighed with exasperation, walked to her bed, and sat. The blanket covering her bed was blue. Very, very close to the shade of blue of his eyes. I wanted to burn it. I wanted to hug it.

"It's my fault for getting hurt this way. I thought… after he said all those things to me about wanting to protect me, that I'm important to him, that he wouldn't let anything bad happen to me and that he's never felt this way before about anyone and he's scared he'll screw it up. What was I supposed to think? What's all that mean? But it's my fault because I believed him, and I expected so much, built it all up in my head."

She shook her head. "Don't be stupid, Kar. I have three kids and a big-ass mansion and I'm pregnant with our fourth kid with my crush. And he doesn't even know I exist. And Mr. Complicated just pretty much confessed his feelings to you. If I were you, I'd have already picked out the venue for our wedding and where we're going for our honeymoon. But that's just me." She winked. "You can't blame yourself for thinking all these things after what he told you."

I let out a laugh. "I love you."

"I love you too, girlfriend. I think you do tend to have really strong reactions, but it's who you are. And if you've dished out your worst at him already and if he comes back, you know he's the one."

"Where are you getting all this good advice from anyway? Did you have a secret marriage I didn't know about?"

"All those Asian drama shows I've been watching trained me to be a master. I don't have a love life, so I live vicariously through them." She waggled her eyebrows. "You know what I think?" she continued, sitting beside me on the bed. "He has some complicated issues he needs to take care of before he can be with you. Who knows? I think you've met your match, Kar. Of course it won't be easy. Did you expect it to be? You'd take it for granted if it were. You've been working so hard all your life that I don't think you'll welcome anything easy."

I frowned, digesting her words. "I think…he's going to break my heart if I give him more."

"Then let him fix it again. Isn't that part of falling in love?"

If it was, I wanted no part of it. I knew this because the week passed without a word from him.

If and when I saw him again, he'd better start praying.

Chapter 22

Kara

IT HAD BEEN TWO WEEKS SINCE I'D SEEN HIM LAST. TWO long weeks of exhaustion. I had thrown myself into work, accepting shifts left and right, asking my coworkers if they needed me to cover their shifts at the nursing home. I did my assignments and even aced a couple of my exams. Yay, me!

He was practically nonexistent to me. He was like my sneakers. I knew I was wearing them all day, but I never noticed them. They were just a part of my body. And I didn't even really think about them until I took them off at night.

At school, Caleb and I had this signal now. I'd pass by the lecture hall and see him there. He'd shake his head at me, meaning Bigfoot wasn't back yet. I didn't even ask him, but for some reason he thought I was still interested to know. I wasn't.

I still had his blue sweater. If I didn't wash it for the first couple of days—okay, more than a couple—because I wanted to keep the scent clinging to it, I figured that was nobody's business but mine. Eventually, I just buried it under my bed and hoped dust mites would make it their personal paradise. That was where he deserved to be.

I'd donate it if I could—or burn it—but he could come back to me later and add it to my bill.

The ordered part for his motorcycle was supposed to arrive early last week, but Dylan had ordered the wrong part. And now we had to wait for the part again. I had sent SOS a text as a professional courtesy. But I didn't even care anymore.

I was over feeling insecure. Wondering what I'd done wrong, obsessing if there was something wrong with me that pushed him away when it was his issues that were to blame.

There was nothing wrong with me. I was more than enough. I was a strong, independent woman who was not afraid to struggle to reach her dreams. And if he could not appreciate that, well, *hasta la vista, baby*. There were other fish in the sea that could handle a woman like me. I was done with him. Capital *D-O-N-E*.

That conviction was put to the test after I finished my shift at the coffee shop. It was late afternoon, and it was the weekend. The sun was still up, the weather uncharacteristically nice. I was used to rainy weekends now, as if Mother Nature were playing a sick joke. Teasing us with good weather during the week, only to give us rainy weekends. She could be a real bitch. But today, she was my glittering fairy godmother.

So I decided to be a wild child and go shopping. Okay, window shopping. I crossed the street to the strip mall, and thought if Tala was available right now, I'd pick her up so we could crash a party. The students in our program hosted a party every weekend. It was easy to find on social media.

I used to go to those things before, back when the

shop was doing well and I didn't have to work so much. My childhood friend Damon had a band and would drag me to the venues where he played. I even worked at a bar before where Damon had gigs every Friday night. The tips were great, but the nightlife wasn't for me at the time. Although it would be nice to go to the bar and forget about my problems, at least for a night.

I thought I had forgotten that part of myself, but...

I stopped in my tracks. Wow, I hadn't felt this in a long, long time. I actually really wanted to shed my grandma skin and just have fun.

What do you think made you find this part of yourself again? The one who likes to have fun and forget her responsibilities for a while? Or should I ask...who?

No one. I just realized that it was nice to be wanted— and to actually want someone, but not just anyone. It was important to choose the right person, because being with the wrong one could easily ruin you.

What would it be like to date someone who was actually kind, sweet, understanding, who wouldn't disappoint me and run away, who wasn't complicated, who was open and genuinely wanted to get to know me?

"Do you normally stand in the middle of the parking lot and daydream?"

I blinked and stared at broad shoulders wrapped in a baby-blue dress shirt. My eyes traveled up and up and took in the brown neck, the square jaw that was freshly shaven, the handsome face with soulful brown eyes, and the soft, curly black hair.

"Because it's cute," he finished. He smiled and a dimple on his right cheek popped out.

I smiled back at him and wondered why he was

flirting with me when I very probably looked like Oscar the Grouch after my shift at the coffee shop. I should've reapplied my lipstick before I left, mopped up some of the grease on my forehead and nose, but I hadn't planned on going anywhere but home after work.

"Kara? Kara!"

My eyes reluctantly moved from his face to the source of the voice behind him. It was Tita Didi from church. The adorable but shameless matchmaker who kept on pushing me to date her coworkers and nephews.

"Tita," he said. I glanced back at the man when he said that. Oh no. Was he one of her nephews?

"I told you I'd get the car. You didn't have to walk all the way here," he said, looking at the older woman with exasperation and fondness.

She waved her hand. "I need the exercise." Then she turned to me, grinning like the cat that ate the canary. "You met my nephew Thomas? This is destiny. This is perfect, perfect! I've been wanting to introduce the two of you. Do you have work tonight, Kara, sweetheart?"

"No, but—"

"That's good. Let's go have dinner together, kids. Come on, come on."

She wrapped her short arm around my waist and propelled me to one of the sushi restaurants at the strip mall. I threw Thomas a helpless look and he just grinned, looking pleased with the situation.

"Kara, this is my nephew Thomas. He's a nurse and he's going to study medicine next year. And he's so handsome and he's single, Kara."

Okay, Tita Didi. Calm your tits. Please don't make this awkward.

I wondered if she thought I was man hungry or she just really wanted to pair me up with someone out of the goodness of her heart.

"I told you about Kara, right, Thomas? She's just so amazing. You two have a lot in common so why don't you get to know each other better?" She rose, hanging her designer bag on her arm. "Just the two of you today, okay? I forgot that I'm supposed to meet my friend at the hair salon in five minutes. It's just next door so don't worry about my ride, sweetheart," she told him. "My friend will drive me home. Enjoy your dinner and just have fun, okay? Bye, kids." She gave us air kisses and left.

When she was gone, I gave Thomas a knowing look. "You know she's full of it, don't you?"

He looked at me for a moment, his lips tucked together, his brown eyes shining with laughter. And then he let it out. He had a deep laugh that rumbled in his chest.

"I'm sorry. She does this all the time." He looked embarrassed. It was adorable.

"I know. This isn't the first time she's ambushed me like this."

His eyes shone with laughter. "No one is safe from Tita Didi."

"Last time, she set me up with a guy who didn't blink."

He looked at me for a moment, not saying anything, not blinking. Ah, damn it. This was another weirdo she'd set me up with. And then his eyes twinkled and he blinked several times. I couldn't help but laugh.

"Hi, guys." The server placed the menu on the table, along with order cards and a pen so we could choose what kind of sushi we wanted. "Can I get you something to drink first?" he asked.

Thomas looked at me. "Ladies first," he said.

"I'd like a coconut bubble tea, please. Double the bubbles."

I would have ordered a milkshake if they'd had it on the menu.

"Great choice. And yours?"

"I'll have green tea, please," Thomas said.

Green tea. I realized I'd never hung out with a guy who ordered green tea. Was he a health freak? He was on the slim side, but his shoulders were broad, his arms filling out the dress shirt he was wearing.

"Perfect. I'll be right back with your drinks."

"Thank you," we both said.

I wasn't sure what else to talk about after the server left, so I asked, "So…you're Tita Didi's nephew, right?" I grabbed the card and the marker, placing a number one beside the veggie caterpillar roll, tempura yam roll, and shiitake mushroom roll.

"She's my mom's sister," he answered.

"You two looked close."

"She doesn't have any kids."

My eyebrows rose. "So you hang out with your aunt at the mall? Nice guy. Didn't know you guys still exist."

His brown eyes were amused. "Oh, we do exist. Just some of us didn't wake up early and missed Nice Guy 101 class."

He was witty too. I handed him the pen. A lock of his hair dropped on his forehead as he looked down and wrote on his order card. He raked it back with his fingers. It was black and curly, so it would totally be normal if it reminded me of someone I was so totally over. Except that it was the wrong shade. Cameron's hair was darker, almost blue black, especially when hit by the sun. And it wasn't tightly curled like Thomas's. Cameron's were like loose angel curls.

Damn him. Get the hell out of my head, Bigfoot!

"Have you guys decided on what to order?"

The server jerked me out of my thoughts as he placed our drinks on the table.

"I don't think you remember me," Thomas said when our server left.

My eyebrows drew together. "Have we met?"

"Not properly introduced. I go to the same church. I saw you slap your brother in the face once."

I drew a blank for a moment and then I laughed, remembering that time when I was so sleepy—when was I not, really—and Dylan woke me up and my hand automatically slapped him. I didn't know anyone had noticed.

"Oh yeah, we do that for fun," I deadpanned. "My brother likes it."

He smiled. "Got a mean streak in you."

"Do you have brothers and sisters?"

He nodded. "Five sisters and five brothers. I'm the baby."

"No way. There's eleven of you?"

"My childhood was an adventure."

The server came with our food, and we discovered that we were both vegetarian. He told me funny stories of how his siblings pranked him, told him to wash the dishes and sweep the floor because he was the youngest, how he never got to hold the TV remote control, and how he missed his siblings when they all grew up and left their parents' house. And eventually he left too. We talked about what it was like to grow up as mixed babies in Canada—his ma was Filipino and his dad was African Canadian.

He was open, friendly, and we had a lot in common. We shared stories about difficult patients and the sweet, kind patients who made working in the health industry worth it. It seemed that the universe was actually listening to me for once when I asked for someone like him. He was the complete opposite of someone I had completely written off. This person I had written off wouldn't even dream about telling me about his childhood.

"Am I boring you?" he asked.

I blinked. "Damn. No, I'm sorry. I just…"

He had a boyish face, one that told me he had an army of family and friends and girls who absolutely adored him. His warm brown eyes invited me to tell him whatever I wanted.

"I'm a jerk, aren't I?" I asked.

"Why don't you tell me what's bothering you? I won't tell. Scout's honor." He made the three-finger salute.

I stabbed a sushi piece with my chopsticks, chucked it in my mouth. What was the harm? He was a stranger and he looked trustworthy enough, although… "I have this…friend," I started.

He nodded, smiling, his eyes shrewd. "I like these 'I have this friend' hypothetical things."

I gave him a dry look. "It's really my friend."

"Uh-huh. So this friend is a lady?"

"Yeah, and she met a man."

"Sounds like something I'm expert in."

"Expert? You get friend-zoned a lot, don't you?" I asked.

He chuckled. "Ouch. But we'll talk about me next time. This is your moment. Take center stage, please."

Please. I knew someone who never said *please*, except for that night.

"Have you ever cared about somebody you really hated a lot? The more you hate them, the more you want them? And you pretend you're fine, but deep inside, you know you're really not? Have you ever cared about someone so much that you just want to push them off a cliff?"

"Hmm. I can't really say for sure I've experienced this phenomenon." He set down his chopsticks. "Should I be worried? Do you need help?"

"Not me. My friend."

"Oh, yes. Sounds like your friend really cares about this man."

"Maybe. Right now, she wants to kill him, but she can't even tell him because he's not around. He just…left."

"Where is he?"

"She doesn't even know. He left without telling her."

"Give me a background. So they broke up?"

"Not really. They were together, but not *together*, really."

"Ah. I think I get it. They spent a lot of time together but were never boyfriend-girlfriend because they never talked about it. But it's obvious they have feelings for each other. Then all of a sudden, he stops texting and calling and he's disappeared on her. Am I getting this right so far?"

"Damn. You're good. You're right—you are an expert."

He patted his chest with his fist. "Thank you. Listen, I think you already know this—"

"Not me. My friend," I reminded him.

He gave me a knowing look. "Fine. Your friend. Tell her she deserves better than that. Every girl does."

Aw.

"But why do you think he left?"

He sighed, leaned back in his chair. "It could be anything, really. You want me to guess?"

I nodded.

"Maybe he got scared."

"What do you mean?"

"Maybe he was falling for your friend and he got scared so he left. He doesn't want a commitment, not ready to settle, all those things an immature mind can't comprehend. But…"

"But?"

"It could also be that he doesn't really like your friend. Or if this guy is a complete asshole, it could be he got bored and moved on because he doesn't see her as challenging enough. Or she's too challenging, too difficult to deal with, and he doesn't think it's worth the trouble. Or…"

Ouch. That hit home.

"Or?"

He scratched his chin. "Or he thinks she's not going to sleep with him."

"Oh."

"I couldn't really tell you," he continued. "But there's one thing I'm sure of. Tell your friend that she shouldn't be too mad at herself for falling for this guy. Everybody has feelings, and if these feelings are real, it's hard to put them away. It's difficult to get over them, but it will happen. I'm sure of it."

He sounded like he knew what he was talking about. We exchanged numbers and promised that we'd go out for coffee soon. I was glad to have found another guy friend. I had missed Damon and his male company and his advice. It was good to get advice from a guy's point of view.

I thought about the things he'd told me when I got home and was in the bathroom. I had thought about all those things too, but just hearing them made them even more real.

Thomas was right. I already knew that I deserved better—and that my feelings were real and it could take a while to get rid of them.

I looked up at the clock in the bathroom. I had put one there to time myself. I could spend hours in here, sitting in the tub, on the toilet, doing my makeup.

It was ten at night and I should get some sleep.

———————————————

Days passed in a blur. The only thing I looked forward to was the interview I had at a construction company. Dylan said it was a friend of a friend who'd told him about the opening. And it was double what I was getting at the coffee shop, and then some.

The morning of the interview arrived. I dressed to impress with a crisp white dress shirt, deep-green blazer and slacks. The construction company office was fifteen minutes outside the city limits. I programmed my phone's GPS so I wouldn't get lost and followed the instructions until it told me: "You've arrived at your destination."

"Bish, what do you mean I've arrived at my destination? Here?"

I glared at my phone as if expecting it to answer. I pulled up to a dirt road, kept going until I located a gigantic open gate.

It was probably fifteen acres of land. I could see three buildings and a trailer. It didn't look like a construction company. It looked more like a supplier of soil/stone.

"Did I get the address right?" I double checked, and it was. "Either I'm tripping or you are," I told my phone.

The sound of big machinery, the smell of dry dust and soil and grease. Large hills of different-colored stones were organized meticulously in long rows. Huge trucks were coming and going from the lot—from eighteen-wheelers to tandems packed with huge amounts of soil or lined with boxes, probably filled with stones.

It was like a colony of worker bees—activity was everywhere. Everybody had a purpose. No one outside was standing still.

I looked at the three buildings and decided to go for the first one. It was a big, square modern building, with a slanted tin roof and earthy colors of red and brown wood paneling on the exterior walls. It was a gorgeous building, a testament to their workmanship. The other two structures looked marginally the same except with different types of roofs and exterior walls.

I knocked. When no one answered, I pushed open the door.

People were everywhere. I smelled coffee, papers, sweat, and dust. Conversations hummed, phones rang, printers and fax machines beeped. It was brimming with energy.

It was a big modern space, with a huge conference

room walled with privacy glass and two rooms at the back. A black steel staircase led to a loft above the rooms. Light-gray concrete walls and flooring, exposed beams. It looked very industrial, but the finishing touches in the furniture added warmth.

On the front left side of the space was an enclosed room, walled with the same glass. It looked like a customer lounge, complete with a TV and chairs. Four massive desks sitting in a row along the wall dominated the right side of the space.

"Can I help you?" A girl who looked my age came up to me. She was wearing a hard hat, like most of the people I'd seen outside, a neon orange reflective jacket, and dirty jeans.

"I'm Kara Hawthorne. I have an interview scheduled in"—I looked up at the moon-size clock in the middle of the room—"five minutes."

"Oh yeah, Deb's expecting you. Just head on to the back. See the last desk over there? That's Deb's."

"All right. Thanks."

"No problem."

I wasn't nervous before, but I was nervous now. This should be easy-peasy for me. I'd done a lot of interviews and I was an expert on how to answer their questions. But as I approached the very pregnant redhead at the back, my heart started to drum in my chest.

You got this.

I'd never worked at a soil company or construction company before, but it shouldn't be any harder than the other jobs I've had.

It's double your hourly rate plus change. You have to bag this job. Plus, you might be working with designers and architects and engineers, and who knows what could happen in the future? You've always loved designing. Maybe you could pick up a thing or two.

Deb spotted me before I could approach her.

"You Kara?" She assessed me with shrewd, green eyes. She was beautiful, probably in her late thirties, and had a no-nonsense aura about her. *Work, work, work,* her eyeglasses, pencil behind her ear, short red hair, and chocolate-brown jacket said. I liked her already.

"Yes, ma'am."

She smiled. "Punctual. It's not usually this jungle crazy. You've caught us on a good day."

I didn't mind crazy, I wanted to tell her, but she was already placing the phone to her ear. "Head on upstairs. I'll tell Rick you're here," she said as she punched in numbers. "He's the owner."

I nodded and went upstairs. I felt a little like I was going to the principal's office as I took the stairs. The room had the same look as the whole building—modern but warm. Big, dusty windows showed the activity from the outside.

There was another massive desk in the middle of the room—same as the ones downstairs. On top of it was a huge pile of folders, almost teetering from the height and weight of it, receipts and Post-it Notes, a mug of coffee beside a desk lamp. Two chairs sat in front of the desk. Jackets hung on metal hooks on the wall. It was a well-used workspace. It gave me a good feeling.

What if I didn't get this job?

Of course you will! They'd be crazy not to hire you. You have a huge range of skills. You can even eat a whole tub of ice cream in one sitting. You can do this!

The door opened, and a tall man strode in. He stopped, looking at me with surprise in his bright-green eyes.

He had the look of an established and handsome man. He was probably in his early fifties, with a salt-and-pepper beard that was trimmed neatly and an old, faint scar running from his left eyebrow down to his cheek and stopping at his strong jaw. He was lanky but had a muscular build. His hair was swept back, and it was shockingly silver. He reminded me of a very attractive silver-haired fox.

"Why, hello there."

"Good morning. Kara Hawthorne," I said just as I heard Deb yell "It's Kara!" from downstairs.

His eyes lit with pleasure. He offered his hand. "I'm Rick. Pleasure to finally meet you, Kara. Have a seat, girl. You want something to drink?"

He had a very calm demeanor. Automatically, my body relaxed. I sat.

"I'm good. Thanks."

"So," he started, sitting on the chair in front of me instead of the one behind the massive desk. "You came very highly recommended."

I did? I better ask Dylan who his friend was who had recommended me. Maybe I could give him a free oil change at the shop.

"Just got a couple of questions."

Here we go.

"You know how to answer the phone?"

I stiffened. Was he being sarcastic? I narrowed my eyes at him. I hoped to God this wasn't a prank or I'd go gorilla crazy on someone for wasting my time this morning.

"I was born answering phones," I said seriously.

He leaned back in his chair, smiling widely.

"Do you know how to use computers?"

"Even in my sleep."

"Don't tell Deb this, but this job isn't really that hard."

"I heard that!" Deb screamed.

"Sometimes you have to have a loud voice to be heard here, especially when you're talking to the guys. Can you scream real loud?"

Now I smiled. "Like a banshee."

"Perfect," he said. He offered me an hourly rate and my eyes bugged out. It was a little more than I was expecting. "As you probably noticed," he continued, grinning at my reaction, "we not only operate in construction, but also in the soil business. Makes it easier and saves us a lot of costs for landscaping." His voice was raspy, as if he'd been smoking for a long time. "Technically, my construction company's located in the city. We have another office there—a little spiffier than what we have here. But it's more for clients than anything, really. I'm mostly here, and so I'd need you here too. Deb will tell you what you need to know. I'm not sure exactly how long she'll be gone for, but she'll let you know. Do you have any questions for me?"

How long she'd be gone for. The job was temporary. For a few months at least—hopefully a year if Deb took all of her maternity leave. Canada gave more than a year for maternity leave for mothers if qualified, which I thought was amazing. She could also split the leave with her husband if they wished. Or she could go back to work too if she liked.

I bit my lip, debating.

"What say you, girl? Would you like to join us?" Rick asked.

Suddenly, I heard someone coming up the steps. I turned around, and everything around me ceased to exist but for that one man approaching the landing.

It felt like someone had taken a sledgehammer to my heart, breaking it into pieces before it started beating again. I curled my hands into fists as everything blurred for one moment and then stood in painful clarity.

Cameron entered the office, stopping dead in his tracks. His eyes zeroed in on me.

"Kara?" Rick asked. "You want the job?" he repeated.

I peeled my eyes away from Cameron. I stood up and offered Rick my hand. "I'll take it."

Chapter 23

Kara

"I'll take it," I told Rick.

I gritted my teeth, so painfully aware of Cameron standing behind me.

The look of shock on his savagely beautiful face when he saw me had only lasted a moment before it shifted to yearning and need as he took me in. And then his walls came up and there was nothing.

Rick shook my hand, grinning widely and looking very pleased with himself.

"I'll come back later," Cameron said.

His voice, deep, rich, and so darkly masculine, sent ripples down my spine. It had been three weeks since I'd last heard it…but it felt longer than that.

"We're done with the interview, boy. Take—"

But Cameron was already halfway down the stairs. I heard Rick sigh, then he looked at me.

I'm good. Just good. One hundred and one percent bomb-ass good.

"Kara, could you get him for me?"

What?

My eyes shot to Rick. His were gleaming—with amusement or challenge, I wasn't sure.

"I need him to do something for me. That boy can move fast if he wants to, can't he?"

He sure did. He could move real slow too if he wanted. Not that I knew anything about that. Well, not anymore.

I had been thinking of what I would say to him or how I would act when I saw him again. Or if I would even acknowledge his existence. I always came up with either blasting him with a cold shoulder or burning him with fire.

I guess we'll find out.

I spun around, ready to run to the stairs to chase after him, when inspiration struck.

I walked to the railing, placed my hands there. Taking a deep breath, I yelled at top of my lungs, "Hey, Bigfoot!"

Everyone in the office stopped and stared up at me. I waved my hands and bared my teeth in a wide grin.

Cameron was almost at the door when he stopped in his tracks. Slowly, he turned. And then our eyes met. If there was a pull I felt from his gaze, I mentally squished it with my heels.

"Get your ass back up here!" I yelled again.

When he looked like he wasn't going to move, I added, "The boss wants you!"

I left it at that.

When I turned back to Rick, he was grinning from ear to ear.

"Man, oh man. You are *so* hired," he said. "You're going to fit just fine here."

"We own an auto shop. I've been working with men all my life, so I don't think you should worry about me fitting in."

"Is that right? If you don't mind me asking, why do you need this job?"

I didn't bat an eye. I wondered why he hadn't asked me important questions like this in the interview. Actually, he didn't ask me anything at all. It was almost like I already had the job the moment he shook my hand. Either he was desperate to fill the position, or whoever recommended me was at the top of his trust list.

"We're only breaking even," I told him honestly.

I didn't turn when I felt a presence behind me. Cameron. What the hell? I didn't even hear him climb up the stairs. How did he do that?

With his massive size, you'd think he'd be clumsy or walk with dumb, heavy footsteps. Not a chance. He moved with catlike grace and stealth, sneaking up on me without warning. I should trip him next time.

"Cam," Rick said.

Cameron didn't say anything, just stood somewhere behind me, waiting.

"Son, why don't you show Kara around the property?"

My head jerked up. *Is this man up to something? Does he know about me and Cameron?*

I couldn't see Cameron having a heart-to-heart talk with anyone, but what did I know? I didn't know him well enough to assume anything. In fact, I didn't know him at all. Maybe he was more open to Rick. I wondered who he was in Cameron's life.

You don't want anything to do with him anymore, remember? Move on, sis.

"Introduce her to the guys. Get her a hard hat," he said and grabbed his own from the desk and put it on.

"Have you decided on that big project you were telling me about?"

"Still thinking about it. I would need your help with it if I take it on."

"Always here for you, Son. Just let me know."

Son?

This was Cameron's dad? But their last names were different, although having different last names didn't necessarily indicate nonrelation. They didn't look alike at all though, except for their height. Even then, Cameron was a tad taller. So maybe Rick just liked to call him that. What did it even matter? Ugh.

What kind of bad stinking luck did I have to be working at the same place as he did? And then I remembered that time when he wasn't so reserved, he'd mentioned that he owned his business and that he also worked for a friend. Maybe that was Rick. Again, what did it even matter? Double that ugh.

"Welcome to the family, Kara. Come back to the shop after your tour and talk to Deb. She'll tell you what you need to know." Rick winked at me conspiratorially—as if we both shared a secret Cameron didn't know and we were going to get him in trouble. He walked behind the desk and grabbed his jacket on the chair, shrugged it on. "I have to run to the site. Have fun, kiddos."

Then he left. And I was alone with Cameron.

I could feel his presence on my back. The air throbbed with it. There were people below us. I could hear the buzz of conversation and movement, but they felt far away. I closed my eyes, took a deep breath.

Steel, baby. You are made of steel.

The instant I opened my eyes, I turned to face him.

The blue of his gaze felt like a sucker punch to my stomach.

I had already made up my mind that it wouldn't affect me. I was so convinced that it wouldn't, I underestimated his effect. So when his focus turned on me, when that piercing gaze fixed on me, it hit me unexpectedly.

His dark, curly hair was tied in a messy man bun—the first time I saw him wear it like that. He had a heavy five o'clock shadow on his jaw, as if he'd given up on shaving. There was a grease stain on his cheek, as if he'd been working on a vehicle. He looked rakish, a devil-may-care look about him. A man with rough edges and an angelic face.

A white hard hat was tucked under his arm and a backpack slung over his shoulder. He was wearing a black muscle T-shirt that emphasized his broad shoulders, the toned muscles of his arms. It was also stained with grease. The jeans and steel-toed boots he had on weren't any better. He looked like a sexy construction worker about to pose for a racy magazine. And he'd have all the months in the calendar.

I hadn't seen him in work clothes before. I hadn't seen him work at all, and seeing him now showed me a different side of him that I didn't want to see.

I didn't want to see any more sides to him—especially the good sides. I knew that no matter how many times I told myself I was over him, how easy it would be to fall back again.

"Kara," he said my name in that way of his. Softly, gently. It rolled off his tongue like rich, liquid dark chocolate.

I fought the delicious shiver that slithered down my spine.

No. Not again. Not fucking ever.

Easy to fall back again, yes, but not impossible to stop it.

He moved his arm and tried to place the hard hat on my head. I stepped away and glared at him.

"You're not touching me. In fact, stay away from me. Two feet," I said, gesturing at the space between us. "Two. Feet. You got that?"

The amused look in his eyes infuriated me. As if nothing had happened between us. As if he didn't leave without even saying goodbye.

If I expected an explanation or an apology from him, I knew it wasn't going to come.

He crossed his arms over his chest, bracing his feet apart. "That's going to be impossible."

"No, it's not. Just keep repeating it to yourself every few seconds. Like a chant. It should help your brain to remember it."

A crooked smile appeared on his mouth.

I looked away.

"Here," he said, handing me his hard hat.

"I want a new one. Something you haven't infected."

I was being childish. The way I was reacting to him, the way I was so defensive. I didn't like it. If I was really over him, I had to show him he didn't affect me. Not a bit.

But it hurt.

I heard him sigh. "Follow me."

I scowled at his sexy back muscles doing their double sexy thing as I followed him down the stairs. I nearly tripped when I noticed what was holding his hair.

It was my blue hair tie.

The one that reminded me of his eyes. The one that I was wearing almost a month ago when he pulled it from my hair.

Confusion swirled inside me.

Don't put any meaning into it. He probably reached for it out of convenience. He probably didn't even know it was yours. For all you know, he's a hair-tie thief. One for every girl he's boned. Like Dexter's blood samples. Get it?

Well, he hadn't boned me, and I would never let him, so that would be a big, fat, stinking no.

I followed him as he opened one of the rooms below the loft, let me enter first. It was a windowless storage room—gray walls, hard hats, jackets, dirty boots, metal lockers, shelves with file folders, and a shower at the back end of the room. He didn't seem to hear the threatening click of the door as it closed on us. But my body did.

I stopped at the door, feeling a sensual animalistic danger around him.

I watched as he walked past me and stopped at a locker. I had forgotten how tall he was, how he took up too much space and air in the room. His torso was long and svelte, his forearm muscles rippled and hardened as he pulled the locker doors open. Then he faced me, gesturing in front of him with his arm.

"Take one if you like," he said.

When I didn't move, he raised a brow.

Can you handle me? it seemed to say. A challenge.

I narrowed my eyes at him. To prove him wrong, I marched in front of him and regretted it instantly. In this room, where I was alone with him, his scent was strong. It wrapped around me, a seductive, cool, blue smell.

You have to fight it! Can't give in, girl. Don't give in.

It was quiet in the room, a little cold. That was why I shivered. Because it was cold. It had nothing to do with him standing near me.

I shook my head, clearing my thoughts, and searched the shelves inside the locker. The hard hats were located on the top shelf. I was tall, but not inhumanly tall like he was.

"Want help?" he whispered.

I felt dizzy. And it was because I hadn't eaten yet. It was absolutely not because of his proximity. Absolutely not the heat emanating from his body. Absolutely not the delicious timbre of his dark voice.

"I don't need your help."

I raised onto my tiptoes and felt for the highest shelf without looking. When I felt a hard hat come free, I looked up and screamed when it fell.

He was there behind me right away. I was locked between his arms as his hands quickly caught the hard hat before it could do damage. I jumped back and sucked in a breath as our bodies made contact.

I was trapped. The locker doors and his arms blocked my sides. And behind me was a hard, immovable wall of male muscle.

I could smell him so strongly—that very appealing smell that always reminded me of raw masculinity. I could feel the warmth of his body and the strength he controlled so meticulously.

We didn't move. One, two, three damned seconds of weakness. I allowed myself this and only this.

"Get off me," I said after a moment. My voice sounded thick.

He didn't budge at first. One, two, three, four seconds. Then he did. I jerked away, far, far away, from him.

"I told you not to touch me," I said.

He clenched his jaw, then looked down. There was a smirk on his mouth, but when he looked up, his eyes looked hard. "You were the one who touched me first."

I glowered at him. Fine. That was true. My brain needed oxygen to function, and he was sucking it all out of the room.

"Here." He offered the hard hat to me. "I touched this one though. Now it's infected. Want to get another one?"

I grabbed the hard hat from his big, idiot hands and left that damned room.

Now I felt hot. And angry at myself for letting him affect me so strongly, so powerfully that I had let myself wallow in his touch for those significant seconds. I let it happen, and that was what ate at me. Because giving in even for a tiny moment could be my downfall. One blow to an already cracked surface—no matter how thick or strong that wall looked, one blow was all it needed to topple it all down.

"Wear this." He handed me a white mask with a yellow, thin garter. "We're going to drive around the lot and it's dusty out there. This should help."

"I don't need it."

"Take it," he insisted.

"No."

He sighed loudly, then proceeded to open the front door. He held it for me as I walked outside. I squinted, the sun blinding me.

I blinked up in confusion as it darkened suddenly. And I realized that he had placed his palm in front of me, blocking the brightness of the sun.

My eyes moved to his face. He was looking at me. His eyes looked so very, *very* fucking blue that my throat felt tight.

"Why?" I blurted out.

Another sign of weakness—asking him a stupid question about his actions. About his *feelings*.

I saw him swallow. And just before he could answer, I walked ahead of him.

Why are you walking away? Are you scared that he'll answer? Or that he won't?

I ignored the voice in my head.

"I don't have all day," I said. "Let's go."

"Not that way."

I stopped and turned around. He pointed at a dusty company truck parked at the other end of the building.

I bit my tongue and headed to the truck. He opened the door for me, waiting for me to get in before he closed it.

Why couldn't he be a jerk and stop being a gentleman now? For once, why couldn't he give me what I wanted and leave me alone?

Before he could slide inside the truck, someone called out his name. An older man slapped his back in that man-to-man greeting. I couldn't hear their conversation clearly because the windows were up.

His phone in the cup holder lit up and I saw his text.

Dad: Your mother has gone back to Toronto. I took care of it.

I'd seen his phone before, and it wasn't this. This phone looked new and was a different model. Maybe it wasn't his.

I jerked my head away, looking outside the window when he opened the driver's side door.

He got in silently, the roominess of the truck accommodating his size. His long legs looked comfortable as he started the vehicle, as he stepped on the gas.

I wondered if he remembered the times we were in my car, just like I was remembering them now.

If they even meant anything to him.

Stop this! Don't make any more assumptions about you and him. You know where that led.

I didn't trust myself around him. I wanted to hurl accusations at him, questions that I desperately wanted answers to. But I didn't.

That's a first.

He threw me a glance, but I turned and faced the window instead. He stopped the truck.

"Give me a few minutes. The guys have been waiting for me to get back," he said and got out of the vehicle.

Three men wearing hard hats approached him. This time, I lowered the window so I could hear their conversation.

I saw how they respected him, how they went to him for reassurance, to ask what they needed to do about this problem or that. It seemed like he had answers for most of their questions. And when he didn't, he promised them he'd find out. He'd pulled out a small notepad from his back pocket, a pen from his front pocket, and jotted it all down.

I didn't like finding out how competent he was. How responsible. At least in his work ethic.

Apparently, it didn't apply to other parts of his life.

"How was that project out of town you've been working on? Rick said that was supposed to take only a couple days," one of the men said. He had a dirty gimme cap on, rather than a hard hat.

"We ran into some complications," Cameron said. "The plumbing, the electrical. Some materials were missing."

"Someone was stealing?"

Cameron shrugged. "It's all taken care of now."

The man stroked his beard. "Took a while, I was told."

Cameron nodded. "A few days."

"You finished it though. Good job, boss." He slapped Cameron on the back. "You going to have a beer with us this time?"

Cameron shook his head but smiled at him. "I'm going to have to pass, Mack."

"You always do. Got a girl you gonna go home to, eh?"

Suddenly Cameron turned his head and caught me looking at him. I didn't remove my gaze and matched his stare.

"If she'll let me," he replied.

My heart tripped. He was confusing me. Every time I was ready to leave, he'd say something to bring me back again. But I didn't want to. Not anymore. Not like before. I'd show him...

"Well, make it so that she does! Get your ass out of here. Some of us gotta work."

Cameron was silent as he got inside the vehicle, as he started the truck and stepped on the gas. I stared straight ahead, pretending to be interested in what I was seeing, but the truth was…I was so *aware* of him beside me, that I…*ached*.

"We refer to this place as The Yard."

I jumped when I heard his voice, but he just kept going.

"The office downtown is called The Necktie."

I would have laughed if my heart didn't feel heavy. If he could act nonchalant about everything, so could I. "How come?"

"The downtown office is where we meet clients, do presentations. Mostly."

I'd heard this before from Rick. "So?"

"So you have to wear a tie," he answered. I could hear a smile in his voice. "Rick's rules."

I smirked.

"You'll get calls from clients asking to set up an appointment with Rick, or if he's not available, with me or Elijah. He's one of our foremen. You'll meet him eventually."

The three buildings, he explained, had different purposes. The first building where I went was the office. The second was for the workers—lunchroom, washroom, a place where they could cool down when the heat gets too extreme in the summer, basically a big locker room. The third was storage.

He pointed out places as we drove around The Yard, the machines and what they do, the process of sifting debris from the soil, the types of soil and stones customers usually ordered.

"You won't be taking order calls from customers wanting stones," he explained. "That's the job of the other three women. You'll be taking care mostly of the construction side. Deb will explain it to you."

"Is Rick your dad?"

Where the hell did that come from?

"I wish he were," he answered after a moment.

He didn't offer anything after that. It was a skill, the way he dodged questions and answered them without giving away anything.

I knew he was like this with everyone, not just me, but it was still frustrating. And if I let the drama queen in me take control, I'd feel hurt because I was like everyone else. I was no one special.

Where the hell were you? What did you do? Why didn't you text?

Am I still important to you?

Was I ever?

But I didn't ask any of that. Every one of those questions sounded pathetic. And needy. And I didn't want to be. Pride kept me in check.

When he parked the vehicle back in the same spot, I shot out of it and headed for my car.

I had to get the hell out of there right now. Being with him was playing with my emotions. And then I realized I still had to talk to Deb.

"Shit."

I felt his eyes following me as I walked back to the office. I waited until Deb was done on the phone. She apologized and said she was too busy today to brief me, but she handed me a folder and asked me to come back in a couple of days and we'd work out everything then. She'd phone and let me know when she wasn't swamped this week, and we could work out the days when I could start my training. The folder she handed me contained most of the information I needed.

"Let me guess—Rick didn't ask you much," Deb said. The phone rang, but she ignored it.

"He didn't tell me much either."

She rolled her eyes good-naturedly. "I knew it." Then she told me my hourly rate, which Rick had told me at least. "That works for you?" she asked, grinning.

"Oh God, yes!"

She laughed, and we said goodbye. I left the office, feeling better than I had in days—no, weeks. When I received my first paycheck, I should celebrate with a milkshake. I should buy pizza for the guys at the garage and takeout for Dad and Dylan. I should phone Tala and take her out for a movie. Damn, when was the last time I went to the theater? I couldn't even remember.

With this money, I could save up faster to buy off Andrew's share. Get rid of the parasite for good. I couldn't wait!

When I saw Cameron outside talking with another man with a hard hat, I lost my smile. Muttering under my breath about dark, evil spirits, I rushed to my car.

"Kara," Cameron called out. "Wait up."

I turned and looked at him impatiently.

How can you stand there as if nothing happened?

"What?" I snarled.

How can your damn smile still affect me? I hate you.

"I need a ride home," he said. "You still owe me."

My jaw dropped.

"I just need to clock out. Be right back."

I watched him jog to the second building.

I must've damaged my eardrums last time I cleaned them. The internet had warned me not to use cotton swabs, because it would only push the earwax deeper, but of course I never listened. That must be it.

I didn't really hear him say I still owed him a ride home, did I?

I rushed to my car and started it.

Nothing wrong with those ears. You heard him right the first time, girl!

The balls! I could choke him with my bare hands.

I grabbed my phone and checked the time. It was 1:15 p.m. Time to leave. Just as I was going to speed my ass out of the parking lot, an eighteen-wheeler decided to block my way.

I closed my eyes in defeat, hitting my forehead repeatedly on the steering wheel. "You gotta be fucking kidding me."

And then I heard a knock on the passenger side door. It was him, of course.

He looked like he'd washed up a little bit. His face looked cleaner, the grease stain missing. He'd lost the man bun, his dark curls in an adorable disarray on his head. He had changed into a gray shirt and dark jeans.

"I'll ask him to move his truck if you let me in," he offered.

His voice was muffled by the closed window, but I heard what he said. And the laughter in it.

"He'll be here for another half hour," he added.

I scowled at him. He grinned.

This is your chance to prove that he doesn't affect

you. Do it. Show him who's got the upper hand. If you can control yourself, that is. Or you can keep making a fool of yourself by blowing up on him again. See if he doesn't ignore you and leave again.

I need you to shut your piehole right now. I don't need you in my head.

Nothing really happened between you two. There were no promises. Why are you so hurt about it?

Because I had let him in. I wouldn't have opened up to him if he hadn't pursued me, told me all those lies. I wasn't dreaming. I wasn't making it all up.

This time, the inner voice in my head was quiet. Might as well let Cameron in then. I would prove to him how much he didn't affect me.

I unlocked the door and got out of my car.

"You're driving, Bigfoot."

"Bigfoot, huh?"

"If you don't want to, then forget about—"

"All right," he said quickly, looking surprised and pleased that I'd agreed.

He went to talk to the truck driver first, and of course, the eighteen-wheeler moved right away. He seemed to be used to getting his way here. He was the prince. The dark-haired, taciturn golden boy.

He was helpful and somehow approachable with his men—when he chose to be, but I also noticed from his conversations how he kept everyone at arm's length. He didn't seem to hang out with them after work hours. I remembered the man said he never went out for beers with them. What the hell did he do when he wasn't at school and working?

He slid into the driver's seat. I refused to acknowledge

the twinge in my chest when he adjusted the seat to accommodate his long legs. It was all so familiar.

The reaction I had watching him do this that first week was so different from my reaction this time. Now I was…sad.

He cranked the window open a little, then started the car and reversed. A few seconds later, we were on the road. He drove one-handed.

His chiseled jawline. His big hand on the steering wheel. The scrapes on his knuckles. His long fingers. A lock of his dark hair against his skin. The movement of his leg as he stepped on the gas.

I looked away, gritting my teeth.

I turned the radio on, noted the time, and blasted the volume. It didn't dispel the tension in the car completely, but it made it easier.

Just like when he drove me around The Yard, I faced the window so I didn't have to look at him. I turned off the radio, noted the time again. I lasted eight minutes.

"You lied to me," I blurted out.

I saw his body go on full alert. "What's the lie?" he asked quietly.

"Your vehicle, you jerk. You told me you don't have a vehicle."

His body visibly relaxed. A small smile was even flirting on his pretty mouth. "I never said that."

"Yes, you did."

"You asked me if I owned the truck. I said it wasn't mine."

Was that what he really said?

"How could you even remember that conversation?"

I couldn't even remember what I ate yesterday.

"I remember," he said softly. "Because I remember every conversation we've had."

Oh no. No, no.

My traitorous heart skipped a beat. I didn't want this. I wanted to be cured of his curse. His black magic on my heart. I needed to be exorcised. I needed a priest.

"Why?"

Did I really ask that? Why did I ask that?

Because you want to hear how important you are to him. What you mean to him. If you do mean anything to him.

"You know why," he said gently. Then he turned his head to look at me. His eyes pulling me again. Back to where I was before. "You know."

Suddenly I was feeling angry. So mad my chest was heaving from breathing so hard, so fast.

"Pull over to the side of the road. Now!"

As soon as he did, I shot out of the car. I couldn't be around him. I just couldn't. I was losing my shit, and there was no way I was going to allow myself to blow up on him the way I had the night before he left.

I started walking. I heard the car door slam closed.

"Where the hell are you going?" he yelled behind me.

"It's none of your fucking business!" I yelled back.

I curled my hands into fists. The sun was glaringly bright in the sky. We were still outside of the city. The vehicles here drove over the speed limit. I could hear them zipping past, the ground shaking.

I didn't care. If I had to walk home, I would. I couldn't be around him anymore. But I wasn't stupid. I definitely didn't want to die. I stayed away from the road but walked as fast as I could.

Suddenly he was beside me, close to the road. I knew he was protecting me from the vehicles, but it only made me angrier.

I wanted to get over him. I wanted to be rid of him. And every time he did something kind or sweet, my treacherous heart gave in, little by little.

"You're going to walk home? Is that your plan?" he demanded.

"What do you care? You don't get to know anything about me when you can't even…when you can't even—"

"When I can't even what?"

I was so close, *so* close, to punching his pretty face. I walked faster. He matched my pace.

"I lost my phone," he said suddenly.

I stopped in my tracks and shot him a glare. "I didn't know you could go so low and lie to me like that."

"I'm not."

If it was true…that was why I'd seen a new phone in his truck.

"You mean you lost your phone right after I texted you that night?"

"No," he answered after a moment. "Not right after."

"Then you just didn't want to reply."

He raked his hands through his hair. "It's not about wanting."

"What then?"

"It was better that way," he replied. "At the time."

I was done. Totally done.

"Fuck you, Cameron. Leave me the hell alone."

I started walking again, trying to calm myself down. I hated how fast he could make me angry. I was aware of my temper, but nobody could light it up as fast as he could.

He walked beside me but stayed a few feet away. Thoughts raced in my head. One after the other.

Bottom line was, riding with him in the same vehicle wasn't going to work. We had to repair his motorcycle. Fast. I could deal with him at the new job. I just had to make sure other people were around us all the time and I would treat him the way I treated other people I worked with. That was a good plan.

"Hey, listen," I said. I felt calmer now. Considerably.

He studied my face and must have seen the storm had passed. He moved closer so he could hear me properly.

"So if I believe that you really did lose your phone—"

"I did."

"—that meant you didn't get my text. Dylan ordered the wrong part, but I fixed that already. I'm sorry," I said, nearly gagging at the word *sorry*. "It will take three weeks again. Unfortunately."

"I guess you're going to have to keep driving me around."

My eye twitched. "No, I'm not. That deal was broken when you left!"

"I'm sorry," he said softly. "I lied to you about the truck."

That caught me off guard.

"It was the only way you'd…stay with me," he continued. He sounded so vulnerable, I felt my heart squeeze. "I know you don't owe me anything, but…can we still keep it?"

"Keep what?"

"Our arrangement," he answered. "Please?"

I swallowed the lump in my throat.

"Why then?" I asked, my voice sounded thick.

"Why what?"

"Stop acting like you don't know what I'm asking you."

His face suddenly lost its vulnerability and was replaced by his stone-cold mask. It was all I needed to remember all the things that happened before. Anger easily took over.

"How long do you think you're going to use that excuse of an arrangement?" I snapped. "I'm tired of it!"

He didn't answer.

"How long?" I repeated.

He threw me a look. "As long as it takes."

"As long as what takes?"

"For you to like me again."

I curled a fist against my stomach when I felt a flutter there. "That's never going to happen. Ever."

"Yeah," he said. "Because I'm just like everybody else."

There was a bitterness in his tone I'd never heard before. But I noticed the pain in it too.

You're just like everybody else.

I'd said that to him the night before he left. I realized now how hurtful it was, but it was my truth back then. He'd hurt me too. Worse, he left without saying a word.

"Are you mad at me? Are you fucking kidding me?" I shouted. I walked away, fast, and then I was running.

I glanced behind me and saw Cameron keeping pace a few feet away. He was giving me space, but that wasn't enough. I needed to not see him. I needed another world to live in without him.

Suddenly, I spotted a familiar car slowing down close to me. I ran near to the road, waving my arms. The car stopped and I got in.

In my peripheral, I saw Cameron run toward me, heard him shout my name. I closed the door of the car and forgot about him.

"Thanks for the ride, Mrs. Chung."

Her grandchildren lived in that area, and it was a very fortunate coincidence that she happened to be driving by.

"Oh, you're welcome, Kara dear. Do you know who that guy was? He was following you."

"Maybe he wants to sell me something."

"Fruit, maybe?" she suggested. "He sure looked handsome, didn't he?"

When she pulled in front of our shop, I gave her a small smile and slipped out of the vehicle. I waved goodbye and watched my ride drive away. I was about to turn and walk to my house when I saw my car barreling down the street.

Cameron's death stare was on me as he pulled my car into the lot. He slammed the door closed and headed over to me purposely. His eyes burning with temper.

"Tell me what the fuck you're trying to prove," he said quietly. Dangerously.

"I don't need to prove anything to you. You on the other hand have a lot to prove."

"He could've been a murderer!"

"Could have. But obviously wasn't because I'm still alive."

"And you asked him to drop you off at your place. At your place! Now he knows where the hell you live. Don't you have any fucking self-preservation?"

His eyes were bright with anger. There was a sick kind of satisfaction inside me to see him lose control. For once.

"First of all," I shot back, "you're one to lecture me about self-preservation when you were the one who jumped in front of my car! I could've run you over and then I would've gone to jail!"

He shot me a glare.

"Second of all, I'm not stupid enough to get into just anyone's car. I knew who the driver was. Third of all, you have no right to tell me what to do." Suddenly, my mouth felt dry. "You left without a fucking word," I said. Finally.

He was breathing hard. His eyes had darkened. His walls were up.

"Tell me why the hell you left, Cameron."

He took a deep breath, his gaze fixed on my face.

"Kara," he said softly.

He sounded so vulnerable, so open, so needy when he was like this. I felt my resolve weakening. He moved closer. Then held my face in his large hands, his thumb stroking my cheek, sliding down to my bottom lip in a caress filled with longing that tightened my throat. "Kara."

No. But I closed my eyes, my body fighting so hard not to lean against him, not to give in.

"There is no other woman in this world that could drive me to my fucking knees but you."

I felt his lips touch mine so softly, so fleetingly, my heart yearned.

I opened my eyes and watched him silently turn and walk away.

Chapter 24

Kara

SOME MORNINGS, I REALLY DIDN'T WANT TO GET OUT OF BED. On those days, I just shut my brain off and went through the motions. It helped when I didn't think of everything I had to get done and just focused on one thing at a time.

Wake up, coffee, eat breakfast, get ready. Go to class, coffee, eat on the go, drive to work or do some errands, coffee, worry, do my assignments and review. Eat, shower, worry, go to bed. Repeat.

But today was different.

Today, it wasn't just my body that ached. It was my heart.

I wished I had enough money to move to another province, to another country, to another planet. Maybe the time machine would be invented in my lifetime, and I just hoped I could afford to buy or rent one. Oh, the fun I could have.

Already I could hear the sounds of my dad making breakfast in the kitchen. The thought of him working so hard was the reason I forced myself to move. I knew even after his work at the garage, he would take on some odd jobs for extra cash. Tonight, he was supposed to paint the local gymnasium. If my supervisor at the nursing home didn't call me tonight, I'd help him out.

I pushed myself up from bed and headed to the kitchen.

"Good morning, sweetheart," my dad greeted as I sat at the kitchen island. "Here you go."

I grabbed the coffee he handed me, sipped, breathed it in, sipped some more.

"Cereal or toast?" he asked, like he did every morning because that was all my stomach could take in the morning.

"Toast, please," I mumbled, my face in my coffee.

"Coming right up. So," my dad began as soon as he placed the toast in front of me and topped off my coffee. "How's my favorite daughter?"

"I'm your only daughter."

"I think in another dimension I probably have ten daughters," he said, wiping the counter. "But you'd be my favorite."

I am my father's daughter through and through.

"I was just thinking of buying a time machine."

My dad's eyes sparkled with humor. "If you go first, check out my future self and let me know if I'm still hot, eh?"

I winked at him, forcing myself to cheer up. "You bet." I watched his back as he went to the sink, washed the rag, hung it over the long neck of the faucet to dry. "Hey, Dad," I said and waited until he turned to face me. "I got the job."

When my dad smiled, really smiled, his whole face lit up. It was hard not to smile back. "Oh, baby girl, I knew it. Congratulations! Want pizza tonight to celebrate?"

I nodded happily. "My treat." I was planning on buying them takeout on my first paycheck, but what was wrong with now? I'd buy them pizza tonight and on my first paycheck.

He frowned. "Oops. Sorry, I just remembered I have extra work tonight. How about tomorrow night?"

Oh, right. The gymnasium.

"That sounds good. I'll drive to the gym after class and give you a hand if I don't have work tonight."

"That's okay. Dylan will help me for a couple hours and Erwin is coming too. About this new job—"

"Mornin'," Dylan mumbled as he walked sleepily into the kitchen.

My dad scooped food from the pan and handed him a plate of pancakes and bacon. Dylan grabbed a juice from the fridge, sat next to me, and proceeded to inhale his food. I had no idea how he could eat so much in the morning.

"All right, kids, I gotta open up shop. I'll see you both tonight. Stay safe." He patted both our heads, walked to the door, and put on his jacket, shoes, and cap, and went out.

"Hey, Dyl," I said. "I got the job."

He nodded sleepily, drank his apple juice. "I knew you would."

"So, who's your friend who recommended me?"

He stabbed at his pancakes and shoveled another huge forkful into his mouth while his eyes were still half-closed. I always worried he'd choke to death eating half-asleep, but he'd seemed to be managing pretty well since he started eating solid food. I took a sip of my coffee.

"Cameron."

I choked, spat my drink back in the mug, and started coughing. "What?"

His eyes widened in alarm. "Shoot. I wasn't supposed to tell you."

"Cameron?" My throat was burning. "Cameron Saint Laurent? Like the guy whose motorcycle you hit-and-run?"

He nodded grimly. "He actually texted me about it a few weeks ago, and I brought it up to you, but you were acting all psycho. I just remembered it again when I texted you about the interview. Don't tell him I told you."

"B-but how the hell?" I sputtered. "I mean how did you guys even talk?"

"It's cool. I found his phone number and started texting him. I mean I don't think he's a text kind of guy. He doesn't even reply most times, and when he does, it's like one or two words, but we manage."

"Oh God." I groaned, collapsing on the kitchen island with my cheek on the cold surface. "No, no, *no*."

I knew how naive and sheltered my brother was, but I hadn't expected him to want to be friends with Cameron. Certainly not worship him.

"He's actually a really good guy, Kar—"

He stopped as I pushed my chair back, scowling at him.

I spotted the bacon on the side of his plate. I knew he always saved it for last. I growled at him, and he must have seen something in my face because his eyes widened in horror. Without mercy, I snatched his bacon and placed it in my mouth.

"Nooo!" he cried. "Why?"

"Don't talk to him again!" I marched to the bathroom,

spat out the bacon in the toilet and flushed it. I went to my room and looked at my phone.

My heart skipped a beat when I saw a message in my inbox. It was from an unknown number.

Where are you?
It's Cameron.

Did he get a new number? I ignored his texts, changed his name back to *SOS*, then changed it to *Asshole Cameron* instead. It had a nicer ring to it. Then I turned my phone off and got ready for school.

My mood followed me to my classes.

When class ended, I gathered my things and walked out in the hallway. As usual, I leaned against the wall, waiting for everyone to get the hell out of my way, so I didn't have to bump shoulders and smell people. Ten seconds, twenty, thirty. I fished for my phone in my backpack. Biting my lip, I turned it on.

Right away, it vibrated with incoming text messages. I bit my lip harder.

One was from Tala and the other from Thomas.

Tala: Just tell him how you feel! You never stopped yourself before, why now?

Thomas: Thanks for the discount on my oil change. Your dad was great. I'm taking you to my favorite ice cream shop next time.

I quickly replied to them. I'd been texting and

hanging out with Tala and Thomas more ever since Cameron disappeared. They had even met last weekend, and I was glad they liked each other. It helped to be distracted by them.

If I felt disappointment because Cameron didn't text me, I ignored it.

You didn't reply to him in the first place. Why would you expect he'll text you again?

Because I wanted to see if he meant what he said yesterday.

And a text will do that?

To start.

You wouldn't have replied to him anyway.

I wanted him to do more than text.

Well, heads up!

I raised my head. My heart, feeling droopy earlier, jumped against my ribs. There on the same bench where I'd seen him before was Cameron. In the same loose-limbed, sprawling position.

His massive body looked relaxed. Muscular legs spread, elbows bent and resting on the back of the bench. He looked calm, but when my eyes met his, there was a storm in them.

We looked at each other. Just looked. Taking in all the details.

My gaze shifted behind him. He was surrounded by the basketball team, but he ignored everyone. Caleb caught my eye. He pointed at Cameron, grinning at me. *He's back*, he mouthed, motioning for me to hang out with them.

I glared at him and shook my head, wanting to stuff his mouth with a dirty sock. *Be quiet!* I wanted to yell.

He was like a little kid. It would have been adorable if only I didn't want Cameron to find out I had been looking for him. When I saw Cameron look behind him, Caleb stopped moving and pressed his lips together, looking guilty. I rushed out of there.

"Damndamndamn," I groaned as I walked to the cafeteria and chose a table.

I wondered if Caleb already told him I had been looking for him while he was away for more than two weeks. He probably had.

I groaned, feeling sorry for how stupid I was. I shouldn't have asked Caleb.

Funny how when I was ready to talk about my feelings, Tala wasn't here. She texted me back and said she was going to miss her classes today because she had to take care of family matters. She sounded busy, so I told her we'd catch up sometime this week.

It was frustrating how life threw these plot twists at me.

Apart from the three students in the far corner and the culinary arts students prepping the buffet table for lunch, the cafeteria was empty.

I wasn't sure if part of the culinary arts students' practicum was to serve meals at the cafeteria, but I knew when they were present, the meals were always good. But today I couldn't even summon the enthusiasm to eat.

I dumped my phone and my backpack on the table and laid my head on top of it.

"Where were you this morning?"

"Shit!" I jumped as Cameron occupied the seat across from me.

He leaned back, watching me with anger in his eyes.

I straightened up in my seat, glaring at him.

"I told you I wasn't going to pick you up anymore," I told him wearily.

"That's going to be a problem."

"The only problem is that you're still here and—"

There is no other woman in this world that could drive me to my fucking knees but you.

"And?" he prompted. He looked tired, as if, like me, he didn't get any sleep last night. But damn he looked so good.

"And…and…"

My phone lit up. His eyes dropped to it, reading the text message.

"Who's Thomas?" His voice sounded hard.

For a moment, I thought about lying and telling him Thomas was my boyfriend. I was so tempted to. But in the end, I decided against it. Lying wouldn't bring me anything but more heartbreak.

"He's the guy who doubted that JC had risen from the dead."

"What?"

I grabbed my phone and sent Thomas a reply.

"You can't wait to send him a message when you can't even reply to mine?" he accused hotly.

I let out an incredulous puff of breath through my nose. "And you replied to mine?" I shot back. "You're asking a lot of things from me when you haven't given anything back."

The muscle in his jaw ticked.

"It's best if you leave me alone," I said quietly.

He looked down, his hands curling into fists. When

his eyes returned to my face, there was an emotion in them that tightened my throat.

"Tell me why you left," I said.

He rubbed his mouth with his hand, his gaze taking in my features, as if he was memorizing every one of them. But when he stayed quiet, I grabbed my backpack and my phone and walked away.

"Fuck!" I heard him hiss in frustration.

But I ignored it, even when my heart was yelling at me to turn back around and talk it out with him.

The day dragged. I felt itchy all day, suffocated in the four walls of the lecture hall. I couldn't concentrate on anything and desperately wanted to leave campus. But when my last class ended, it took ten minutes of dragging my feet, trying to decide whether to stay, before I decided to head to the parking lot to my car.

I knew Cameron had practice tonight. Should I stay and wait for him or just leave? I looked at my phone for the thousandth time today. Still no texts from him.

It was eight thirty, and I noted that he still had a half hour before his practice ended. It was dark outside, but the lampposts illuminated the parking lot. There were only about fifteen cars left in the massive parking lot, probably most of them from the basketball team. Did Cameron bring his own vehicle tonight?

"I'm leaving. I'm not waiting," I muttered under my breath as I stashed my phone in my purse. When I looked up, I gasped.

Cameron was leaning against the side of my car, waiting for me. He had his hoodie up, covering his face, but I knew it was him. There was no way I wouldn't recognize that devil-may-care way of his stance, the confidence in his movements as he pushed away from my car.

He looked up, and the need I saw in his gaze spoke to me more than his words, but then he masked it quickly, hiding himself from me again.

This is not going to work.

"I didn't expect you to," he said, "but I hoped you would wait anyway."

I swallowed the lump in my throat. He'd heard me.

"I thought you had practice tonight," I said.

"I did."

"You didn't go?"

He didn't answer. I closed my eyes, praying for patience.

"If you're not going to talk," I said under my breath, "just go. I want to go home."

"I don't know why the fuck I can't let you go," he said suddenly.

My chest felt tight.

"I—"

My phone pinged with a text and he stopped whatever he was going to say. Then his eyes narrowed.

"Same guy who texted you this morning?" His voice was cold again. How fast he switched moods. "I know I was gone for a few weeks, but I didn't expect you to move on so fast." It was a statement. He believed it. "Makes me fucking wonder if I should even be here."

He raked his hands through his hair as he looked down at the ground. When he looked up, his eyes were accusing.

My temper ignited. "Go to hell!"

I had no idea where he was coming from. *I don't*

know why the fuck I'm here? And that look he gave me made me furious. As if I had no right to move on, as if I cheated on him when he was the one who left. We weren't even in a relationship.

Makes me fucking wonder if I should even be here? He might as well have told me I wasn't worth it. It fucking hurt. I couldn't go on like this. This had to end.

"I wish I hadn't met you," I said softly.

He looked stunned for a moment, and whatever emotion followed was shadowed when he lowered his eyes from me.

"I was fine before I met you," I said. "You're confusing me, but worse than that is you're hurting me. And I feel so pathetic because I've been so careful, so fucking careful, protecting myself from people like you. But you're so good, so convincing, because in such a short amount of time, I let you in my life. You asked me to trust you, but you won't give the same thing you're asking of me. You're hot one minute, then cold the next. You say one thing that touches my heart, but then you break it by not saying anything at all—by *disappearing* without a word.

"I wish you didn't tell me any of those lies that night before you left," I continued. "I wish you'd just left, then it would've made it easier for me to forget about you. Then I wouldn't have to worry or feel like I've done something wrong to push you away. I wouldn't have to miss you or keep expecting you to text or call."

I was showing him my heart again, opening it up so he could shred it…again. Why didn't I learn? But he had to know, and maybe after this, it would be over. And the thought that it would be over scared me. So I got angrier to mask the fear and fought harder.

"If this is a game you're playing," I continued, my voice breaking, "just stop. I know you don't feel the same way about me, and I'm not saying this to burden you. It's my fault too. I built you up in my head, expected things I shouldn't. And I'm responsible for my own feelings. But now I just want all of this to stop. I don't want to care about you anymore. It's heartbreaking to care about you. You make it so hard. So just fucking stop. Get the hell away from me."

I got in my car, slammed the door closed. My tires squealed as I drove out of the parking lot. And this time, I didn't look back.

When I parked in front of the local gymnasium, my anger had left me, replaced by a whole lot of tiredness and numbness. Today had been a long day, as usual, but the emotional storm that Cameron brought into my life felt more exhausting.

I grabbed my phone and read the text message Deb had sent while I was in the parking lot with Cameron. She gave me a date when I could start and I replied yes.

I slid out of my car and walked to the gym entrance. I saw my dad priming the poop-brown walls with white.

"Hi, Dad."

He jumped, the paint roller almost jumping out of his hand. We were jumpers in the family. Even Dylan was—most especially Dylan.

"You scared the bejesus out of me!"

"Sorry." I laughed and the sound made me wince. It

sounded rough. I dropped my backpack on the floor and crossed to him.

The gymnasium was probably over five thousand square feet. It was old, dark, and dingy. The new white walls would definitely light it up. It was unfortunate that they had built rooms near the entrance, where it disrupted the flow of the space. If they took down those walls and moved them to the rear, beside the stage, it would open everything up. It was huge. I wondered how long it would take my dad to finish painting. And how tired he'd be.

"Where's your helper, Dad?"

He dipped the paint roller in the pan. "He just left. Jamie phoned him, and she said their kid's pretty sick."

"I hope Junior's okay," I said. "He was just eating ice cream with his daddy in town when I saw him last."

"Junior will be fine. Boy's as healthy as a horse. Takes after his pa." He ran the paint roller on the wall expertly. Up, down. Up, down. He looked over his shoulder at me, smiling. "Been a long time since we went for ice cream, eh, Kara Koala?"

I nodded. I pushed up the sleeves of my sweater, retied my hair in a bird's nest on top of my head, picked up the other roller, dipped it in the paint, and slapped that shit on the wall.

We worked for a while, my dad piling on his dad jokes, me laughing uproariously. My shoulders and legs were screaming from the activity, but I knew my dad's muscles were worse. Last time I gave him a massage, they were as hard as bricks.

"You laugh, but your eyes look sad," he said suddenly, not looking at me. "You ever going to tell me what's going on?"

I took a deep breath and kept painting. "What did you want to be when you were a kid, Dad?"

"Oh, well. Let's see." He blew out a breath. "I guess I wanted to be a race car driver."

I threw him a look. "You would've been a great race car driver, Dad."

He blushed. "Thanks, baby girl."

"You didn't pursue it because she got pregnant with me," I said. "Right?"

Now I really felt sad.

"I wanted you more than I wanted to drive fast cars," he said simply. He stopped painting for a moment and looked at me. "Whatever choices I made in life, good or bad, they were mine and mine alone. And if I didn't choose whatever it is, it's because I didn't want it bad enough. And I chose you and your mom."

"But she left you anyway."

He shrugged. "She left you too. And Dyl. That's her choice. You see? She wanted that man bad enough to leave us. And she went for it. The one thing that made me really angry at the time was that she hurt you and Dylan."

"And you. Her loss."

He nodded. "That's right."

"Are you sorry you stayed? I mean, you could've been anything you wanted if it weren't for us dragging you down. I knew from Charity that you were going to race cars. You had your sponsors; you'd been training. And then my mother happened."

He shook his head. "Haven't you been listening to me, Kara?" He studied my face for a moment. "Tell me what's really bothering you."

I took a deep breath, let it out. Took another one.

"I'm confused. I want something really bad, but I'm not sure if it's the right thing for me, Dad. Actually, I keep telling myself it's wrong, and maybe it is, but how come my heart feels so tired but my heart is still looking for it? The truth is maybe I just want to make it right, but it's really wrong." I let out a humorless laugh. "I don't make sense, do I?"

He placed his roller on the plastic sheet on the floor, held out his hand so I could give him mine. He placed my roller next to his.

"Let's have a seat on the bleachers," he said, gesturing to the other side of the gymnasium. "I want to tell you something."

"All right."

We sat beside each other, and he was quiet for a moment. I could feel that he was trying to gather his thoughts, wrapping them in a neat bow before presenting them to me. My dad had always been careful with his words.

"Kara," he started. "You have to fight for the things you want in this life. Fight for them with everything you've got because there will be a lot of people who will try to stop you. Your worst enemy is yourself.

"It's not a bad thing to want a good life," he continued. "For your family, for you. It's not a bad thing to want to reach for your dreams and do everything you can to achieve them. But do them with a good heart and a clear conscience."

He sighed long and deep, letting it out in a steady stream of air.

"You know the bad things in life you've experienced? The most despicable thing you can do is do the same bad things to other people that were done to you. Because you already know what it feels like, you know the suffering more than anyone, and yet you choose to do it to others. Life can beat you up real bad, sweetheart, but don't let your heart harden to the point where you've lost it. To me, that's disgraceful and heartbreaking."

I wondered if he was talking about my ma. I knew it had broken his heart when she left.

"Learn to forgive so you can move on to the greater things that are waiting, that are meant for you to grab with both your hands. Once you've grabbed them, hold on to them as hard as you can. No matter how difficult or confusing. If your mind and your heart are at war, make a choice. Pick the one that you want bad enough, the one that you'll regret most if you didn't."

"I will," I told him, my voice rough.

"I know it. I forgave your ma a long time ago. How can I stay mad when she gave you and Dylan to me? The one thing I don't want you to be is sad. Whatever it is, I want you to be happy. The last person who will stop you from doing what you want is me. Go for it. Go for whatever it is. Dylan and I will survive. I know you're worried about the shop. What will happen will happen. Are you worried about taking this other job? You know Charity likes to help us out. She'll fill in when you're away. And if she can't, you know we boys can manage. Don't worry too much. Be a kid, be a grown-up, be a woman, but most of all, be you. Just be you. Whatever it is that you want, that's what I want you to be."

I was so exhausted by the time Dad and I got home. Dylan had cooked potatoes, chicken, and rice, but I was barely awake. I skipped dinner and showered, brushed my teeth, and went straight to bed. Before I closed my eyes, I couldn't resist grabbing my phone. I checked my messages. I had messages from Tala and Thomas.

But none from Cameron.

I just felt numb and so worn-out.

Thomas: My patient just offered me a thousand dollars to go on a date with her.

I sent him a reply and closed my eyes.

I didn't pick up Cameron the next morning. The lack of texts from him told me a lot and, at the same time, told me nothing. When I passed by the lecture halls at school, he wasn't there.

When my supervisor at the nursing home phoned that night, I took the shift they needed covered without hesitation. I had work at The Yard the next day, but the shift at the nursing home was only for four hours tonight, and I could come home after that and nap for five hours, then attend my morning classes before driving to The Yard. It would work out. It always did.

The next day came and I convinced myself to feel excited, to see that the day was sunnier and that everything would be okay. It was my official first day at The Yard. I went to my morning classes, hoping that I'd see Tala this time, but she texted and said she still couldn't make it to campus today. I wanted to phone her and find out what was going on, but she said she would be out all day and would let me know soon what was going on.

I told myself to not look for Cameron, but I did anyway. Like Thomas said, accept that the feelings I had for him were real and it would take time, but I'd get over him eventually. I had to believe that I would.

My phone vibrated.

Thomas: Break a leg on your first day!

I texted him a quick thanks and drove to work. We'd sat together in church and had gone out for coffee after with Tala. He'd been a good friend and I was thankful, especially right now. I'd sensed a loneliness in him behind his easygoing smiles. Maybe that was why I allowed him in my circle. I was drawn to people masking their loneliness with laughter. Maybe because I was like that too.

The Yard was noticeably less busy when I pulled up to the office. Employees had a designated parking space at the back of the building, which I was grateful for. I imagined myself getting out of my car just as an eighteen-wheeler came barreling through and making me a splatter in the dirt. Or food for the birds. Yummy.

Deb was less busy this time. She introduced me to everyone in the office and showed me where everything was. When we entered the storage room where Cameron took me to get my hard hat, I felt sad all of a sudden.

I hadn't seen him or heard from him since that scene in the parking lot. It was only two nights before, but it seemed longer. Sooner or later, I knew I'd see him at The Yard. Or maybe not. Maybe he'd pull another disappearing act. He should join the circus. Then maybe he could disappear forever in one of those disappearing magic tricks.

You miss him.

Was there any point denying it? It wasn't going to work out anyway. I needed more than what he could give me, and I didn't want to force him to give more than what he was ready to give because he might resent me eventually.

And I didn't want to stay with him when he couldn't trust me because I might resent him eventually.

My heart ached thinking about him. I was tired of thinking about him.

"You did horrible on your first day," Deb said in a sarcastic tone, patting my back. There was a playful smile on her face. "Make sure you come back on your shift this weekend, you hear? I won't accept anyone else to take my place."

I laughed. "Yes, ma'am."

It was almost the end of my first day. It had been fantastic. I really liked Deb. She was a sharp lady, with a dry humor that I appreciated. She had to leave fifteen minutes early today to see her doctor. Her husband was already waiting for her outside.

"You catch on quickly. I like that. So, listen, it's up to you if you want to stay and file or you can leave now. Just make sure you clock out. I'll see you on Saturday."

"Bright and early," I said. "Thanks a lot, Deb."

She stroked her stomach, pushed up from her chair with a groan. Grabbing her purse, she waved goodbye to everyone who was left at the office. There was only me and Jerika manning the desks, and two other guys in the conference room. I watched Deb as she waddled out of the office with that adorable pregnant-lady walk.

She opened the front door, and just before it closed someone stepped inside.

Cameron's eyes met mine.

He held my gaze captive. One thought after another raced through my mind in the three seconds that we looked at each other.

One second.

I miss you.

Two seconds.

I hate you.

Three seconds.

I fucking miss you.

Then I yanked my gaze away and looked down at the files in front of me, seeing nothing but his face in my mind.

God, he looked so damn beautiful. That black T-shirt again that molded to the contours of his upper arms and chest, the dark, dirty jeans, the steel-toed boots, the hard hat. A working man's clothes. A beautiful archangel's face.

Of course he'd be here. This was his workplace too, but I hadn't seen him at school or at work all day. To see him now was so unexpected.

My phone vibrated.

Thomas: Be there in ten minutes. Finishing up my charting. There's a café close by. Let's go there and you can tell me all about the progress of your friend's problem.

I focused on Thomas's text message, but my brain wasn't absorbing it. I read it again. His work was a three-minute drive from The Yard. Since I was done with work, I agreed to meet him for coffee. He texted back and said the café was hard to find and offered to pick me up instead, so I wouldn't get lost. I'd save on gas money, so I agreed.

I looked up again, but I couldn't find Cameron anywhere. When it was time, I gathered my things and clocked out. I stepped out of the building, my heart skipping a beat as I remembered that moment when Cameron covered my eyes when the sun was too bright.

This time there was no sun. And there was no Cameron.

Thomas pulled up in front of the office. He waved to me, smiling. I waved back. I was just about to walk to his car when a firm hand wrapped around my wrist. I looked up and found an angry Cameron.

"Are you getting in that guy's car?" His eyes looked hard, his voice cold.

I raised my chin. "Yes!"

"Who is he?"

"It's none of your—"

"Kara," he said softly. Was it my imagination or was there pleading I heard in his voice? "Don't go."

My heart. My heart. Please don't give in now.

"Why?"

"Because I don't want you to go with him."

There was a ringing in my ears. The hope and delight I felt from his words only made me angrier. More at myself now than him.

"Sorry, boss. I'm done with my shift. Now let me the hell go."

I shook him off, and he released me. With wooden legs, I walked to Thomas's car and got in the passenger seat. I could feel Cameron's eyes drilling a hole in my back.

"Kara," Thomas said carefully. "Is that your boyfriend? I mean your *friend's* boyfriend?"

"Yeah." I strapped my seat belt on, refusing to look to see if Cameron was still there. My hands were shaking. "That's him."

"I think I made a huge mistake," Thomas whispered.

"What do you mean?"

"I like you as a friend, but I don't know if I want to get beat up by that. He's a monster. He looks like he wants to break all of my bones, then feed them to the dogs."

"That's why you have to step on the gas and let's fly the fuck out of here."

He let out a nervous laugh. "Good idea."

I wanted to look back, wanted to know if he was still there, watching us drive away. I wanted to know why he stopped me, why he said those things he did. And why he didn't say the things I wanted him to say.

"Go back," I said.

"What?" Thomas threw me a glance.

"I'm sorry, Thomas. Head back to the yard. I have to ask him something."

"I knew it." He sighed. "You always have this sad look in your eyes every time I see you. If he's the only one who can remove that sadness, if he's the only one who can make you happy, go for it. I'll support you as a friend and drive you back."

I reached for his hand on the steering wheel and squeezed.

"Thank you, Thomas."

My heart jumped when I saw Cameron still standing in the same spot, as if he knew I was going to come back.

Make a choice, my dad said.

Then I will.

Chapter 25

Cameron

SHE WAS COMING BACK. SHE HAD TO, BECAUSE IF SHE DIDN'T, I was going after her.

There was no way I would let her go. Not with that guy. Not with *any* guy.

Not yet.

Not *ever*.

Did she expect me to let her go?

She probably did. She probably thought I had let her go completely when I left. And for a while, I had fooled myself that I could. That I did.

But one look at her that day in Rick's office and all thoughts about letting her go went out the window.

Being with me might complicate her life more than it was already. She was already struggling, I could see that as clear as day. But I was selfish. I was greedy. I wanted her.

I wanted her anger, her annoyance, her mean streak. Every fucking thing I could get.

I was weak when it came to her. I realized that now. Fighting it just made me a miserable son of a bitch.

I had no reason to believe that she would come back

to me. I had given her every reason to stay away, but something inside me…hoped. And kept wanting.

I stood in the middle of the yard, like a stupid motherfucker, waiting.

And hell…she said she never went out with guys. Who was that guy who picked her up? What was wrong with her car? She had an auto shop, for goddamn sake. What did she need a ride for? She could just ask me.

I fisted my hands, feeling the bite of my nails against my palms.

She had to come back.

I had sworn I wouldn't wait for anyone anymore, but she made me break that promise I had made to myself.

I could feel the sting of the wind on my skin, but I was burning up. If she wasn't going to come back, I would go to her.

I was just going to hop into my truck and chase after her when I saw the white Jeep pull up in the yard.

My chest felt tight as I watched her shoot out of the vehicle, march her way to me.

Kara.

My Kara.

My Spitfire.

The tightness loosened up a bit.

She was mad as hell. Her face was flushed, her mouth in a tight, straight line. The fire in those hazel eyes—those eyes that starred in my dreams every night—as they homed in on me raced through me like an electric shock.

She was mesmerizing and terrifying, like a big tidal wave in the middle of the ocean where your lifeboat was floating in peace. She would appear out of nowhere, swallow you whole, and obliterate every sign of you on earth.

She came back for me.

———————————

There had never been any woman who looked as beautiful to me as she did at that moment. I could not take my eyes off her.

Whatever was building between us had been destroyed when I left. But I was here now, and I was here to get her back, whatever it took.

She parked her long legs in front of me. She was breathing hard, and it wasn't because of the distance she'd walked. It was her anger toward me. I'd take it. I'd take anything.

She raised her chin defiantly and looked down her nose at me.

She couldn't hide her emotions if she tried. Somehow, it always came out—whatever she was feeling, whatever she was thinking. I couldn't fucking get enough of it.

"Give me a reason why I should stay here with you," she demanded.

I looked at her. And I told her the truth.

"I miss you," I whispered. "I miss you so much it's driving me fucking crazy."

Her eyes softened, but she didn't move. I knew it was going to be hard convincing her to be with me. I expected it, but I wasn't going to give up easily. Not this time.

"Let me fix it," I said, but it was a plea. My voice sounded gruff to my ears.

She just looked at me, not saying anything. It started

to scare me. Was she going back to that guy? Was he the guy who was texting and calling her?

Over my dead fucking body.

I held out my hand to her. "Will you take my hand?" I said softly. "Kara?"

I saw her take a deep breath, close her eyes for a moment. And when she opened them, she placed her hand in mine.

We were on the road a moment later. I insisted we use my company truck. It was a little cold outside, so we had the windows closed. I was driving toward the one place no one knew I had. If there was anyone I wanted to show it to, it would be her.

She faced the passenger window, not giving me a glimpse of her lovely face. She was still mad at me. I couldn't blame her. I hadn't answered any of her questions.

"Where are we going?" she finally asked. And still she wouldn't look at me.

"You said you barely know me," I started.

Now she faced me. I wished I could park somewhere, so I could just hold her face in my hands, feel her skin, and just look at her, Touch her. Kiss her. Taste her.

"So I'll take you to a place that's important to me," I finished.

She looked intrigued. Good. But she turned and faced the window again.

If my chest felt tight again, I ignored it. She was here with me. That was all that mattered.

"Who was that guy?" I asked.

"I'm not answering any of your questions until you answer mine," she told the window.

"Fair enough."

I tapped the steering wheel. I felt itchy, spoiling for a fight. Preferably with that guy she wouldn't tell me about.

"Kara." Damn, I could hear the impatience in my voice.

"Yes?"

"Who was that guy?"

Now she laughed. A knowing, teasing laugh only a woman could make. She threw me a look. "Wouldn't you like to know?"

Damn, she had a mean streak. And damn if I didn't crave it. I was miserable without it when I left. But right now, it was driving me crazy.

"Ask me something you want to know then," I told her.

She faced the window again. Dismissing me.

That hurt. She didn't want to know anything about me anymore. Had I damaged everything between us? Didn't she want me anymore?

"Tell me why you left," she said after a moment.

She said it so softly, her voice so maddeningly small, that my chest ached.

"I'll show you when we get to where we're going. Will you wait till then?" I asked.

She nodded but, again, didn't say anything. Did that mean she wouldn't tell me about that guy until we were there?

I sighed loudly, blowing my hair off my forehead.

"He's just a friend from church," she said. I heard a smile in her voice.

"He's not…your boyfriend?"

"Well…"

I shot her a look. Her hazel eyes were full of mischief. Just the way I liked it, but not when she was torturing me like this. Not about another guy.

"Do you see now how it can drive you crazy not knowing what I'm thinking? When I won't tell you anything?"

I kept my mouth shut. She got me there. I knew it. I knew it now.

"It's frustrating, isn't it? Doesn't it make you want to assume things? Make you feel awful that you're contemplating the worst?"

"Yes," I said.

"I won't know what you're thinking if you don't tell me."

"Okay," I murmured. "I understand."

She seemed placated by that because she said, "He is a boy friend."

"What?"

"A guy friend. I like him."

"You. Like. Him."

"Yeah," she said cheekily. "I like him."

Her tone said *What are you going to do about it, big guy?*

"I could crush him like nothing," I growled.

She laughed. A very feminine laugh that did something below my stomach.

"You sound like a jealous boyfriend."

"I *am* your boyfriend."

Her eyes widened in shock. "What? No, you're not!"

She was right, but that hurt a little. She didn't sound

repulsed by the idea, so I figured I still had a chance. I'd have to convince her.

"You don't have a boyfriend."

"Not *yet*."

She was teasing me, baiting me to respond. She knew I was jealous, and this was driving me crazy, but she wouldn't show any mercy.

I guessed I deserved that. Again, I wisely kept my mouth shut.

She was wearing another dress today. It was pale pink, and she'd paired it with black stockings—the *sheer* kind. The kind that drove a man wild.

My eyes roved down to her legs. She had long, long legs. Shapely ones. The skirt of her dress rode high above her upper thighs, showing the little sweet V shape where the length of her legs met. My hands itched to touch.

"I'm hungry," she said suddenly.

I sucked at my bottom lip. *Me too.*

"I have"—Jesus, my voice sounded rough—"some food in my cooler. It's in the back."

"You bring a cooler to work?" There was curiosity in her voice. I didn't realize how much it meant to me that she wanted to know me until she took it away earlier.

"I have to eat something every hour or so," I answered. "I get hungry a lot."

I could feel her eyes travel down my body.

"I could see that." She muttered something else under her breath that sounded like "Is that why you're big?" but I couldn't hear her properly.

She unbuckled her seat belt and shifted so she could reach over the back seat, her arm accidentally grazing mine. I clenched my jaw.

When she returned to her seat, she placed the cooler on her lap. She didn't seem affected by that little contact. At all.

"Seat belt," I growled.

She ignored me and opened the cooler.

"Whoa. Did you put your fridge in here or what?"

"I'm pulling over if you don't put your seat belt on."

"Fine." But it took her another minute before she did it.

"Holy crap. These are some monster sandwiches. What kind are these?"

I rarely cooked and I wasn't very good at it either. I usually just slapped some bread, a lot of lean meat, and cheese together and called it a meal. There were probably five big sandwiches in the cooler. I wasn't kidding when I told her I got hungry every hour.

"Ham, chicken. I don't know. Food stuff," I said.

"I'm vegetarian."

"What's a vegetarian?"

She glared at me for a moment, staring at my face, then laughed. "I'm serious. I'm hungry," she grumbled.

"There's a service station up ahead. I'll get you something there," I said.

She grabbed something in her purse, squirted something in her hand, and rubbed it all over them. It smelled like alcohol and peaches. A hand sanitizer probably.

"So what should I get you?" I asked, wanting to keep her talking. The sadness in her voice was fading. I wanted her to be happy, like she was before. With me. "I'm not sure if they serve smoked wild alfalfa sprouts a la carte there, but I'll try."

She pinched my arm.

"Ouch!"

That hurt. That really hurt. She wasn't pulling any punches. I rubbed my arm, then quickly returned my hand to the steering wheel.

"When I'm hungry, I become the Hulk. Don't joke around. I'm serious."

I glanced at her and saw the little pout on her lips. Damn she was cute. I missed her. I missed her a damned lot.

She was pulling the sandwiches apart, checking what was in them. "You have an egg sandwich?"

"I thought vegetarians don't eat eggs?"

"You're thinking of vegans. They don't eat animal products at all. I'm a vegetarian. There are different kinds. My kind eats eggs, milk, and cheese."

I shrugged. "All right." But I made a note of it.

"So, any egg sandwiches here?" She was still rummaging.

"That means boiling eggs, so no."

She sighed.

"There are peaches," I said quietly. I wondered if she'd figure out I ate them because of her, then I realized there was no way she'd know. "At the bottom of the cooler. Keep looking."

"No way. Cool."

I heard her biting on one, then she moaned.

My mouth watered.

"Omigod, these are so ripe. Yummy," she said happily.

"Give me one. I'm hungry now too."

I wasn't sure if she would. We'd been apart for weeks, and I wasn't sure how she would react to such an intimate request.

When she offered it to me, I felt something warm inside my chest.

I took a big bite, my tongue grazing her finger. She pulled away, and I could feel her intense gaze on my face. I pretended not to notice. I chewed, swallowed.

"Again," I said.

"No." She pulled away. She hadn't forgiven me yet. I understood. But it made me…sad. And dampened the happy mood we had.

It was all right. I would fix it soon.

"My hands are sticky. I need tissues," she said and opened my glove box. I heard her sharp inhale. She reached for something inside it.

"I saw you wearing this on Monday," she said. "Did you miss me that much?"

She had the blue hair tie I stole from her in her hand. It had been a month ago, but it seemed longer than that. My eyes shifted to hers. Her hazel eyes were glittering. *Grass green*, I thought with a hitch in my heart, *more than brown*.

"Yes," I said gruffly.

"Then why…"

"I was an idiot. I'm sorry, Kara," I whispered.

I swallowed the tightness in my throat. I wanted to pull to the side of the road, park there, so I could right the wrongs that happened between us.

"You made me worry," she said.

"I'm sorry." It seemed such an inconsequential word. I wanted to show her how I felt, not say it.

"I don't want your sorry," she said. "I want an explanation."

I stopped myself from rubbing a hand over my

face. "I'll tell you what I can when we reach our destination."

She quieted, content for now. She wouldn't be for long.

The thought of opening up made my heart flip in my chest.

I had seen psychiatrists when I was a kid. My dad had insisted that Raven send me to see professionals after the incident when I was eight. When Raven refused, he threatened to take custody of me. That scared her into action.

All of the doctors I'd seen tried their best to make me talk about what happened, but I had refused. In fact, I hadn't talked for a couple of years after the incident.

I still didn't want to. But for Kara I would try.

It hurt to talk about it. Every time I thought about it or tried to talk about it, it felt like there was a pit of nothingness in my stomach and acid was filling it up.

She perked up in her seat when I turned my signal on, slowed down, and pulled up to a service station.

"What do you want to eat?" I unbuckled my seat belt, grabbed my wallet from the compartment in the middle console. "I'll get it. Stay here."

"I'll go with you," she said and simply jumped out of the truck.

I smiled. She didn't like to be told what to do and would do the opposite if I even brought it up.

She looked exhausted. I wondered if she'd been picking up shifts at the nursing home again, if she'd quit her job at the coffee shop. Hopefully now that she worked for Rick, that would lessen.

"How long is the drive to this place?" she asked as she went straight to the small eatery beside the service station.

"About another hour."

Her eyes widened in alarm. "What? What time do you expect us to go home tonight?"

"I'll take you home."

"I thought it was a half hour away or something. What about my car?"

"It'll be there in the morning. I'll give you a ride. Don't worry about it. Grab your snacks and let's go."

"Don't tell me what to do."

"Fine." I hid my smile.

I'd keep telling her what to do. I wouldn't be able to help it just as she wouldn't be able to help throwing it back to my face. It was perfect.

"Fine," she said, just for the hell of it.

She always wanted the last word. With me, anyway.

She took her time, and I could tell it was because she was still upset. She could be exasperating, but even that I liked about her. I liked everything about her.

I bought a few things from the convenience store and stored them in the back seat. She munched on tofu hot dogs and sweet potato fries when we were back on the road.

"I like that they had that small eatery beside the service station."

"It's for truck drivers mainly."

She nodded, took a big bite of her hot dog bun. "The older woman who owns it said her husband was a truck driver, and she knew how hard it was to find a hot meal on the road, so she'd set up the eatery. Isn't that nice?"

"You got all that from buying your hot dog and fries?"

She sipped her drink. "You'd be surprised what people will tell you if you ask."

I kept quiet.

"Are we there yet?" she asked.

"No."

"How long still?"

"As long as it takes."

"Come on. Tell me."

She tugged on my shirt and I threw her a look. She was smiling like a little girl. She was playing with me.

"I hope this night doesn't end," I whispered.

"Sorry, what did you say?"

She didn't hear me. "Soon," I said instead.

"I'm feeling sleepy, Cameron."

My throat felt tight. She said my name. She must be really tired because I hadn't heard her say my name for what felt like a long time.

"Go ahead and take a nap. I'll wake you when we get there."

I thought that she had fallen asleep, but she mumbled something. Maybe she was dreaming. Her voice was too low, and I couldn't hear her. And then she said it again.

"I missed you too."

As I drove farther away from the city, the heavy, black cloud that had been following me dissolved. The last time I felt this good was the last time she'd smiled at me, weeks ago.

I glanced down at the woman beside me. She was sleeping and snoring lightly. And I realized why all the bad stuff seemed to be pushed away. It wasn't because we were going far from the city, but because she was right beside me.

She'd been the reason all along.

My heart jerked in my chest as I slowed down on the street of my childhood. A very short part of my childhood, but the one that would always be a part of me. The one that changed me.

"Are we there?" she asked.

She'd woken up ten minutes ago and had been sipping the now-cold coffee I bought for her at the service station. It was ten minutes past six in the evening now, but it was still a little bright outside.

I nodded, gauging the reaction on her face as I pressed a small square remote and the gates opened. They opened smoothly, soundlessly. They were the first thing I'd installed. I wanted protection for it. A symbol to everyone that someone now owned the place.

I pulled up the long, winding driveway and pressed the remote again to close the gate behind us. I had planted huge pine trees on both sides of the driveway and all around the property a few years ago. They'd grown tall and wide, and not only served as protection, but as walls from the outside, hiding the place from passersby. I'd posted *PRIVATE PROPERTY* and *NO TRESPASSING* signs all along the old, black iron fence.

"Wow. It looks like we're going to visit a vampire," she said excitedly.

"Could be werewolves too."

"Really?" she chuckled. "It's so…secluded. What is this place? Who owns it?"

"I do."

"What?"

"I bought this place a few years ago. As soon as I saved enough money for it."

"Really? Someday I want to buy my own place too. Maybe even something like this if I won the lottery. How much did you—Omigod, is that…? Wow." She goggled. I wondered what she thought of it. "I don't think I've ever been inside a mansion before. Are we going inside? It's haunted, isn't it? We should definitely go inside. Hurry up."

I chuckled. She looked like an excited little girl about to open her presents. I didn't know what reaction I'd expected from her, but I never thought she'd be delighted to see it.

It was a derelict manor. I had only started fixing it. I'd had it since forever, but I'd always put off repairing it.

But when I'd left her, I started like a madman.

"Can we take a look at it later?" I asked. "I want to show you something first."

"You mean there's something more interesting than this?"

"Yeah," I said. "I'll show you."

"It better be good, Bigfoot."

I smiled at her and she smiled back.

I kept driving, following the paved road that led behind the mansion. Here, the trees were thicker and older. The paved road turned into a narrow gravel path until we reached a clearing. And then it gave way to a large open backfield.

There in the middle of it stood a small modern cabin. I'd renovated it over the years. It had been the game-keeper's cottage before and wasn't in as bad a condition as the mansion, but I wanted to put my stamp on it. I had ripped everything out and started with bare bones.

Now it was an A-frame structured cabin, with a slender metal roof slanting to the ground on both sides like a tent. The wall-to-wall privacy glass had cost a fortune, but it was worth every penny when I woke up in the morning to find the interior bathed in natural light and the view of the open field spread out before me.

"I love it," she said softly, her eyes warming as she took in the building and the view behind it, which is where I wanted to bring her. "It looks so modern but warm. I love the black trim and the stained-wood exterior walls. I love the front deck. Maybe you could put a couple of rocking chairs there. What's behind it?"

I parked the vehicle in front of the cabin. The porch lights flicked on, bathing the cabin in warm light.

I hadn't answered her question yet when she asked another one. "Is this where you…went off to when you left?"

"Yeah," I answered. "It's where I thought of you. A lot."

She became pensive.

"But it's not what I brought you here to see."

"Okay," she said. "Show me."

She got out of the vehicle before I'd even unbuckled my seat belt. I watched as she shivered her way to my side of the car, waiting for me. She wrapped her arms around her middle, rubbing her sides. The wind blew her hair, covering parts of her face.

My heart ached as I watched her.

She knocked on my window impatiently. I chuckled, grabbing the blanket I kept in the back seat before I stepped out of the truck.

She'd already started walking ahead of me.

"Kara," I called out.

She looked over her shoulder, and I could tell she was feeling sad.

"Come here," I said.

A small frown marred her brow. "Why?"

"Please."

I hated saying *please*. But for her I didn't mind.

It seemed to placate her somehow. She hesitated at first, but she stepped forward once, twice, until she was walking toward me, and stopped an arm's length away.

I stepped forward. I saw her shift back, and I could see that her walls were up again.

Our truce was over. And she was expecting payback.

I wrapped the blanket around her shoulders. She let out a relieved sigh.

"Thanks," she mumbled, tightening the blanket around her.

I nodded. She was always welcome.

"Come with me," I said.

I was going to show her the maze. And what happened just beyond it that changed the course of my life.

Chapter 26

Cameron

"COME WITH ME." I WANTED TO ASK FOR HER HAND, FEEL HER fingers seeking mine once more, but I could tell from the way she held the blanket tight around her that she wouldn't welcome my touch at this moment.

It made me anxious. If I told her what happened just beyond this maze, would she run away from me?

Should I even tell her?

Maybe this wasn't such a good idea.

Too late now, motherfucker.

Yeah, that's right. We were already here, and I had promised her I would tell her.

My heart pounded. The night air was a little chilly, but I felt the sweat break out on my forehead, trickle down the side of my face.

"What is this place?" she asked as she walked beside me. I led her to the back of the cabin.

"It's a maze."

Her jaw dropped, then she smiled. "Wow. Do you have a treasure map?"

"I can make one for you," I said.

I would have smiled and would have enjoyed showing her around if we were in different circumstances.

I stopped just at the entrance of the maze. I'd put up a trellis there. It was too cold for the flowers now, but thick, brown vines wrapped around the structure.

The maze was as it always had been—massive, beautiful, secretive. The tightly packed greenery was high and dense, making it almost impossible to squeeze in between. When I was a kid, I could squeeze my way through in certain spots, but now it was impossible. I'd tried.

"They say this maze is cursed," I told her.

I glanced at her to see her reaction. I wondered if it would spook her, but her smile had turned into a grin.

"What are we waiting for?" she said, her eyes sparkling. "Let's go in."

Damn. She's fucking awesome.

"Who else knows about this place?" she asked. "I mean…have you brought anyone else—"

"Just you."

I stepped forward, then stopped in my tracks when I felt her hand reach for mine.

I looked down at our joined hands, then up at her. This was the first time she'd willingly touched me after I left.

"I'm glad. Cameron," she said, "if you're not ready to tell me, I understand."

Something warm and tight was forming inside my chest as I looked at her. What was she doing to me?

I grew up being very careful not to show anyone what was important to me. I had to keep everything locked inside me tightly, securely. Because once you showed the world what you valued, they got you by the balls. The world would know your weakness. And the world would use it against you. The world always did. You'd be crippled. Then where would you be?

"Why are you looking at me like that?" she asked.

"Like what?" I asked hoarsely.

"Like…you don't know what to do with me."

Because something was changing, I realized. It wasn't just a small shift. And I had no idea what to do about it. Because when I looked at Kara's face, her eyes, so honest, so damn real, and strong and good, it made me believe the world had a place just for me. And this time, it was something that was good.

"I'm wondering if you're real."

She didn't speak for a moment, then she smiled. "It was hard getting you to open up to me. Damn near impossible," she admitted. "I'm happy that you brought me here. It's a start."

I tried not to show it, but I wondered if she'd seen by the expression on my face how hard this was for me.

I closed my eyes, brought her hand to my lips, and kissed her palm. She was so warm.

I wondered why in all those years I had never talked about what had happened just beyond this maze and why I wanted to now.

"You don't have to tell me now. Whatever it is. You can tell me when you're ready," she said, her voice low and gentle.

I looked in her hazel eyes, saw the understanding and strength. And I knew. I had been waiting for her to come in my life.

I didn't know why these thoughts were in my head, and right now, the *why* wasn't important. She was beside me. That's what mattered.

"I want to tell *you*," I said gruffly.

"All right."

We stepped inside the maze and started our trek. When we reached the part where the trees formed a canopy, shielding the ground from the elements, she stopped.

"It's beautiful," she said, her eyes wide as she released my hand and twirled around slowly to take in her surroundings. "A little creepy when I see the dark parts ahead, but seriously beautiful. Is this maze the reason why you bought this land?"

It helped that she was asking me questions. I didn't know where to start.

"A huge part of it, yeah," I answered. "Kara?"

"Hmm?"

"I'm glad you're here with me."

Was it too much to tell her that? Was it too fast?

The smile on her pretty mouth was everything sweet and soft.

"I made a choice," she said, reaching for my hand again. "And I chose to fight for you."

She had no clue—absolutely no clue—how much that meant to me.

Not too fast. Just right. Just damn right.

I stopped, gently pulled at her hand to prevent her from walking away from me. I turned to face her, wanting to touch her face. Wondering if she'd let me.

"I know I hurt you," I whispered, realizing how easily I could get lost in her eyes. "I'm so fucking sorry for what I did."

She bit her bottom lip. My eyes focused on it. It had been a long time since I felt her body, had her taste on my tongue. The last time I kissed her only intensified my hunger.

I couldn't stop myself. I pulled her closer. I heard her

sharp intake of breath as I wrapped my arm around her small waist and drew her against my body.

"I'm hungry, Kara," I said roughly.

She swallowed. Her eyes had turned glassy as they dropped to my lips.

"Can I?" I murmured.

Her gaze lifted to mine. "Yes."

I watched the play of emotions on her face. I was anticipating the things I could do to her, the pleasure I could give her. The last time I had her on top of me didn't go well.

I was too hungry for her, almost desperate to be inside her, and I had let that desire control me and had forgotten that she hadn't done it before.

I wouldn't make the same mistake twice.

It was all about her now.

And hell if it didn't make me feel like a damned caveman that she'd let me be the first to touch her.

I knew this maze like the back of my hand. Behind her was a small secret passage. It was a narrow space, a cocoon surrounded by high and dense shrubs and trees. There was a bench there where I could lay her down and kiss her until she was writhing in pleasure. And until I've had my fill.

I had a feeling that day wouldn't come anytime soon. Maybe not ever.

I placed my hands below her ass, squeezing, wanting my fingers to go higher, find and play with her wet heat, but I'd wait until she was ready.

I tightened my grip on the back of her thighs and hitched her up. Her long legs wrapped around my waist as I walked us into the passage. She placed her chin on my shoulder, hiding her face from me.

Was she embarrassed?

The dress she had on rode high on her hips. Damn, I loved it when she wore a dress or a skirt. It was easy access and made me imagine what she'd do, what her alluring face would look like when I touched her.

"Just a kiss," she said in a soft breath.

I sprawled on the bench and groaned as she sat on top of me. I could feel her heat, wanted it on my lips, on my tongue.

I licked my bottom lip. "Just a kiss," I promised.

My hands banded on her hips, lifting the dress more so I could look at the piece of lace covering between her legs.

My hands shook. It was white lace. *Damn, damn, damn.* She couldn't have known what it would do to me.

"Kara?" I murmured in her ear.

"Hmm?"

"Where do you want me to kiss you?"

She let out a soft, little moan when I lifted my hips up against her.

"Cam," she rasped. "What are you doing to me?"

"Nothing yet." I kissed her neck, rubbing my lips on her skin, just lightly, faintly, so that she could barely feel it. "Soon."

My breath hitched against her skin when she ground her hips against me. *Fuck.*

"Shall I kiss you here?" My fingers stroked the long line of her throat, sliding down between her breasts. She closed her eyes, but her lips parted slightly.

"Or here?" I slid my finger down her stomach, stopping just below her navel. Her eyes flew open.

"Just a kiss, Kara," I murmured. "Anywhere you like."

Her legs tightened against my waist. A sign that she

was aroused. There was no question that she could feel mine. It was straining against my jeans. Soon it would start to feel more than uncomfortable. But right now, the pain felt good.

She wrapped her hands around my shoulders and buried her face in my neck. She was breathing hard. "Damn, Cameron. I want to know how to handle you."

"You are, baby," I said in her ear.

"I…want to."

"Let me taste your lips then."

I plunged my fingers in her hair, securing the back of her head as I brought her mouth down to mine.

She tasted like a woman. My woman. She tasted like a peach. Soft, juicy, sweet. I lapped at her bottom lip slowly, making a sucking sound as I drew it between my lips, biting it lightly, licking at it.

She let out a soft breath. I slipped my tongue inside her mouth, discovering her tastes, seeking more of her as I played with her tongue. She was hesitant at first, shy, and I had no idea why the hell that made me feel a rush of affection and desire for her to open up to me, share a part of herself with me willingly. I let out a moan.

She made a little noise at the back of her throat. She tangled her fingers in my hair as she licked at my mouth, sucked on my tongue just the way I had with hers, and then I lost it.

So fucking good.

Calm down. I forced myself to slow down, concentrating on her needs and not my own. If it were up to me, her dress would be ripped to shreds by now. And her legs would be on my shoulders.

My hands stroked her neck, her shoulders, then paused

just below her collarbone. Slowly so as not to spook her, I used my thumbs to stroke the delicious small swells of her breasts. When she moaned, I devoured her, slanting my mouth against hers, swirling my tongue inside her mouth again and again. My thumbs moved down and caught her nipples against the fabric, rubbing, pinching them with my fingers. I wanted to suck on them.

She yanked her mouth from mine.

"Cam!"

We were both breathing hard, but she didn't pull away. Instead, she rested her head on my shoulder.

My sweet, sweet Spitfire.

"I'll stop if that's what you want," I said, my voice thick with desire.

"I don't know if I want to stop," she breathed. She pulled back a little and looked at me. "I…I've never done this before, but I want…"

More, her eyes said. I placed a small kiss on her shoulder and smiled against her skin, letting out a long breath. If this made her speechless, we should definitely do it more.

"Did you enjoy it?" I murmured.

She nodded.

"Kara?"

"Yes?"

"I want to make you come."

She took a deep, shaky breath.

"Can I?" I asked.

She turned her head so that her cheek was resting on my shoulder and her lips were touching my neck.

I ran a fingertip down her arm. "Are you wet?"

"I…don't know," she whispered.

"Can I feel you? I want to know if you are."

She swallowed audibly. "If…if I'm what?"

"Wet," I said in her ear. "Between your legs."

She moaned again, arching her back unconsciously.

"You're…you're hard," she blurted out.

"Yeah."

"Does it…hurt?"

"Uncomfortable," I replied.

"Is it…okay?"

"My cock?"

Then she started laughing, giggling like an adorable schoolgirl who had cut classes and didn't get caught.

"Yeah," she answered, still laughing. "Is it?"

I let out a sigh. "I need to…adjust it."

"Okay?"

"Hmm. You need to get off me first. Unless you want me to continue."

She sucked in a breath and didn't say anything, but her body did. Her hips moved.

I gripped her hips, then guided her against my arousal. I sucked on my bottom lip, grinding up against her. Wanting more.

"Stop!" she said, laughing, swatting my arm playfully.

"I'm sorry," I said teasingly. "Are we finished?"

Her lashes fluttered. "Let me up, Cam."

I could feel her body yearning for my touch. But I thought of the last time I had her on top of me and what I'd promised her. I let out a long breath, lifted her up, and placed her gently on the bench. She weighed as much as a feather.

Her face was flushed, but she didn't look away, watching me as I adjusted myself in my pants.

"Better?" she asked. Her voice sounded raspy.

Not really. "Yeah," I lied.

I was sure she'd drive the hell out of here using my truck and leave me if she knew what was in my head. What I was imagining doing to her. What I was imagining her doing to me.

She got up, pulling her dress down, fixing her hair. I felt the loss of warmth and the weight of her body as I pushed up from the bench, stood beside her.

"Here," I said, handing her the blue hair tie so she could put her hair up if she wanted to.

She shook her head. "Keep it. I want you to."

I smiled and put it in my pocket. I wanted to keep it. She'd given it to me. And now she couldn't take it back.

I pushed open the wooden secret door and let her pass first. We walked for a bit. She was quiet, but she was making these little sighs now and then. I lowered my head so she wouldn't see my smile. She was thinking about what happened in the secret passage.

"Do you have any hair ties from other girls?" she blurted out suddenly.

I frowned. "No. Why would I?"

She grinned. "Good answer."

"It's not a good answer," I said, walking beside her deeper into the maze. "Or bad. It just is."

Why did she want to talk about this? Feeling uncomfortable, I stole a glance at her. Was she going to blow up later about this, or did she just genuinely want to know?

I went out with girls before, and I thought I had a pretty good idea what they were like, but with her, I never knew what was coming.

She looked at me as if she was still waiting for an answer. I reminded myself that she wanted me to open up more.

I wanted to know more about *her*. But she was right. It wasn't fair if I kept asking her for things I wasn't willing to give. I hadn't even been aware I was doing that until she mentioned it.

"I never kept anything from the girls I slept with before," I confessed, sighed, then checked to see her reaction. "If that's what you're asking me."

"Maybe you just keep stuff from the girls you *haven't* slept with before."

Why did she want to know this?

When I asked her that, she answered with a little shyness that I found so damn adorable, "It's part of your past and I'm curious."

I looked at her for a moment, studying her face. "I don't spend time with a girl I'm not going to sleep with. I don't see the point. I know that makes me an asshole, but I have to tell you that they don't want to spend time with me either."

"How would you know?"

I shrugged.

"I think some of them might want to spend time with you, but you just won't. There are girls who want more than just sex, you know. How come you spend time with *me* then?"

I gave her a knowing look. "You're the exception."

"Why?"

Did she really have to ask?

"You're just…different."

She nodded as if she understood. "Like weird different."

"No," I answered truthfully. "Refreshingly different. You're...real." I remembered the very first time I saw her at my neighbor's house. The one she nicknamed Dingle Dick. "Fearless. Fucking beautiful. I can't compare you with anyone else because there's no one that could measure up."

Her eyes widened, then softened.

I shrugged. "It's the truth."

"What if I don't sleep with you?" she asked. "Ever?"

"Then I'm just going to have to keep begging until you do."

She grinned, enjoying the image she saw in her mind. "You might need to wait a long time."

"How long?"

"A long, long time."

I sucked my bottom lip in my mouth. "You think so?"

She narrowed her eyes. "That wasn't a challenge."

I smirked. "Then you shouldn't have kissed me in the first place."

"What if I don't sleep with you?" She raised an eyebrow, unlacing her fingers from mine and walking ahead of me. "I might not. I mean you can expect anything you want, but it doesn't mean it's going to happen."

Oh, it was going to happen. From the moment I saw her, I wanted no one but her. And I knew I would want no one for a long, long time. We could barely resist each other now. I could feel it by the way her body shifted toward me, the way her eyes lingered on me, the way she kept biting that irresistible bottom lip. The only question was when she was ready. I would never force her. She had to come willingly to me.

"What if *I* don't want to sleep with you?" I teased.

She tossed her hair and shot me a look over her shoulder heavy with womanly knowledge.

This woman would have me begging on my knees anytime of the day and enjoy it.

I put my hands together and looked up to the sky. She threw back her head and laughed.

I smiled at the sound. She looked more carefree tonight, as if she'd left all her burdens back home and just brought herself. It was a pleasure seeing her this happy. I wanted her to be like this every damn day.

"Do you know your neighbors who live across from you?" she asked suddenly.

I chuckled. She was definitely talking about Dingle Dick. "I was just thinking back to the first time I saw you."

"You were?" She sounded happy about that. "I first saw you on campus. In the lecture hall."

"The first time I saw you was in front of my house. You were on a mission to cut off my neighbor's balls. The one you named Dingle Dick."

"Dingle Dick?" she laughed. "How did you even know? He did mention that…"

I frowned. "He mentioned what?"

She waved her hand. "Tell me about this encounter. I don't remember seeing you."

"Ouch," I said. "You don't remember?"

It was a dead end where she was heading, but I didn't say anything. I wanted her to discover the maze on her own.

I pressed the remote in my pocket and the lights I'd installed in the maze came on.

"Pretty lights." She looked at the blue lights on the ground, then the fairy lights I'd recently installed in the trees, thinking of her. I wondered if, during the time I was installing the lights, after I left her, I'd always known that I'd bring her here eventually.

Yes, I realized, I did.

She turned around at the dead end, walked to her left, and kept going. If she kept going straight, she'd hit a secret passage. I looked at her long hair swaying behind her back as she walked ahead of me. The sway of her hips tempting me.

"I'm sorry I didn't see you. I have this thing…" She looked over her shoulder at me and caught me checking out her ass. She rolled her eyes.

I grinned.

"Sometimes I block out everything around me except for my current mission in life, so that's probably why I didn't see you at the time."

"I know. I noticed."

"Really?"

I nodded. She stepped back so she could walk beside me.

"I went back to…look for you after you left…" she said quietly.

My eyes lifted to hers. She went to my house to look for me?

"Big Tony was there."

"Big Tony?" I repeated.

She chuckled. "Your neighbor."

"Ah."

"He said you told him that I would harass everyone in his life if he didn't pay his bill."

"I had to improvise. He's a piece of shit for not paying his bill."

"He paid. Thank you for that. Although couldn't you have made up something else? Like maybe I was a secret assassin or something. And, Cameron?"

"Yeah?"

"Thanks for getting me the job. At Rick's."

I frowned. "You know?"

"I asked Dylan when he'd just woken up. Why didn't you just tell me about the job?"

"You wouldn't have accepted it if you knew it came from me. You'd have been suspicious and rejected it," I said. "Are you angry?"

"That you got me the job?" She shook her head. "No, I'm not angry, Cam."

"I never stopped thinking about you. When I came back, I didn't know if you'd ever let me see you again. Talk to you again. I knew our deal was off after what I did. I didn't have a plan and I was going fucking crazy thinking of you. I had forgotten I had asked Dylan to tell you about the job before all…this happened. So when I found you at The Yard that day, I was caught off guard. I didn't expect to see you. And when I did, I was desperate to hold you and never let you go. But I was more… afraid you'd reject me."

"Was that why you acted like nothing happened? I thought you just didn't care."

"Of course I cared. I'm just good at…looking like I don't."

She gave me a small smile.

"I told Dylan not to tell you I referred you for the job," I said.

"You can get him to talk about almost anything in the morning when he's still half-asleep."

I laughed, remembering what she was like in the morning. "You're a zombie until you drink your coffee."

She flushed. "I guess you know that by now about me, huh?"

"I want to know more about you," I said.

"I want to know more about you too."

She smiled at me, and I smiled back.

I noticed she didn't have her blanket anymore. It must have fallen when we were in the secret passage. I took off my jacket and placed it on her shoulders. And this time, instead of shrugging it off and throwing it back at me like she did that first time I walked her home, she held it closer to her.

"Thanks." She gave me another smile. I wanted her to keep smiling at me. "Can I ask you something then?"

I nodded. *Just don't ask me to leave you alone. Like you did before. Even if I deserved it.*

She looked down at the ground as we walked before she asked, "Why didn't you text me before you left?"

I didn't answer right away, wanting to give her a real, honest answer by thinking about what I was going to say to her.

"Sometimes," I began, massaging my knuckles with my other hand. "I need to get away from…everything."

That sounded useless, but I didn't know how else to explain it to her. I wished for words, better words I could give her to remove the sadness in her eyes.

I looked down, gathering my thoughts, and tried again. "There are things in my past that still haunt me. And I have to deal with them the way I know how."

"Is this where you went?" She gestured at the maze.

"I went to finish a project up north first. And then I drove here. But yeah, I stayed here for a while."

"I see."

I must have taken a while gathering my thoughts because I heard her sigh.

"I'm not used to telling anyone where I'm going, Kara." I stopped and leaned against a tree trunk. "Not since I was a kid. And even then…"

She leaned against the tree across from me. She gathered all her hair and piled it on her left shoulder. It streamed down her front silkily. She made a captivating picture, standing there, watching my face.

"I'm not making an excuse," I continued. "It just is. I didn't think about telling you that I was leaving because I never had to do that before. I'm not used to anyone looking for me." I raked my fingers through my hair, uncomfortable at having to explain. "The people I've allowed in my life know I don't want them to look for me."

Her eyes drifted down. Was she hurt by what I said? The thought of her waiting for me to call or text squeezed my heart painfully.

"Kara, I'm sorry I left without a word. I had no idea how it would affect you. I know you like me. That you're very attracted to me. But I didn't know you… had feelings for me. That you cared."

I let out a breath. It was hard opening up, even with her. It was hard. "I stopped thinking. I'm sorry. I didn't think I was important enough to you to… I didn't think at all."

I was staring at her face the whole time, but she never once lifted her eyes up to mine. I kept quiet and waited until she looked at me.

When at last she did, she said, "I think I understand. And I'm sorry because I know I demand and expect things to happen right away, disregarding how hard it is for you to open up. I'm learning, too. This is all new to me too. But…" She trailed off, chewing on her bottom lip.

I pushed away from the tree and walked to her. Her eyes were on me, her face open, beautifully vulnerable to me.

I cupped her face in my hands, leaned down to kiss her lips. Her taste was a balm to an open wound.

"I was worried about you," she said. "Can you tell me next time, if you leave again? Just send me a text, a call, an email. Send a bird with a note. Anything."

I chuckled, kissed her again.

"I'm sorry you were worried about me. I'm an ass, but I don't want to be an ass to you. I hate hurting you. When you told me I was just like everybody else…" I paused, feeling my chest tighten. "It…hurt me. And I realized that I couldn't let you go that night without letting you know how important you are to me."

I rubbed my face with my hands, wondering if I was doing this right. If I was making an idiot of myself. But her hazel eyes told me to keep going.

"I don't want to be just like everybody else to you."

"You're not." She reached for my hand. "You're not, Cameron."

"I know you said you care for me and that I don't feel the same about you. You're wrong." I stroked her hair, her neck, her face. "Whatever I have for you inside me is stronger than anything I've felt before. I tried to forget you, but it's impossible. I had no one I wanted to call mine…before you. I didn't care about anyone. There are only two people I've let in my life." I tipped her chin up. "And now there's you."

She sighed softly.

"I've never been good with words. But I'll show you. I want to show you."

She closed her eyes as I kissed her eyelids, her cheek, her nose. "You're doing good so far," she said. "Really good."

I kissed her lips, her chin. "Am I?"

She nodded and opened her eyes.

"I'm ready to tell you now," I said. "About the maze."

"All right."

I looked down for a moment, feeling my heart pound against my chest. There was a familiar ringing in my ears every time I remembered what happened just behind the maze. Something I kept forcing my mind to forget.

I stepped forward, leading the way this time. When she grabbed my arm, I paused and met her eyes.

There was an understanding there and a whole lot of strength that reinforced my own. She slid her hand into mine, squeezing tightly. As if somehow she felt my apprehension.

"I got you, Cameron," she whispered. "I got you."

Goddamn it. *Goddamn it.* I gripped her jaw, yanking her to me. I kissed her again, hard and fast. Something that would tell her how much I wanted her. Her fingernails dug into my back as she rubbed her body against me. I would take her right here if we didn't stop now.

"Baby," I murmured in her ear, gathering her close to me. "You have to stop now, or I'll fuck you right here."

I wanted to do more than that. I wanted to possess her. Not just her body but...*more.* Just more. I seemed to want more from her than I ever wanted from any woman I'd been with. It couldn't even compare. It left me frustrated. It left my heart *aching*.

She pulled away, licking her lips. She brushed her hair off her face as she tried to catch her breath. Then she nodded. "Let's go."

She walked close to me, still holding my hand. We were close now.

"How did you find out about this place?" she asked.

"Raven and I moved here when I was a kid."

She frowned. "Who's Raven?"

"My mother."

"You call your mother by her given name?"

I nodded but didn't offer her an explanation.

"How about your dad?"

"They'd divorced by then. She moved around a lot, and she took me with her everywhere. It was an adventure for her."

"Did you like it?"

"Hell no."

She squeezed my hand.

"My parents are loaded, and after the divorce, my mom fleeced my dad for every drop she could. She didn't need the money, but she needed to punish him. They hated each other."

"It must have been hard for you," she said.

I shrugged. "It was my normal."

I couldn't say I missed anything because I didn't know what to miss. I grew up with parents who hated each other's guts. I thought everyone's parents were the same.

"We stayed here the longest, but she hated it here too."

Talking about Raven twisted something in my gut.

"The only reason we stayed here was because she met a man. But I was…" I searched for the word. "Content here."

"Did you have a lot of friends here?"

I chuckled, but there was no humor in it. "I don't do friends."

"You hang out with Caleb."

A small laugh came out, and this time it was real. "He didn't give me a choice."

"Best friends forever, huh?"

I gave her a smile. I pushed her back gently behind me when I saw tree branches in the way. I shoved them back and gestured for her to go on, holding them back so they didn't scratch her.

"The boys in my class talked about this place a lot. They said it was haunted and anyone who entered the maze would be cursed. The people in this town believed it, so no one came here."

"But you did."

"Yeah," I said. "I did. It felt like mine even when it wasn't. I felt safe here. And it was the only time I felt happy." But I felt my body go numb when I said, "A boy in my school came here too."

She sensed what I was feeling because she pulled me closer to her, as if she were trying to protect me.

"I first saw him behind the school grounds. He was getting beat up by these bullies. Three to one. I hated seeing that shit. Fucking cowards. So I beat them up."

"You beat up three bullies? How? Bet you were big back then too, huh?" she teased.

I knew she was trying to lighten the mood, and I appreciated it, but nothing could make this better.

"I wished I was bigger when I was a kid," she went on. "It would have been easier to defend myself." She gave me an approving look. "That's pretty awesome of you though."

She wouldn't think so after she heard everything. I felt sick in the pit of my stomach.

"How old were you then?"

"Eight," I replied.

"And your friend?"

"Same age as me."

"And how old were those bullies?"

"One was in my grade, the other two were older by a couple of years."

"It's easier to assume the bigger and older bullies were the worst, but that's not always the case."

I looked at her, waiting for her to tell me more, but she shook her head. I studied her face. It sounded like she had dealt with bullies when she was younger. The thought of her getting bullied made me angry because I wasn't there to defend her. But I bet she fought hard and defended herself pretty damn well.

"I'll tell you about my childhood woes next time. Keep going, Cam."

I wondered if she was aware she'd called me *Cam*. She did before too, when we were kissing. I would have smiled if we were elsewhere.

"So you defended this boy against these shitheads. What happened next?"

I could see the bend now. A few more turns and we'd be there.

"He wanted to be friends. I kept avoiding him. I didn't want a friend and told him I'd beat the crap out of him if he kept at it, but he wasn't intimidated."

"You did save him from those assholes. You were his savior, so that automatically made you his friend." She smiled, encouraging me to keep going.

"Probably. In any case, he kept following me. Until one day we just started hanging out."

"Sweet."

I clenched my jaw. There was nothing damn sweet about it.

"He found out about the maze from me. I showed it to him. He was scared at first, like most kids, but I told him I'd been hanging out here almost every day for the past few months. I didn't want to show him at first. I was selfish with it, but he wanted to hang out with me. I wasn't going any place else. I was addicted to this place. I wanted to find out every secret door, every nook and cranny. I was going to memorize everything about this maze. I had a map."

She didn't say anything, just listened.

"But he was better at it, though." I smiled a little, remembering, but it felt stiff. "He found more hidden spots than I did. He was smaller than me, thinner, almost malnourished, really. It was easier for him to squeeze through the bushes. I found out later on he was a foster kid and his foster parents didn't feed him. Sometimes they'd kick him out and make him sleep outside."

I heard her gasp of outrage. She was quiet for a while and then she asked, "You let him stay with you, didn't you? You gave him food. You took care of him."

"I shouldn't have. I should've made him stay away from me. I shouldn't have let him be my friend."

"Why?"

Her eyes were direct and nonjudgmental as they searched my face.

I could see the exit now. A few more steps.

"We're here," I told her.

I pushed open the secret door hidden behind thick vines and debris—and stepped out into an open wide field. There was nothing but fields of grass.

"Cameron," she said softly. "Tell me why. Tell me why you don't think he should've been your friend."

I could feel my body harden, then go numb. And when I faced her, I knew she wouldn't see any hint of emotion on my face.

"He's dead," I told her coldly. "He's dead because of me."

Chapter 27

Kara

"HE'S DEAD BECAUSE OF ME."

Cameron's voice was flat. My eyes snapped to him, horrified by what I'd heard. His face had gone blank, devoid of any emotion.

I waited for him to tell me more, but he had gone silent. He was staring intensely at a spot in the distance, but when I looked over, there was nothing there but an empty field.

"Cameron," I said as gently as I could, but he didn't react. As if he had already retreated to a place where I couldn't find him.

I reached for his hand, to hold on to him, but he pulled away.

I stepped back in response. I didn't think he'd moved away from my touch before. I understood that he needed space right now, but still, his reaction stung. It was clear that he was in great pain, but he was trying his damnedest to hide it from me.

He was still staring at the same spot in the distance, as if he was watching a scene play out in his head. Maybe he was.

I don't know how long we stood there in silence. It

could have been a minute or a half hour. I didn't say anything, just waited for him.

I looked at him and saw a tall, beautiful man with a broad back, carrying the weight of the world on his strong shoulders. But a body and heart could only take so much. One of them was bound to feel exhausted sooner or later. And someday his strength would give out. What would happen to him then?

"Cameron," I said. "Tell me what happened here."

When at last he looked at me, his eyes glistened with intensity. I couldn't explain why I felt his pain right there and then, as if it were a solid thing floating in the air. It wrapped around us, covering the field with sorrow.

"We were supposed to meet that day," he began. His voice, unlike his sad eyes, was hard and cold. "But I couldn't get away."

I could tell it was hard for him to talk about it. I looked back at the field again, wondering why he bought the land if something horrific happened here.

Was it out of a sense of guilt? Of responsibility? A self-imposed punishment? But he said he'd been content here too. That it had been the only place where he had been happy.

"Why couldn't you get away?"

He stepped forward, his back to me. He curled his hands into fists. I could tell it was in anger. I just wasn't sure if it was directed at himself or something else.

"I couldn't get away because I was locked up," he answered.

My head snapped up. "What?"

"Raven locked me up in the house. And this time I

couldn't get away because if I tried and she caught me, there would be hell to pay."

"Your mother locked you up?" My heart started to beat fast and that familiar feeling of anger rushing in my veins was taking over. I imagined Cameron as a kid— alone, lonely, hungry, locked in his house. What kind of mother would do that to him? What kind of childhood did he have? "Did she hurt you?" I asked.

"Not really," he replied, but he sounded impersonal. As if he were answering an interview question. "She'd hit me sometimes when she was drunk, but that was because I was in the line of fire. She never hit me while sober. She said she loved me too much."

"No, she didn't!" The feeling of wanting to hit something was getting stronger by the minute. "How could she love you too much when she abused you? She—"

"It doesn't matter," he said.

It doesn't matter? "How can you say that?"

"It's over. She can't control my life any more, even if she tried."

I seethed. "Where is she now?"

"You're amazing, do you know that?" Now he smiled at me, but it didn't reach his eyes. "You're so angry for my sake."

"If you were in my shoes, wouldn't you be?"

He nodded. "I would."

"Tell me the rest."

"There was an abandoned car here before," he started, gesturing at the place he'd been staring at. "Right there. In that exact spot. I see it in my head. It's been years, but it's still so clear in my head. It's so fucking clear."

There was only an open field there now with sparse dry grass. That car only existed in his memory now.

I knew what it was like to keep pain and anger inside—knew it so well. It would fester until all you felt was anger every damned day. It ruined everything, and it wouldn't give anything good a chance.

He *needed* to talk about it—this pain he'd been keeping for a long time. It was time to let go of it, or at least start letting it go.

"Tell me about that day," I said. "Did you manage to get out? Did your friend go back to see you at your house?"

"No," he said.

Suddenly he looked tired. He crossed his arms and lowered his head.

"Sit down, Cam," I said. He needed to get off his feet. He'd been working nonstop. I could tell. I could tell he had lost some weight. His cheekbones were sharper, his jaw more prominent. He said he ate a lot, and from what I'd seen in his cooler, he was right. But he was probably working a lot too, burning all his energy, not getting enough sleep. Worrying.

I sat on the dry grass, waiting for him to do the same. Eventually he did, just a little ways from me, as if he needed space to think, to gather his thoughts.

"He was supposed to come to my house," he began after a moment. "We were going to eat first, maybe watch some TV, play some video games. Then go to the maze to finish the rest of the map. It was almost complete."

The wind blew, whipping his dark curls against his forehead. I shivered.

"Raven was supposed to be gone that day. Another

trip to an exotic resort. Whatever. She'd usually be gone for days. That's why I asked Pete to meet me at my house."

Gone for *days*. That meant he was often by himself. Just a little boy. Was it a wonder he closed himself off to the world? He'd said he knew I was attracted to him, but he never thought I cared for him. It made sense he would think that. My heart hurt.

"But she didn't go. Her boyfriend broke up with her and she blew up. Just another one of her normal tantrums, I thought, but I realized that it was beginning to be a bad one. She got drunk, broke things in the house. She locked me up in a room down in the basement. She didn't want me to leave. She hated being alone. She thought I wouldn't be able to escape and no one would hear my screams if she locked me down there."

I let the anger roll through me. There was no goddamn excuse for anyone, especially a mother, to do that to her child.

"She didn't physically hurt me. Just locked me up," he added. As if that would change what I thought about the whole thing. As if that made it okay.

It was still abuse in my book. A child shouldn't be exposed to that kind of treatment or behavior from an adult who was supposed to protect him. I had my dad to protect me and Dylan. Cameron didn't have anyone.

"Pete came to my house. They'd never met before. I could hear them. Raven was screaming at him, asking him things, cursing him. She said I wasn't home, so I assumed he went straight to the maze. A few minutes later, I heard Raven leave. And then I escaped."

Dread filled my limbs. I knew something bad was

going to happen. I could hear it in his voice, the way it lowered and hardened.

"He was about to leave when I got to the maze. And I asked him to stay. I remember he was holding this green notebook. It was just something I had lying around my room. I gave that damned notebook to him and he took care of it. He said it was the very first present he'd gotten. He fucking cherished it as if it were priceless. Like it was..." His voice broke. He lowered his head.

"It was a gift," I said hoarsely, my heart aching for him. "From a friend."

"A *friend*," he said in a mocking tone. Full of self-hatred and blame.

It was dark now, and the stars had started to come out.

"We stayed a few hours in the maze, exploring, mapping. He was getting tired and he wanted to go home, but there was only one section of the maze left. If we kept going it would all be done. I told him I was staying until I finished it. And I knew he'd stay too. I knew he wanted me to be his friend enough that he'd stay."

"And then what happened?" I asked when he stopped.

"We never got to finish it."

"Why?"

"He found another exit. Another hidden door. The same one you and I came out of. At the time, I thought there was only one exit, which led to the lake on the other side of the property." He rubbed his eyes. "We were excited. All these possibilities. Maybe there were more exits. He'd already found this one, the one behind us, so maybe we could find more."

I nodded, picturing two young boys enthusiastically exploring and mapping a secret maze.

"He found the secret door," he went on, "and I opened it. And here we are sitting right where it all happened."

"What happened, Cam?"

"We found an abandoned car. It was just there in the middle of the damned field." He gestured absently. He looked so alone. So lonely. So damn sad. An angel who'd lost everything he held dear.

"He didn't want to explore it for some reason," he went on. "He felt uneasy about it, but I dismissed his concerns. I'd driven once before, stolen my dad's car, wrecked it even. My dad nearly killed me for that. Raven was on him before he could slap me. She hated anyone hurting me."

Except for her, I thought bitterly. No wonder Cameron had his emotional scars. He grew up with a monster.

"We climbed inside the car to explore. There wasn't much inside—no keys, so we couldn't start it. But eventually, I did find something very interesting, a box of road flares in the trunk."

My heart skipped a beat.

"I wish I'd never opened that trunk," he said miserably.

"You were a kid. Any kid would've explored an abandoned car. I know I would have."

He turned to look at me, and I wanted to kiss him so badly. I wanted to chase away the horrible memories in his eyes.

"Those kids that bullied him showed up, the ones I beat up. There were five this time."

A chill went down my spine.

"They were still a few yards away when we spotted them. I wanted to go back to the maze. We knew that place inside out. We would lose them in there easily. We would be able to escape. But Pete was scared. He locked himself in the car."

"Did you…did you leave him and go to the maze?"

He shook his head. "I stayed there, screaming at him to open the door so we could both go."

I should have known he wouldn't leave his friend.

"But he wouldn't listen. He was paralyzed with fear."

He stared at the spot where the car had been.

"What happened next?" I asked when he didn't continue.

He shook his head to shake off the memories. "I fought them. I didn't just do it for Pete. I didn't want them to call me a coward if I ran away and left my friend in the car."

He looked so angry, and I knew it was targeted at himself.

"I'd beaten them before. Surely I could do it again. But I didn't. They beat me up. And they found the flares."

I held my breath, terrified to hear the rest of his story.

"They weren't there for Pete. I knew that. They were there for me. For *me*. They wanted to get their pound of flesh, scare me, beat me up some. But it got out of hand."

His hands fisted, the veins in his arms popping in anger.

"One of them lit one of the flares, but it burned his hand, and when he dropped it, it rolled under the car. It was the middle of summer. All that dry grass and heat."

A horrified sound came out of my throat.

"It burned the dry grass around the car and it filled it with smoke. Lots of smoke. I screamed at Pete to open the fucking door, but he wouldn't. I could hear him coughing, gasping for breath. I tried to break the windshield, the windows, but I was too weak. I could see my hands bleeding, trying to break the glass, but it was no use. I grabbed a rock, anything, but nothing worked. Pete was looking at me, just looking at me. He wouldn't move. He wouldn't fucking move."

He dropped his head in his hands and stayed like that for a while. But this time I touched him. And this time, he didn't flinch. He lifted his head to look at me, and we stared at each other for a moment.

I leaned over so I could wipe the tears off his cheeks and lay a soft kiss on the side of his mouth. He closed his eyes, seeming to absorb my touch.

"Finish your story, Cam."

He nodded. "I must have passed out," he continued in a hoarse voice. "When I woke up, there were police and firefighters everywhere. There was a paramedic seeing to my hands. He said I had burns, but I didn't even feel anything. I wanted to find Pete."

When his eyes turned to me, they were filled with sorrow and pain and guilt.

"But he was already gone," he whispered. "He was gone."

Chapter 28

Kara

THERE WAS NO QUESTION IN MY MIND WHAT I NEEDED TO DO. I crawled on his lap, wanting to get as close to him as I could, offering him the warmth of my body. I wrapped my legs around his waist and my arms around his neck, resting my cheek on his shoulder.

He stiffened for a moment, and my heart ached realizing that he wasn't used to people touching him for comfort. I squeezed my arms around him, letting him know I wasn't going anywhere. And then his arms were there, pulling me closer against his body that had turned hard and cold.

I wasn't sure I'd get used to the feel of his brawny arms embracing me. It felt new. But it also felt like home. And it felt right. Like I was supposed to be here. I closed my eyes and just held him.

He was so solid, so strong and powerful that even though I was the one who wanted to protect him, he was the one who made me feel protected just by being in his arms.

"Cam," I said gently. I waited for him to respond with words, but he didn't. Instead, his grip around me tightened. I could feel his fingers pressing against my back, pulling me closer to him. "It's not your fault."

His body trembled.

I knew that, sometimes, all you needed was someone to tell you that it wasn't your fault. Some sort of assurance that someone believed in you, especially when you didn't believe in yourself.

I wasn't sure if that was what he needed, but it was what I could give him. My words paired with my touch would hopefully convey my faith in him.

"I'm so sorry that happened to you and to your friend," I said. "It was a tragedy. There was no way you could have known what would happen that day or else you would have done everything in your power to stop it. You're a protector. You protect the people you care about. You did everything you could to save him."

He didn't answer, just held me. I tried to pull away so I could see his face, but his hand slid up from my back to grip my neck gently but firmly, silently telling me to stay where I was.

I closed my eyes and let him take comfort from my embrace. Then I said, "Nothing that you or anyone could say to me would change my mind about it."

I felt his body start to relax, the stiffness in his shoulders and arms dissolving. I smiled as I felt him kiss my hair.

Who would have known he was affectionate like this?

"Kara," he said softly. "Kara."

"Yes?"

I waited for him to say something, but he didn't. And I realized he wasn't going to. He pressed against me instead, his arms pulling me closer as if I wasn't already close enough.

"I wish I had better words for you so you can

understand how it's not your fault," I said. "But I want you to know that I'm here. I'm right here, Cam. And I'm not going anywhere."

I let my body rest against him, listening to him breathing. We stayed like that for a while. A sense of calmness and comfort came over me.

"It's enough," he said after a moment, his voice thick with emotion. "More than enough."

"You still blame yourself, don't you?" I asked.

He didn't answer.

I sighed. "I really hope you don't blame yourself because you asked Pete to stay."

When he was telling me his story, he had repeated that he had asked Pete to stay several times. I knew there was a reason for it, that he blamed himself for it.

I pulled away from him so I could look at his face, and this time he let me. His lion eyes looked so dark, so intense when he let me see his emotions. I cradled his jaw in my palms.

"Cam, why wouldn't you ask him to stay? And why wouldn't he stay? You were kids. Kids play all the damn time. They break rules and stay up late. They don't go home when it's time to go home, and they play outside as long as they can. They break curfew. You know how many times I did that? Don't you dare blame yourself. Those five kids who beat you up, who bullied Pete, think of their role. I hope to God they're sorry for what happened. But never, ever blame yourself. Think about it, goddammit."

"Do you think I haven't thought about all those things? I have, Kara. Many times. More than you could count." His eyes shifted back to the spot where it happened. "Why—" His voice broke. "Why do you think he did it?"

"Did what?"

"Why didn't he get the fuck out of the car? It was as though he just gave up. What if…"

I felt sick. He was right. I didn't think that there could be another reason why Pete stayed in the car. I thought he was paralyzed with fear, but then…

"What if he intentionally stayed in the car?" His eyes filled with horror. "I should have known. I…I should've recognized the signs if he…if he wanted to…"

Escape everything by choosing to stay in the burning car.

"You were just a kid," I whispered, my heart breaking for him. And for Pete. "Answer this for me, how would an eight-year-old kid be so aware of death, let alone recognize the signs that his friend wanted to commit suicide? If that was really his intention. And, Cam, would you blame an eight-year-old kid for not being able to pry open a car that's made of steel and glass and on fire? That kid did everything he could to save his friend. His hands were bleeding and burned, but he kept trying until he was so exhausted he passed out. Would you blame him?"

I didn't expect him to answer, and he didn't.

"I didn't know Pete, but whatever his reason was, I don't think he would want you to blame yourself for this. Not when he knew you didn't leave him there. You stayed and fought for him. He knew his friend stayed and fought for him because he mattered to you."

His fingers closed around my wrists, and I thought he would reject my touch again, bring them down to my sides. But he surprised me. With his eyes staring at me, he brought them to his mouth, kissed the inside of my wrists.

"I have no idea why you're suddenly in my life," he said, his voice gruff. "But I don't fucking care anymore. I'm done fighting it. I want you to be with me. With me, Kara."

This man. I closed my eyes and rubbed my cheek against his shoulder.

"Good," I said, smiling. "I want you to be with me too."

He stroked my hair, his hand sliding down to my neck, massaging it with his long fingers. I sighed in contentment.

"It's getting cold." I couldn't have been warmer with his body heat and embrace shielding me from the cold, but what about him? He had given me his jacket and he was only wearing a shirt. "Why don't you show me your cabin?"

He nodded but stayed where he was for a few moments before he decided to get up. He didn't want to let go of me yet.

"All right," he said. "Let's go."

But I didn't let go of him. I held on.

"I want to be your monkey," I murmured into his neck. He wasn't the only one not ready to let go.

"My beautiful spitfire monkey."

My heart thudded against my chest when I heard him say *my*.

He gripped the backs of my thighs as he stood up, groaning a little. How did he even do that? He was so strong.

When he entered the maze carrying me, I realized what he had to walk through. I told him I'd walk, but his grip just tightened.

"You weigh the same as a feather," he murmured in my ear. "I'd carry you anywhere, Kara."

I smiled into his shoulder, savoring his words. He said he'd never been good with them. He was wrong. He might not say a lot, but when he lowered his walls and showed me a glimpse of his heart, his words dug deep.

He was quiet as he walked us to his cabin. I assumed he knew a shortcut in the maze because it didn't take long at all until he was walking us up to his porch steps and the light flicked on.

I heard a series of short beeps as he put in his code to open the door, and then a longer beep before the click of the lock released.

It was dark inside. It smelled clean and new and woodsy. Good scents. Masculine scents. My eyes adjusted to the dark, and I had an impression of high ceilings, open space, and generous glass windows.

He toed off his shoes at the entrance. He didn't bother turning the lights on but walked straight until he was gently laying me on the bed. But he didn't join me.

"I need something to drink," he said. "You want something?"

He was pulling away. I could feel it. Wrapping himself in his misery. We'd just talked about being open to each other, but I knew it would take time for him to get used to doing that. He was feeling vulnerable and the right thing to do was to give him space now, let him be for a while.

I sat on the bed, watching him move around his place. He turned on a soft, dim light before kneeling in front of a fireplace. I couldn't see what he was doing, but I had a view of his back and arm muscles shifting.

The musky, sweet scent of wood floated in the air as the fire started crackling.

He rubbed his hands together, wiping them on his jeans. Then, slowly, he uncoiled his body and rose.

"It should warm up soon," he said without looking at me.

I followed him with my eyes as he walked to the small kitchen. The light from the fridge slashed a bright rectangle on the hardwood floor as he pulled it open.

He reached inside, then twisted the cap off a bottle of water and drank, his throat muscles working. He grabbed another one and approached me, opening it and offering it to me. I took a sip and handed it back to him. He capped it and placed it on the floor.

Kneeling beside the bed, he carefully took off my shoes. I wanted to slide my fingers into his dark curls, pull him to me, but I resisted. He set my shoes beside the water bottle.

He let out a sigh and rose gracefully. He reached for the collar of his T-shirt and pulled it up and over his head. He dropped it on the floor, looking weary. I felt the mattress sag as he sat on the edge of the bed. He leaned forward, propping his elbows on his knees, then pulled off his socks.

My heart ached for him. He looked so alone, so lonely. I had a feeling he'd been harboring all these toxic emotions inside himself, and although he'd told me he had people in his life—probably Rick and Caleb—how much did he share with them? I could be wrong, but I had a feeling not much. He seemed so closed off.

"Cam," I said. "Don't go there by yourself. Let me in."

I crawled in his lap again. He was warm now and his masculine scent—the cool, blue scent—was stronger. I inhaled. "I'm here now."

His arms wrapped around me. No hesitation this time. Just acceptance. Like he'd been expecting it and I was welcomed.

It gets easier every time.

"Kara," he said, his voice gruff with emotion. "I don't think I can let you go."

I swallowed my heart back down. "Then don't."

"Stay here with me," he whispered, his voice filled with need. "Just like this. Just right here. Just tonight."

"I'm not going anywhere. Let's lie down."

He slid up on the bed, taking me with him. He cradled me as he stretched out, pulling me on top of him. I shivered at the feel of his hard length pressed against me. The warm, soft skin of his chest under my palms.

I shifted so that I lay half on the bed and half on him. He seemed to like that because he wrapped his wide hands around my waist and turned me on my side, then he pulled me closer, plastering my back to his chest. His arm snaked around my stomach, under my breasts.

"Kara," he whispered. His lips softly grazed the back of my neck.

"Right here with you, Cam. Go to sleep."

He let out a deep, long sigh, his broad chest expanding, then deflating. And then he was asleep in an instant.

It must have taken all of his energy to tell me everything in the maze. Being mentally exhausted could be worse than physically exhausted.

He wasn't used to sharing his thoughts or problems

with anyone. I was the same, but we could start being more open with each other. I could trust him. He could trust me.

The thought filled me with warmth, like submerging myself in a warm bath. Only ten times better. I closed my eyes, sighing deeply, and fell asleep with a smile on my face.

When I woke up, I felt confused. I blinked in the semidarkness, at the sound of crackling fire and the glow from the fireplace. And then felt the heat coming off Cameron's hard body wrapped around me. I closed my eyes, savoring the feeling of him beside me.

He wasn't snoring. In fact, he'd been quiet in his sleep. I turned my head slowly so I could see his face. I wished there had been more light so I could see him clearly.

I slowly extricated myself from him, taking care not to wake him up. His arm was heavy as I lifted it off my stomach. When his fingers grazed my nipple, I gasped sharply and almost jumped. Damn. I snapped my eyes to his face to check if I woke him up. He didn't move. Finally I eased away and stood beside the bed. And just stared.

Naked from the waist up, he was sleeping with a frown on his brow. His body was so long and muscular—a warrior's powerful body. He was so beautiful. His dark curls stark on the white pillow. His tanned skin healthy.

I let out a quiet breath, wondering how I ended up here. With him. With someone like him. He'd never been in my cards, I thought, as I searched for his car keys, never even anticipated him.

I found them on the counter by the fridge. Tiptoeing

so as not to wake him up, I opened the front door and nearly closed it behind me before I suddenly remembered it was locked with a code, not a key.

Shrugging out of his jacket, I placed it between the door and frame to keep it open and ran to his truck. I made quick work of jumping inside and grabbing my things and his cooler. A couple minutes later, I was back inside the cabin.

I sat on the floor by the door, rummaged inside my backpack for my phone, and read my dad's texts.

Dad: Hey, KK, don't forget pizza night tonight!

Dad: Are you working OT?

Dad: I'll save you some so you have something to eat when you get home. Got the vegetarian with double cheese. Drive home safe. Love you!

Shit.

It was the middle of the night. I sent a quick text telling him I'd be home tomorrow. I'd never missed pizza night before, but he was used to me not replying to his messages. That usually meant I was at work. There were other messages from other people, but I decided I'd check them later. I placed my phone back in my backpack and quietly walked to the bed.

I held my breath as I watched him shift onto his back and slowly open his eyes. His gaze was dark.

"Where did you go?" he asked, his voice husky from sleep.

I found it so sexy. There was a raspy quality to it that made my stomach muscles clench. That made me swallow the lump in my throat. That made me think of secret lovers and kisses in the dark.

I slid beside him on the bed, and his arms welcomed me so naturally. I sighed against his chest. He was so warm and both soft and hard.

"I got my things from your truck. I had to text my dad."

He didn't respond.

"Did you think I left?" I was teasing.

Again, he didn't respond. There was a twinge in my chest. Did he really think I would?

"I won't leave you," I told him.

His jaw clenched. "I won't be surprised if you do."

"Don't," I said quickly. "Don't say that bullshit. The only thing that would make me leave is you."

I shifted so that our bodies were pressed close. I wanted to make him feel how important he was to me, how much I wanted his touch. How much I wanted him. Just him.

"I need you," I whispered. "I…want you, Cameron."

His eyes flickered with understanding. "Kara," he rasped, then moved on top of me.

He was already hard. I could feel him pressing against my thigh. I wanted to feel more of him. To explore him. I wanted to make him feel the pleasure he had given to me, I wanted to see his face as I gave it to him.

"Can I make you come?" he asked, eyes watching my face intently.

Yes.

I clenched my thighs to stop myself from pushing against him. "If you say please."

He narrowed his eyes at me. "Why do you want me to say that word?"

"I like hearing you say it."

"Make me," he said.

My heart thudded against my chest. It was a challenge. And it turned me on. So damn much. What was it with him?

Was it because he was untamable? He was so wild, so…raw.

His hands banded around my wrists and he pulled them up above my head.

"Make me, Kara."

I was breathing hard. He released my wrists. His hands stroked down my arms, the sides of my breasts, my hips as he knelt between my legs, nudging my thighs apart. I bit my lip as I slowly spread my legs for him.

He pushed up my dress's skirt, took off my sheer stockings, and stared.

Before I could even feel self-conscious, his hands slid under my ass and cupped both my cheeks, jerking me forward. I let out a loud gasp as my center met his arousal.

He pumped his hips against me several times before he caught my mouth in a searing, carnal kiss. His tongue was wild, seeking the recesses of my mouth before he dragged it down my neck, making sucking sounds, making *moaning* sounds that drove me to the edge.

Through the fabric of my dress he closed his mouth on my nipple and I cried out. I tangled my hands in his hair, pulling, pushing him against me. His other hand slipped under my dress, his thumb lightly skimming between my legs before sliding upward. He pushed my bra down and toyed with my other nipple with his fingers.

"Wanna come?" he whispered.

"Cam, omigod."

"Wanna come, Kara?" His eyes, so dark, so intense, were focused on my face. "Say yes."

"Yes," I whimpered.

"Christ. I want you so fucking bad," he groaned before he tugged my dress up and off.

He lowered the cups of my bra, pushing my breasts up as an offering to his mouth. He kept on sucking, flicking his tongue over the tips of each nipple, torturing me.

There must be a release to this torment. It kept on building inside me, bigger and fuller and tighter. He didn't stop sucking, and when his hand slid down to press between my legs, it hit me instantly. I was crying out, shaking, digging my fingernails into his back as the sweet, sweet release of ecstasy came.

Chapter 29

Cameron

"YOU'RE BEAUTIFUL."

She was. I'd never seen anyone more beautiful. Especially right now, when her face was glowing from the aftermath of her orgasm.

She closed her eyes. There was a secret smile on her lips.

My back stung from the imprint of her fingernails. She'd dug them in deep.

My spitfire.

Her arms and her long legs fell limply on the bed. I stroked her stomach, her sides, fascinated at how big my hands looked on her body. I could hold almost her entire waist in them.

I massaged her arms gently, her legs, taking care that she was comfortable, then grabbed the folded blanket we hadn't used and covered her with it.

The look of satisfaction on her face made me want to make her come again. Her climax came so quickly that I wondered if it was always going to be like that. Was that her first? It made me want to give her more pleasure, find out if that was true.

But I knew she wasn't ready for that yet. I wanted to

pump myself inside her, feel the eager thrust of her hips as I let myself get lost inside her wet, tight heat…

"I'm taking a shower. Be right back." I pushed up from the bed before I did something we'd both regret in the morning.

She'd said she wanted to wait, and I meant it when I said I would never push her. She had to come willingly to me.

But damn. The sight of her spread on that bed, all rosy and soft and so fucking beautiful…

I clenched my jaw. A cold shower would be a good idea right about now, I thought as I headed to the bathroom. She was ruining my self-control.

I glanced at the clock, noted it was one in the morning. We'd only slept for a couple of hours.

Needs and wants, I thought as I turned on the light, took off my pants, stepped into the shower. There usually wasn't a confusion between the two for me. I could differentiate and prioritize them quite easily. With Kara, everything got blurred but for one thing—there was an absolute demand inside me, an almost desperate one, to keep her in my life.

I had slashed myself open, willingly, in front of her and spilled my guts—secrets that I'd been harboring inside for years that ripped me apart every time I thought about them. Much less spoke of them.

But I knew that was what she wanted from me. And I was desperate enough to do anything to keep her.

There had been no choice for me after that. It was either tell her or lose her.

And the thought of losing her was unbearable. And this time I knew it would happen if I didn't do anything.

It surprised me how I felt after telling her everything. It felt…less dark around me. As if a heavy shadow had taken a few steps back. It was still there—I could still feel it hovering—but it was somehow less ominous now. It didn't seem an all-consuming presence as it was before.

What shocked me more than anything was that she *stayed*.

She fucking stayed.

I knew there was a huge possibility that she would leave when she'd heard the whole terrible story. I told her everything anyway. Because she had asked it of me. And if there was even a slight chance that she would stay, hell, I'd take it.

There had never been anyone like her before in my life. Everything I'd experienced with her was all new to me. I had no baseline, nothing to compare it to. And I was afraid I'd screw it all up. In fact, I was sure I would screw it up.

I wasn't sure about a lot of things, and that was fine, but there was one thing I was certain of—with absolute fucking clarity. The moment I woke up and saw her, with those big hazel eyes filled with emotion that choked me up, there was this overwhelming need to touch her, claim her for myself, make her feel how important she was to me. And I was going to show her the only way I knew how.

Not with words or promises, because I had never been very good with those, but with my touch. Make her feel even a tenth of what I felt for her, give her something I could only give her.

And she had welcomed me, given a part of herself to me. I knew how much it meant to her. I remembered her telling me how she'd never dated anyone before and that she was still a virgin.

And for her to give herself willingly to me made my breath hitch. Made me feel that I... *meant* something to her. Something important.

I want to be your monkey. I chuckled. She did this thing where she'd rest her cheek on my shoulder and rub. Like a sweet cat. It was so unexpected. Freakin' drove me insane.

She was so sweet, so hot. Her small breasts were perfect, so responsive. I loved the way she gripped my hair, how unaware she was doing it, and how she gave herself fully to sensations.

Gotta think of something else.

No matter how many times I thought about it, I couldn't get over how she was still here after what I'd told her in the maze.

It's not your fault. Nothing that you or anyone could say to me would change my mind about it, she'd said. Did she mean it?

I'd heard it all before—from the doctors I'd seen when I was a kid, how it wasn't my fault, how I should start to heal and let go. Their words all felt meaningless. None of them got through to me. They were professionals who got paid to care. That wasn't real. Not to me.

But she was. It was her presence—her resilience and compassion—that meant more to me. More than anything. I needed her right now. Under me, moaning, calling out my name. I wanted to feel the press of her legs against my hips as I...

Think of something else.

But, Christ, I wanted this woman like I'd never

wanted anything before in my life. There was no rational explanation for it. It just *was*.

What the hell is this?

My bike. I missed my damn bike. I couldn't wait to ride it again. The speed, the freedom. Once it was repaired, everything would go back to normal again. I pictured it in my head. Parked in front of the cabin, it would look black and sleek and gleaming.

And there she was coming out of my cabin, wearing nothing but white lingerie. In my head it was sheer white. And lace. It made my mouth water. Ice-pick high heels.

She'd throw me that come-and-get-me look over her shoulder. She'd crook her finger at me, her fiery hazel eyes on me, as she hooked her leg over my bike and straddled it like she was going to…

Damn.

I pressed my hands on the tiles, clenched my teeth. *The bike. Get back to the bike.*

Maybe she'd look better naked. In my mind, her lingerie disappeared. She was naked now, blinking slowly at me, silently asking me to take her.

I gave up and rubbed one out.

I dried myself quickly, put on the same jeans, and stepped out barefoot into the living room.

She was sleeping.

I sat on the floor quietly, watching her face as she slept. She looked peaceful, with a small smile on her face.

I reached out and gently moved the lock of hair on her cheek. Then she opened her eyes slowly.

It felt like getting a quick, sharp stab. Right in the

damn heart. That first moment she opened her eyes. And that moment of recognition in her eyes. And that moment when she smiled. As if she was happy she woke up and found me there. I was at a loss for words.

There was a tightness in my chest, and the more I watched her face, the tighter it got.

"Hi," she said.

I would have spoken if I knew my voice would work.

"Aren't you going back to sleep?" she asked drowsily.

But I was feeling…off. I couldn't put my finger on it.

"I'm not—" I cleared my throat. "I'm not tired." My voice sounded clipped.

Why the fuck do I do this?

She blinked at my face. I had to get away from her line of sight. She'd noticed something wasn't right and she was starting to wake up.

I rose from the floor and walked to the fireplace, adding more kindling to it. It might get colder tonight, and I wanted to keep her warm.

Was she warm enough now? Did she need a thicker blanket? I frowned at the flames.

What the hell is this? What the hell am I feeling?

I was an expert at blocking things out—thoughts and feelings. These things were dangerous if I let them take rein. But ever since I'd met her, I couldn't find the switch to turn them the hell off.

I tensed when I heard the rustle of sheets on the bed as she pulled herself up.

"Hey, Bigfoot."

Damn. Damn. Damn. I lowered my head. Fought it. Failed. I gave up and smiled.

"Don't run away," she said.

I looked at her over my shoulder. And my heart thudded against my chest.

Her hair looked dark in the firelight. It tumbled over her shoulders, as if she'd just woken from a wild night of sex. Her eyes, feline eyes I couldn't get out of my head no matter what I did, watched me now, waiting, wondering.

"Are you sorry you told me?" she whispered.

Told her about the maze? Never.

"No."

"Then what is it?" she asked. "Because you're doing it again."

I had no explanation for her. I couldn't even understand what I was feeling, so how could I even begin to explain?

I crossed over to her, my eyes on hers. She surprised me when she scrambled up, kneeling on the bed facing me. I stopped in front of her.

"I don't mean to do it again," I said.

The fire popped and sizzled behind me.

"Is it hard to talk about it?"

"Yeah."

We were whispering in the dark. I could see the light from the flames playing on her alluring face. Slowly, I reached out and stroked her cheek, slid my hands down, and held both sides of her neck as I rubbed her nape with my fingers. She closed her eyes, her body leaning in for more.

"But we both know you can get anything out of me if you want to, don't we?" I said. It wasn't a question.

Now she smiled. A knowing smile. She tipped her face up to me, silently demanding a kiss, and I kissed her softly, taking my time, nibbling on her bottom lip.

My hands traveled down to her shoulders, her arms, then gripped her hips, and I lifted her up. I loved how she automatically hooked her arms and legs around me, how trusting she was that I wouldn't let her fall.

"Did I give you blue balls?"

I smirked. "Yeah. Big time, but you made up for it when you screamed my name."

"I did not!" she blustered. "I think you screamed *my* name."

I nuzzled her neck. "We'll do more when you're ready." *Don't think about that.* "Can't sleep?"

It took her a moment to reply. "No." Her voice was raspy, and I wondered if she was thinking of the *more*. I wanted her to be. "Where are you taking me?"

"Kitchen. You have to eat."

"No, I don't," she said just as her stomach growled.

I chuckled. "Yeah, you do."

I knew she had a slim frame, but I wondered if she was too thin because she worked too hard and forgot to eat. She also drank a lot of coffee. I assumed it was to keep up with her work and other responsibilities. I didn't want her to get sick.

"Are you saying I'm too thin?" she teased. "Is that why you can't get enough of my body?"

My Spitfire.

"I can't get enough of *you*."

"And he says he's not good with words."

It was the truth. I didn't have to look for words when it was so plain to see, when it was that simple.

Amused at both of us, I propped her on the kitchen island.

"You like my words?"

She nodded, her fingers playing with my hair. I dipped my head to kiss her, bit her bottom lip that I couldn't get enough of.

"I do," she said. "Let's start with your physical attributes. You're very, very attractive. I really, really like your hair. And your eyes. And your nose. And the way you bite your lip or your knuckles when you're excited or just because. And your hard back muscles. Don't forget about your forearm muscles. The sexy veins. And your hot body. And…"

I laughed. "You *are* hungry."

"Well, make me something to eat then, chef."

"All right. You have to let go of me first."

"Make me," she said.

I sucked my bottom lip in my mouth and stared at her. Her eyes widened. So she remembered that, didn't she?

"Okay, okay." She let out a nervous laugh, placed her hands on my chest, and nudged me back. "Sorry, that wasn't an invitation. Food first. Food."

"Fine." I kissed her again before releasing her. I turned the lights on in the kitchen, then walked to the counter, where I found the plastic bags containing the stuff I'd bought for her at the service station and rummaged through it. She must have brought them in with her.

"I don't know if you remember, but I don't eat pork. Or beef. Or…" She raised her brows when I turned and looked at her. She pounded a fist on her chest. "Vegetarian lady here."

"Of course, I remember." I turned back to the groceries and pulled out the items and placed them on the counter. "I got you three cartons of eggs and a loaf of bread at the store."

"Aw." She let out a slow, sweet sigh behind me. "Wait, three? How long were you planning on keeping me here?" She laughed. A happy sound that made me smile. She was so damn cute. "Any cheese?"

"They didn't have any. You like cheese?"

When she didn't reply, I turned to look at her again.

"I love cheese. That time when you and I…in the bathroom. I'd just had the veggie lasagna from the cafeteria. It happens every time."

I laughed softly. I didn't think I'd ever forget that. "Why do you eat it then?"

"Are you kidding? It's so freaking good it's worth the pain. I'm going to die sometime in the future, and I don't want to say I missed out on the good stuff."

I shook my head at her, then went to find a pan. I didn't normally cook, but I knew I'd bought one for emergencies. I'd stored it here somewhere.

"So…that girl in the bathroom. Was she the same girl who kissed you in the hallway?"

"I haven't had sex since I met you."

"Good. You want a medal?"

"I think I deserve one."

She smirked.

"I don't know about you, but I don't like to share," she said. Her voice stern.

"You mean me?"

"Of course you."

I grinned. *Good.*

"Would you share me? The way you glared at Thomas probably scarred the poor guy for life."

Share her? What the fuck did she think? The thought made me want to punch something.

I slammed the cupboard closed. Harder than I meant to. "Thomas."

"Calm down, Wolverine. No growling. He's a good guy. A friend," she added quickly when I scowled. "Just a friend."

I found the pan in one of the bottom cupboards. I placed it on the stove, turned the dial on low heat, poured in just enough oil to cover the pan. *Where the hell is the spatula?*

Friend, my ass.

I opened drawers, slammed them closed.

"Men and women can't just be friends."

"Yes, they can," she insisted.

Exasperated, I glared at her over my shoulder. "We typically don't spend time with women we don't want to have sex with."

Where the hell was the damned spatula?

"Gross. And that's not true for every guy." She narrowed her eyes at me. "Is that the only reason you want to spend time with me?"

"Of course not, but it's one reason. I want to sleep with you."

She scoffed behind me.

I opened the same cupboard I'd opened the first time. It was there. Dammit.

I went back to the counter, grabbed a bowl, and cracked an egg too hard. I sucked at cooking. I sucked at it more when I was distracted, and she was one hell of a distraction. I was already pulling a bunch of cracked shells out of the egg white.

"Sharing you with another guy?" I growled. "Over my dead fucking body."

I glared at her over my shoulder. She was grinning. She liked that, didn't she? I narrowed my eyes. I could see on her face there was no arguing with her about her friend though. I went back to cracking eggs. Damn shitty convenience shitty store shitty eggs.

"I like your honesty, but your argument about guys and girls can't just be friends is invalid. Error 404," she said.

I brooded for a moment. "I think about you all the fucking time."

I froze when she wrapped her arms around my waist from behind. So unexpectedly. So suddenly. Then I relaxed and smiled when she rested her cheek on my back, rubbed like a cat.

I fucking loved *that*.

"You're so random. I love it. But let's not argue about my friends. I only have a few," she said against my back. "Can I help?"

I let out a sigh. "Here." I gave her the bowl.

"Whoa. Are we going to eat all of these?" She goggled at the bowl.

"I only cracked eight. There's still four left in that one carton," I pointed out.

"That's a lot."

"How many do you usually cook?"

She looked up from the bowl. "I don't cook. *Ever*. It scares me."

I sighed again. "All right, just pick out the egg shells."

She scrunched her nose at the bowl. "You're not very good at cracking. I don't think I am either, but I can fix this. I'm an expert at picking out eggshells."

But she just made it worse. She punctured the yolks, making it hard to find the eggshells. She laughed, giggling like a little girl messing up her chores and unapologetically having fun with it.

"Let's just cook it like this!" She threw her hands up in defeat. "This is a hard job and these eggs are rude."

I shook my head at her, chuckling because she was so damn adorable. "Watch this for me. I'm going to make toast for your sandwich."

"Don't leave me here. I'll burn this place down! Cam!"

"Calm down. I'm just right here."

"Didn't you attend Nice Guy Class 101? You don't tell a girl to calm down."

"I'm not a nice guy."

I opened the fridge, searching for condiments for her sandwich. I had nothing here but water bottles and a box of leftover pizza I'd had last week.

I spotted my cooler sitting on the floor. How… caring and thoughtful and just damned sweet was she? I knew I was smiling as I opened it, grabbed a sandwich, and scarfed it down. Then I sniffed something in the air.

Something burning.

"Holy shit, Kara, what the hell?"

I hurried to the stove and turned it off.

"Did you turn the burner on high?"

She lifted her head from the bowl to glower at me. "Do you see anyone else here? Of course it was me!"

"Well, you don't turn the stove on that high!"

"It was taking too long! And you left me here! I told you I can't cook!"

"For a minute! Jesus."

"Stop yelling at me!"

"You're yelling at me too! Fuck!"

We looked at each other. Stopped. She laughed first. A big, boisterous laugh that shook her shoulders. She doubled over, holding her stomach. I laughed with her, gathering her in my arms because I couldn't help it.

The pan was still smoking. Soon the fire alarm was going to blare if I didn't do something. Blowing out a breath, I lifted the pan from the stove and yelped. Cursed continuously when I burned my hand.

"Shit, shit, shit!"

I'd forgotten that this pan was metal—what was I thinking buying this crap?—and that I needed a pot holder to hold it.

I was too busy watching her, too busy smiling at her—I was forgetting every damn thing.

"You okay?" She ran to the sink, turned the faucet on. "Come here, you poor baby."

"This is all your fault." I scowled at her.

"How is this my fault?" She glared back.

"You like to argue with me all the time."

"No I don't," she shot back. "You're the one who likes to argue with me all the fucking time."

I raised my brows at her. "See what I mean?"

She gave me the death stare for a few seconds. "You make me want to fucking curse all the time. Why are you so argumentative?"

I raised an eyebrow. She rolled her eyes and beckoned me to her. Still scowling, I stopped in front of the sink. I watched as she held onto my wrist, placed my throbbing hand under the blast of cold water. Her fingers were long and slender, and I wasn't sure which felt good—her touch or the cold water on my skin.

It wasn't even a burn. I barely touched the hot part of the handle. I removed my hand from the water and touched her mouth with my thumb, spreading the water onto her bottom lip. It trickled down her chin. We stared into each other's eyes, savoring this moment of aloneness together. I leaned down and kissed her lips. Sucked the water from her chin.

"You're so good at that," she said languorously.

"At what?"

"Kissing me."

"Want another one?"

She blinked slowly. "Food," she said loudly, stepping away. "Kiss later."

I smirked and turned back to the counter, at the mess we'd made.

"We can just boil them," she suggested.

"But then we have to peel the shells off," I said.

"I know, right?"

We looked at each other again. She bit her lip, her eyes shining with laughter.

"We don't know what the hell we're doing," she said, wiping her eyes on my shirt. "And it's fine because it feels great to be here with you right now." She sniffed. "I'm still hungry though."

"All right. Sit over there and be quiet."

She gave me her serious face, not letting it pass that I was telling her what to do again, but she couldn't follow through and laughed again.

"It better be good, Bigfoot."

She hopped onto the kitchen island. I washed the pan

and wiped it dry. Put it on the stove. I threw out the egg mixture we'd both messed up and grabbed the carton of eggs. I cracked them carefully this time.

"How did you survive without cooking your meals?" she asked.

"Takeout. Lean meat, sandwiches mostly. Fresh veggies, fruits."

There weren't any eggshell bits this time. I scrambled them with a fork and poured the mixture in the pan. The satisfying crackle made me smile. I popped a couple pieces of bread in the toaster.

I noticed she hadn't said anything for a while. I looked over my shoulder and found her watching me. There was sadness in her eyes.

"Kara?"

"My mom," she started, her voice thick. "She used to cook all the time, but she never really liked it. Eggs and bread every morning. And then one day, it all stopped."

This I wanted to know. Everything. About her.

"She left when I was just a kid. Dylan barely remembers her." She took in a deep breath, released it slowly. "But I do."

"What do you remember?"

"That she was a bitch." She gave out a small laugh, but it was strained. "I remember one thing. It was her birthday, and my dad was going to take her out to a fancy dinner. I remember he bought her a fur coat. She'd always been hinting at him to buy her one. You know, hints like she'd cut out pictures from magazines and leave them lying around the house for my dad to see. Or say something like 'This coat would really look pretty on me.' Stuff like that. She never said what she wanted straight out. I don't mind using the hint technique, but she was over the top. It was always a guessing game with her."

She kinda did the same thing, I thought. Like her mother with her cut-out pictures, Kara did with her Post-it Note reminders in her home, except that instead of hints, Kara's messages were direct and told exactly what she wanted. And I adored that about her.

"It probably drove your dad nuts."

She lifted her long legs onto the counter, crossing them in front of her. Her eyes blazed with anger. I stared.

She gestured with her arm. "I think those eggs are done."

I turned back to the stove. She was right. I reached for the spatula and plate, scooped out the eggs.

"No," she said. "It didn't drive my dad nuts. My dad's a very patient man. He loved her."

I didn't tell her I had no clue what that was like. I didn't think I'd ever seen my parents hug each other. They couldn't even stand being in the same room.

"But on her birthday, he got her this fur coat. She was really excited. She unwrapped the gift box really, really slowly, carefully pulling off each piece of tape. Folding the paper meticulously. I wrapped that fur coat myself and I wished to God I'd only used three pieces of tape."

I chuckled. "How many pieces of tape did you use?"

I grabbed the toast and fixed her sandwich, brought the plate to her.

"Thanks," she said, smiling up at me. She took a huge bite. It was satisfying to watch her eat. Maybe I'd look up vegetarian recipes and cook her a couple of meals just to see her eat more. It shouldn't be too hard.

Yeah right. Probably burn the whole place down. I'd stick with sandwiches for now.

"Lots of tape," she continued. "It took her a while. And when at last it was all unwrapped, she shook it out. And you know what she did?"

I waited for her to continue while I got her a bottled water from the fridge. I didn't have anything else. I should ask her what she liked to drink, other than coffee, and stock up. For next time.

"What?"

"She went outside and threw that fur coat—that expensive fucking coat that my dad had been saving up for—on the ground. Right on the dirt. And stomped on it. She broke my dad's heart.

"You see, it wasn't the fur coat she wanted. 'I've been leaving hints every fucking day to you, Mike,'" she continued, her voice sounding higher than normal, copying her mother's voice probably. "'And you buy me this piece of shit coat? Did you get it for a bargain? Did you get it from a consignment shop? Someone owned this piece of shit before, and you dare give it to me as a present?' Like she's better than a queen and she levitates above everyone else because she's so fucking special. My dad and I loved to shop at secondhand stores. I don't care. I'm in love with a great outfit, but I'm well aware that what you put out into the world is more important than what you wear."

I unscrewed the cap on the bottled water and handed it to her.

"I saw my dad's face," she continued. "He was hurt, and he got mad this time. Not because she didn't like the coat, although that's probably one of the reasons, but because Dylan and I were there, watching it all happen. She left him eventually for a vacuum salesman. Her loss."

She drank water and placed the bottle on the counter. "It was hard for my dad to raise two kids on his own. So he got a job, saved up, then went into business with his older brother, Andrew." She looked like she wanted to spit. "Another leech, if you ask me. He and my dad both own the garage. Fifty-fifty. You want to know why I work so hard? So I can buy him off. I already talked to Andrew about it, and we have a deal."

"How much does he want for his share?"

She narrowed her eyes at me. "Why?"

I looked at her, and I knew there was no way I could hide my intentions. Might as well tell her. She was too smart for her own good.

"I can give you the money."

"Are you nuts? Hell no! Then all my hard work would've been for nothing. *No.* I'm so close. So close."

"You didn't get mad when you found out about the job at The Yard."

"That's different."

"How so?"

"I know I'm qualified for that job and I'm a hard worker. You couldn't go wrong with someone like me."

I nodded. "You're more than qualified for that job."

She grinned at me, then took a couple more bites of her sandwich, nodding in approval. "Not bad, Bigfoot."

I grabbed her bottled water, tipped it to my mouth so she wouldn't see my smile, and almost spilled.

She chewed for a minute. I knew she was busy contemplating something. Kara didn't think quietly. Her face showed her emotions.

"Everyone is asking me why I work so hard. The people at work gossip about me, talking about why I do so much overtime and where my money goes. I don't care. I can take all that. I've been bullied worse than that when I was younger. They think they can stop me, hurt me with harsh words, they better think again. I'm made of steel, baby. Steel. I've had worse, and that mean-girl bullying shit sure as hell won't get to me."

"They're gossiping about you because you work hard?"

"I have seniority over them. When there's OT available, I take it. Almost all the time. So they're mad at me because they can't. They think I'm a bitch, and you know what? I don't give a crap. I don't have time to join them at gatherings outside work either because I have a lot of shit to do. So on top of being a bitch, I heard I'm also a snob. Yummy. Get over it, bitches."

I let out a small laugh. She was on a roll. I loved seeing the sparkle in her eyes, the fire and passion that always came out in everything she did.

"In my extended family, Dylan and I are the only ones who don't have a degree. My dad doesn't either. My mother running away with another man was the icing on the cake. So most of my relatives look down on us. I detest family dinners with them—especially with my dad's brother, Andrew. They all feel superior. I hate condescending advice masked as concern and fake love. It's so cheap. It's crap. I reject it."

I know, I thought but didn't say anything.

She continued, "That breaks my dad's heart because he loves those assholes. And it hurts me because I love my dad so much. Degrees and money could be useful, but they don't buy morals or values or a heart. I get up every morning and force myself to work because I see that amazing man, my dad, working harder than anyone I've ever met from his family. I respect the hell out of him. I want to be like him." Her voice cracked. "I work hard not because I want to prove to everyone that I can do it. I work hard because I want to prove to *myself* that I can do it. And I will. I can save my family from this. Money has always been tight. I can help my dad out. I can give him what he deserves. Dylan too. He's always been a softie, and he takes it hard when people say bad things about my family. There are so many things that could stop me if I let them."

She lowered her eyes and took a deep breath before lifting her gaze to mine. "But I can't let anything bother me—I *won't*. Because I don't want to sacrifice my world just to be in other people's. I want my own world, filled with all the people I care about."

I watched her silently as she finished her sandwich, sipped water, and wiped her mouth with the back of her hand. Like a little kid.

But she was a woman. A woman with the heart of a child. A child who wore her heart on her sleeve but had learned to protect it with thorns.

Was it a wonder why no matter how hard I tried to let her go, I couldn't? Why I wanted desperately to be in her world?

"Kara," I said gruffly. "Am I in it?"

She looked up, and our eyes met and held. Everything that I wanted, without knowing I had wanted it, was in her eyes.

"You know you are, Cam," she whispered. "You just hid from me for a while. But you're here now."

I stepped forward. She wrapped her legs around my

waist. I placed my hands on the small of her back, pulling her closer to me.

"I am," I murmured. "I want to…stay."

"Then stay."

She rested her chin on my shoulder, wrapped her arms around my torso. "But I want you to do something for me."

Anything. "What is it?"

"I want you to…accept the things that are true to me and don't go behind my back to do what you think is best for me. I can work hard, take all the crap people dish out at me, and flick that shit off. Besides, I can dish it out harder. So don't worry about Andrew. I don't want you lending me money. I have savings."

"All right. I must've put a dent in it with my motorcycle."

"Well, I had to use my tuition for next semester."

"Shit. I'm a son of a bitch. I'm paying you back."

She pulled back. "Are you now?" Her tone said no. She played with the ends of my hair, twirling it around her finger. "You know I always wondered, ever since I saw you, what it would feel like to touch your hair. It's so black. And perfectly curled and soft. What shampoo are you using?"

I chuckled. "Whatever's in the bathroom."

She pulled.

"Ouch. I don't know. Whatever I can grab at the store. I'm not picky."

She rested her cheek on my shoulder again, rubbed. "Hey, Cam?"

"Hmm?"

"Why did you do that?"

"Do what?"

"Blackmailed me into driving you around. You didn't need me. You have your own vehicle."

"I…" I paused. She already knew why, but I knew she just wanted to hear me say it again, and I didn't care because I was more than happy to do anything that would make her smile. "I think I just knew. I wanted you. I want you."

"You mean that very first time you saw me?"

I stroked her back, kissing her shoulder. "Yeah," I whispered. "I saw you that day, and I knew I had to see you again."

"Well, keep seeing me and don't go anywhere again."

I nibbled on her shoulder.

"Cam?"

"Yeah?"

"I'm full and now I'm sleepy."

"Come on, then." I gripped her hips and lifted her up. She wrapped her arms and legs around me.

I laid her on the bed, stretched out beside her, gathering her in my arms.

"It feels so…new. Being here with you," she said softly. "It feels right."

It fucking does.

She wiggled her butt against me, and I clenched my jaw as she tried to find the perfect comfortable position. "Night, Cam."

I sighed against her hair, curled my arm around her. "Night, baby."

"See you in the morning."

I kissed her hair and pulled her closer. I had never in my life held anyone or even wanted to hold anyone like I was holding her, but it seemed like I couldn't get enough of it now.

I thought that she had fallen asleep, but she wiggled her butt again. I let out a sigh.

"Kara," I said in a serious tone.

She let out a happy puff of air. "Tell me about your childhood. Just a little. Give me a happy memory."

I was quiet for a moment. She laced our hands together, fitting my fingers with hers. She traced from the tip of my finger to my knuckle slowly and continued with the same treatment on all of them. Her soft touch evoked a response from me.

"Happy memory," I said.

I felt her nod. "Anything."

"Coming home from school in the afternoons," I said after a moment.

"Can't wait to play your video games, huh? Freedom."

"No, it's not that," I answered.

"Freedom. How can anything be better than that?"

I smiled against her hair. She would think so.

"What could be better than that?" she pressed.

"My mom waiting for me in the kitchen," I said. "Cooking something for me."

She stilled, then squeezed my hand after a beat. "And then? Describe it for me. What did she make?"

"Anything. Spaghetti, maybe? With meatballs. Huge ones. The size of a baseball and a lot of them."

"Your mom must be a good cook."

"She can't cook worth shit. It's not a memory. I conjured it up," I told her. "I don't remember any happy childhood memory except for my time in the maze. And I don't want to talk about that right now."

"Understood."

"Tell me about yours," I said, sensing her sadness.

I shouldn't have said anything.

"A happy one. About your dad and Dylan."

"We used to go to the beach during the weekend when my dad wasn't busy with work. We'd make sandcastles or Dylan and I would hold him down on the sand, and he'd pretend we were so heavy he couldn't get up, then we'd cover his body with all that wet sand. I'd make this mermaid tail for him and he'd say it was the most wonderful thing."

She told me another one after that, and another. I lost track of time. She made me laugh, and I had never laughed as much in a year as I did with her that night. She made me...happy. And I could only hope I made her just as happy.

"Kara," I said softly. "Let's go to sleep."

"All right." She pulled my arm around her and wiggled her butt against me again in an effort to be closer. "We'll make good and happy memories," she whispered. "Promise."

As I drifted asleep, I realized for the first time in my life, I actually believed the best was yet to come. With my spitfire.

Read on for an excerpt from

Chasing red

Caleb

THE DANCE FLOOR GLOWED AS RED AND GREEN LASER BEAMS shot out from the rotating lights in the ceiling. It was Friday night, and the club was packed with people dancing and jumping to the DJ's throbbing music. The floor pulsed beneath my feet, and the heat radiating from the mass was inescapable. My eyes roved over the tightly packed crowd. They reminded me of penguins huddled in the cold—on crack.

"What the hell's wrong with you?" Cameron yelled in my ear, giving me a friendly punch to the arm. His ice-blue eyes glittered in the dim light. "That was the fourth chick you turned down tonight, and we just got here."

I shrugged. Saying that I was bored with the meaningless sex and monotonous flirting seemed pretty pathetic.

All right, the sex I didn't mind, but I was feeling restless, looking for something else lately. A challenge, maybe. The thrill of the chase.

I chugged my beer. "If you ate the same shit every day, you'd get bored of it too," I replied.

Justin barked out a laugh. His blond, gel-soaked hair stayed in place as he comically motioned with his head and then with his beer to the dance floor. "Check that out, man. Holy shit!" he exclaimed, letting out a high-pitched whistle.

In the middle of the dance floor, a girl was dancing—no, scratch that—gyrating so sensuously that I couldn't help but stare. She moved like… Sex comes to mind. Her short, tight dress covered her hourglass body like a second skin, seducing the dozens of eyes turned on her.

And it was in make-me-sin red. Damn.

I might have drooled a little as she bent over and did something dreamy with her hips. Her long ebony hair swayed against her tiny waist, and her legs looked a mile long in those spiky heels. There was something captivating in the way she danced, a defiance that flowed with the silky movements of her body. I felt my heart skip one fast beat against my chest when she looked up and our eyes met.

"Shit. I'm going to take this girl home with me," Justin yelled excitedly.

That was low and annoying enough to distract me. I hated cheating, and Justin had a girlfriend.

Cameron shook his head at Justin, looking up when a redhead asked him to dance. He laughed and whispered something in her ear. The redhead giggled. Cameron nodded to me and they left.

"Hello, team captain."

A soft body sidled up to me, reeking of intense floral perfume. I looked down into the heavily made-up eyes of Claire Bentley. I can appreciate the magic makeup does to a girl's face, but not when she looked like she was punched and was now sporting two black raccoon eyes.

"Claire. How's it going?" I gave her a small smile, but it only encouraged her to grab on to my arm.

Ugh, no. Why did I sleep with her again?

"Oh, you know, nothing much." She batted her eyelashes, pushing her breasts into my side. I couldn't help but glance quickly at her cleavage. Her breasts were staring at me. Ah, one drunken night and those lovely things must have been enough reason for me at the time.

The strap of her dress slid down her shoulder. She looked up at me from beneath her lashes, and I wondered if that was a practiced move. Still, I thought it was kind of sexy. If she were someone else, I might be interested. My eyes strayed past her shoulder to the dance floor, searching for that girl in the red dress. Claire's grip on my arm tightened, yanking my gaze back to her.

"You owe me a drink, Caleb. I dropped mine when you walked by." Her tongue snaked out to touch her top lip.

I hid my wince. She was trying too hard, and I didn't want to be trapped in her claws all night. Racking my brain on how to shut her down without offending her, I desperately looked around for Cameron or Justin. Neither was in sight. Assholes.

"Hey, baby." My eyes widened in surprise as the girl I'd been shamelessly ogling on the dance floor earlier wrapped her arms around my waist, maneuvering me out of Claire's grasp. When her eyes shifted to mine, I forgot how to breathe.

She was stunning.

"He's with me," she told Claire, but her eyes were still locked with mine. I was mesmerized by the way her mouth moved. Her lips were wide and full, colored a very, very hot red. "Aren't you?" Her voice was soft and low, reminding me of dark rooms and hot, smoky nights.

I felt my heart leap inside my chest for one insane second—it might have been a full minute or two. She wasn't beautiful in the classic sense. Her face was striking and eye-catching, with high, sharp cheekbones and long, dark brows above catlike eyes filled with secrets. I wanted to know every one of them.

When I didn't respond and just stared, her brows drew together in confusion. The dusky gold of her skin glowed under the dim light, making me wonder how it would feel. I caught her arms quickly before she moved away, placing them around my neck. I was right. Her skin was soft and smooth. More was all I could think.

Leaning close to her, I let my lips brush her earlobe and whispered, "Where have you been?" A smug smile split my lips as I felt her shiver. "I've been looking for you my whole life." Leisurely, as if I had all the time in the world, I glided my mouth from just under her ear to the hollow of her throat.

Before I could do anything else, she stepped away.

"She's gone. You're safe," she said, smirking. "Now you can buy me a drink for saving you."

I placed my hands in my pockets to stop myself from reaching for her again. I already missed the feel of her in my arms. "Sure, what would you like?"

She shook her hair back, and I couldn't stop watching her. I was captivated. "Something strong. Tonight, I want to be someone else. I want to…forget."

That was my cue. I slid my hand around to the small of her back, pulling her toward me so our faces were only inches apart. "You can be anyone you want with me." Her scent seduced me. It was addicting. "Why don't we leave this place and go somewhere I can help you forget, Red?"

Her eyes turned cold before her palms flattened against my chest. She pushed me away. "Nice meeting you too, asshole." She turned on her heel, waved, and left me staring after her like a lost puppy.

What the hell just happened? Did she just reject me?

The feeling was so unfamiliar that all I could do was watch her until she disappeared in the crowd. She swayed a little, like she'd had too much to drink. I almost ran after her to make sure she was all right, but she'd probably just spit at me. I figured her friends would take care of her.

But what the hell did I do wrong? She was sending all the right signals that she was interested. Maybe I should have actually gotten her the drink first.

"Caleb!" Another girl yelled behind me, but I was no longer in the mood for anything but my bed.

Funny how I had been wishing for a challenge tonight, but when one stared me in the face, I screwed it up like an idiot.

I closed my eyes and inhaled the refreshing air as I stepped out of the club. I had parked my car at the end of the lot and walked hurriedly to it, afraid someone would see me and drag me back inside. I'd rather chew my arm off than go back in there.

My steps faltered as I spotted the silhouette of a woman leaning against one of the filthy brick walls of the club parking lot. She'd probably had too much to drink. I would have been happy to leave her in peace, but when I glanced at her again, I noticed a man leering at her from a few feet away. My protective instincts kicked in as the man straightened and walked toward her.

The woman shifted, and the dim light from the streetlamp touched her face. My pulse kicked up a notch as I recognized her—Red.

I didn't need to think twice and went straight for her.

Acknowledgments

Kara and Cameron's story is not over until their happy ending, but I hope you enjoyed reading how they met and fell in love. These characters brought so much love and laughter to me, and I hope they brought the same to you.

Thank you to the amazing Wattpad team, especially Caitlin O'Hanlon and Ashleigh Gardner, for doing the heavy lifting. Also to Aron Levitz and Eric Lehrman for holding up the other side. To Allen Lau and Ivan Yuen, for giving writers a platform to share their stories with the world.

Thank you to the wonderful Sourcebooks team, especially my editor, Cat Clyne, who just gets me and my characters, for your patience and understanding. Special thanks to Laura Costello, Rachel Conte, Heather Hall, Gretchen Stelter, and Carolyn Lesnick for your valuable feedback and hard work. I learned so much from you. Thank you to Dawn Adams for your creative mind.

To my Wattpad readers who tirelessly cheered me on to write Kara and Cameron's story, who never forgot, who've been there since the beginning, a big hug and so much love to all of you.

To all my readers who support me and what I'm doing, you are the voices in the dark that remind me to keep reaching for the light. I'm so grateful for all of you. I love you all.

To my family and friends, whom I love dearly. Thank you for the love and support.

To my Adam, whose comments I can't get enough of, for always listening, reading my drafts, and helping me with plots and making me pancakes. For never letting go of my hand no matter how hard the journey is, my heart is yours. You are the most important person to me.

And to God, who makes everything possible.

Love,
Isabelle